Praise for THE CHEMICAL GARDEN TRILOGY

★ "[A] harrowing debut. . . . DeStefano has an observant and occasionally pitiless eye, chronicling the cruelties, mercies, and inconsistencies of her young characters."

—*Publishers Weekly*, starred review, on *Wither*

"Creepy and elegant, shocking and romantic, dreadful and rewarding, and delivers unexpected twists."

—Lisa McMann, *New York Times* bestselling author of the Wake trilogy and *Cryer's Cross*, on *Wither*

"Lauren DeStefano crafts an all-too-believable future. I loved the world, the romance, the writing—exactly the kind of book I've been craving to read."

—Carrie Ryan, *New York Times* bestselling author of *The Forest of Hands and Teeth*, on *Wither*

"Rhine's struggles and pain are real, and her story is both heartbreaking and hopeful. I couldn't read this book fast enough."

—Beth Revis, *New York Times* bestselling author of *Across the Universe*, on *Fever*

"A satisfying ending."—*Booklist*, on *Sever*

"*Sever* is well written and is a satisfying . . . conclusion to the trilogy."

—*VOYA*

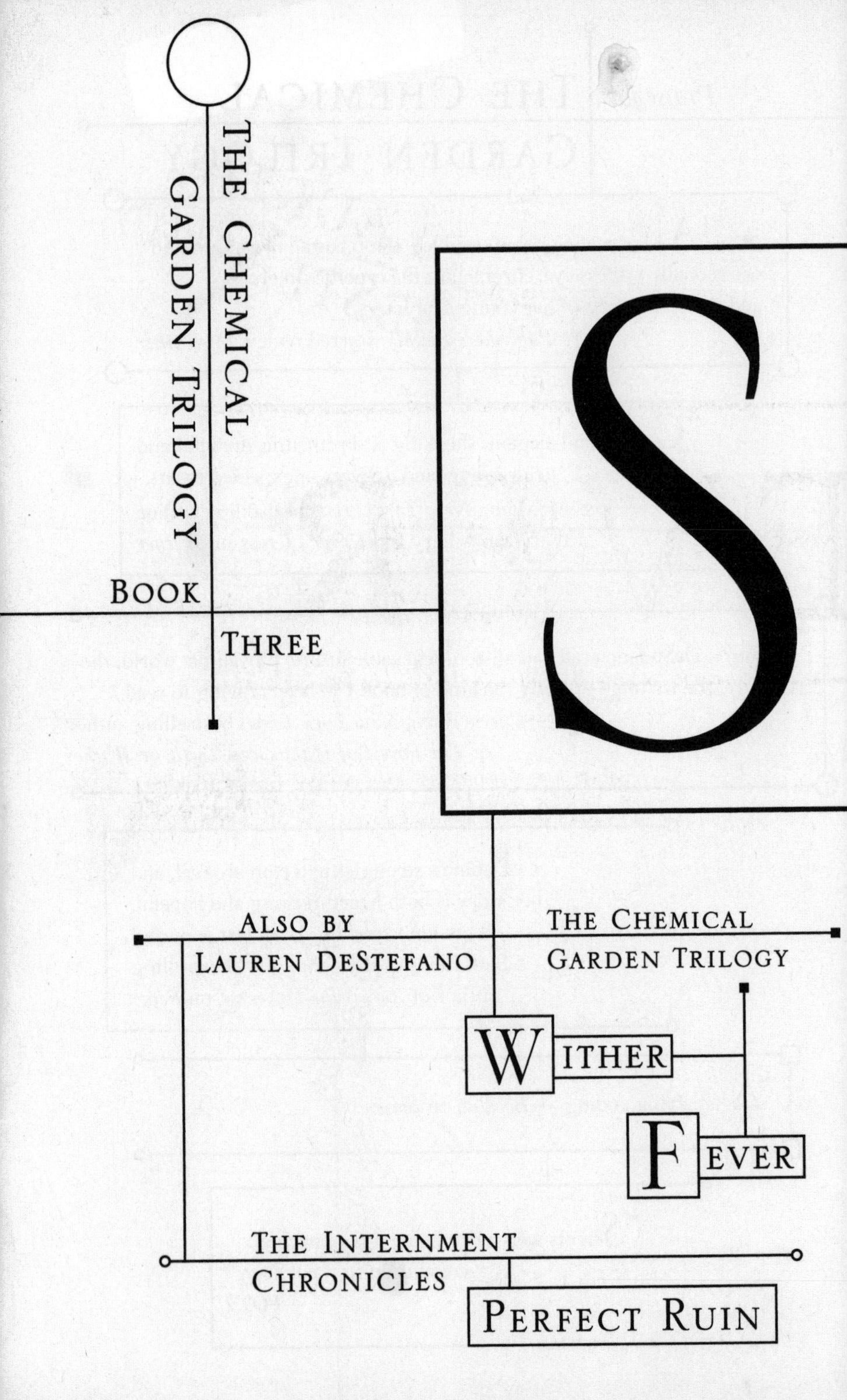
The Chemical Garden Trilogy
Book Three
S
Also by Lauren DeStefano
The Chemical Garden Trilogy
Wither
Fever
The Internment Chronicles
Perfect Ruin

Lauren
DeStefano

EVER

SIMON & SCHUSTER BFYR

New York London
Toronto Sydney New Delhi

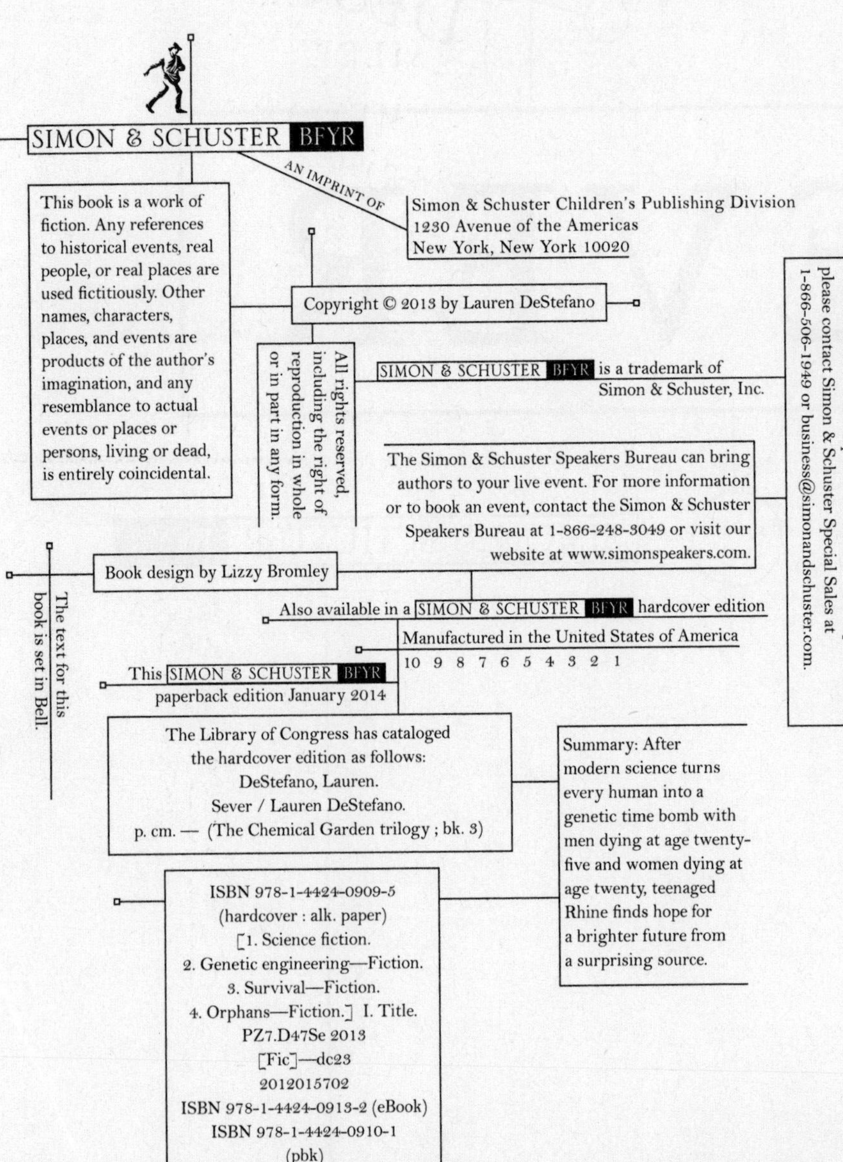

SIMON & SCHUSTER BFYR
AN IMPRINT OF
Simon & Schuster Children's Publishing Division
1230 Avenue of the Americas
New York, New York 10020

This book is a work of fiction. Any references to historical events, real people, or real places are used fictitiously. Other names, characters, places, and events are products of the author's imagination, and any resemblance to actual events or places or persons, living or dead, is entirely coincidental.

For information about special discounts for bulk purchases, please contact Simon & Schuster Special Sales at 1-866-506-1949 or business@simonandschuster.com.

The Simon & Schuster Speakers Bureau can bring authors to your live event. For more information or to book an event, contact the Simon & Schuster Speakers Bureau at 1-866-248-3049 or visit our website at www.simonspeakers.com.

Book design by Lizzy Bromley

The text for this book is set in Bell.

Also available in a SIMON & SCHUSTER BFYR hardcover edition

Manufactured in the United States of America

10 9 8 7 6 5 4 3 2 1

This SIMON & SCHUSTER BFYR paperback edition January 2014

The Library of Congress has cataloged the hardcover edition as follows:
DeStefano, Lauren.
Sever / Lauren DeStefano.
p. cm. — (The Chemical Garden trilogy ; bk. 3)

Summary: After modern science turns every human into a genetic time bomb with men dying at age twenty-five and women dying at age twenty, teenaged Rhine finds hope for a brighter future from a surprising source.

ISBN 978-1-4424-0909-5 (hardcover : alk. paper)
[1. Science fiction. 2. Genetic engineering—Fiction. 3. Survival—Fiction. 4. Orphans—Fiction.] I. Title.
PZ7.D47Se 2013
[Fic]—dc23
2012015702
ISBN 978-1-4424-0913-2 (eBook)
ISBN 978-1-4424-0910-1 (pbk)

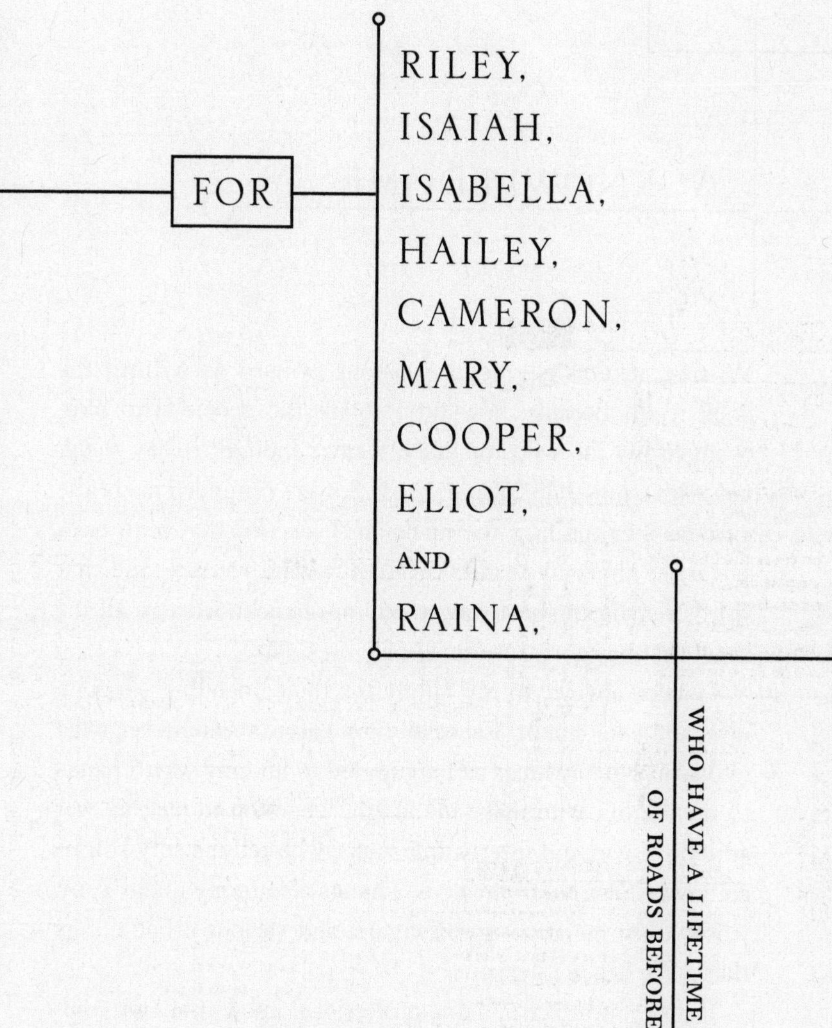

FOR

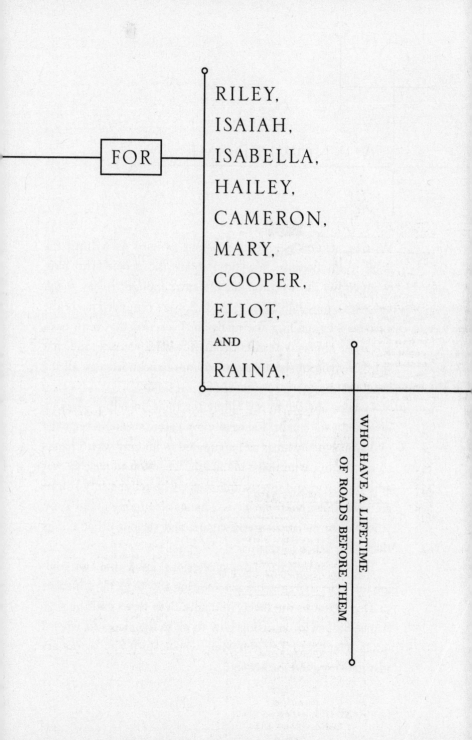

RILEY,
ISAIAH,
ISABELLA,
HAILEY,
CAMERON,
MARY,
COOPER,
ELIOT,
AND
RAINA,

WHO HAVE A LIFETIME
OF ROADS BEFORE THEM

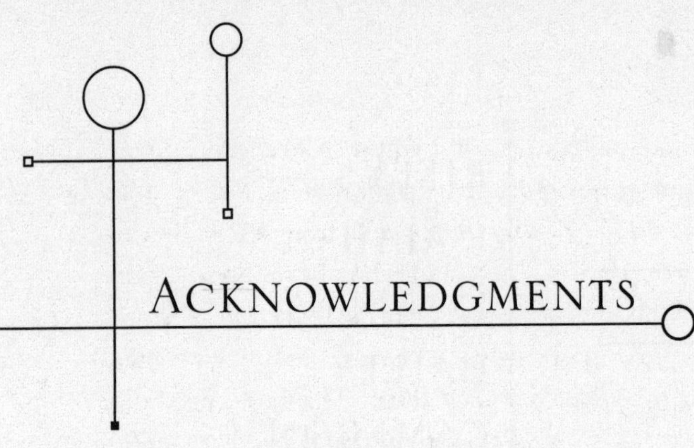

ACKNOWLEDGMENTS

Writing acknowledgments is about as hard as writing the book itself. Because how do I thank the people who have changed my life so completely? I once thought to say thank you with a mini bonsai tree whose flowers reminded me of the gardens surrounding the mansion. I learned that mini bonsais make short-lived gifts (You know who you are) and that words remain the best way to attempt to acknowledge all the heart that has gone into this book.

Thanks, always, to my family for their unending support, love, and excitement. Especially my parents, who never tried to discourage my ideas as I struggled to find my way. Thanks to the kiddos, who make me laugh, who stop to pick up wet autumn leaves and interesting rocks, who tell me silly stories and make me glad to be alive. Thanks also to my uncle Tony, who taught me about guns, cigars, and various other things that make Linden nervous.

Thank you to Harry Lam, professional know-it-all, for reading this story in fragments and knowing how to fix the unfixable.

Thank you to the lovely and silly Beth Revis and the sage Aimeé Carter for knowing how to make the pieces fit when I don't. Thanks to Tahereh Mafi, whose spirit and words are just flat-out good for my soul.

Thanks a million times to my editor, Alexandra Cooper, who, in addition to being phenomenal at what editors do best, also entertained many, many phone calls from me while this installment was being written, and who always knows what to say. Thank you to Lizzy Bromley, artist extraordinaire and all-around genius, for the beautiful covers, and to Ali Smith, who so brilliantly photographed them. Thanks to everyone who routinely takes the elevator to the floor that houses Simon & Schuster BFYR and sees to it that their stories get the star treatment. To visit that floor is to understand what a love for stories looks like.

Thanks forever to the wonderful Heather Shapiro and the entire team at Baror for making this story a part of the world.

Thanks to my agent, Barbara Poelle, for whom proper words of gratitude will forever elude me, and who, with a bit of her everyday magic, has turned my stories into things that can be held.

Thankfully, acknowledgments are longer-lived than potted plants, and so, as this story enters the world and spends its years on the shelves, let it always be known that this story came from a story of its own; it is the product of a lot of love, many phone calls, many tears, much laughter and excitement. In the three years that this series has been in progress, the lives of everyone behind it have changed, showing us funerals, weddings, births. The conquering of fears. Moments of cruel despair. Moments of radiant sun.

This story has been our constant.

It was never a journey I had to take alone. For that, and for everything: Thank you.

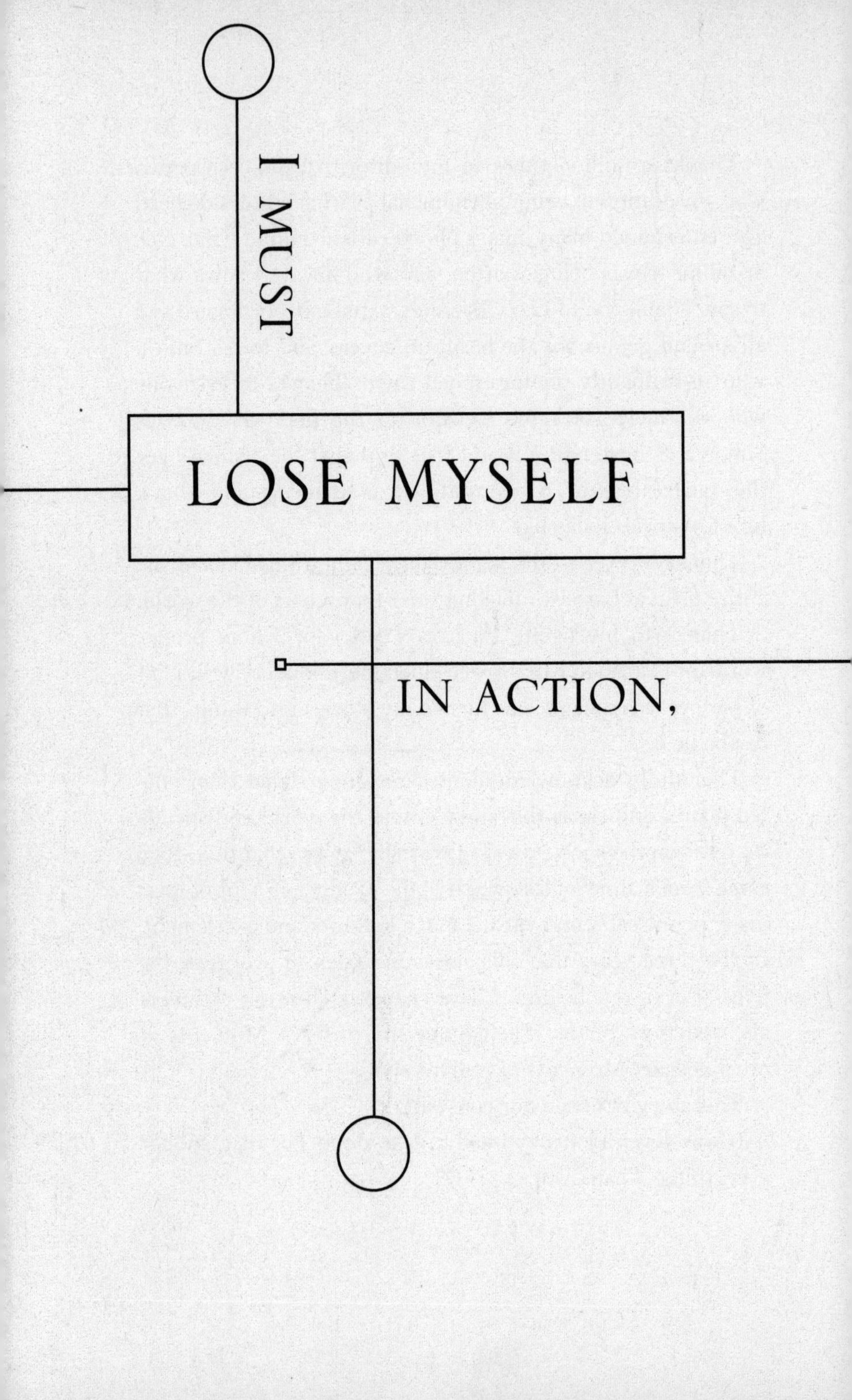
I MUST
LOSE MYSELF
IN ACTION,

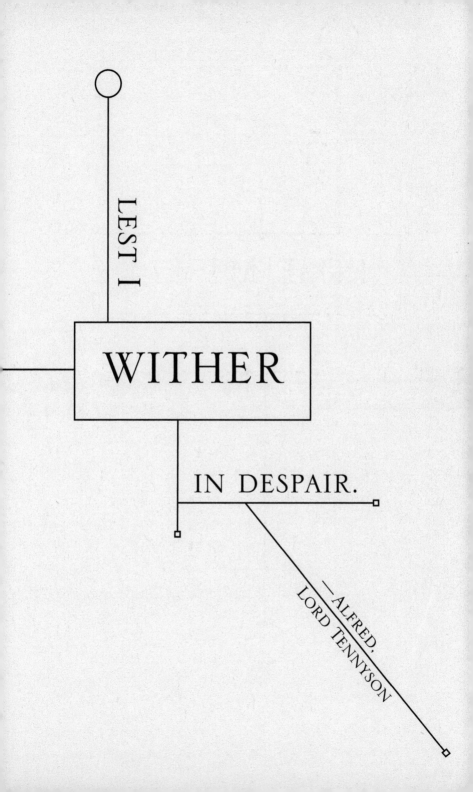

LEST I

WITHER

IN DESPAIR.

—Alfred, Lord Tennyson

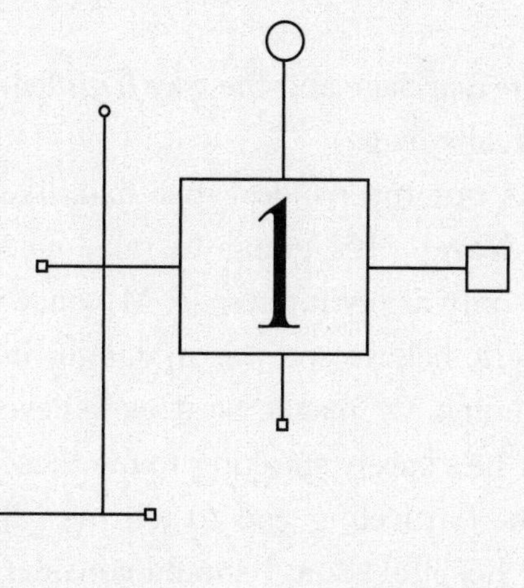

IN THE ATLAS the river still flows. The thin line of it carries cargo to a destination that no longer exists. We share a name, the river and I; if there's a reason for this, it died with my parents. The river lingers in my daydreams, though. I imagine it spreading out into the greatness of the ocean, melting into sunken cities, carrying old messages in bottles.

I have wasted too much time on this page. Really I should be in North America, charting my way from the Florida coastline to Providence, Rhode Island, where my twin brother has just bombed a hospital for its pro-science research on embryos.

I don't know how many are dead because of him.

Linden shifts his weight restlessly. "I didn't even know you had a brother," he'd said when I told him where I was going. "But the list of things I don't know about you is growing longer every day, isn't it?"

He's bitter. About our marriage and the way it ended. About the way it's not really over.

My sister wife looks out the window, her hair like light through autumn leaves. "It's going to rain," she says quietly. She's here only at my insistence. My once-husband still doesn't quite believe she was in danger in his father's, Vaughn's, home. Or maybe he does believe it; I'm not sure, because he's barely speaking to me these days, except to ask how I'm feeling and to tell me I'll be discharged from the hospital soon. I should consider myself lucky; most of the patients here are crammed into the lobbies or a dozen to a room, and that's if they're not turned away. I have comfort and privacy. Hospitalization of this class is reserved for the wealthy, and it just so happens that my father-in-law owns nearly every medical facility in the state of Florida.

Because there is never enough blood for transfusions, and because I lost so much of it when I sawed into my leg in a maddened delirium, it took me a long time to recover. And now that my blood has regenerated, they want to take it a bit at a time and analyze it to be sure I'm recovering. They're under the assumption that my body didn't respond to Vaughn's attempts to treat the virus; I'm not sure what exactly he told them, but he has a way of being everywhere without being present.

I have an interesting blood type, they say. They wouldn't have been able to find a match even if more people donated their blood for the meager pay the hospital gives.

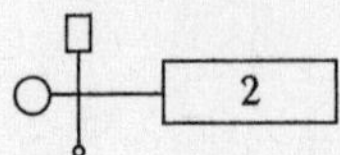

Cecily mentioned the rain to distract Linden from the nurse who has just sterilized my arm. But it doesn't work. Linden's green eyes are trained on my blood as it fills up the syringe. I hold the atlas in my blanketed lap, turn the page.

I find my way back to North America—the only continent that's left, and even it isn't whole; there are uninhabitable pieces of what used to be known as Canada and Mexico. There used to be an entire world of people and countries out there, but they've all since been destroyed by wars so distant they're hardly spoken about.

"Linden?" Cecily says, touching his arm.

He turns his head to her, but doesn't look.

"Linden," she tries again. "I need to eat something. I'm getting a headache."

This gets his attention because she is four months pregnant and prone to anemia. "What would you like, love?" he says.

"I saw brownies in the cafeteria earlier."

He frowns, tells her she should be eating things with more sustenance, but ultimately succumbs to her pouting.

Once he has left my hospital room, Cecily sits on the edge of my bed, rests her chin on my shoulder, and looks at the page. The nurse leaves us, my blood on his cart of surgical utensils.

This is the first time I've been alone with my sister wife since arriving at the hospital. She traces the outline of the country, swirls her finger around the Atlantic in tandem with her sigh.

"Linden is furious with me," she says, not without remorse, but also not in her usual weepy way. "He says you could have been killed."

I spent months in Vaughn's basement laboratory, the subject of countless experiments, while Linden obliviously milled about upstairs. Cecily, who visited me and talked of helping me escape, never told him about any of it.

It isn't the first time she betrayed me; though, as with the last time, I believe that she was trying to help. She would botch Vaughn's experiments by removing IVs and tampering with the equipment. I think her goal was to get me lucid enough to walk out the back door. But Cecily is young at fourteen years old, and doesn't understand that our father-in-law has plans much bigger than her best efforts. Neither of us stands a chance against him. He's even had Linden believing him for all these years.

Still, I ask, "Why didn't you tell Linden?"

She draws a shaky breath and sits more upright. I look at her, but she won't meet my eyes. Not wanting to intimidate her with guilt, I look at the open atlas.

"Linden was so heartbroken when you left," she says. "Angry, but sad, too. He wouldn't talk about it. He closed your door and forbade me from opening it. He stopped drawing. He spent so much time with me and with Bowen, and I loved that, but I could tell it was because he wanted to forget you." She takes a deep breath, turns the page.

We stare at South America for a few seconds. Then she says, "And, eventually, he started to get better. He was talking about taking me to the spring expo that's coming up. Then you came back, and I thought, if he saw you, it would undo all the progress he'd made." Now she looks at me, her brown eyes sharp. "And you didn't want to be back, anyway. So I thought I could get you to escape again, and he would never have to know, and we could all just be happy."

She says that last word, "happy," like it's the direst thing in the world. Her voice cracks with it. A year ago, here is where she'd have started to cry. I remember that on my last day before I ran away, I left her screaming and weeping in a snowbank when she realized how she'd betrayed our older sister wife, Jenna, by telling our father-in-law of Jenna's efforts to help me escape, which only aided his decision to dispose of her.

But Cecily has grown since then. Having a child and enduring the loss of not one but two members of her marriage have aged her.

"Linden was right," she says. "You could have been killed, and I—" She swallows hard, but doesn't take her eyes from mine. "I wouldn't have been able to forgive myself. I'm sorry, Rhine."

I wrap my arm around her shoulders, and she leans against me.

"Vaughn is dangerous," I say into her ear. "Linden doesn't want to believe it, but I think you do."

"I know," she says.

"He's tracking your every move the way he tracked me."

"I know."

"He killed Jenna."

"I know. I know that."

"Don't let Linden talk you into trusting him," I say. "Don't put yourself in a situation where you're alone with him."

"You can run away, but I can't," she says. "That's my home. It's all I have."

Linden clears his throat in the doorway. Cecily bounds to him and ups herself on tiptoes to kiss him when she takes the brownie from his hand. Then she unwraps its plastic. She settles in a chair and props her swollen feet up on the window ledge. She has a way of ignoring Linden's hints about wanting to be alone with me. It was a minor annoyance in our marriage, but right now it's a relief. I don't know what Linden wants to say to me, only that his fidgeting means he wants it to be in private, and I'm dreading it.

I watch as Cecily nibbles the edges of the brownie and dusts crumbs off her shirtfront. She's aware of Linden's restlessness, but she also knows he won't ask her to leave. Because she's pregnant, and because she's the only wife left who so genuinely adores him.

Linden picks up the sketchbook he abandoned on a chair, sits, and tries to busy himself looking through his building designs. I sort of feel sorry for him. He has never been authoritative enough to ask for what he wants. Even though I know this conversation he's itching to have will leave me feeling guilty and miserable, I owe him this much.

"Cecily," I say.

"Mm?" she says, and crumbs fall from her lips.

"Leave us alone for a few minutes."

She glances at Linden, who looks at her and doesn't object, and then back to me.

"Fine," she sighs. "I have to pee anyway."

After she leaves, closing the door behind her, Linden shuts his notebook. "Thanks," he says.

I push myself upright, smooth the sheets over my thighs, and nod, avoiding his eyes. "What is it?" I ask.

"They're letting you out tomorrow," he says, taking the seat by my bed. "Do you have any sort of plan?"

"I was never good at plans," I say. "But I'll figure it out."

"How will you find your brother?" he says. "Rhode Island is hundreds of miles away."

"One thousand three hundred miles," I say. "Roughly. I've been reading up on it."

He frowns. "You're still recovering," he says. "You should rest for a few days."

"I might as well get moving." I close the atlas. "I have nowhere else to go."

"You know that isn't true," he says. "You have a—" He hesitates. "A place to stay."

He was going to say "home."

I don't answer, and the silence is filled with all the things Linden wants to say. Phantom words, ghosts that haunt the pieces of dust swimming in beams of light.

"Or," he starts up again. "There is another option. My uncle."

That gets me to look at him, maybe too inquisitively, because he seems amused. "My father disowned him years ago, when I was very young," he says. "I'm supposed to pretend he doesn't exist, but he doesn't live far from here."

"He's your father's brother?" I say, skeptical.

"Just think about it," Linden says. "He's a little strange, but Rose liked him." He says that last part with a laugh, and his cheeks light up with pink, and I strangely feel better.

"She met him?" I ask.

"Just once," Linden says. "We were on our way to a party, and she leaned over the driver's seat and said, 'I'm sick of these boring things. Take us anywhere else.' So I gave the driver my uncle's address, and we spent the evening there, eating the worst coffee crumb cake we'd ever tasted."

It's the first time since her death that he's brought up Rose without wincing at the pain.

"And the fact that my father hates him just made my

uncle that much more appealing to her," Linden goes on. "He's too pro-naturalism for my father's taste, and admittedly a little strange. I've had to keep it a secret that I visit with him."

Linden has a rebellious side. Who knew. He reaches out and tucks my hair behind my ear. It's done out of habit, and he jerks his hand back when he realizes his mistake.

"Sorry," he mumbles.

"It's all right," I say. "I'll think about it." My words are coming out fast, bumbling. "What you said— I mean— I'll think about it."

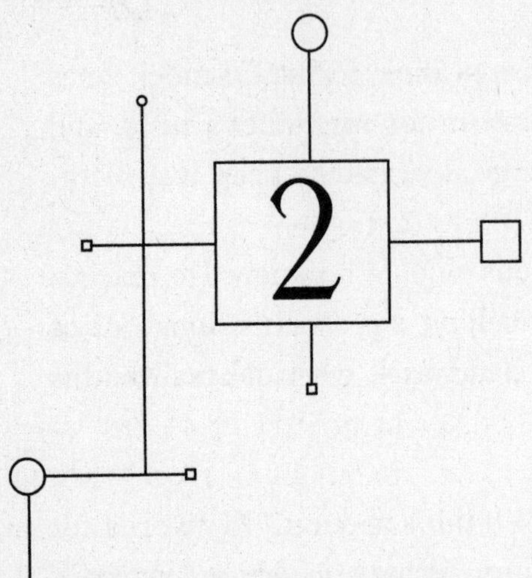

2

CECILY HANGS out the limo's open window, her hair flailing behind her like a ribbon caught on a hook. Bowen, in his father's arms, reaches out to catch it. I'm astounded by how much he grew while I was away. He's a teddy bear of a boy—stocky and friendly and apple-cheeked. He was born with dark hair and beaming blue eyes that have since gone hazel. His hair has lightened to a coppery blond that I imagine mimics Cecily's when she was a baby, which we'll never know for certain. He has her defiant chin, her thin eyelashes. With every day that passes, prominent traces of Linden dissolve from his face.

He is beautiful, though. And Cecily is mad for him. I've never seen anyone love anything as much as she loves that baby. Even now, though she's facing the sky that rushes past, she's singing a lullaby for him. I recognize it as a poem from a book in the library on the wives' floor. Jenna used to read it aloud.

And frogs in the pools singing at night,
And wild plum-trees in tremulous white;
Robins will wear their feathery fire
Whistling their whims on a low fence-wire . . .

The sun is setting, making the world orange. I rub my fists over my knees, uneasy. I can't believe Vaughn let us use the limo for this. Maybe he's trying to stay on Linden's good side, to manipulate him by being contrite and reliable. I keep expecting the driver to turn on us and take me back to the mansion. But he has taken us so far into the countryside that I'm beginning to let go of that fear. It's been minutes since we passed any buildings. There's only grass, and the occasional lone tree that comes and goes like an explosion.

Cecily interrupts her song to ask, "Where are we?" and lean back into her seat.

"Someplace rural," Linden says. "It's hard to say. I never knew the street names."

Cecily reaches for the baby, and then holds him over her head, blowing absurd-sounding kisses on his belly; his giggles make her grin.

"It's this turn," Linden tells the driver. "Off the road. Follow the tire tracks."

Even the limo, with its smooth ride, jostles over the uneven terrain. And a few minutes later we've come to the only thing in sight: a two-story brick house that looks as old and stable as the mansion, but much smaller.

Surrounding it are half a dozen tarps arranged like black car-shaped ghosts. There's a dilapidated shed and a windmill. The roof is covered in reflective panels.

Cecily crinkles her nose and turns to Linden. "We can't leave her here," she says. "It looks like a junkyard."

"It's not as bad as all that," he says.

"There's tinfoil on his roof!"

"They're solar panels," Linden amends patiently. "So he doesn't have to use so much electricity."

Cecily opens her mouth to object, but I say, "It's only for a couple of days. It looks fine." I don't mention that, while this is a step down from the luxuries of the mansion, it's as nice as any of the homes I grew up near. And solar panels aren't uncommon in Manhattan at all, where many can't afford electricity.

The limo stops, and I open my door quickly, afraid of sleeping gas or locks or snakes that could come slithering through the vents to strangle me.

It's early evening now, and without civilization for miles I can see darkness stretching toward me from every direction. The stars are bright, splayed across every shade of pink and blue, tracing a lone, oblong cloud.

Linden comes up beside me, follows my gaze skyward. "When I was little," he says, "my uncle told me the names of all the constellations. But I could never find them."

"But you know which one's the North Star," I remind

him. I remember that he told Cecily about it, and she was discouraged by his lack of romance.

"Right there," he says, following the line of my arm as I point.

"That's the tail of Ursa Minor," I say, moving my finger along the corresponding stars. "It's my favorite because I think it looks like a kite."

"I actually see it," he says quietly, as though astonished. "But I thought Ursa Minor was supposed to be in the shape of a dipper."

"Well, I think it looks like a kite," I say. "That's how I'm always able to find it."

He turns toward me, and I can feel his breaths, so faint and unassuming that they only move the finest hairs around my face. I don't dare take my eyes from the stars. My heart is pounding. Memories rush through me. Memories of his fingers unbuckling my shoes, inching under the strap of my red party dress. His lips on mine. The darkness of my bedroom swimming with ivy and champagne glasses the night we came home late from the expo. Snow dusting his shoulders and his dark hair the night we said good-bye.

Cecily slams the car door, snapping me back to reality. "If Rhine is staying here tonight," she says, "I am too, to make sure she doesn't get murdered by whatever lunatic runs this place."

I open my mouth to chide her for being so rude. To say that Linden's uncle was nice enough to let me stay, and that asking for anything more would seem ungrateful. And also to point out that she's barely as high as my shoulder, and how exactly would she fend off a lunatic if I couldn't?

But the words won't come out. The thought of my only remaining sister wife going back to that mansion is making my palms sweat. She was safe when Vaughn kept her oblivious, but now that she's seen the workings of his basement and she understands what he's capable of, I worry for her safety.

"My uncle isn't a lunatic," Linden says, and opens the car door again to pull out the suitcase that was sliding around the floor on the way here.

"Why does your father hate him so much, then?" Cecily says.

Linden's father is no judge of who is or is not a lunatic, but I don't say this either. I lean back against the trunk of the limo because I'm starting to feel light-headed, and the stars are throbbing, and Linden is right, I do need to rest before I venture into the world again. Everywhere I look, there's nothing. The world is so far away. All that effort, all those miles undone. I was in Vaughn's basement of horrors for more than two months. Two months that felt like ten minutes. Gabriel must think I'm dead. Just like my brother thinks I'm dead.

But there has been so much sadness, so much disheartenment, that my body has worked up a defense mechanism to keep me from thinking about it. My head goes numb, and my bones start to ache. Hurricane winds spiral in my ear canals. A sharp pain has streaked my vision with a lightning bolt of white.

Cecily and Linden are talking—something about what counts as eccentricity versus insanity, I think, and the conversation is getting terse as they interrupt each other. Linden is a creature of saintlike patience, but Cecily has a way of wearing anyone down.

"You okay?" Cecily asks me, and I realize that they've moved a couple of yards ahead of me, toward the house. Linden turns to watch me, Bowen's diaper bag slung from his shoulder, and a suitcase in his hand; he packed some clothes for me from my old closet.

I nod and follow after them.

Nobody answers when Linden knocks on the door. He knocks harder, then tries looking into the only visible window, which has its shade drawn. "Uncle Reed?" he calls, and knocks on the glass.

"Does he know we're coming?" I ask.

"I told him last week when I visited," he says.

"How often do you come out here?" Cecily says, wounded. "You never told me."

"I've kept it secret. . . ." Linden trails off, mouthing something to himself as he tries to see around the window shade. "I think I see a light inside." He knocks again, and when there's no answer, he opens the door.

Cecily cradles Bowen's head protectively, and casts a pensive stare into the darkness. "Linden, are you sure?" But he has already gone in ahead of us.

I follow him, my sister wife shuffling close behind and gripping the hem of my shirt.

It's so dark that I can barely make out Linden's shape as it moves ahead of me. It's a long hallway, the wood creaking under our feet, and there's the smoky smell of cedar and must. Then there's a faint orange light flickering in a room at the end of the hall.

We gather at either side of Linden in the doorway. We've come to a kitchen—at least I think that's what it is. There's a sink and a stove. But rather than cabinets there are shelves cluttered with things I can't make out in the darkness.

There's a small round table, upon which a candle flickers in a mason jar. A man is seated there, hunched over something that looks like a giant metal organ. Its wires, pipes, and gears are the arteries, and it's a mechanical heart, bleeding black oil onto the table and the man's fingers.

"Uncle Reed?" Linden says.

The man grunts, working some intricacy with a pair of pliers and taking his time before looking up. He sees me first, then Cecily. "These are your wives?" he says.

Linden hesitates. But he doesn't have to answer, because the man returns to his work rather unceremoniously and adds, "I thought you said there were three of them."

"Just two," Linden says, with so little emotion it gives me pause. It's as if Jenna never existed. "And this is my son," he adds, taking the baby from Cecily's arms. "Bowen."

The man—Reed—pauses, astonished by something. But then he only grunts. "Doesn't look like you," he says.

Cecily plays with a light switch on the wall; it doesn't work. "Please don't touch anything," Reed says, and wipes his hands with a dingy rag that only spreads the oil around. He moves to the sink, and the faucet shudders before it spits out an unsteady stream. I can't be certain in the candlelight, but I think I see flecks of black in the water. Reed mutters curses.

Then he pulls a cord over his head, and bleary light fills the room from a bulb that swings from the ceiling. The shadows jump back and forth, animating jars and pipes and senseless pieces that fill the shelves. There's a refrigerator in one corner of the room, but there's no electrical hum to it, no indication that it's on.

Reed comes closer, inspects the child in Linden's arms. Bowen's eyes are dazed, transfixed on the swinging bulb. "Nope, nothing like you," Reed reaffirms. "Whose is he?"

"He's mine," Cecily says.

Reed snorts. "How old are you? Ten?"

"Fourteen," she says through gritted teeth.

I get a whiff of something heady and smoky when Reed moves to stand before me. It's making my eyes water, but I'm just grateful that he looks nothing like Vaughn. He's not as tall, and he's a little overweight, and his gray hair is as wild as waves breaking on rocks. "I thought you were dead," he says to me.

I must be worse off than I thought, because surely

I just imagined that. But then Linden says, "That isn't Rose, Uncle. Her name is Rhine. Remember I told you the other day?"

"Oh, right, right," Reed says. "I'm bad with names. I'm usually much better with faces."

"I've been told I look like her," I offer.

"Doll, you could be her ghost," Reed says. "Do you believe in reincarnation?"

"She can't be a reincarnation of Rose," Cecily says, indignant. "They were both alive at the same time."

Reed looks at her like she's something he just stepped in, and she inches closer to Linden's side.

"Tell me," Reed says, turning back to me, "because my nephew's story was confusing. You're running away from him, and he's helping you?"

"That's one way to put it," I say. "But I'm not running away. Not really. I'm looking for my brother." A lump is forming in my throat, caused by Reed's stare and his smell and the interrogating hue of that light. "The last I heard, he was in Rhode Island. He's gotten into a—situation, and I need to find him. I won't be any trouble in the meantime." My words are coming out one atop the other, fast, and Linden puts his hand on my arm, and for some reason it calms me.

Reed looks me over, his mouth squished to one side of his face like he's thinking. "You have too much hair," he says. "You'll have to tie it back so it won't get caught in the machines."

I have no idea what he's talking about, but I say, "Okay."

"I told him you would help out a little," Linden says. "It won't be anything arduous. He knows you're recovering."

"From the car accident. Right," Reed says. I don't know what story Linden fed him to explain my injuries, but judging from his tone he doesn't believe it, or care to. "There's a room upstairs where you can put your things. My nephew can show you. The floors make a terrible creaking, so I'll have to ask you not to walk around at night."

That's apparently our cue to leave, because he turns his attention to the contraption on the table. Linden herds us down the hallway.

"Oh, Linden," Cecily whispers, her words almost lost to the creaking of the steps. "I knew you were mad at her, but you can't be serious about leaving her here."

"I am doing Rhine a favor," he replies. "And she can take care of herself." He looks over his shoulder at me. I'm two steps behind him. "Can't you?" he says.

I nod like I'm not at all unnerved by this new cold side to him. Not cruel like his father. Not warm like the husband who sought me out on quiet nights. Something in between. This Linden has never woven his fingers through mine, never chosen me from a line of weary Gathered girls, never said he loved me in a myriad of colored lights. We are nothing to each other.

Reed may have forgotten my name, but he apparently remembered that I was coming, because the spare bedroom is lit up by three candles—one on the nightstand, two on the dresser. They and a twin bed are the only furniture in the room. There's a cracked mirror on the far wall, and my reflection drowns in the darkness of it. Rose's ghost. I almost expect it to move independent of me.

Cecily drops the suitcase and the diaper bag on the floor, and a cloud of dust bursts from the mattress when she sits on it. She makes a big show of choking on it.

"It's fine," I say, shaking out the pillow.

"I'm afraid to even ask if there's a bathroom I can use," Cecily says.

"At the end of the hall," Linden says, rubbing his index finger along the bridge of his nose; it's something I've only seen him do when he's frustrated with his drawings. "Take a candle with you."

After Cecily has left the room, I sit on the edge of the bed and say, "Thank you, Linden."

He looks at his reflection in the mirror. "My uncle won't ask any questions, if you don't," he says. "About why you aren't staying at home with me, that is."

The silence is tight and unnatural. I grip the blanket in my fists and say, "Are you and Cecily going back there?"

"Of course," he says.

He still won't believe me about everything that happened in the basement. About Deirdre. I vaguely remember whispering about her in my medicated delirium, and about Jenna's body hiding away in some freezer. He rubbed my arm, whispering words that sounded like moth bodies flying into glass windows. Nonsensical things I tried to cling to. Maybe, lying there, I was so pitiful that he felt no choice but to love me. Now he says I can take care of myself. Now I'm the liar trying to destroy the perfect world his father set up for him, who ran away, broke everything. And it's getting late, and it's time to part ways.

But the words come out of me anyway. "Don't go."

He looks at me.

"Don't go," I say. "And don't take Cecily back there. I know you don't believe me, but I have a terrible feeling that—"

"I can take care of Cecily," he says. "I would have taken care of you, too. If I'd known you were so worried about my father."

Bowen has fallen asleep against Linden's chest, and Linden shifts him to the other arm. "My father thought that if you didn't want to be married to me, he could have you. It's because of your eyes. He wanted to study them, and he took it too far. He can be that way." His eyebrows knit together, and he looks at his feet, struggling to make sense of what he's saying, to force logic where there is none. "He isn't the monster you think he is. He just—he gets so into his work that he forgets people are people. He gets carried away."

"Carried away?" I spit back. "He drove needles into my eyes, Linden! He murdered a newborn—"

"Don't you think I know my own father?" he interrupts. "I'd trust him before I'd believe anything you say. You couldn't even do me the dignity of telling the truth."

There was a night, months ago, when I almost did. It was after the expo. I was half-drunk, my hair sticky and perfumed and teased, the bed tipping under me. He climbed over my body, and he kissed me. I could hear tree branches murmuring to one another in the moonlight. And Linden said, so close that I could feel his breath on my eyelashes, *But I don't know who you are. I don't know where you came from.* His eyes were bright. I wanted so badly to tell him, but something about that entire night seemed so beautiful, so bizarre, that I didn't trust it with my secrets. Or maybe I just wanted to play along, to wear his ring and be his wife for a little while before the magic took the light from the moon.

Now I say nothing. There's no brightness in his eyes for me.

"If you didn't love me," he says, "you should have said it. I would have let you go."

"You might have," I admit. "But not your father."

"My father has never been in charge of what I do," he says.

"Your father has always been in charge of what you do," I say.

He looks at me, and I stop breathing. Something comes

surging up behind his eyes, some argument of love or vengeance. Something that's been building every second I've been away. And I want it, whatever it is. Want to hold it in both hands like his leaping heart that's been ripped from his chest. Want to warm it with my body heat.

He says, "When Cecily comes back, tell her I'll be waiting by the car."

Then he's gone.

"I don't want to leave you here," Cecily says when I relay the message. "This place looks like it could give you cancer or something." She's remembering that word, "cancer," from a soap opera Jenna used to watch. It's a disease that was eliminated from our genetics.

"I don't think cancer was something you could catch," I tell her.

"That's my point," she says.

We must be making too much noise, because Reed bangs on the ceiling.

Cecily huffs and sits on the bed next to me. After a few seconds she puts her arm around my shoulders and stares at her stomach. At four months along she's already looking tired and swollen. Her cheeks and fingertips are flushed. Her face and hair are damp from where she's splashed herself with cold water, something she does after a bout of nausea.

"Have you been sick a lot?" I ask her.

"It's not so bad," she says softly. "Linden takes care of me."

I'm worried about her. I wonder if it has even occurred to her or to Linden that she hardly had a rest between pregnancies. Vaughn surely knows how unsafe this is, and he allowed it, which worries me even more. I'm scared that she'll enter that dark hall, descend the stairs, and be forever in Vaughn's clutches. I think she's scared too, because she doesn't move. I don't know how much time passes before Linden comes looking for her.

"Ready to go?" He stands in the doorway, mostly in shadow.

"I'm staying the night," she says.

They have some sort of conversation with their eyes. A husband-and-wife thing—something I could never quite get the hang of. Cecily wins, because Linden picks up the diaper bag and says, "I'll be back for you in the morning, first thing."

A few minutes later, through the window, we watch the limo drive out of sight.

The mattress is lumpy and hard, and Cecily, who is back to snoring the way she did in her later trimesters, spends the night thrashing and turning. She kicks me so many times that I eventually take a pillow and settle on the floor. But every position on the hard wood aggravates the recovering gash in my thigh. In my dreams, it bleeds and seeps through the floorboards, and Reed pounds on the ceiling because blood is raining down on his work. The engine on the table comes to life. It pulses and breathes.

In the darkness Cecily whispers my name. At first I

think it's part of my dream, but she persists, increasing in frequency and intensity until I say, "What?"

"Why are you on the floor?" I can just make out her face and arm leaning over the mattress, tangle of hair coming over one shoulder.

"You were kicking," I say.

"I'm sorry. Come back up. I promise I won't anymore."

She makes room for me, and I cram in beside her. Her skin is sticky and hot. "You shouldn't wear socks to bed," I tell her. "They keep heat in. Last time you were pregnant, you always got feverish at night."

Her legs move under the blanket as she kicks her socks off. It takes her a while to get comfortable, and I can tell she's trying not to disturb me, so I don't complain as I'm knocked around the mattress. Eventually she settles on her side, facing me.

"Did you get sick earlier, when you went to use the bathroom?" I ask.

"Don't tell Linden," she says, yawning. "He's squeamish about that stuff. He worries."

That's to be expected after what happened with Rose's pregnancy. But it's not as though I can tell her that. And soon I find, despite my worries, that I'm exhausted enough to fall asleep.

Just as I'm beginning to dream, she says, "I think about those other girls in the van with us. The ones who were killed."

My dreams fade away from me, and I wish desperately

that they'd return. Even a nightmare would be welcome over that memory. It's not something my sister wives and I ever talked about, the odd and horrific thing that bonded us to one another. I especially wouldn't expect to hear about it from Cecily, who has always wanted to be the happy housewife.

"I just wanted you to know that," she says. "I'm not a monster."

I turn my head to look at her. "Of course you aren't."

"You called me one," she says. "The day you ran away."

"I was upset," I say, pushing the sweaty hair from her face. "But what happened to Jenna isn't your fault."

She draws a shaky breath, closes her eyes for a long moment. "Yes, it is."

Here is where I expect her to cry, but she doesn't. She only looks at me. And it strikes me again how much she's grown in my absence. Maybe she had no choice. There were no sister wives to console her, the father-in-law she trusted had only been using her, and it's not as though she could explain any of this to her husband.

I struggle for words of comfort, but nothing feels sincere enough. And no matter what I say, Jenna is still gone, and so are the other girls that were Gathered, and the girl Silas and I found lying in a ditch. Cecily still won't live to see Bowen grow, and my brother has spiraled out of control in his grief, and I'm no closer to finding him than I was last year.

I am entirely powerless.

"The whole time we were married, I treated you like you were too small to understand what was happening to us," I say. "But I felt small too. I couldn't control the way things were any more than you could."

"You looked so confident," she says. "I envied you from the day we were married. I've decided I'm going to be more like you." She says it with conviction. "I'm going to be stronger."

The last thing I am is strong.

"Get some sleep," I whisper.

"Rhine?"

"What?"

"I told Linden to believe you. I told him it's true that Housemaster Vaughn is doing awful things downstairs."

I feel hope. Linden might not have any reason to believe me, but he'll listen to Cecily. Even if it's just to humor her so she doesn't go hysterical on him. "You did?"

"He wouldn't listen at first," she says. "It was while you were in the hospital. But I begged him to go and see for himself."

"Did he?" I ask.

"Yes," she says. "But—when he came back, he said there was nothing down there. A few of Housemaster Vaughn's chemicals and things, lots of machines and attendants working on them, but no bodies. No Deirdre. He says you must have been hallucinating, or making it all up."

Hope swims away, leaving me with less than nothing.

"But you saw those things too," I press. "Did you tell him that?"

Now she's the one brushing her fingers through my hair, trying to console me. "I only saw what was happening to you," she says. "I wish I'd seen more. I wish I'd seen Deirdre, or Rose's domestic, what was her—"

"Lydia," I say.

"Right. Lydia. I wish I could prove it." She's talking to me in that hushed, cooing tone usually reserved for her son. Trying to lull me to sleep, or compliance.

And then I realize why.

"You don't believe me," I say.

"Oh, Rhine, Housemaster Vaughn did such terrible things to you. You were so delirious, and so sick. Maybe there's a chance some of it—"

"It was real," I say, sitting up. "It was all real."

She sits upright herself, facing me in the darkness. She's frowning. "There was nothing down there, Rhine."

"He hid them, then," I say. "The bodies. The domestics. If Gabriel were here, he'd tell you the same thing."

Cecily straightens her posture, hopeful. She wants to believe me. "Did he tell you there were bodies down there?"

"Not exactly," I say.

"What did he tell you?"

My stomach sinks. I collapse back onto the pillow, defeated. "Not much," I admit. He was so high on opiates at first, and then it was one problem after the next, really. "He didn't have a chance."

Cecily lies beside me, rubs my arm reassuringly. We both go silent. I struggle to cope with the fact that I am the only one who saw what Vaughn kept in the basement. But even worse than that, I want to believe what Linden and Cecily do, that none of it really happened. Maybe it didn't. Maybe Deirdre really did get sold to another house when I left, and Adair and Lydia too. Maybe they're comfortable and safe, and I'd conjured Deirdre up to cope with the loneliness as I lay strapped to that bed. She visited me often.

I start to make a list in my head of all the things I know. Vaughn killed Jenna; he admitted as much. Rose's body was in the basement that day the elevators gave out. I saw her. I recognized her nail polish, her blond hair. There was a tracker in my leg. Deirdre told me about it. Didn't she? I think of all the attendants who came to work on me while I was in the basement. In my memory they all have the same blank expressions; they're all voiceless, uncaring. Deirdre was warm. She spoke gently, made me feel safe, which was a bizarre thing in that place.

The list collapses in on itself, words and memories jumbling into a bloody mess. It's so frustrating the way the pictures keep on changing.

In the end it's Cecily I reach for. At least I can be certain she exists. Her skin is sweaty and warm as I scrunch up the sleeves of the nightgown she borrowed from me. I worry about how overheated she gets, like there's a fire inside her. I think she drifted off to sleep and I woke her, because she mumbles something nonsensical before opening her eyes. "You don't have to believe me," I tell her. "You just have to believe that Vaughn is capable of those things."

"I do," she says. "Linden doesn't. I think he chooses not to. He's sensitive, you know?"

She strokes my cheek with the side of her hand—a repetitive, wispy motion. Like little ghost kisses.

"I thought Housemaster Vaughn wanted to do good things and save us all," she says. "I was wrong. And admitting that meant admitting he won't find an antidote and none of us has much time. You said you have to find your brother—so you should go do that. And Linden and I have Bowen, and this baby. I want to spend as much time with them as I can. I want to be with them until the end."

These are all things she wouldn't have dared to say last year. But now she's unflinching. Her voice doesn't even catch when she adds, "If all those things you saw are real, there's nothing we can do about them. We have our own lives to take care of, and there's only time to do so much with them."

What she says is terrible and true. She grabs my hand. We squeeze each other's fingers, and I wait for her to realize the magnitude of what she's said. I wait for her to squish up against me and sob. But from the reason in her tone, I sense that those words have been in her for a long time. That while I was away, she had plenty of time to get used to them.

And when the sob does come, several minutes later, it's mine.

My sister wife has already fallen asleep.

I dream of Linden in the doorway. He looks at me a long while, the green in his eyes changing every second. "The stars do look like a kite," he admits. "But everything else you've said is a lie."

In the morning I awaken to Cecily jumping from the bed, her feet crashing onto the floorboards like baritone notes, to get to the window. "Quiet," I tell her, cringing at the sudden light when she yanks the window shade, forcing it to recoil with a slurping noise.

"No, no, no. You have to hide," she tells me. Panic in her eyes. The sound of an engine purring under the window.

I stagger to my feet, every muscle sore, and walk to the window. And outside is the limo, a figure standing beside it waving us down. Linden said he'd be here to collect Cecily in the morning, but as my grogginess subsides, I realize that Linden isn't here.

Vaughn is.

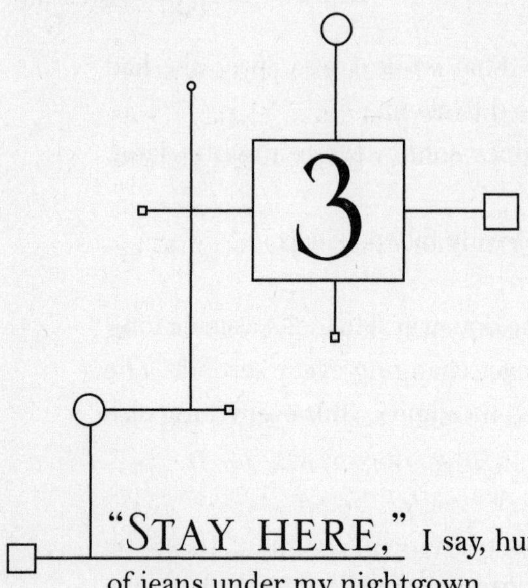

"STAY HERE," I say, hurrying to put on a pair of jeans under my nightgown.

"Wait!" Cecily calls after me as I'm running down the stairs.

"Stay!" I tell her.

Outside, the early morning air is cold, and I hug my arms for warmth. Dewy grass clings to my bare feet as I move toward him. He smiles. "Ah, so she awakens," he says. His voice disrupts the gray sky. A burst of black-birds rushes past.

I maintain my distance, keep my tone neutral when I ask, "Where's Linden?"

"Your husband had an early meeting with a potential contractor," he says. "He sent me for you and Cecily."

"Sure he did," I say, bracing one foot behind me to take a step back.

"You're still angry with me," he says. "I understand.

But, Rhine, darling, you're such a fascinating creature. You should be flattered; before you came along, I was sure I'd seen everything. I couldn't help but get carried away."

Carried away. I laugh humorlessly, a cloud bursting from my open mouth.

"Let's just be honest with each other. If it weren't for me, you'd be dead," he says.

"Thanks to you, I almost was," I say. "What will you do if I refuse to go along this time? Burn down this house?"

"While I do think a fire would be an improvement, no. The choice is entirely your own," he says, sounding sincere. "I thought you and I could put this sordid mess behind us. How does resuming first wife status sound?"

I open my mouth, aghast, but no words come. How did he even find me here? The tracker has been removed from my leg. Did Linden really send him here after me? I know he's angry, but I don't believe he'd do anything so venomous.

The screen door slams behind me, and then I realize it. Cecily. Vaughn can't trace my steps anymore, but she is still his property. How does it work? Is there a computer somewhere that spells out our location on a digital map? Or some kind of beeping device that sounds an alarm when we're nearby, like a metal detector hovering over coins? My parents used to have one of those; it was often how my father found scrap metal to build things with.

She moves to stand beside me, coiling her arm around mine. "She isn't going back," she says.

"You don't want your sister wife to come home?" Vaughn says. "But you've been so lonely. So lonely, in fact, that you were sneaking down to visit her every time I left the house."

She draws a deep breath. She's scared, though she's trying not to let on.

"Don't go with him," I say into her ear.

The screen door slams again, and I catch a whiff of smoke. Reed has a cigar in his mouth. Grease and brown splotches stain his white shirt. "Nobody was going to invite me to the reunion?" he says to Vaughn. "You can't have it both ways, Little Brother. If I can't come onto your property, you can't come onto mine."

"I've just come to collect something that belongs to me," Vaughn says. "Put something decent on, Cecily. Run a brush through that hair, and let's go." She's still wearing one of the nightgowns that Linden packed for me, the unbuttoned collar dipping over her shoulder.

"I'll leave when my husband gets here," Cecily says. "Not before then."

"You heard the kid," Reed says.

Vaughn opens his mouth to say something, but the sound of a baby crying interrupts him. And the words he was going to say turn into a grin. Cecily stiffens.

Vaughn opens the passenger door and says, "Come on out and talk some sense into your keeper."

Elle, Cecily's domestic, steps out of the car. She's holding Bowen to her chest, and his face is red and wet with tears. Cecily reaches for him immediately, but Vaughn steps in her way. "It's chilly out here, darling," he says. "And you're pregnant. You don't even have the sense to wear a coat. What makes you think you can get by without me to supervise your prenatal care? You've already missed your vitamins this morning."

"He's right," Elle says a bit too softly. She's looking at the ground, and her words sound rehearsed. She's smaller than Cecily—nine, maybe ten years old, and of all our domestics she's always been the most timid. I'm sure it was no challenge for Vaughn to intimidate her.

Cecily purses her lips together, composing herself. I think she's trying not to cry. "You can't keep my son from me."

Vaughn laughs, taps her nose the way he did when she was a newlywed, when she adored him because she didn't know any better. "Of course not," he says. "You're the one who's been away from him."

She steps past Vaughn, and he grips her forearm when she tries to reach for her son. I see the strain in his arm from the force of holding her. Her jaw swells with spite. He has never grabbed her before; he's always been able to command her with his serpent's charm. "Come home, or don't," he says. "But know that I won't allow my grandson to stay here in this cesspool."

He looks at me and adds, "As always, the invitation

is extended. It wouldn't be home without you."

"Whose home?" I mutter. I take a step back, into the choking smog of Reed's cigar. He says nothing, standing on the top porch step. This isn't his battle.

Cecily looks at me with the same regret as on the day I told her our father-in-law was responsible for Jenna's death, when snow was falling between us. And my heart breaks the same way it did then. "I have to go," she says.

"I know," I tell her, because I realize it too. She has Bowen and an unborn child to care for, and a husband to love. I have my brother and Gabriel to find. Cecily and I can't keep each other safe. We have to let go.

Vaughn releases her, and she comes at me, hugging me with so much force that I stumble. I wrap my arms around her. "Take care," she murmurs into my ear. "Be brave, okay?"

"You too," I say.

She lets go of me when Bowen's cries jump up a few octaves. Vaughn escorts her to the car and waits until she has climbed inside, before instructing Elle to hand her the baby.

Cecily clings to her son, but watches me over his wispy curls. Her lower eyelids have gone pink, a wavering line of tears tracing them. We know how unlikely it is that we'll ever see each other again. If Linden had come to collect her, at least we'd have had time for a real good-bye.

Vaughn climbs in beside her and closes the door, and

I'm left staring at my own reflection in the darkened windows. Until even that is gone.

Reed steps beside me, and together we watch the limo get swallowed by the horizon. He offers me a puff of his cigar, but I shake my head, letting the numbness take over my head, welcoming the pain into my bones. Waiting for this sadness to disappear like both of my sister wives.

"Don't feel bad, doll," Reed says. "My mother never cared for Vaughn either. Though, bless her soul, she did try." He claps my shoulder. "Better get washed up. There's work to do."

The water trickles from the showerhead; it runs bleary and chunked with rust. But it's not very much worse than what I was used to in Manhattan, and I'm able to get reasonably clean by not standing directly under it and splashing myself when it's at its clearest. I take extra care with the gash that runs along my inner thigh, the skin pinched together with stitches.

When I go through the suitcase Linden packed, I find that he left a roll of gauze and a bottle of antiseptic in one of the inner pouches by my toothbrush, where I'd be sure to see them. He was still thinking of me, caring for me in that passive way of his. Everything is neatly folded too. A lesser husband would be angry after what I put him through, would hope the wound became infected and the entire leg fell off.

I dress the wound, and try to roll up the rest of the gauze as neatly as I found it, but I can't duplicate Linden's meticulousness.

Remembering what Reed said last night about the machines, I tie my hair back with one of the many rubber bands hanging on the doorknob. Rubber bands on doorknobs, and bolts and rusty nails in glass jars, stacked into pyramids in corners. The entire house is a sort of machine, as though gears are turning between the walls.

The downstairs hallway smells like fried lard, becoming more pungent when I reach the kitchen. "Hungry?" Reed asks. I shake my head.

"Didn't think so," he says, pouring grease from a frying pan into an old can. "You seem birdlike. Even your hair is like a nest."

Maybe I should take offense, but I don't mind this image of me he's painting. It makes me feel wild, brave.

"Bet you never eat," he says. "Bet you drink up the oxygen like it's butter. Bet you can go for days on nothing but thoughts."

That gets a smile out of me. I can see why Vaughn wouldn't like his brother, and why Linden would.

"So," he says, turning to face me. "My nephew tells me you're still recovering. But you look recovered to me."

Linden did say his uncle wouldn't ask many questions, and he hasn't. But he has a clever way of getting answers with carefully worded statements.

"I am," I say. "Mostly. I'll only be a day or two, and

I can be useful in the meantime. I know how to keep a house running. How to fix things."

"Fixing things is good," he says, walking past me. I follow him down the hallway, out the front door, into the breezy May air. The grass and the bright weeds of flowers sway on the wind like the hologram that came from the keyboard as Cecily played. A stop-motion drawing in colored pencil, unreal.

It's gotten warmer since this morning, and there's the almost plastic smell of grass. I think of Gabriel, how this time last year he brought me tea in the library and read over my shoulder. He pointed to the sketches of boats on the page of the history book, and I thought that it would be nice for us to sail away, the water dividing endlessly in the sunlight. Breaking in half and then breaking in half again.

I push back my worries. I'll come to find him soon; that's all I can hope for.

Reed shows me to the shed beside his house, which might have once been a barn. It's enormous enough. "Even things that aren't broken can be fixed," he says. The darkness smells like mold and metal. "Everything can become something it's not."

He looks at me, eyebrows up, like it's my turn to say something. When I remain quiet, it seems to disappoint him. His fingers flutter over his head as he presses forward.

It's hard to see. The only light comes through gaps in the wooden planks that make up the walls.

Then Reed pushes on a far wall, and it swings open. It's a giant door, and at once the place is flooded with sunlight. Awkward shapes around me become leather straps, guns mounted up by nails, car parts hung like carrion in a butcher shop. The floor is nothing but packed dirt, and there's a long worktable covered with so many odd things, I can't make sense of them.

"Never seen anything like it, I bet," Reed says, sounding pleased with himself. I get the sense that he takes pride in being perceived as mad. But he doesn't seem mad to me. He seems curious. Where his brother unravels human beings, weighing their organs in his bare palms, prying back eyelids, drawing blood, Reed unravels things. He showed more care with that engine on his table last night, more respect for its life, than Vaughn ever showed with me.

"My father liked to make things," I say. "And fix things. But woodworking, mostly."

I don't know what's making me talk so much. In the almost year I spent at the mansion, I don't think I revealed so much truth about myself as I have this morning.

I'm homesick, I suppose, and talking to a total stranger is my way of dealing with it.

Reed looks at me, and I catch the green in his eyes. He's like his brother there. They both have that distance, living in the world their thoughts create. He stares at me a long time and then says, "Say 'ridiculous.'"

"What?"

"The word 'ridiculous,'" he insists. "Say it."

"Ridiculous," I say.

"An absolute ghost," he says, shaking his head and dropping into a seat at his worktable. It's really an old picnic table with attached benches. "You look just like my nephew's first wife. You even have her voice, and 'ridiculous' was her favorite word. Everything was ridiculous. The virus. The attempts to cure it. My brother."

"Your brother *is* ridiculous," I agree.

"I'm going to call you Rose," he says with resolution, picking up a screwdriver and working the back off an old clock.

"Please don't," I say. "I knew Rose. I was there when she died. I'd find it creepy."

"Life is creepy," Reed says. "Kids rotting from the inside out at age twenty is creepy."

"Even so, my name is Rhine," I say.

He nods for me to sit across the table from him, and I do, avoiding a gray puddle of something on the bench. "What kind of name is 'Rhine,' anyway?" he asks.

"It's a river," I say. I upturn a bolt and try to spin it like a top. My father used to make them for me and my brother. We'd spin them at the top of the stairs, and crush our shoulders together as we watched them jump down one step to the next. His always got there first, or else mine slipped through the banister and fell away. "Or it *was* a river, a long time ago. It ran from the Netherlands to Switzerland."

"Then I'm sure it still does run there," Reed says, watching the bolt spin away from my fingers and promptly collapse. "The world is still out there. They just want you to think it's gone."

Okay, maybe he is a little bit mad. But I don't mind. Linden is right. Reed doesn't ask many questions. He spends the rest of the morning keeping me busy with menial tasks, never telling me what it is I'm doing. As near as I can tell, I'm disassembling an old clock to make a new one. He checks on me sometimes, but spends most of the time outside, lying flat under an old car, or climbing inside to start its engine, which only splutters and creates black clouds through the tailpipe. He hides away in an even bigger shed farther back, higher than the house and more makeshift, as though he built it as an afterthought, to cover what's inside.

But I don't ask about that, either.

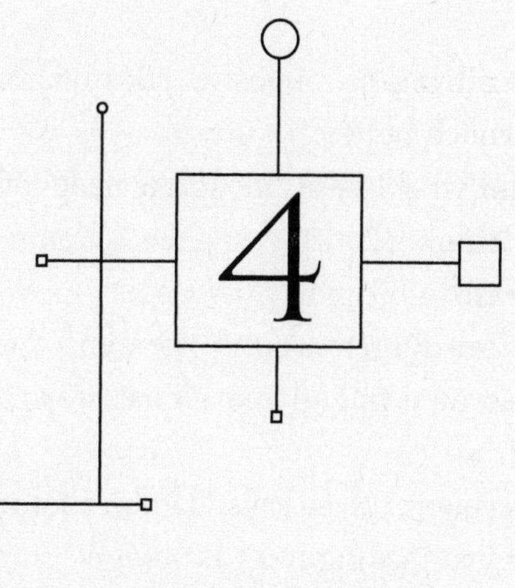

IT'S LIKE THAT for the rest of the day, and the next day, and the next. I don't ask questions, and neither does Reed. He places tasks before me, and I do them. One piece at a time. Never knowing what I'm assembling. I watch him, too. He spends a lot of time under cars or in that lumbering shed with the door closed.

I never have much of an appetite, and the safest things to eat in his kitchen are the apples, anyway, being that they're the only things I recognize. They're not the ultrabright green and red fruit I got used to in the mansion. They're speckled, flawed, and mealy, the way I grew up thinking they should be. I'm still not sure which way is more natural.

On my fourth morning, when I climb out of bed, I notice that the dizziness and the flecks of light are gone. The pain in my thigh has dulled, and the stitches have started to disintegrate. "I think I'll leave tomorrow,"

I tell Reed while we're sitting on opposite sides of his worktable. "I'm feeling much better."

He's taking a magnifying glass to some heap of machinery—a motor, I think. "Did my nephew arrange for transportation?" he asks.

"No," I say, tracing my finger around the rim of a mason jar filled with screws and grime. "That wasn't part of the agreement."

"So there was an agreement," Reed says. "Doesn't seem like it. Seems like you're just making it up as you go."

Story of my life. There's no real way to counter that, so I just shrug. "I'll be all right," I say. "He knows there's no reason to worry about me."

Reed glances at me for a moment, his forehead creased, eyebrows raised, before he returns to his task. "The fact that you're here says he's worried about you," he says. "Doesn't want you anywhere near his father, that much is clear."

"Vaughn and I don't exactly get along," I say.

"Let me guess," Reed says. "He tried to pluck out your eyes for science." He says that last word, "science," with such exaggerated passion that I laugh.

"Close," I say.

He stops working, leans forward, and stares at me so intently that I can't help but look back at him. "It was no car accident, was it?" he says.

"What do you keep in that shed?" I counter. Since we're asking questions.

"An airplane," he says. "Bet you thought they were extinct."

It's true there aren't many airplanes. Most people wouldn't be able to afford traveling that way, and most cargo is transported by truck. But the president and select wealthy families have them for business or leisure. Vaughn, for instance, could afford one if he wanted. But my guess is that what Reed calls an airplane is a patchwork of different parts, and not something I'd want to board.

I look at the table. He answered my question; now he's waiting for me to answer his.

"Vaughn was using me to find an antidote," I say. "Something about my eyes being like a mosaic, or something. I don't know. It's hard to follow him." And at the time, I had so many drugs running through me that I thought the ceiling tiles were singing to me. Those days were so vivid at the time, but now, looking back, the memory is a shadow at the end of a long corridor. I can't remember much of anything.

"Doesn't sound like something my nephew would allow," Reed says. "Don't get me wrong, the poor boy is as oblivious as a rabbit on a lion reserve, but still."

Animal reserves are a thing of the past, but somehow this comparison feels right.

"He didn't know," I say. "And when I told him, he didn't really believe it was as bad as it was. He still won't. So we've decided it's best to"—I pause, looking for the right words—"part ways. He and Cecily have the new baby coming, and I need to find my brother." And Gabriel, but that would require even more explaining, and I'm already starting to feel exhausted and achy just thinking about what's been said so far.

The dull aching becomes a stab of pain in my temple when Reed asks, "Then, why, doll, are you still wearing his ring?"

My wedding ring. Etched with fictional flowers that don't begin and don't end. More than once I've thought about cutting into it with something sharp. Making a line, severing the vines just so they stop somewhere.

"Can I see your plane?" I ask. "Does it fly?"

He laughs. It's nothing like Vaughn's laugh. There's warmth in it. "You want to see the plane?"

"Sure," I say. "Why not?"

"No reason not to, I suppose," he says. "It's just that no one's ever asked before."

"You have an airplane in your shed, and no one has ever asked to see it?" I say.

"Most people don't know it's there," he says. "But I like you, not-Rose. So maybe tomorrow. For now, we have other things to do."

That night I lie in Reed's yard. It stretches on farther than I can see, empty, aside from the tall grass and the bursts of wildflowers. I lie on the dirt and think, *There is where the orange grove would be. And over there, the golf course, with its spinning windmill, its lighthouse gleaming.* And farther down would be the stables, abandoned now, where Rose and Linden used to keep their horses. And here, where I'm lying, would be the swimming pool. I could coast on an inflatable raft as imaginary guppies flicked their bodies around me in glimmers of color.

I thought I'd left that place behind me. But it keeps rebuilding itself in my mind.

Something rustles nearby and I turn my head, watching the grass move. I get the terrible sense that it's trying to warn me.

I sit up and hold my breath, trying to listen. But a gust of wind is rolling through. I think it's saying my name. No, that voice didn't belong to the wind, though it would make more sense than the truth.

"Rhine?"

I lean back on my arms, tilt my head all the way to see the figure standing behind me.

"Hi," I say.

The moon is full and beaming like a halo behind his head. His curls are his dark crown. He could be a sort of prince.

"Hi," Linden says. "Can I sit?"

I collapse onto my back, liking the way the cold earth feels against my skull. I nod.

He sits next to me, careful to avoid my hair that's splayed around my head like blood. A bullet to the forehead, boom, blond waves everywhere.

"Didn't think you were coming back," I say, focusing on the kite in the stars. I look for other kites, or people to fly them.

Linden lies beside me. All I can think is that he's going to get grass stains on his white shirt. He's going to dirty that lovely hair. I feel like he's trying to prove a point that he can be like me—not so neat and perfect.

"I didn't send my father, the other day," he says. "I didn't know he was going to do that."

What he doesn't say is that his father probably tracked my whereabouts using whatever device he implanted in Cecily. Linden saw for himself the one that had been implanted in me.

"Thought you said you knew him so well," I mumble. Without looking back, I can feel his stare.

"He was trying to spare me," Linden says. "He knew how difficult it would be for me to see you."

"So you were spared," I say. "Why did you come back?"

"My uncle called me this afternoon," he says.

"I didn't know you even had a phone," I say. Somehow this feels like a violation, a reminder that while Linden treated me as an equal during our marriage, that was only part of the illusion. I was always a prisoner.

"He told me you were leaving," Linden says. "He said you just planned to walk off and leave everything to chance."

"Something like that," I say.

"That's not much of a plan," he says. "What are you

going to do for money? Transportation? Food? Where will you sleep?"

I shake my head. "It doesn't matter."

"Of course it matters."

"This is why Reed was stalling, isn't it? He wanted to talk to you before I left." I suppress a cry of frustration. "Please just let this be my problem," I say. "Not yours."

He's silent after that. The silence adds a foreign element to the air, polluting the moonlight, making my throat tight, the crickets extra loud. Planets are leaning in to listen. And finally I can't take it anymore. "Just say it," I tell him.

"Say what?"

"Whatever it is you want to say to me. There's something ugly in there you've been wanting to let out. I can tell."

"It's not ugly," he says gently. "Or angry at all, really. It's more of a question."

I prop myself on one elbow to look at him, and he does the same. There's no hostility in his eyes. There's no kindness, either. There's nothing but green. "That night, at the New Year's party, you said you loved me. Did you mean that?"

I stare at him a long time. Until his face disappears, and he's just a shadow.

"I don't know," I tell him. "If I did, it wasn't enough to make me stay."

He nods. Then he gets up, dusts the backs of his legs,

and offers his hand to me. I let him pull me to my feet.

"Don't leave tomorrow," he says. "Please. Give me a chance to figure something out. If I just let you go, Cecily will be livid."

"She'll be okay," I say. "You don't owe me anything."

"Then think of it as doing me a favor," he says. "I'd like for Cecily to not be angry with me."

I hesitate. "How long?"

"A couple of days, maybe less."

"All right," I say. "A couple of days. Maybe less."

His lips waver, and I think he's going to smile, but he doesn't. The last time I saw him, he was brimming with words and thoughts, anger and intensity. I could feel them humming inside him. But now they're all gone. I wonder where he put them. I wonder if he shouted them into the orange grove with the supposed ashes of his dead wife and child. When he opens his mouth, all he says is, "If you're going to be out here, you should really wear a sweater. I packed one for you."

Then he turns to leave. The limo is idling in the distance.

"It wasn't all a lie, Linden," I burst out when he's a few yards away. My voice is weak, getting smaller with each word. "Not everything. Not all of it."

He climbs into the backseat, giving no indication that he believes me.

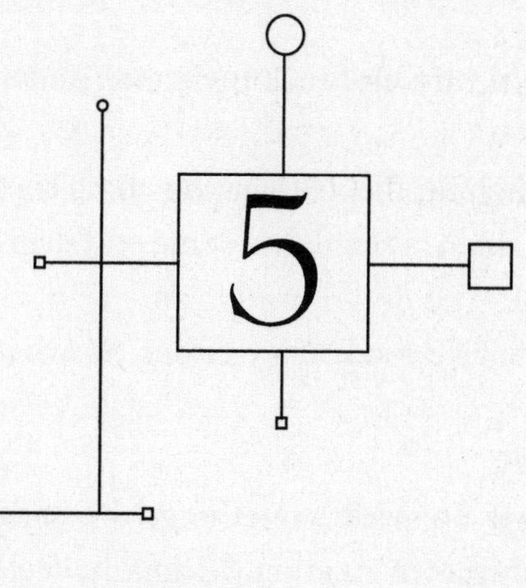

5

REED SITS across the kitchen table, watching me as I turn the apple in my fingers. Maybe he's right about my never needing to eat. I can't remember the last time I had a real appetite. Even the delicacies served to me on the wives' floor wouldn't appeal to me right now.

I keep my eyes down. I don't want Reed to see my defeat. I don't want him to see that Vaughn has had a victory over me, because almost all of my misfortunes can be traced to that man. Being separated from my brother. Losing Jenna. Watching Cecily go with tears in her eyes. Leaving Gabriel to fear the worst. Linden's coldness toward me. I keep staggering forward because I have to, but what Linden said last night is true: It's not much of a plan.

"Are you going to eat that, or submit it for fingerprint analysis?" Reed says.

I set the apple down neatly, and tuck my hands under the table.

He tilts his head, watching me. He's eating some sort of deep-fried stew. The smell is repulsive; some of it drips onto his plaid shirt.

"Okay, then," he says. "No food today either. So what will sustain you?"

"Oxygen," I say softly.

"You need to spice it up with something," he says. This is his way of making conversation. I think he feels sorry for me.

"A question, then," I say.

He sets his spoon into the bowl with authority. "All right. Go for it."

I look aside, thinking of how I want to word this. "You and Vaughn don't seem anything alike," I begin. "I guess my question is—was he always this way? You said your mother didn't really care for him."

Reed laughs gruffly. "He was quiet all the time. I don't mean like he was being polite or solemn. I mean like he was planning something."

"He's still like that," I say. I try to imagine Vaughn as a child or even as a young man, but I can't. All I see is a version of a young Linden with blackness where his eyes should be.

"But he didn't have much purpose until his boy died," Reed says. "That's when he reprogrammed the elevators so that only he could access the basement. I never knew what was going on down there."

"Did he used to let you visit?" I ask, thinking of what Reed said a few days ago about Vaughn not allowing Reed onto his property.

"I used to live there," Reed says. "When our parents died, they left that house to both of us. Our father was an architect, and it was an old boarding school he'd reconstructed. That's why it's so enormous. You'd think, with all that space, there'd be room for both of us. But we seemed to get in each other's way. We both like things just so."

"Linden's grandfather was an architect," I say quietly, more to myself than to Reed. It makes me happy to know Linden inherited that brilliance. It skipped his father and buried itself in him, like it knew he would do better things with it.

"Linden takes after him in a lot of ways," Reed agrees. "Vaughn hates when I point that out. He likes to pretend he's the only family that boy's got. Won't even talk about Linden's mother, or Linden's brother that died before he was born. It's one of the things we butted heads about. My brother and I were already walking a fine line with each other, but I suppose the last straw was when Linden fell ill."

I raise my head at that. Linden told me about a time when he was very sick as a child. He could hear his father's voice calling him back to consciousness, but he was too scared to answer. He'd made the decision to let go, but he survived anyway.

Reed stares at something over my shoulder, his pupils turning to pinpricks. "That poor boy," he says distantly. "I really thought it was the end of him."

"What was it?" I ask, and he snaps back to attention and looks at me. "What made him so sick?"

"I can tell you what Vaughn said, or I can tell you what I think," he says.

I press my eyebrows together. "You think Vaughn was responsible?"

"Not on purpose," Reed says. "I don't think he meant to harm him. But I think he was running some experiment that went haywire. I called him out on it, and he asked me to leave."

"So you did?" I ask.

"I did," he says. "I'm better off with my own place anyway. I would have liked to take my nephew with me, but Vaughn would have had my head for it. There's nowhere I could take that boy where Vaughn wouldn't have found him."

"I know the feeling," I mumble.

"Look at that," Reed says. He slaps his palms on the table, rattling the bowl, startling me. "You asked for an answer to one question, and you got an entire story. Feeling sustained yet?"

In answer I take a bite from the apple.

"Finish your breakfast and then tie that hair back. I have a new project for you."

"New project?" I say before taking another bite.

"A cleaning project," he says. He drops his bowl into the sink and then winks at me. "I think you have a knack for making things shine."

Once I finish the apple and throw the core into the compost pile that Reed started just outside the kitchen window, and swat away a good deal of flies, Reed leads me past the usual shed and keeps going toward the bigger one.

"What I'm about to show you is top secret stuff," he says. I can't tell whether he's kidding. "I wouldn't want anyone coming out here chopping it up for parts."

He fiddles around with a padlock, somehow coaxing it apart without a key. Then he pushes the door open, moves aside, and makes a flourishing gesture with his arm for me to enter first.

It's dark until he flips a switch, and tiny bulbs strung along the ceiling and walls illuminate the space.

"What do you think, doll?" Reed says.

"It's . . . a plane. In your shed." I can't hide my astonishment. He told me it would be here, and here it is, yet it still surprises me. It's rusty and mismatched, but it has a body and wings, and it takes up almost the entirety of the shed. "How did you get it in here?" I ask.

"Didn't," he says. "Most of it was already here. I figure it probably crash-landed forty, fifty years ago and was abandoned. So I decided to fix it up, see if I could make it fly. Of course the weather proved to make things difficult, so I built this shed over it."

The whole thing sounds too absurd for him to have made it up. "How will you get it out?" I say. "How will you even start it without being poisoned by the fumes?"

"Haven't gotten to that part yet," he says. "But no matter; she's not ready to fly."

I stare at it, and for some reason my shoulders shake and I start to laugh. It's the first real laugh I've felt in days. Or weeks. Or months, maybe. Reed is either a genius or completely mad, or both. But if he's mad, then I am too, because I love this airplane. I've never seen one up close before, and the stories I've heard never prepared me for the power such a magnificent thing implies. I want to climb inside of it. I want it to carry me up, the grass getting greener and greener the farther away it becomes.

Reed is grinning when he tugs the handle of the curved door. It looks like it once belonged to a car and was melted into shape. With a horrible rusty noise, it opens from the top, like a curled finger rising to point at me.

The door opens to a small cockpit. There are monitors and buttons and what appear to be two half-circle steering wheels. "The supply room's in the passenger cabin," Reed says, pointing me to a curtain that serves as a door.

The passenger cabin is all beige and red, like a mouth. It seems almost human. When I was bedridden in the mansion, Linden read a story to me that was about a scientist named Frankenstein who created a man from the body parts of the dead. Somehow Frankenstein gave this creation a pulse and made it breathe. I imagine it must have looked like this odd assemblage of pieces.

The plane is a lot bigger than it looks from the outside. The ceiling is high enough that Reed, who's taller than me, can nearly stand up straight. There's some room to walk around. The seats are red, mounted to the wall. There are four of them, in pairs of two, facing each other. The carpet is beige and stained, like the walls.

What Reed calls a supply room is actually a closet. Opening its door reduces the passenger cabin by half. "Needs to be organized," Reed says, standing at the curtain that separates the cockpit from the passenger cabin. He watches as I open one of the cabinets. Shoe boxes tumble out at me and spill their contents onto my shoes. "I was thinking that'd be your job."

It's easy, repetitive work. Sorting medical equipment apart from the dehydrated snacks and labeling their boxes. Reed works on the outside of the plane. I hear him banging parts into place and smoothing them down, trying to blend all the pieces together. He says he's going to paint it when he's done. He says it'll be beautiful. I think it already is.

I open another box, and it's full of cloth handkerchiefs. I recognize them immediately. They're exactly like the ones at the mansion: plain white, with a single red sharp-leafed flower embroidered onto them. Gabriel gave me a handkerchief with this pattern, and I kept it for the remainder of my time at the mansion. The same flower that marks the iron gate.

"Oh, those?" Reed says when I ask him about them. He doesn't look away from his work. He's sitting on one of the wings, pressing down a sheet of copper and using a screwdriver to mark where the screws will go. "I thought they'd make good bandages; put them with the first aid stuff."

"Where did they come from?" I ask.

"They used to belong to the boarding school," he says. "A ton of things were left behind when my parents bought the building—handkerchiefs, blankets, things like that."

"But what kind of flower is it?" I say.

"It's a lotus," he says. "Doesn't look exactly like one, if you ask me, but that's the only logical thing it could be. The school was called the Charles Lotus Academy for Girls."

"Charles Lotus? As in, his name was Lotus?"

"Yep. Now get back to work making things sparkle. I'm not letting you live here eating up all the apples and oxygen for free, you know."

The rest of the day is a malaise of chores. I pack the handkerchiefs away and bury them at the bottom of all the medical supplies. I don't want to ever see them again. It's my fault for hoping they symbolized something important. For believing anything that comes from the mansion could mean anything good.

I take a shower and go to bed early. The sky is still pink, undercooked. I bury myself beneath the blanket. It isn't very thick; I shiver most nights, but right now the blanket feels like the heaviest thing in the world. It comforts me. I don't just want to sleep; I want to be crushed down until I disappear.

In the morning there are voices. Something hissing and spitting on the griddle. Footsteps are pounding up the steps, and a voice calls after them, "Wait!" but the footsteps don't comply. My door is pushed open, and there's Cecily. The sunlight touches every part of her, making her into an overexposed photograph. Her smile floats ahead of her, a double bright line. "Surprise," she says.

I sit up, trying to force consciousness back into my brain. "What are you— How did you get here?"

She hops onto the edge of my bed, jostling me. "We took a cab," she says excitedly. "I'd never been in one before. It smelled like frozen garbage, and it cost a ton of money."

I rub my eyes, trying to comprehend what she's saying. "You took a cab?"

"Housemaster Vaughn has the limo," she says. "He's at some conference for the weekend. So we came to see you."

"We?"

"Me and Linden." She frowns at me. "You don't look

well," she says. "You didn't contract sepsis from this place, did you? It's so filthy."

"I like it here," I say, collapsing back onto the pillow, pretending not to notice that it reeks of mustiness. I wonder who slept here before me. They probably died last century.

"It's worse than the orphanage was," Cecily says. She pats my leg as she stands, and heads for the door. "Anyway, get up, come downstairs. We brought you things."

I take my time about getting dressed after she goes. I'm in no hurry to see the emptiness in Linden's eyes when he looks at me.

I guess I've forgotten to brush my hair, judging by the way everyone looks at me when I enter the kitchen. And Cecily kindly informs me that my shirt is inside out.

"She hasn't been eating," Reed says apologetically. "I tried waving the fork around her head and everything."

I drop into a chair opposite Linden. He's holding Bowen, who is reaching for the things on the shelves. He wants the jars that have caught the morning light; I think he believes they hold little pieces of the sun.

"Of course she hasn't been eating," Cecily says. She stands behind me and gently works the tangles from my hair. "She doesn't want to die."

Reed lights his cigar and bumps Linden's shoulder with his fist. "I can't tell you how wonderful it is to be blessed by the presence of your wives."

Cecily drops my hair. She reaches across the table and

snatches the cigar right out of Reed's teeth and squishes the ignited tip into the table.

"What the hell!" Reed snaps. The house rattles. Bowen stops reaching.

"I'm *pregnant*, you moron," Cecily says. "Don't you know anything about gestation? And in case you're blind, there is also a five-month-old baby sitting right next to you."

Reed stares at her, aghast. And then he narrows his eyes as he stands and leans forward across the table, until his nose is an inch from hers. And I really think he's about to strangle her—Linden tenses, ready to stop him—but Reed only growls and says, "I don't like you, kid."

She presses her hand to her chest. "Break my heart," she says, spins around, and makes her exit.

Reed rescues the smoldering cigar and tries to relight it, grunting with each failed spark. "Will never know what you see in that one," he says to Linden.

"I'm sorry," I say, standing and scooping the ashes into my hand, and then dumping them into the sink. "She's just sort of an acquired taste."

Reed bellows with laughter. "Acquired taste," he says, clapping his arm around Linden. "See now, *this one*, I like. You're letting the wrong one get away."

Linden's cheeks go pink.

Cecily returns with a backpack slung over her arm. It also bears the lotus embroidery on one of the front pockets.

She grabs my shoulders and guides me back into a chair, then sets a foil container in front of me and opens the lid. I'm hit with a blast of sweet-smelling steam. The head cook's berry cobbler, topped with giant crumbles of sugar. Cecily presses a plastic fork into my hand and says, "Eat."

Linden says, "Let her be. She can take care of herself."

"Obviously she can't," Cecily says. "Look at her."

"I'm fine," I say, and to prove it I take a forkful of cobbler. Some small, distant part of me acknowledges that it's delicious, rich with fat and nutrients I've been in need of. But a more frontal, prominent part of me is having a hard time just getting it down my throat.

Cecily resumes working on my tangles.

The silence is tense, and Reed breaks it by saying, "Well, I hate to leave a party. But I've got work to get to." He makes a production of sticking a fresh cigar between his teeth as he heads for the door. "Help yourself to anything you'd like." He eyes the cobbler and then looks at me with his eyebrows raised. "Though, it looks like you've brought your own supplies."

Floorboards creak under his feet as he walks down the hall. As soon as he's gone outside, Linden says, "Cecily, that was incredibly rude."

She ignores him, humming and setting my hair neatly against my shoulders like she's laying down an expensive dress. I'm glad my sister wife is here. She's a chore sometimes, but she comforts me. I want to lean against her and let the weight I've been carrying fall away. But a part of me is angry that she has returned. I already said good-bye to her, accepted that we had no choice but to part ways. I don't want to have to say good-bye again.

I can feel Linden frowning at me. I can't bring myself to look at him.

"You're not eating," Cecily fusses.

"Leave her alone," Linden says.

The tension is too much. Too tight. I feel myself bursting, but somehow my voice is very soft when I say, "Yes, why don't you? Why don't you both leave me alone?"

I look up at Linden, then Cecily. "Why did you come back?"

Cecily tries to touch my forehead, but I lean away from her. I stand up and walk backward toward the sink. Their stares are strangling me somehow.

Cecily looks at Linden and says, "Do you see?"

"See *what*?" I say, and this time my voice is a little louder.

Linden swallows something hard in his throat, composing himself, readying that diplomatic tone of his. "Cecily," he says, "why don't you take Bowen outside? It's a warm day. Show him the wildflowers."

It unnerves me that she agrees easily to this. She gives me a frown as she goes, and then sings something to Bowen about daffodils.

"I'm sorry," Linden says after she has left us alone. "I warned her not to smother you. She's just been worried about your well-being."

I know this. Cecily worries. It's her way. She's the youngest of all Linden's wives, yet she has always loved to play mother hen. But Linden is the practical diplomat in this marriage. He should be reminding her that I'll be gone for good. And sure, she'd argue with him. She'd slam a few doors and refuse to speak to him for a while. But how long could that really go on? Locked up on that wives' floor by herself, the loneliness would make her forgive him soon enough.

"You shouldn't have brought her here," I say. "You shouldn't be here either. We both know there's nothing to figure out. You're only prolonging our goodbyes." And I don't add that every day he keeps me here is another day my brother thinks I'm dead and is capable of destruction. And still I can't bring myself to escape in the night, behind his back. Not again, especially after all he's done to help me.

He looks at the wall over my head. I can't read his expression. He opens his mouth to speak, but only a fraction of a syllable makes it out. I concentrate on a crack in the linoleum floor that looks like the apex of a leaf.

"I can't believe the things you told me about my father," he says. "You understand that, don't you? I can't side against him."

He seemed to be on my side while he was carrying me away from his father's clutches and trying to stop the bleeding. He seemed to be on my side when he slept in the chair at my bedside and told me he wouldn't let his father cross the threshold of that hospital room while I was inside it.

But the upsetting part is that I do understand. While Vaughn controlled my sister wives and me with gates and holograms, he controlled his son with something deeper than blood or bones. Vaughn is Linden's only constant. How can Linden have any choice but to love his father, to believe there's good in the man who raised him?

I'm no one to judge. There is no number of buildings my brother can destroy, and no number of lives he can claim, that would undo my love for him.

I nod.

From somewhere very far away, in a world where there's only green and deeper green, Bowen shrieks with laughter.

"I've brought some things for you," Linden says. "I was going to bring more of your clothes, but I thought they'd only weigh you down if you were traveling. So I packed a first aid kit and some bus fare. You should be careful about letting anyone see that you're carrying money." He laughs, but it comes out more like a cough. "But you probably know that, don't you?"

"You didn't have to do that," I say. Then, thinking better of it, I add, "But thank you."

He gets up and pushes his chair back against the table, then Cecily's chair, then mine. "You and Cecily can share the bed. I'm going to sleep on the divan in my uncle's library. I'll set up Bowen's bassinet in the bedroom, but you won't have to worry; he mostly sleeps through the night."

"You're really staying the weekend, then?" I say.

"It'll be good for Cecily," he says. "She's been stir-crazy lately." He lingers in the doorway for a moment, his back to me. "It'll give both of you a chance for a proper good-bye. It'll help her to let go of you."

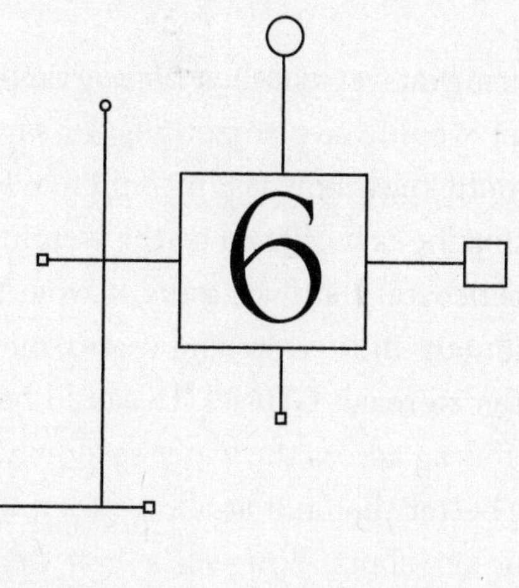

CECILY STANDS at the bedroom mirror, frowning. Her shirt is rolled to her chest, and she dusts her fingers over the pink ribbons of shining skin that run up her stomach. "Horrible, aren't they?" she says. "Bowen stretched me out as far as I could go."

I'm sitting on the bed, staring at the book I've taken from Reed's library. He doesn't have as many books as his brother, and they're all tattered and old. I get the sense that he inherited the rejects of the collection. Some of the history books have pages ripped away, and passages that are blacked out. There was a book about the discovery of America—I was drawn to it by the image of a ship on the cover—but the pages were filled with furious notes calling the text a lie, theories scrawled in smudged, sloppy lettering I couldn't read. I didn't want to read it anyway; I just wanted to look at the ships and try to remember Gabriel's fingers in my hair.

I turn the page, staring at yet another photograph of a cargo ship. Gabriel would have something to say about it, I'm sure. He would know how fast it could move across the water. This ship looks burdened by the weight of its cargo, though. I bet that if I stowed away, it would be easy for me to hide among those towering crates, but it would take me months to reach Gabriel. It would be torturous, feeling myself drag across the water so slowly.

But slowly would be better than not at all.

Cecily is still going on about how she's lost her youth, and how her body will never be the same, but how happy she is to be a part of it all. Some kind of miracle, reinforced hope. I don't want to look at her naked stomach, which is starting to take the shape of an upside-down question mark; her knuckles and cheeks and feet are always bright red. She gave birth to her first child with difficulty, fazing in and out of consciousness, crying when she had the strength, white from blood loss. I don't want to think about her going through it all again. The whole thing terrifies me.

But it's unavoidable. Since Cecily arrived with her son, this room has smelled like a nursery. Powder and some indeterminable sweetness that lingers on infant skin. It has taken over the room like it has taken over her life. The child here is no longer her.

"Aren't you tired?" she asks, falling onto the bed beside me and kicking off her socks before getting under the blanket. "Don't you want to change into your pajamas?"

"Not yet," I say. "I think I'll read for a while. I could go somewhere else if the light bothers you."

"No, stay," she yawns, and rests her head on my knee and closes her eyes.

Within minutes she's breathing that disquieting pregnancy snore that makes me worry. We were brought to Linden as breeding machines, and Vaughn saw no greater opportunity than in the most naïve among all the girls to tumble from that line: Cecily. I've no doubt that's why she was chosen. He saw that determination in her eyes, that vulnerability. She would do anything, anything to belong to his son after a lifetime of belonging to no one at all.

What is happening to her? What does it do to a young girl to birth two children in less than a year's time? There's a rash across her cheeks; her pianist's fingers are swollen. In sleep she clings to my shirt the way Bowen clings to hers. The way a child clings to its mother.

I rake my fingers through her hair as I go on flipping the pages.

I've gone through all the pictures of boats a second time, never bothering with the words, when there's a soft knock at the door. I know it's Linden. Reed never comes upstairs at night. In fact, I'm not sure where he sleeps, or even if he does.

"Come in," I say.

Linden inches into the room through the slight gap in the doorway. His presence is barely there. He looks at Cecily and me, and I feel like a model in an unfinished portrait. *The Ashby Wives.* There were four of us once.

"Is she asleep?" Linden asks.

"I'm awake," Cecily murmurs. "I had a dream we were ice-skating." She sits up, rubbing her eyes.

"I wanted to see how you were feeling," Linden tells her, looking right past me. I'm nothing—candlelight on the wall. "Did you need anything to drink? Are your feet sore?"

She says something about needing a back rub, and I take my book and slip out of the room just as easily as Linden slipped in.

I've memorized which floorboards in the hallway don't creak, thereby leaving Reed undisturbed as he toils about his mysteries below me.

The window is open in the library, and the books and walls and floorboards are all cool with the night's breeze. I hear crickets as though they're in the shelves. The stars are so bright and unobstructed that their light fills the room, making everything silver.

I replace the boat book and run my fingers over the spines of the other books, not really looking for anything. I think I'm too exhausted to read, anyway. There's a pillow and a blanket on the divan, and it looks inviting, but I don't feel right about getting into the bed Linden has made for himself. I focus on the book spines.

"My uncle used to let me pretend they were bricks," Linden says, startling me. He eases a thick hardcover from the shelf, hefts it in either hand, and then places it back. "I liked to build houses out of them. They never came out exactly like I'd planned, but that's good. It taught me that there are three versions of things: the one I see in my mind, and the one that carries onto the paper, and then what it ultimately becomes."

For some reason I'm finding it difficult to meet his eyes. I nod at one of the lower shelves and say, "Maybe it's because in your mind you don't have to worry about building materials. So you're not as limited."

"That's astute," he says. He pauses. "You've always been astute about things."

I'm not sure if that's supposed to be a compliment, but I suppose it's true. So much silence passes between us after that, with nothing to sustain the atmosphere but impassive crickets and starlight, that I become willing to say anything that will end it. The words that come out of me are, "I'm sorry."

I hear his breath catch. Maybe he's as surprised as I am. I don't look up to see what his expression is.

"I know you think that I'm awful. I don't blame you." That's it—all I have the courage to say. I fidget with the hem of my sweater. It's one of Deirdre's creations, of course. Emerald green embroidered with gold gossamer leaves. Since having my custom-made clothes returned to me, I've been sleeping in them. I've missed how comfortable they are, how getting dressed into something that fits every angle and curve feels like rematerializing into something worthwhile.

"I don't know what to think," Linden says quietly. "Yes, I've told myself that you're awful. I've told myself you must be—that's the only explanation. But my thoughts always go back to the you I remember. You, lying in the orange grove and saying you didn't know if we were worth saving. You held my hand then. Do you remember?"

Something rushes through my blood, from my heart to my fingertips, where the memory still lingers. "Yes," I say.

"And about a thousand other things," he says, pausing sometimes between his words, making sure he has them right. I get the sense that words are not sufficient tools for him to build what's going on in his head as he stands before me. "While you were gone, I tried to take all of those memories and turn them into lies. And I thought I'd done it. But I look at you now, and I still see the girl who fed me blueberries when I was grieving. The girl who was in a red dress, falling asleep against me on the drive home."

He takes a step closer, and my heart leaps into my mouth. "I try to hate you. I'm trying right now."

I look at him and ask, "Is it working?"

He moves his hand, and I think he's going to reach for a book on the shelf above me, but he touches my hair instead. Something in me tightens with expectancy. I hold my breath.

When he pushes forward, my mouth falls open,

expecting his kiss even before it comes. His lips are familiar. I know the shape of them, know how to make mine fit against them. His taste is familiar too. For all the illusions and colors and sweet smells of that mansion, and of our marriage, he has always tasted like skin. His breaths are shallow. I'm holding his life against my tongue, between my rows of teeth. He's offering it up.

But it doesn't belong to me. I know that.

I draw back, gently step out of his hands that gripped my shoulders and were just edging their way to either side of my throat.

"I can't," I whisper.

One of his hands still hovers near me, a satellite. I imagine what it would be like to tilt my head into his open palm. The flood of warmth bursting through me.

He looks at me, and I don't know what he sees. I used to think it was Rose. But she's not here with us now, in this room. It's just him and me, and the books. I feel like our lives are in those books. I feel like all the words on the pages are for us.

I could kiss him again. I could do much more than that. But I know it would be for the wrong reasons. It would be because my family is far away, or else dead, and because I miss Gabriel; in my dreams he's something small I dropped into the ocean, and I wake knowing that I might never find him again. But Linden is here. Brilliantly here. And it would be too easy to make him a substitute for all those things, to take advantage of his desire for me.

But then logic sets in. Logic and guilt.

I won't hurt him the way I did before, manipulating his affections while I worked for the freedom I wanted.

He seems to understand. His fingers close into his palm, and he lowers his hand from my side.

"I can't," I say again, with more certainty.

He steps closer to me, and my nerves bristle like the long grass outside. Everything is rustling with expectancy.

"We never consummated our marriage," he says softly. "At first I thought you only needed time. I was patient." He presses his lips together for a moment, thinking. "But then it didn't matter so much. I liked just being with you. I liked the way you breathed when you were asleep. I liked when you took the champagne glass from my hand. I liked how your fingers were always too long for your gloves."

A smile tugs at one side of my mouth, and I allow it.

"Looking back, those feel like the most important parts. They were real, weren't they?"

"Yes," I answer, and it's the truth.

He touches my left hand and looks at my eyes, asking permission. I nod, and he holds my palm flat against his and then holds my hand between us. His other hand traces the slope of my wedding ring and pinches either side of it between his thumb and index finger. When I realize what's happening, my pulse quickens, my mouth goes dry.

He slides the ring down my finger, and it hitches on

my knuckle, like part of me is still trying to hang on. My body lilts forward, tethered to the ring for only an instant more before letting go.

This was it. This was why I kept wearing my wedding ring, why it never felt right to remove it myself. There was only one person who could set me free.

"Let's call this an official annulment," he says.

I can't help it. I throw my arms around him and pull him tight against me. He tenses, startled, but then he puts his arms around me too. I can feel his closed fist where he holds the ring.

"Thank you," I whisper.

Minutes later I'm lying on the divan, watching my ankle swing back and forth over the edge like a guillotine. Linden paces the length of the room, tracing the book spines.

I look for the moon through the open window, but it's hiding behind clouds.

Linden says, "What's your brother like?"

I blink. It's the first time he's asked me about Rowan. Maybe he's trying to get to know me, now that he knows I'll give him the truth.

"He's smarter than me," I say. "And practical."

"Is he older? Younger?"

"About ninety seconds younger," I say. "We're twins."

"Twins?" he says.

I hang my head over the arm of the divan, looking at him upside down. "You sound surprised."

"It's just—twins," he says, leaning against a row of paisley cloth-bound books. "That changes the entire way I look at you." He keeps his mouth open, struggling for the right words.

"Like I'm half of a whole?" I say, trying to help him.

"I wouldn't put it like that," he says. "You're a whole person by yourself."

I look out the window again. "You know what scares me?" I say. "I'm starting to feel like you're right."

Linden is quiet for a long time. I hear his clothes rustling, the chair creaking under his weight. "I think I understand," he says. "When I lost Rose, I kept going, I still do, but I'll never be what I was when she was alive. It'll always feel like something's . . . not right, without her here."

"That's sort of what it's like," I agree. Even though my brother and I are both still alive, the longer we're apart, the more I feel myself changing. It's like I'm evolving into something that doesn't include him. I don't think I can ever be the person I was before all this.

It's quiet again after that. It's a comfortable quiet, though. Peaceful. I feel unburdened, and after a while I start to imagine that the divan is a boat moving over the ocean. Sunken cities play music beneath the waves. The ghosts are stirring.

Someone turns on the light, and my thoughts scatter away as I blink at the brightness. This is one of the few rooms with functioning lightbulbs, though they flicker.

"Linden?" Cecily says.

She's standing in the doorway, her knuckles white from clutching the frame. Everything about her is white: her face, the quivering misshapen O of her lips, the night-gown that she's got bunched up to her hips as though she's unveiling her body to us.

But sliding down her thighs is an abundance of red. It's pooling at her feet, from the trail of blood that followed her into the room.

Linden moves fast. He scoops her up by the backs of her knees and shoulders. She comes alive with a scream so awful that he has to brace his hand on the wall to keep from falling. She's whimpering while he's rushing her down the stairs.

I hurry after them down the long hallway, making footprints in the red puddles and thinking about how small she is, about how much blood it takes to keep a girl her size going, how much of it she can stand to lose. Redness is leaking rivers over Linden's arms like veins atop his skin.

He says my name, and I realize what he wants. I push ahead of him and open the door.

Outside, the night is warm, sprinkled with stars. The grass sighs in indignation as we crush it with our bare feet. Wings and insect legs make music, which moments before had been lovely through the open window in the room full of books.

In the backseat of the car, which reeks of cigars and

mold, I take Cecily's head in my lap while Linden runs off to find his uncle to drive us.

"I lost the baby," Cecily chokes.

"No," I say. "No, you didn't."

She closes her eyes, shudders with a sob.

"They'll know what to do at the hospital," I tell her, though I don't believe a word of it. I'm only trying to calm her, and maybe myself. I hold her hand in both of mine. It's clammy, ice-cold. I can't reconcile this pale, trembling girl with the one who stood before the mirror hardly an hour ago, fussing over her stomach.

Thankfully, Linden is back soon.

The drive to the hospital is rocky, thanks to Reed's reckless driving and the lack of a paved road. Linden holds Bowen, whose eyes are wide and curious, and shushes him even though he doesn't cry. I've always thought Bowen was intuitive. He just might be the only child of Linden's to live.

I feel a gentle pressure around my finger, and I look down to realize Cecily is touching the place where my ring used to be. But she doesn't ask about it, the bride who has always made it her mission to know everything about everyone in her marriage. She has been eerily silent this whole ride.

"Open your eyes," Linden tells her when she closes them. "Love? Cecily. Look at me."

With effort she does.

"Tell me where it hurts," he says.

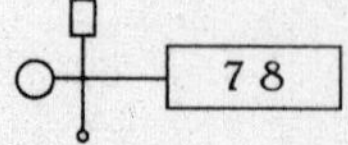

"It's like contractions," she says, cringing as we hit a pothole.

"It's only another minute from here," Linden says. "Just keep your eyes open." The gentleness is gone from his voice, and I know he's trying to stay in control, but he looks so frightened.

Cecily is fading. Her breaths are labored and slow. Her eyes are dull.

"'There will come soft rain,'" I blurt out in a panic. She looks up at me, and we recite the words in unison, "'And the smell of the ground, And swallows circling with their shimmering sound.'"

"What is that?" Linden says. "What are you saying?"

"It's a poem," I tell him. "Jenna liked it, didn't she, Cecily?"

"Because of the ending," Cecily says. Her voice sounds miles away. "She just liked how it ended."

"I'd like to hear the whole thing," Linden says.

But we've arrived at the hospital. It's the only real source of light for miles. Most of the streetlights—the ones still standing, anyway—have long since burned out.

Cecily has closed her eyes again, and Linden passes the baby off to me and hoists her into his arms. She murmurs something I can't understand—I think it's another line of the poem—and her muscles go lax.

It takes a few seconds for me to realize that her chest has stopped rising and falling. I wait for her next breath, but it doesn't come.

I've never heard a human make a noise like the cry that escapes Linden's throat when he calls her name. Reed runs past us, and when he returns, he's got a fleet of nurses behind him, first generation and new. They rip Cecily from Linden's arms, leave him staggering and reaching after her. I can't help but think this attention is due to her status as Vaughn's daughter-in-law. Reed must have made that clear.

Bowen starts to wail, and I bounce him on my hip as I watch Cecily's body through the glass doors. The hospital lights reveal the gray of her skin. And, strangely, I can see her wedding band as though through a magnifying glass; the long serrated petals etched into it are like knives. They catch every bit of hospital light, the gleam stabbing my eyes. Then she's laid onto a gurney that turns a corner, and she's gone.

She's dead. We'll never get her back.

The thought hits me in the back of the knees, shaking me with its certainty.

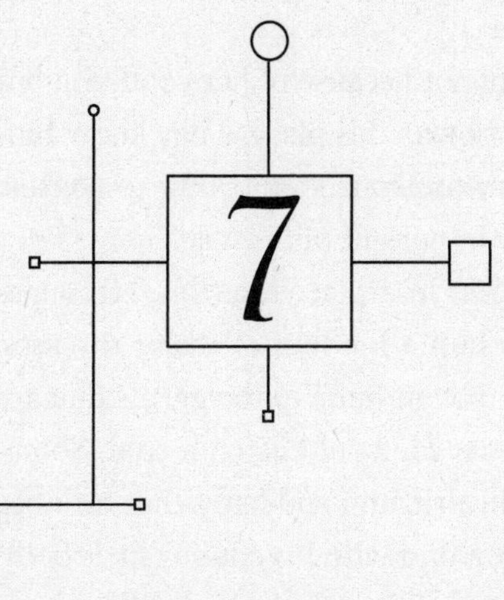

7

I'M SITTING ON the floor of the hospital lobby, waiting. That's always the worst part, the waiting.

Bowen has fallen into a quiet lull, ear to my heart. My arm hurts from supporting him. But I can't think about that. I can't think about anything. Voices and bodies move past.

The lobby is crowded. The chairs that line the walls are full of the coughing and the sleeping and the wounded. This is one of the few research hospitals in the state; my father-in-law often boasts about it. They take the wounded, the emaciated, the pregnant, or those who are dying of the virus—depending on which cases are interesting enough to be seen, and depending on who is willing to have blood drawn and tissue sampled without being compensated for it.

A young nurse is standing with a clipboard, trying to decide who is in the worst shape. Cecily was hurried down that sterile hallway not because of her condition but because her father-in-law owns this place. They know Linden here; last I saw him, someone was trying to console him as he wrestled away in pursuit of his wife.

I shouldn't have Bowen in a place like this. His superior genes will promise him a life free of major diseases, sure, but he isn't completely immune to the germs that are surely hovering around us. He could catch a cold. Someone has to think of his health, and suddenly that task has been placed in my hands, along with his chubby little body.

I raise my head and search for Reed. Eventually I spot him emerging from the same hallway that took my sister wife. Linden is pacing ahead of him, head down, face drained of color. I rise to meet them, and I realize my knees are trembling. And suddenly I don't want to hear what they have to tell me. I don't want to return Bowen to his father. I want to take him and run away from here.

Linden's hands have been scrubbed of the blood. His face is splashed wet. The hem of his shirt is wrinkled, and when he begins twisting it in his fist again, I understand why.

"They couldn't get a pulse—" he says, and presses the heels of his hands against his eyes, hard. "I wanted to be with her, but they pushed me away."

All I can think is that Cecily was supposed to outlive us all.

But when I open my mouth, what comes out is, "Bowen shouldn't be here."

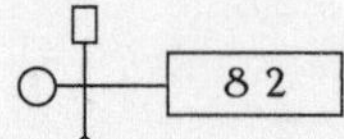

Reed understands. Reed has always understood me. He takes the baby, and he's so careful with him, even smiles at him.

"She was fine when I kissed her good night," Linden says.

I should be saying something to comfort him. That was always my role in this marriage, to console him. But we aren't married anymore, and I can't remember how to be.

"I don't want them to dissect her," I say. I know I shouldn't be so morbid, but I can't stop myself. If Cecily is dead, then all the rules are broken. "I don't want your father to have her body. I don't—" My lip is quivering.

"He won't get her," Reed assures me.

Linden whimpers into his palms. "This is my fault," he says. His voice is strange. "We shouldn't have tried for another baby so soon. My father said it would be okay, but I should have seen it was too much for her. She was already so—" His voice breaks, and I think the word he croaks out is "frail."

In more rational circumstances, hearing the intimate details of what went on between my sister wife and my former husband would embarrass me, but feelings of any sort are miles from me now.

"I need air," I say.

"Wait," he starts to say, but I stumble on anyway, until a pair of hands grabs my arms. I stare at the nurse's name tag, uncomprehending, unable to read. He's probably younger than I am. There were nurses at the lab where my parents worked too, and it always astounded me how serious they could be, how well they knew medicine.

"Mrs. Ashby?" the nurse asks, his voice too gentle.

I shake my head, eyes on the floor. "Sorry," I whisper. "No."

Linden comes up behind me. He says words I don't understand. And the nurse says words I don't understand. And I can't catch any of what's being said until I hear a cruel pang of hope in Linden's voice when he asks, "Can we see her?"

I whip my head around to stare at him. He wants to see her? Doesn't he understand that a body isn't a person? Doesn't he understand how awful that would be—how awful it already was to watch her get swept away a few moments ago?

"But it will be a while yet before she's lucid," the nurse says. And suddenly—I don't know why—his name tag makes sense. Isaac. The whole world reemerges from the darkness that had been closing in around me.

My heart starts pounding in my ears, my throat. I try to hang on to what's being said now.

Somewhere, on a table in a sterile room, my sister wife took in a sharp breath. It happened just as they were drawing the sleeves from their watches to call a time of death.

Her heart forced blood out from her chest, back to her brain, her fingertips, her cheeks.

Cecily. My Cecily. Always the fighter.

A squeaking noise escapes through my teeth, joy and relief.

We're guided down a hallway, our footsteps echoing around us at all angles like claps.

Linden and I huddle together to see her through the small window in her door. We can't go in yet. She can't be agitated. Her body is still working through the shock of losing a pregnancy in its second trimester; all of this is fascinating to the promise of research, which is what this hospital is all about. The doctors want to know everything about the new generations, and such a violent miscarriage invites all sorts of interest. There are monitors recording her heart rate. The nurse is explaining that her temperature will be checked every hour. They're taking thorough notes on any slight change in her body chemistry.

But I don't see the intrigue in any of those things. I don't see more research fodder. All I see is my sister wife, barely hanging on.

There's a plastic mask over her mouth, misting with her breaths. Her cheeks are flushed, and her eyes lazily rove along the wires that connect the machines to her body. Her heartbeats are small green bursts on the monitor. She looks so alone and lost in her dreams.

I press my hand to the glass, and the ghost of my frowning reflection is superimposed over her bed.

"Will she be all right?" Linden asks. I don't think he's heard any of the nurse's rambling.

"You'll be able to see her in the morning," the nurse says.

Old tears still glisten on Linden's face. His lips move, sending inaudible prayers to phantom gods. The only words I can make out are "thank you." He takes my hand and leads me to the lobby, where we will wait for the morning light to come and fill Cecily's hair with its usual fire.

Why did this happen? Any number of reasons. She's young, the first generation doctor tells Linden. And, superior genes or not, pregnancies in rapid succession can take a toll on a young girl. I can tell he's being disapproving. So many of the first generations hate what has happened to their children and their children's children. They look at us and see what we should have been, not what we are.

Doctors speak in impersonal, clinical terms: fetus, infection, placenta, hypothesis, patient. This textbook approach does wonders for taking the emotional edge out of it. The most likely hypothesis here is that the fetus has been dead for days, and, left unchecked, an infection spread through her blood like a wildfire. Eventually her body caught up and worked to expel the source of the problem, and she went into labor. She started hemorrhaging, and, finally, she went into shock. While we were trying to keep her awake in the car, her body was already shutting down. We were inevitably going to lose her without proper treatment. It all sounds so official and possible the way the doctor explains it. Like I'm reading one of my parents' lab reports.

It's that simple. It ends there, with no mention of the fact that if she hadn't mustered the strength to get out of bed and drag herself down the hall, it would have been too late when we found her. How much time would we have squandered, talking about annulments and fraternal twins as she died alone at the other end of the hall? I file that thought as far back into my brain as I can, out of sight.

"I don't understand," Linden says. "There were no signs."

"She was flushed all the time," I volunteer, remembering how hot her skin was when we shared a bed. And then I run through the checklist: how heavily she breathed and snored, the way her bones seemed to creak when she moved, the bags under her eyes. Linden is surprised by it. He says he had no idea it was that severe. This doesn't surprise me. Even outside of the mansion, the full picture is lost on him. He sees what he's been taught to see. I can't fault him for that.

Later, when we're alone in the lobby, he says, "This is my fault."

"No," I say. "Of course it's not."

He's trembling. I touch his arm.

"She was just so sad when Jenna fell ill," he says. "The only time she was happy at all was with Bowen. My father convinced me that another baby would make her better."

"What about you?" I ask. "Was a baby what you wanted?"

He looks at his lap, and the word comes out so small. "No." He rubs tears from the side of his face. "I just didn't know how else to make it better."

Poor Linden. He has had, at once, four wives, whom he adored and maybe even loved. But we frightened him, us girls, with our intensity, the weight of our sadness and the sharpness of our hearts. Rose knew him well. She kept her misery a secret and found a way to love him. Jenna and I hid from him; we smiled across the dinner table, let him sleep beside us, and we mourned when we were alone. But Cecily could only love him the way she knows how: all at once. Everything rushing up to the surface. I've seen her sadness, and it's a frightening thing. As her stomach grew with Bowen, I saw it begin, but it was so much worse after she gave birth and after Jenna was gone.

And then I was gone too.

Linden only wants for Cecily to be happy. He showers her with affection and pretty things. But all the while he knows that even he will have to leave her.

The mattress is at a slight incline when we're brought in to see my sister wife. Her eyes are murky. The infection brought on by the miscarriage left her with a fever, and she's glistening with sweat. Her lips and cheeks are hot pink. Her hair is in tangles.

She looks ravaged. Chewed up and spit out.

Linden stands beside me in the doorway, and he fumbles for my hand but then doesn't grab it. I know he's trying to respect the annulment, to get used to us being unmarried. But in this moment I wish he would hold on to me. I need his strength and he needs mine, the way it was before.

"Linden?" Cecily croaks.

With that, he rushes to her. "I'm here, love," he says, and kisses the top of her head, her nose, her lips with a fury of affection that says he's so glad to have her back that he can't get enough of her at once. It's the kind of attention she lives for, but she's so defeated that all she manages is a weary smile.

"You weren't here when I woke up," she says. "I was worried about you."

Linden laughs shakily. "You were worried?" he says. "You gave me the scare of my life last night."

"Did I?" She's trying to blink the lethargy from her eyes. The doctor told us she wouldn't be very alert and that she wouldn't be talking much, but he clearly underestimated her resolve. "Where's Bowen?"

"Bowen is all right," Linden says, and puts another quick kiss on her lips. "My uncle took him back to the house."

"He'll be hungry," she says. She tries to push herself upright, but Linden holds her shoulders down.

"Bowen is being taken care of, Cecily." His voice is

stern. "You'll see him later. Right now you need to rest."

"Don't order me around like I'm a child," she says.

"I'm sorry," he says, taking her hands. "You're not a child."

A child is exactly what she is, but she hides it so well sometimes that even I forget.

But it's no matter what I think. Husband and wife are in their own universe right now, and I'm not a part of their conversation. For the first time I feel the full effect of the annulment.

She looks at me with cloudy eyes. "You were right about everything."

"Shh." I touch her arm. "You should be asleep."

"Who do we think we are," she says to Linden, "to have children when we can't cure our own curse?"

Though her voice is calm, her lip is quivering.

"We'll talk later, love," Linden coos. "You aren't thinking clearly."

"It's as clear as crystal," she says. Her voice is eerie and hoarse. Tears are streaking down her temples.

There's pain in Linden's eyes, though I'm not sure if it's because he's worried or because he believes what she's saying. He says something into her ear in a low voice, and it calms her. She lets him dab at her runny nose with his sleeve. And she has put up a good fight, but the fever and the exhaustion and the drugs are overpowering her.

"I can go back to the house and check on Bowen," I offer lamely.

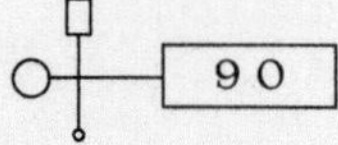

"No." Her voice is fading as she closes her eyes. "No, no, no. Stay where I can see you. It isn't safe out there."

She's delirious, but there might be some truth to that still.

"That's enough now." Linden draws the outline of her eyelids with his finger. There's a nearly imperceptible tremor in his biceps. "Get some rest. We'll be right here."

Her eyebrows raise, but her eyelids stay down. She mumbles, "Promise?"

"Yes," he tells her, desperation in the word. Of course he won't leave her. After all this, I don't believe he'll ever let her out of his sight again. She knows that; she only needed to hear him say it.

True to his word, he doesn't leave after she falls asleep. He just sits there, smoothing back her hair and frowning.

I stay in a chair on the opposite side of the bed, invisible. I don't belong here, but I have no place else to go tonight. I don't want her to wake in the night and realize I'm gone and go into a panic.

As though Linden has been reading my mind, he says, "Thank you for staying." He doesn't take his eyes off Cecily.

"I'll leave when she's stronger," I say.

"I meant what I said before. I want you to be safe."

"I know," I say. "You don't need to worry about me."

"Just the same, I'd appreciate a good-bye this time."

He ventures a glance at me, and he smiles the way he

did the morning after Rose's death. That morning the smile faded the instant he realized I wasn't her. It stays now. He understands that I'm not a ghost. I'm a girl, and one who hasn't always been especially kind to him.

"I promise I'll say good-bye this time," I say. I feel certain I'll cry if I say anything more.

I listen to the monitor steadily relaying my sister wife's pulse, and I think of how far away Gabriel is. I don't know that I could ever love him the way that Linden and Cecily are in love, or the way Linden and Rose were. I never saw the point in exhausting so much emotion on something there are so few years to enjoy. I never planned on getting married, though in weak and foolish moments I let myself pretend there would be time for such things.

But this surge of longing that comes to me now—is it love? I've never felt so alone.

We can change so many times in our lives. We're born into a family, and it's the only life we can imagine, but it changes. Buildings collapse. Fires burn. And the next second we're someplace else entirely, going through different motions and trying to keep up with this new person we've become.

I was somebody's daughter once, and then I was somebody's wife. I'm neither of those things now. This sullen boy sitting before me is not my husband, and the girl he's fretting over isn't me, will never be me.

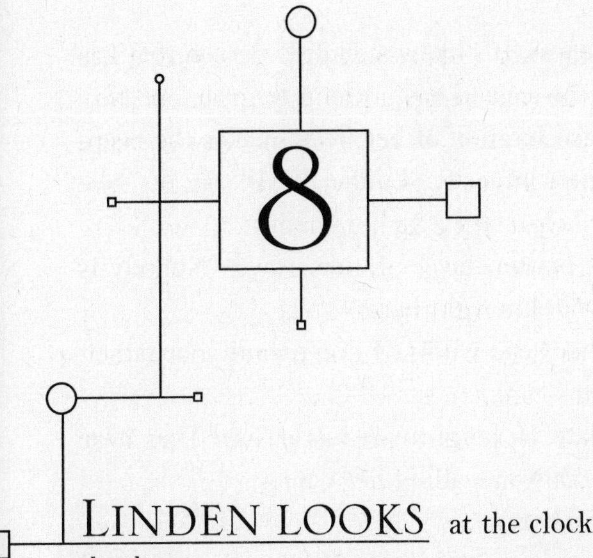

8

LINDEN LOOKS at the clock mounted over the door.

"Maybe you should go to the cafeteria," he tells me.

"Do you need me to get you something?" I ask.

He shakes his head, watches the motion of Cecily's chest as she draws a troubled breath. She's been asleep for hours. "My father will be here soon," he says. "It's best if he doesn't see you. He's rushing over from a conference in Clearwater. He said it would take him a couple of hours, but that was this morning."

My blood goes cold. "You called your father?"

"Of course." He says this louder than he perhaps meant to, because Cecily's eyes open. She stares at us through a haze, and I'm not sure if she's awake. Linden pushes the hair from her forehead and leans close and says, "You're getting the best possible care. My father will see to it."

At that her pupils dilate. I can see her immediate fight

to regain awareness. It's like watching a person that has fallen through the ice and has nothing to grab for. "No," she says. The acceleration of her heart makes the beeping on the monitor intensify. "Linden, no. Please, no." She looks to me for help, and I grip her hand.

"What's the matter, love?" Linden says. "Nobody is going to hurt you. I'm right here."

She shakes her head wildly. "I don't want your father. I don't want him."

But it's too late. Her nightmare has arrived. I can hear his voice in the hallway, calling her name.

And then he's here.

Vaughn brings with him the smell of spring rain and earth. It has always been a smell I associated with life, but right now it's choking. His hair is wet and windswept, his coat dripping, his boots muddying the tiles. "Oh, Cecily," he says, "I'm so sorry about the baby. Perhaps if you listened to me about staying in bed, it wouldn't have happened. You always were too reckless for your own good."

Of course he's blaming her for this.

She's kicking her legs, propelling herself away from him. I've never seen her so frightened. The girl who has spent the last several hours asleep is now squeezing my hand with enough brute strength, I'm certain, to bruise bone.

"Please, love, you have to lie back down," Linden urges. "You're not well."

But Cecily doesn't even hear him. "You did this," she

tells Vaughn. "You'll bury me alive the first chance you get."

The faraway stare in her eyes terrifies me. She's sitting up now, speaking in whole sentences, but she's muddled by delirium.

Vaughn brushes past me and leans over her bed. I think he's going to grab her arm like that morning outside of Reed's house, but he only touches the IV bag hanging over her and checks the writing on it. "They shouldn't have you on something this strong," he says. "I'll get this sorted out."

"No," Cecily says. "No." She turns to Linden, pleading. "You have to make him leave. He wanted me dead. Me and our baby."

The hurt in Linden's eyes is immediate. He blinks several times before he can speak. "Cecily, no . . ."

"Just get him out of here, Linden," I say through gritted teeth.

Vaughn looks at me with dead eyes before regarding Cecily with a surge of affection. "Darling, you don't have a clear head," he says. "We'll get you set up with something milder, and you'll feel better." Then, to Linden, "You and I should talk outside."

Once they're gone, I manage to calm Cecily enough that she lies down. "Don't worry," I tell her. "He isn't coming back."

"He'll try to take Bowen," she says, tears brimming in her eyes.

"That's not going to happen. Have you seen Reed's gun collection? He won't let anyone touch Bowen."

I wipe at her cheeks with the cuff of my green sweater because it's the softest thing I can think of. It catches her tears without absorbing them, and they hang between the fibers like stars.

"I feel strange," she says, "like I'm underwater."

I tuck the bedsheet up to her chin and press the back of my hand to her forehead. "That's the fever."

"Are you sure?"

"Yes," I say. "I know the feeling."

"I was never sick a day in my life before I got pregnant with Bowen," she says. "I never even had a runny nose."

"You'll be better soon," I say, willing it to be true.

"I dreamt Housemaster Vaughn pushed me into the dirt and I started sinking," she says. "His eyes turned into Jenna's eyes. I tried to scream, and my mouth filled up with mud."

It doesn't matter if I keep constant vigil; I can never protect her from what's happening in her dreams.

"That wasn't real." I pull the flimsy hospital blanket over the sheet. "Close your eyes," I whisper, and she does.

I weave small sections of her hair into braids, untangle them and start again. It's something Jenna used to do to our hair when she was bored, which was often, and doing it now makes me feel like Cecily and I are still a part of that trio.

"Don't leave me by myself," she says. "Please."

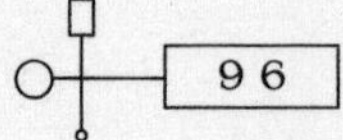

"Of course not. I'm right here," I say.

"He tried to murder me," she says.

"If he tries again, I'll murder him first," I tell her.

"Not necessary." Her voice is slurring. "I'll do it myself."

I keep up the braiding, and eventually the drugs and the exhaustion pull her back under. Her mouth falls open, letting out steady breaths.

She's grown so much since I ran away. Her pert chin has elongated just enough for her face to lose its permanent pout and give her an air of assuredness instead. Her bratty sense of superiority has matured into a cool, practical certainty, which is perhaps why Vaughn grabbed her arm that morning, why he seems to fear he has lost control of her. Her ferocity is palpable now; it's the very strength that brought her spluttering and gasping from death itself, as if to say she were promised twenty good years and she's going to have them.

"Jenna would be proud of you," I whisper. Her eyebrows knit for a moment and then relax.

When Linden returns, his arms are folded across his stomach. There are streaks from tears on his skin. He looks small, rattled. I've only known him to be this way late at night, when he was first mourning Rose; the darkness hid the worst of it then. His shaking breaths make my arms remember the shape of him beneath the blankets. Something deep within me wants to pull him close.

"How is she?" he asks. His voice is congested.

I open my mouth to say that she's okay, but what comes out is, "She's terrified, Linden."

I expect him to argue that she's perfectly safe, but he only nods as he takes his place in the chair by her bed. "My father agreed to leave for now, so she can rest. But he wanted to take her home tonight. He thought she'd get the best care in her own bed, with the doctors we have at home." He watches her eyes roving busily as she dreams. Her eyelids break apart, revealing a sliver of white. "I said it wouldn't be a good idea."

I'm impressed. It's the first time he has overridden one of his father's decisions.

I think about how he spent last night awake, waiting for the moment when he could see Cecily again. I drifted to sleep a few times in the waiting room, leaning against him, and every time I awoke, his face had changed into a different kind of grief. "Linden," I say softly now, "you should at least try to get some sleep."

He shakes his head, watching as I gather Cecily's hair for a new braid.

"My father warned me that you're an interloper. He told me I should make you leave, since we're no longer married and you're not my concern," he says. The thought gives me a chill. Yes, I'm sure Vaughn would love for his son to abandon me, so that Vaughn can swoop in and reclaim me the second I'm alone.

But Linden adds, "I told him that wouldn't be a good idea either."

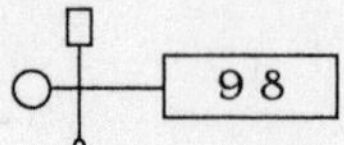

By evening Linden has succumbed to sleep. He sits hunched over the bed, his head resting beside Cecily's on the pillow, his hand gripping her arm as though she might float away from him. I listen to the rain and the thunder, and I think I hear Jenna's voice in them, sounding out a warning. She's been gone for months now. But sometimes it feels like she's more alive than ever. She's one of the indecipherable things that make sounds in the wind, and she's in every kind of dream—the good and the awful.

I go into a fitful half sleep. Coasting along, I hear Cecily's voice, high and operatic and lovely when she sings. I dream of Jenna braiding her own long dark hair as music notes fill the room. We're safe here. Safer than we'll ever be when we're awake.

But with morning comes reality. The rumble of gurneys and trays in the hallway replaces the danger of last night's storm.

"I brought you some tea," Linden says when I open my eyes. He nods to the paper cup on the night table. "It's gone cold."

"Thanks," I say.

"Sure," he says, looking at Cecily, whose face is more relaxed in sleep.

"I think she's doing better," Linden says, miserable, drained, "now that my father's gone." His next breath looks like it hurts. "I thought she loved my father. I thought my father loved her. He has told me that she's like a daughter to him."

I decide that right now is not the time to say anything awful about his father. Linden's having a hard enough time. I sip my tea. It *is* cold, but I feel it immediately in my stomach, stirring things, waking my organs and making me alert.

Whatever Linden is thinking, he doesn't say it. He only stares at Cecily.

"She'll be all right," I say, resolute. "We'll get her a little bell to ring when she needs anything, and by the second day we'll want to throw it out the window."

That gets a smile out of him. I hear the scrape of stubble when he rubs his chin. He opens his mouth like he wants to say something, but then he looks away.

"What is it?" I ask.

"Do you think—" He swallows something painful. "Do you think my father had something to do with this?"

Linden. The thought is sinister for him. Even I didn't want to entertain the possibility. But now that the fear and the shock are subsiding, I know it's the best explanation. Vaughn is so good at his wicked craft that he can ruin his daughters-in-law without even being under the same roof, without even being in the same city. He finds a way into our blood, as deadly as the virus that kills us.

The anger is so much and so sharp that I can't bear it. "It's a sound theory," I say.

Linden doesn't seem to hear me, though. He's staring

ahead when he says, "It would've destroyed me if I'd lost her. My father knows that, doesn't he?"

"He does," I say cautiously. I can see the doubt coming to his face, the way he's piecing things together. Vaughn never told Linden much about his late brother, or his mother. He didn't want Linden to feel a shred of love for them. But Linden can love his wives if he wants to, because if they die, Vaughn knows that his son will return to him, broken and vulnerable and so easy to control.

He looks so haggard. I move my chair beside his and force the cup of cold tea into his hands, hold my palm under it, and guide it to his lips. He takes small obligatory sips, but then I have to take the cup away because his hands are shaking so much that the tea is splashing onto his thighs.

I put my arms around him, and he grabs my shirt in his fists and pulls me close.

"Hey," I say into his ear. "She's going to be okay. That's the important thing. We'll figure the rest out later."

Linden nods and says nothing more, but I can feel his rage. This is where it starts. This is the spark that will eventually consume him.

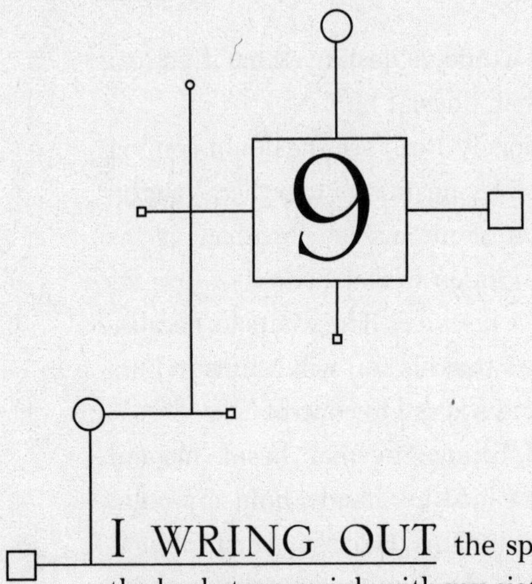

9

I WRING OUT the sponge, and the water in the bucket goes pink with my sister wife's blood.

Reed makes his own soap—these crude oatmeal-based rectangles that leave a beige film on everything. But it's doing wonders for the upholstery in his car. The big bloody stain becomes a dull orange, and then gray. By now it looks like it could be a grease stain, or cooking oil. But I want it gone completely, and so I scrub until my shoulders ache and the upholstery starts to look thinner. After this I'll mop up the red streaks in the hallway, launder the bedsheets, burn them if washing them doesn't take care of it. Bad enough she had to lose the baby in that hospital room all alone. I'll be damned if she has to come home to the evidence, too.

"I think you got all of it, doll," Reed says. His hands are dirty up to the elbows. He said he'd be in his shed. I don't know how long he's been standing there. I don't look up. Keep scrubbing.

"Not all of it," I say.

"Really. It was pretty dirty before, anyway. You can't make it perfect."

"Yes, I can."

"Doll . . ."

I wring out the sponge again. Pink suds drip from my fingers and onto the stain. This is getting counterproductive. I need fresh water. When I pick up the bucket, it slips in my wet hands and spills across the floor of the car. And suddenly I can't move. I can only watch the water get absorbed into the carpet. I'm breathing hard. My muscles ache. My head is pounding. And all I want is for this stupid car to be clean, but it's not going to happen. It's not ever going to happen.

Did I bring this on? In warning Cecily about Vaughn, did I only fuel her defiance against him and put her in his warpath? How bad would it have been to let her carry on in blissful ignorance? She would have been safer under Vaughn's thumb, maybe, and she wouldn't have lost this baby.

I feel sick, and I purse my lips to fight against a dry heave.

Reed climbs into the driver's seat, reaches across and opens the front passenger door. "Come on," he says, and numbly I step out of the car, walk around it and sit in the passenger side. I close the door with a slam that makes everything shudder, and the tears just come. I can't stop them. I'm too tired to even try. I've been sleeping hunched over in a plastic chair, my dreams pervaded by a sharp, rhythmic beeping. My back is sore and I've definitely pulled something in my neck, but how can I possibly fixate on that? I can't, not when Linden's eyes are so puffy, and not while there's so much cleaning to do.

Reed slides his hands around the steering wheel like he's pretending to drive. "Rough week, huh?" he finally says.

I snort and wipe my eyes with my wrist. "Yeah."

"They're letting her out tonight, aren't they? Linden's youngest wife."

"Cecily," I remind him. Names aren't his strong suit. "And she's his only wife now."

"Well, then, that's a bit of good news, isn't it? It means she'll be okay."

When I last saw her, she was in a hospital bed, rocking her son and whispering into his hair. Linden was trying to say something to her, but she kept moving her head away.

I was astounded by how young and how very old she looked at the same time. And then I thought of Jenna—strong, steely, beautiful Jenna, who turned sallow and died in our hands while we just watched. Vaughn can do what he wants with us. He can make us sick, and make us well again, and keep us alive for months after our expiration date if he has a mind to. He can deliver our babies, or kill them in the womb, or smother them if they're malformed.

And I can't stop him. All I can do is clean up.

"I have to get fresh water," I say.

"You should stop now," Reed says. "You're about to drop."

My legs are shaking from the inactivity. Tears are heavy in my eyes. "Until that happens, I have work to do."

"You're of no use to any of us unconscious," he says. "Sit for a while."

"If you make me stay, I'm going to ask all the questions I like, until you're sick of me," I warn.

"Deal."

"And you have to answer them," I say.

"Shoot."

I don't have to think about it; there's something I've been wanting to ask him. "Have you ever been married?"

"No," he says. "I rather like being by myself. Had a dog for a while; it followed me around and never talked. I imagine a wife wouldn't grant me that level of peace."

"You never wanted children?" I ask. "Not even before they knew about the virus?"

"Having children seemed like a reckless thing for someone like me to do," Reed says. "Now that we know about the virus, it's worse than reckless. It's cruel. No offense, doll; you had as much a right to be born as any first generation, but if I wanted to watch something live its course and die, I'd get another dog."

I don't know why, but that makes me laugh. Dogs. I'll

only live a few years longer than a dog. All that effort to save my sister wife, and the bloodstain she left in the backseat will be around longer than she will anyway. Reed has had his solitude disrupted by a house full of kids, and in a few years we'll all be dead, though he's the one with tired eyes and wrinkled hands and gray hair. We are young and energetic, but in six years there won't be a trace of us. The absurdity of it all.

Reed frowns at me.

"Your brother has been filling everyone's head with promises of a cure," I say, recovering from my laughter with intermittent hiccups of it. "He builds all of these hospitals and secret lairs. But not you."

"My brother is mad," Reed says. "Completely off his rocker. Don't get me wrong, but if you strip all of that away, he just doesn't want to bury another son. I have to hold on to that thought, or else I wouldn't believe he was human at all."

"And when he can't save Linden, he'll move on to Bowen," I say.

"Bowen and Linden," Reed says, clapping his hands against the steering wheel and staring straight ahead. "Those are two names I thought I'd never hear in the same sentence."

"What do you mean?" I ask.

"Vaughn doesn't like to talk about the past, you understand," Reed says. "Poor Linden has no idea that his son is named after his dead brother."

That night Cecily is discharged from the hospital. It rains. Reed goes speeding down twisty back roads, the tires of his old car squealing at sharp turns. Through the windshield I can't see a thing, and I wonder how, or even if, he can.

Linden sits in the front seat holding Bowen, and patiently says things like "Uncle Reed, please" and "That was a stop sign."

Cecily's eyes are closed, and she's curled up in the backseat with her head on my shoulder. I can tell that she's awake by the way she tenses when we hit bumps, but she doesn't make a sound, and I know what's keeping her subdued.

When she'd gone into premature labor, she'd been unconscious, hanging to life by a thread. But the doctors had chemicals to do the work for her. Dilate the cervix. Loosen the muscles. Force everything out. I remember from one of Cecily's childbirth books a drawing of a fetus at four months. In the drawing it was sucking its thumb, eyes closed, knees curled, and ankles crossed. Even when Cecily began to get stronger a few days ago, she asked me to stay with her. I was at her bedside when she and Linden asked the doctor about their stillborn child—if they could see it, if it had been a boy or a girl. The doctor said it was long gone, donated to the hospital research lab, which would take anything it found worthy of analysis. The doctor said it should be a comfort to them, knowing their loss might help find a cure.

I remember that both of their expressions went blank. They were so bereft already that there wasn't room for new grief. Linden's hands were shaking when he held his palms to his temples.

They've both endured the worst of it with wayward defiance. The silence between them is like a dam about to burst.

The car squeals to a stop.

"Wait for me to get the umbrella," Linden says. "Cecily, love, pull your hood up."

She sits up, groggy, half of her hair rumpled. I help her with the hood of her coat. "We're here?" she murmurs.

"Yes," I say. "And you can go to bed now. I even came by this morning and washed the dust out of the sheets." I don't tell her about the blood.

"She did," Reed says. "Who knew the washing machine actually worked? I've been using it to store food."

"I made the bed." I frown and push the hair from her face. "The sheets are tucked in extra snug, the way you like them." It was a pathetic gesture to comfort her, too little in the grand scheme of all she's been through.

"Thanks," she yawns. Her head tilts sleepily. Linden pulls up the hood of Bowen's plasticky raincoat and hands him to Reed before helping Cecily out of the car, holding an umbrella over her. Once we're inside, he tries to carry her, but she brushes him off.

"Wait," Linden says, but she moves down the hallway ahead of him. There's been a distance behind her eyes since her heart stopped that night. She somnambulates beyond human reach, ignoring voices that call after her. She has stopped talking about her nightmares, but she never truly awakens from them.

Now her fingertips drag along the wall. Her steps are slow, shaky, but purposeful.

Reed, who has just pulled the cord that illuminates the stairwell with flickering light, steps aside to let her pass. She stops in front of him, more than a head shorter than he is, and meets his eyes. "I'm sorry for how I acted," she says. "I was awful, and you've been nothing but generous. Thank you for letting me stay in your home."

And Reed, who muttered angry things whenever she left the room, softens. "Think nothing of it, kid," he says. Cecily gives him something like a smile and then pushes herself up the creaky stairs.

In the bedroom she collapses facedown on the mattress, and Linden removes her muddy shoes. She turns onto her back, limp as a rag doll, watching with dull eyes as he unbuttons her coat, slides it from her arms, and rubs warmth into her fingers.

He's murmuring nice things to her the whole time, saying that she's important and that she's strong, but she doesn't react, not even when he tells her he loves her.

And then I hear her slight gasp, see the way her bottom lip curls back with a sob. The dam is finally breaking.

When Linden peels away the covers, I backpedal from the doorway and into the hall. They should be alone. Husband and wife. There's no room for an awkward, unmarried third. And I'll be leaving soon anyway. If Cecily knew I was staying for her sake, she'd be pushing me out the door. But I can't leave until I'm sure she's well.

I go down to the kitchen, where Reed is attempting to feed Bowen a bottle while working on some project that involves soil and glass jars. "Compact watermelons," he tells me, not looking up. "If I can make the seed grow in a jar, it'll take its shape. No bigger, no smaller."

"I like it," I say. "Modifying something without changing its genetics."

"Clever you," he says. "Too bad you won't stick around to see how it turns out."

I take Bowen, surprised at how heavy he is for someone so small, and sit in a chair to feed him the rest of his bottle. I watch his lips move, the milky formula that pools between them without ever spilling over. His eyes are winking. He's a perfect little machine, I think, flawlessly engineered, except for one pesky glitch.

It's quiet for a while, and then Reed says, "That child looks like she's been to hell and back."

I like that Reed sees Cecily for what she is.

"She's been to hell," I agree. "I don't know about back."

Reed reaches into the jar and presses a seed into the layer of soil that lines it.

"She's convinced that Vaughn wanted her dead," I say. "She won't have him anywhere near her."

"Is that so," Reed says, not sounding at all surprised. "What do you think?"

"I wouldn't put it past him," I say, tilting the bottle so Bowen doesn't suck up any air bubbles. I remember this from watching my mother handle newborns in the lab. "If a second pregnancy was dangerous to her, maybe he didn't have to do anything; maybe he could just sit back and let it take its course. What I don't understand is why. Maybe he has realized he can't control her anymore, but for her to be dead? What would he gain from that?"

"I heard there used to be hunters," Reed says, "who'd use the whole animal. Cook with its fat, eat its meat, wear its pelt, preserve its organs, and worship its skull. My brother is like that—nothing wasted, nothing without purpose."

"You're thinking of the Inuit," I say. "They used to carve sculptures out of the bones and make thread from the sinew." I read about them in one of my father's encyclopedias years ago. They lived in Canada's arctic regions and survived almost entirely on sea life. Even now I can see the glossy photographs of their heavy fur coats, the long trail of footsteps in the snow behind a little girl in black braids as she held up a fish. I remember how strong they seemed, and how beautiful. It pains me to compare them to Vaughn, but it's accurate. He would gut me and my sister wives like fish, but every organ would have a purpose.

Anger bests me for a moment, and my hand shakes; the bottle slips out of Bowen's mouth, but he sucks it back into place. It doesn't seem right that I'm holding such a fragile creature while I'm thinking such ugly thoughts.

"You know a lot of things, doll," Reed says. "You can't trust everything the history books tell you, though. They lie." He shakes a little glass bottle of seeds, holding them up to the lightbulb that's swinging over his head. The seeds are tiny, unborn things, and I resent them. They'll be planted and they'll grow into exactly what they're meant to be.

"Rhine?" Linden's voice is soft. He's standing in the doorway, pale as death.

"I'm almost done feeding Bowen," I say. "Then I'll bring him up. Unless you want to take him right now?"

"No, let him finish," Linden says, his tone never changing. "Just put him in the bassinet when he's through, if you don't mind. I'll see you in the morning."

He doesn't wait to hear my reply. He turns around slowly and with precision, like he's balancing porcelain plates on his head, and disappears into the darkness of the hall.

Reed frowns through a mason jar. "Look at that boy," he says. "I always hoped he would come around and realize the kind of person his father is. But I never wanted it to make him look like that. Ignorance is bliss—have you ever heard that expression?"

"Yes," I say. Though, my generation hasn't been granted enough ignorance to squander.

"My nephew is a bright boy, but I think he prefers to

stay ignorant," Reed says. "Not you, though. There are always cogs turning in that head of yours."

"A lot of good it does," I say. "I've caused nothing but trouble for everyone."

"The trouble was already there," Reed says. "You've just uncovered it, is all."

After Bowen has finished his bottle, I carry him up the stairs, avoiding the creakiest boards as best I can. The lights are off in the bedroom, but I hear Cecily say, "Your father is definitely doing something down there."

"We didn't see anything," Linden says. Both of them are trying to recover from crying; I can hear it in their voices.

"I would hear things in the walls. People. I don't think Rhine was lying. She wouldn't lie to me."

"Love, I used to think that too. . . ."

"I believe her. I believe her whether you do or not." She breaks with a sob. "Stop it—don't touch me like that, like you pity me."

"We'll talk more about it when you're well," he says.

"I'm not made of glass," she says. "When will you stop treating me like I'm going to break?"

"Okay." He sobs too. "Okay. There's something I never told you," he says. There's a long pause, blankets rustling. "Long before you and I were married, I had a daughter."

His voice becomes just a murmur, so faint I can't even be sure he's still speaking, until Cecily says, "My god," and a new round of sobbing kicks up from the both of them. "Why didn't you tell me? Something like that."

It's hard to make out his words after that, because his voice has been reduced to a teary whisper, "Rose said . . . couldn't believe her . . . didn't want to think it . . . thought it would frighten you."

I hear her respond, "You can always tell me anything. Anything."

Bowen, intuitive little thing that he is, hiccups and lets out the high-pitched whimper that prefaces his tears. He knows there's cause to be sad.

"Rhine?" Cecily calls, and to her credit there's nothing to indicate she's been crying, though the air carries the tension of a conversation cut short by my arrival.

I step into the darkness of the bedroom, and I can just make out their forms in the twin bed. "He's all fed," I say by way of explanation.

Bowen whimpers, and Cecily reaches out for him and says "Thank you" when I hand him off.

"Good night," I say.

"Night," she says, with a cheer that doesn't sound at all forced, and then she snuggles under the covers with her husband and son.

Linden yawns so casually it would seem that nothing is wrong. "Sleep well," he says.

If we were all still married to one another, I wonder if they'd want me to be a part of their conversation. I wonder if any of these horrible things would even be happening.

On the divan in the library, I immediately feel myself falling asleep. This always seems to be my reaction when things are bad. Exhaustion. It's comforting. It's a heavy blanket, making everything dark and soft. Across the hall Bowen is crying, and his parents are forgetting their own tears to tend to him. It occurs to me that they're a family, every bit as real as the one I once had, almost too long ago to remember.

My sleep carries late into the afternoon. When I open my eyes, the clock on the wall tells me it's after two p.m.

I would have slept later if not for the noise of an engine revving outside. Reed trying to bring one of the old cars to life, no doubt.

There's a tray on the floor by the divan, with a teacup of beige liquid and a bowl of cubed fruit floating in its own juices.

"Sorry," Linden says from the doorway. "I know you like fruit for breakfast, but my uncle is big on canning all his food, except for some apples that looked a bit mealy."

I sit up, batting away the hair that's falling into my face. The shade on the window has been drawn, though I'm sure it was open last night. "It's all right," I say. "Thank you."

He nods, looks at me for a few seconds and then at his feet.

"I wanted to make sure you were okay," he says. "It was getting late, and you hadn't woken up."

"How's Cecily?" I ask.

"She's downstairs trying to get the radio to work," he says. "When I left her, she was about to throw it at the wall."

He forces a laugh, and I smile a little. It's comforting to think she's back to normal. As much as she can be, anyway.

Linden looks as though he has more to say, but he's waiting for an invitation, I think. I make room for him on the divan, bundling myself in the scratchy wool blanket.

He sits on the far end, putting more than a foot of distance between us. It takes him a long time to speak.

"I owe you an apology," he says, looking at the clock like it's holding a gun on him. "Everything you said—it was staring me in the face, and I chose not to believe it. I made excuses not to."

I can't blame him for not trusting me. After all, I did most of the lying in our marriage. But I don't want to interrupt him when he's clearly having a hard enough time getting the words out.

"My father showed no regard for your safety. As my wife you should have felt that you could tell me when someone was threatening you. You chose to keep that from me. And I understand your reasoning. I wouldn't have believed you. Just like I didn't believe Rose." He winces when he says her name.

"She tried to tell me things about my father. She told me that she'd heard our daughter cry. And—" He has to stop.

He looks right at me. And once again I feel like Rose's

ghost. He is looking at her hair, her face, trying to make amends with the dead. "A part of me believed it. She was a lot like you: very grounded, never making statements unless she was *sure.* She was always right, too. But still it seemed like too awful a thing to be true. And so—to hear you say it, that afternoon when you woke up in the hospital, it was a little bit like she had come back to haunt me."

My heart is thudding in my throat. I hug my knees to my chest in the blanket, making myself as small as I can.

"I lied to you," he says. "The truth is, I believed everything you were saying. I just didn't want to."

"Of course you didn't want to think of your father that way," I say gently. "Linden, I understand—"

"Please," he says. "Just let me finish." He holds my gaze, forcing Rose away, forcing himself to accept that he cannot apologize now for how he wronged her. There's only me.

"When you told me Cecily was in danger, I didn't want to believe that, either. I thought I could keep her safe. But that night she lost the baby, I—" He looks at his empty hands. "There was nothing I could do."

He has made it this far with a steady tone, but now his hands start to shake and his eyes well with tears. It's been a valiant effort to stay brave; he even made it through talking about Rose without breaking. But for Cecily to suffer is just too much; she's precious to him.

"I should have listened to you." He clenches his fists.

I disentangle myself from the blanket and scoot closer to him. Our shoulders and the crowns of our heads rest together.

He says, "I'm sorry."

"I'm sorry, too."

It's quiet for a while. I let him collect himself, and then I draw back to look at him and ask, "But are you sure? You really believe everything you've just said?"

"Cecily still swears my father is to blame. She thinks he knew about the baby and that he was just waiting for it to kill her. My father, of course, will insist she's being unreasonable."

"Your father is wrong about a lot of things," I say. He was wrong about his own son. He told me that Linden's unrequited love for me had turned violent. But Linden had the chance to turn his back on me—nobody would have blamed him for it—and he didn't.

"It still doesn't make sense," Linden says. "I don't understand why my father would want to hurt her. Maybe it's a big misunderstanding. But I had to choose a side, and I chose Cecily. She told me a lot of things that she was afraid to tell me earlier. She thought I would feel betrayed and cast her away." As I was falling asleep last night, I could hear them whispering down the hall; I wonder if either of them got any sleep.

"She doesn't want to lose her marriage," I say. "It's her whole world."

"Mine too," he says. "We talked for a long time. We

agreed to be honest with each other. And we agreed to support each other, no matter what."

"That's good," I say.

"Which is why, when she told me we should help you, I agreed."

"Help me?"

"We want to help you find your brother," he says. "And that attendant."

"Gabriel."

"Yes. Gabriel." He looks at his lap, then at me.

I'm suddenly unsure what to do with my hands. I tuck them between my knees. My cheeks feel hot, and I feel at once the need to cry and to laugh, but I find I have the energy to do neither.

"I know it isn't my place to ask what's gone on between the two of you," Linden says. "Even before the annulment, I see now that I was wrong to expect all of your affections to be for me."

"It wasn't wrong of you," I say. "We were married."

"Foolish, then," he says. "But I admit that I've wondered, since the day you both went missing, what existed between you and him. I wondered what made you love him instead of me."

"It wasn't what you think," I say, too quickly and too loudly. I force myself to look at him. "I couldn't leave him behind. I loved the idea of being free again, and I loved the idea of Gabriel being free, rather than carrying on in servitude until the end. It doesn't seem right to me, Linden, people only seeing the world through daydreams and windows."

I think I've hurt him. He stares past my shoulder and nods.

"He's been good to you, then?" he says. "Gabriel?"

"Better than I've been to him," I admit.

Still looking past me, he tightens his lips. I can see that they're heavy with something he'd like to say.

He wants to ask if I slept with Gabriel. I think he's wanted to ask me since my return, but he hasn't. It's too forward a question for him.

He clears his throat. "What I really came here to tell you is that I'd still like to help you get home. If you'll allow me, that is. I have a plan this time."

"What's that?" I ask.

"My uncle is going to fix one of his old cars," Linden says. "He modifies them to run on his homemade fuel. It's some big secret recipe of his, so I don't know how reliable it is, but it's better than nothing, isn't it? I can teach you how to drive."

I already know how to drive. My brother taught me on the delivery trucks he used for work. But now's not the time to add another thing to the list of what Linden doesn't know about me, so all I can offer is my most sincere, "Thank you."

Linden sees the hope this has brought me. "It'll mean postponing your trip a bit longer, but it'll still be faster in the long run, and I'd feel much better about your traveling this way, for what it's worth." He reaches to touch my shoulder but then changes his mind, and I get the sense that he's in too much of a hurry to get away from me. But when he looks at me, he smiles wearily as he stands. "Eat, and get washed up if you want to. I think my uncle needs your help out in the shed. I offered to help, but he said I should stick to designing things, not repairing them. I don't think he's quite forgiven me for the homemade radio I broke when I was a child."

"Linden?"

He turns in the doorway to face me.

"I didn't. I realize you didn't come right out and ask, but Gabriel and I—we didn't."

His expression doesn't change but for the flush of color to his cheeks. "I'll see you downstairs," he says.

Once he's gone, I force myself to eat everything in the bowl. I have no desire to, but I know my body is craving it. I can feel the emptiness in my stomach gnawing at my bones. After I've eaten, I shower under the rusty tap. I ignore the want to collapse under the blankets and sleep away the next three years. If Linden and Cecily can make an effort to go through the motions and be strong, after all that they've lost, so can I.

After a week of rain, the days return twice as bright. Blades of grass rise from the heaviness of raindrops in defiance. The sunlight breaks through the gaps in the shed, swimming with bits of dust. Everything smells like flowers and dirt.

Cecily's domestic arrived the other day. I'm not sure what Linden told his father that made him relinquish control of her and let her stay with us, but she seemed unharmed, if quiet, when she stepped out of the limo.

Cecily comes outside sometimes, barefoot. For most of our marriage she's been partial to skirts and elaborate sundresses to impress our husband, but now she wears jeans rolled up to her knees. She lays Bowen on his stomach and tries to coax him to crawl, though all he does is grab at the earth and hold it up to the sun in offering. She decides he must be worshipping his secret god.

"There are so many colors in his eyes," she tells me one afternoon when I come to sit next to her in the dirt. "Sometimes I wonder where he gets that." She grabs a fistful of grass and sprinkles it over her son, who is bobbling on his hands and trying to push himself forward.

"Do you look like your parents?" she asks.

I draw my knees to my chest. "A little like my mother," I say. "She had blue eyes."

"I wonder how far down the line genes go," she says. "Your mother had blue eyes, and maybe her mother, and her mother. It could be this one gene that's gone on for thousands of years just to get to you. You could be the last one to ever have that exact shade of blue."

I don't tell her that my brother has the same shade of blue, and that he'll live longer than I will. Although, the way things are going with the explosions and everything, I wonder if he'll even live long enough for me to get to him.

"How are you feeling?" I ask her. "Are you chilly? I could get you a sweater."

"No," she says. "I feel pretty good right now."

It's been nearly a week since she's been discharged from the hospital, and she's more self-sufficient than ever. She's insisted on having her meals with us at the table, politely declining Linden's offers to bring a tray to her in bed. She's even been cleaning the house, though nobody asked her to and I've never known Cecily to be at all domestic. I found her polishing the mason jars, scrubbing the grit from the countertops, kicking a damp rag across the linoleum. She wrapped tinfoil around the radio antenna until the scratchy white noise turned to music. She's memorized the songs, and she sings in low voices as she moves through the rooms. Sometimes I think I hear her singing in her sleep.

"You should get going soon," she says to me now. "You're not getting any younger."

She knows that I've been dawdling. Trapped in the mansion, I could think of nothing but home. But now my home is gone. I'm frightened of what I might find when I'm reunited with Rowan. I'm frightened of not finding him at all. And perhaps what frightens me the most is accepting that once I leave Cecily and Linden, I'll never see them again.

Time almost seems to stop here on Reed's middle-of-nowhere piece of land. It's oddly comforting.

I shield my eyes and squint to see Linden in the distance.

He's got one of the cars uncovered, and he and his uncle are gesturing to it as they talk.

"So that's my ride," I say.

"It's like looking at an old picture," she says, squinting.

"I didn't know Linden could drive," I say.

"Me either," she says. "But I think he's been practicing."

She scoops Bowen into her lap. His eyes are full of clouds and sky. He reaches for my hair, and I hold up a lock of it for him to grab.

"I used to daydream how nice it'd be if you had one of your own," Cecily says. "A baby, I mean. And Jenna, too." She watches Reed lower himself under the car while Linden toys with things under the hood. "This isn't where I thought we'd all be a year into our marriage. I thought we'd all be happy. Stupid, huh?"

Bowen tugs at my hair, his skin so soft that it sticks to the strands. "No, it isn't," I say. "Nobody could have predicted it would turn out like this."

"What have I done, Rhine?" she says. "I brought a child into this world because Housemaster Vaughn convinced me he could save us. But Bowen is just as doomed as you and me." Bowen clutches her shirt and throws his head back into the sunlight, utterly without a care. I heard once that humans are the only species aware of their own mortality, but I wonder if that's true for babies. Would it even matter to Bowen that his life will end?

Childhood is a long, long road, from which that dark whispering forest of death seems an impossible destination. "Who's going to take care of him when Linden and I are gone?" Cecily says.

I don't know how to answer her. Bowen is the child of a failed plan, just like all of us. "You and Linden will figure something out," I say. "Things didn't turn out how you'd have liked, but nothing ever does. You've found a way to manage so far, haven't you? You're still going."

She shakes her head. "I hate that man," she says. "He ruined everything." Something dangerous and ugly flashes in her eyes. It's only there for a moment, but she doesn't look quite the same after that. And now I know: The winged bride that fluttered ahead of me is gone. She's been conned, ruined, left for dead, and she's not going to forgive any of it. She will soldier on, if only out of spite.

"Even if Vaughn had meant to save us, our marriage couldn't have gone on like that forever," I say.

Cecily watches the daylight shift in Bowen's hair.

"I never wanted to live forever," she says. "I just wanted enough time."

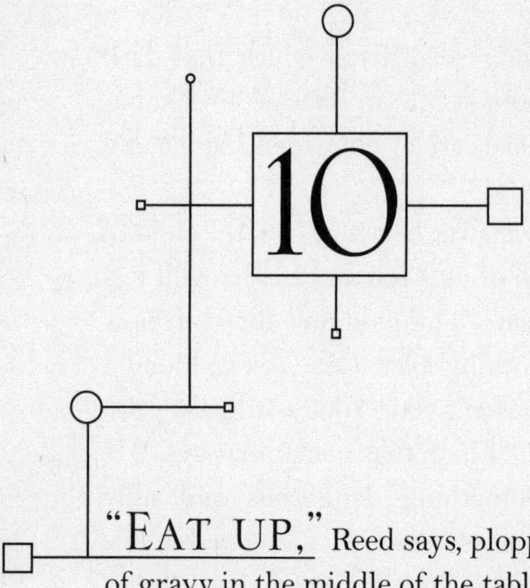

10

"EAT UP," Reed says, plopping a pot of some type of gravy in the middle of the table.

Cecily peers into the murky gray liquid and frowns at a cube of meat that's floating against the rim. "What was this in a past life?" she asks.

"Pigeons and a field rabbit," Reed says. "Hunted them down myself."

"He's an excellent shot," Linden says.

"Can you eat pigeons, though?" Cecily falls back into her chair, looking a mix of disgusted and curious.

"You can eat just about anything," Reed says, dumping a ladleful into her bowl. Like me, Cecily has been sticking to the mealy apples and the most recognizable of the canned fruits and pickled vegetables. We haven't been quite as brave as Linden, who swears his uncle's ventures "aren't so bad."

I can tell that Cecily has more she wants to say, but

she doesn't, because this is the last meal we'll all have together. In the morning I'm leaving. I've decided to return to New York to find Gabriel first. I can only hope he's still with Claire. And I miss him. I miss him every time Linden and Cecily look at each other, or whisper behind a closed door, because it all reminds me that I'm not a part of what they have. I don't belong here.

The pieces of my life can never seem to stay in one place.

Nobody talks. Reed has brought his work to the dinner table. It's some kind of small electronic device that hisses and spits sparks at him.

Linden eats the gray liquid with quiet sips. I swirl my spoon around the inside of the bowl.

Cecily leaves the table and returns moments later with the radio, which roars with static interrupted by high squeals and the occasional muffled voice.

"Do you have to bring that to the table?" Linden says.

"Well, your uncle has that . . . thing." She gestures to Reed's project. "I just want a little dinner music, that's all."

Linden frowns, but he says nothing more. He knows how to choose his battles with Cecily, and he's been much more forgiving since her brush with death. He endures the grating noise.

Finally she finds a station that comes through. There's no music, though. It's some kind of news report. Long before I was born, there used to be whole stations dedicated to music, but there haven't been new songs for years, and the only music that plays is the filler between news broadcasts. Old cheerful songs about frivolous things that mean nothing to me. Cecily likes them, though; anything she can sing along to.

She waves the antenna back and forth until the voices come through more clearly. "Maybe they'll play something soon," she says.

"Doubt it, kid," Reed says. "I've heard this guy. He runs his own broadcasts out of his home."

She frowns and reaches for the knob again, but Linden says, "Wait. Did you hear that?"

"What?" she says. The sound has gone to static again, and she repositions the tinfoil wrapped around the antenna.

Voices cut through, trying to reach us. At first when the words come, they mean nothing. I've heard them all my life. "Genetics." "Virus." "Hope." It's become like white noise, especially having parents who spent their evenings listening to such broadcasts.

I take a spoonful of the gray liquid, purposefully avoiding the cubes of meat. The taste isn't terrible.

"There," Linden says. Cecily moves her hands away from the antenna, and the static has subsided to make way for the voices.

She looks disappointed. "It's only that same guy again."

Linden's listening intently, though.

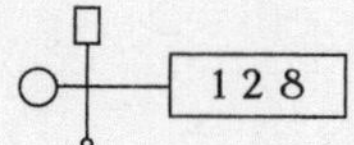

"So-called doctors have been at it for years," the voice on the radio says.

Another voice responds, "The Ellerys' work has developed a cult following among doctors and extremists alike in the wake of these recent terrorist bombings. Their research, which as we all know was cut short by an act of terrorism that killed them, had faded into the grain with all the rest."

The small bit I've eaten immediately feels like it's gone to stone in my stomach. My body goes cold, a sort of numbness clouds my judgment, and I think: *Not the Ellerys* I *know.* How could these strange voices possibly know anything about my parents, who have been dead for several years? They were scientists and doctors, and their life's work was to pursue a cure, but they were small-time compared to nationally recognized doctors like Vaughn.

Oh, but the broadcasters know about Vaughn as well. "Even revered experts like this Dr. Ashby have cited the Ellerys' study of twins. Dr. Ashby theorizes that the Ellerys' children, twins themselves supposedly, were a part of their research."

"If they even existed," the other voice says. "They may have been metaphors."

Cecily is pulling at a lock of her hair that's come free of her ponytail, and I swear her eyes are getting wider as she stares at me and the words on the radio get stranger.

"Dr. Ashby is essentially revamping the Ellerys'

theory that the virus can be duplicated in a way similar to vaccinations. Given in small doses, it can build up the immune system to make its victims resistant."

The men are having such an impassioned discussion, and the static keeps interfering, and Linden adjusts and readjusts the tinfoil trying to make the voices stay. But it doesn't matter, because I can't hear them anymore. There's static in my head, making it impossible to concentrate. The room feels twice as hot, and the lightbulb dangling from the ceiling makes so many shadows. How have I never noticed all these shadows?

"What about these claims by one of the terrorists heading these attacks that he's the Ellerys' only surviving twin? He very well could be who he claims to be."

"How many extremists have claimed to be products of some research project or other? That's if the Ellerys' research isn't an urban legend," the other voice counters. "The Ellerys ran these nurseries as part of their supposed Chemical Garden project, nurseries that also served as research labs. If their children existed, they were probably killed along with the other subjects. The only reason the Ellerys are getting attention now is because of this terrorist claiming to be their son."

The static overtakes the voices until they're gone.

Everyone is watching me. Their eyes bore into me, but I can't face them.

The heavy feeling in my stomach has moved to my chest, and it's hard to breathe. I need to get outside, where there are breezes and stars and no walls. I'm moving even before I realize I've stood up.

I stagger out to the porch. Dizzy, I sit on the top step and try to catch my breath. There are so many thoughts whirling through my head that I can latch on to none of them. I never thought I'd hear my parents mentioned again, much less in a discussion that involves my ex-father-in-law. It's true they all have genetic research in common, but Vaughn is the madman. My parents only wanted to make things right. Didn't they?

How did those men on the radio know about my brother and me?

Rowan said that he was the only surviving member of our family?

What theory that the virus could be duplicated? What are Chemical Gardens?

The questions are bits of blackness, arranging like puzzle pieces until I can hardly see, can hardly think.

And for what? What answers do I hold? My brother and I—the apparently famous Ellery twins—aren't an urban legend. We exist. But we hold no keys, can't offer even a vague promise of a cure.

The screen door slams behind me, making me flinch.

Reed's heavy footsteps make the planks in the porch creak. He's never without his boots, even at night, as though he's always prepared to run at a moment's notice. He's not so different from the people I knew back home, before the sheltered life I led in the mansion.

He's not so different from my brother and me.

He sits beside me, reeking of cigar smoke, although he hasn't had a cigar in hours. Cecily throws a fit if the smoke comes anywhere near the oxygen Bowen breathes. It only enrages her more when Reed counters that the smoke is totally harmless. It used to cause ailments that no longer exist, and a little coughing won't kill the kid, he says.

"You're in some real trouble, aren't you, doll?" Reed says.

I draw my knees to my chest, and my voice comes out broken and small. "I don't know what any of it means." I can hear the static in the kitchen as Linden and Cecily try to bring the station back.

"Does my brother know the Ellerys were your parents?" Reed's expression is unsettlingly grave.

The notion is overwhelming. It's terrible enough that I was ripped from my home, but to have been a specific target rather than a random victim of Gathering? It puts Vaughn's madness into a whole new light. He could have been looking for me all my life.

No. No, it couldn't have been that. Like the men on the radio were saying, there are plenty of scientists, plenty of theories. My parents hadn't broken any new ground. Vaughn wouldn't have heard of them until my brother said what he did, about being their only surviving twin.

My brother, with his unmistakable resemblance to me.

With his eyes that are heteroc
Vaughn would have to do is lo
related.

"I don't know," I whisper. "If Va
come after my brother, too."

I'm too stunned to process any of
even to cry, though my eyes are starting
are trembling.

"No matter what, you're safe here," Ree

"Am I?" I say. "Or is your brother just lett
that while he plans his next move?"

"He'll never get through my door," Reed say
to believe that. Just as Reed never goes without h
he never goes without the handgun that's holste
his belt. But Vaughn has his ways. He comes peace
never raises his voice, never draws a weapon, and he w
virtually every time.

Strange new voices from the radio are coming toward me. Cecily carries the thing out onto the porch. Her face is solemn and sympathetic. "We couldn't get that station to come in again, but there's a news broadcast. There was another bombing yesterday; that's what those men were talking about."

Linden comes after her, frowning. "Why don't you take that back inside, love? Leave her alone now."

"She needs to hear this," Cecily insists. She holds the radio in her hands like an offering. The news is telling a horrible story.

urteen are confirmed dead and at least five wounded ing yesterday's bombing in Charleston, South ina." The same state where Madame's deranged ival is. This of course would mean nothing to the scaster, who goes on, "The trio of bombers has made secret about their activities, and though they haven't sclosed their next target, they have spurred public ral-es and spoken openly on camera about their actions."

There's a sharp pain in my head, like a kite string has lassoed my brain, tugging me to the speakers. And I know that I am about to hear something I have not heard in a very long time. A simple thing, the absence of which has parched something deep within me.

My brother's voice.

He's riled up, shouting into the crowd. The tape recorder that captured the sound is buried somewhere in all the cheering and jeering voices, rustling, picking up the rush of wind. But Rowan is the maestro of this cacophony. I concentrate on my brother, imagining him standing someplace high, and I hear him say, "—research is pointless. All this madness trying to find a cure is more dangerous to us than the virus itself. It kills people. It killed my sister." There's a devastated pitch when he says that last word. The word that symbolizes me. "It's gone too far, and it must end!"

The clip is over, and he's gone.

A sound comes out of me; something like a choke or a whimper.

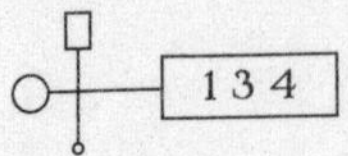

There's no doubting it now. He thinks I'm dead. He's given up on me.

"Rhine?" Linden shoves past Reed and kneels on the step before me. He pushes the hair from either side of my face and cradles my skull with his fingertips. His eyes are searching mine, like he's checking a vase for chips and cracks.

"It was my brother," I manage to say. My voice is strained, like I'm only inhaling, which maybe I am. I can't tell. I've never felt like this. There was the adrenaline and terror of being thrown into the Gatherer's van, and again in the back of that truck with Gabriel, but in the darkness all of that melted down to a sort of malaise after a while. Then came the planning. I'd kept myself together with logic. I'd been taken. I'd escape. I'd make it home, and my brother and my house would still be waiting for me. But my brother has made a crater of our house. He has made a crater of himself and everything he touches.

"You have to breathe," Linden says softly. He's always so careful with me, even when I've hurt him. Bright spots move around him like someone shook the stars from a blanket and they all went flying.

"This is my fault," I say. "We were supposed to look out for each other, and I left him. He's gone now. I'll never get him back."

"Sure you will," Linden says.

"I know the guy who runs that first broadcast," Reed

offers. "I could take you to him. Maybe he'll know something."

Linden moves to sit between Reed and me. "Is it safe?" he asks. "He sounded like he was deranged."

"Linden, you've been bred to think everything is dangerous," Reed says.

"You have to talk to him," Cecily says. "You have to find out about the Chemical Gardens. Maybe your parents knew something real, Rhine. Maybe there is a cure. Maybe it has something to do with you and your brother. You have a responsibility to find out." The hope in her voice is unbearable.

"Cecily," Linden snaps. "Now isn't the time to make demands. Could you try to be a little sensitive?"

"Sensitive?" she says. "Sensitive! When I was pregnant with our son, you told me that he was my job. You said, 'Don't you see how important it is?' Well, I do! Maybe this is a dead end—who knows? But we have to find out. I brought him into this world thinking he'd have a shot at surviving, and I'm not going to just sit here and wait to die if there's still a chance."

Everyone is looking at her now. She seems bigger in the moonlight. Hardened by tragedy. But I see the way the now-silent radio is shaking in her hands. Her jaw is clenched. No matter how realistic Cecily has become, something within her will always ignite at the thought of hope. Even if we all know that hope is pointless, who am I to take it away from her?

Linden opens his mouth to speak, but I put my hand on his arm. "She's right," I say. "We should talk to him."

"You're sure?" Linden says.

His pity and Reed's pity and Cecily's intensity have all become too much. I look away from them and toward the tall grass bending sideways on a gust of wind.

"Yes," I say. "Can I please be alone now?"

Reed is on his feet immediately. "Show's over, kiddos," he says, herding Linden and Cecily back inside.

The windows are open upstairs, and a few moments later I hear Bowen start to cry, and then Cecily singing to him. Linden asks her what she's done with his suitcase, and she tells him it's under the bed.

They're all going to die too soon. I want to be the thing to save them, but I can't.

I sleep, but my dream is a vivid hallucination of Vaughn's hands snatching Bowen out of his bassinet while Cecily and Linden sleep in a bed five feet away. And then Vaughn steps into a shred of moonlight, and he's not Vaughn at all. He's my brother.

I open my eyes, heart pounding. I won't close them again. I rise from the divan and move to the open window. It's so motionless out there. If I don't look behind me, if I look to the horizon, I could believe that the line where the earth meets the sky is the end of the world. And in the quiet I think I hear my father calling something to me.

My mother said I had a different kind of strength, and that's why I needed to look out for my brother. But maybe she didn't know me as well as she thought, because while my brother is starting disturbing revolutions and making fire in the sky, I'm struggling just to catch my breath. I'm not very strong by anyone's standards, especially my brother's.

When we were eight, he and I found a fallen star.

It wasn't really that. I guess it was just some scrap metal that had blown into our yard on a windy night. But in the early morning, when we first saw it, the edges caught the rising sun at odd angles, and it appeared to be on fire. We ran outside in our pajamas, the fire dying more with every step, until we saw that it was just a crumpled piece of metal. My father came running after us, warning us not to touch it. He said it might be dangerous, and I knew that he was right. I saw all the jagged edges and rust, understood the treachery of the dark crevices it bore. Still, I wanted to think there was something special about it.

My brother nudged it with his foot, and almost immediately I could see the red dominating his white sock. He didn't move. He just watched as his blood spread out, until my father grabbed him and carried him inside. Next, I remember him sitting on the kitchen counter while my mother fussed and dabbed at his foot with wet dishrags and antiseptic that hissed and crackled when they touched skin.

I remember looking out at the metal star in the yard, seeing the bright line of blood where it had cut him. I felt betrayed that something so fascinating and pretty had hurt my brother.

"It's okay," he told me later, when his foot was all bandaged. "It's probably a piece from a bomb. It was designed to hurt people."

He was so cool about the whole thing. That's the last time I ever saw him get hurt. He understood very early the ways of war. Approaching weaponry and touching it out of curiosity would never work. No. He had to understand its purpose and then find a way to utilize it.

Maybe he's always been leaning toward this. Maybe our parents' death made him view the virus and all attempts to cure it as his enemy, and maybe I really was the only thing keeping him docile. Maybe my mother knew exactly what she was talking about when she told us to always stay together.

I rest my elbows on the window frame and let that thought sink in.

When the thoughts turn painful, I seek respite in one of Reed's books. I would love a book of American history, but Reed doesn't keep them. He has some silly theory that history was doctored shortly before the first generations were born. He says we can't trust any of the information we're given. His conspiracy theories have become a comfort to me. I like everything about Reed and his strange little world.

The dictionary happens to be the first thing I grab, and I take it back to the divan and start on the first page, working my way from the *A*s. Whenever I encounter a word I've never had cause to use, I whisper it aloud, just to have said it in my lifetime.

I'm two pages into the *A*s when the door creaks open and Cecily peers in. She's gotten better about avoiding the noisier floorboards, and I didn't hear her coming.

"I saw the light on," she says softly. "Bad dream?"

She knows me well. "Lots to think about," I say.

"Want to talk about any of it?" she says. "I could make some tea." Much as she scoffs at Reed's strange menu, she loves his homemade tea. He grows the herbs in cans and cardboard boxes.

But tea or no tea, I don't want to talk about what's on my mind. It's exhausting enough just trying to sort it out. And it's painful enough to know how much hope I've given her, and how devastated she's going to be all over again when she realizes it's false. "I'll pass," I say. "Thanks, though."

She frowns but doesn't cross the threshold. It's an old habit from mansion life. It was a household rule that we couldn't enter one another's bedrooms without asking. None of us ever thought to break it, because we each had our own reasons for following the rules. "You're angry with me."

"I'm not," I say, closing the dictionary. "Honestly, I'm not. What you were saying made sense."

"I could have been nicer about it," she mumbles, abashed. "I can't help it when it comes to Bowen. I get this panicked feeling in my chest—like there's no time to waste."

It's a bizarre thought that she loves her child the way my parents loved me; she's so young and they were so much older and more prepared. I thought.

Now that I'm looking at her, really looking at her, I can see the half-circle breast milk stains on her nightgown. It must have started up again after she lost the baby, because Bowen's long been on formula—this powdered stuff that Cecily filled a suitcase with before she came here. There are bags under her eyes. I was wondering how she'd managed to be so energetic these past several days, twirling through the house belting out lyrics and humming refrains, but now I understand. She's as sad as ever. It's just that she sings anyway.

When I stand, she asks, "Where are you going?"

"Kitchen. I changed my mind about the tea."

We tiptoe down the steps. The lights are off. Reed's snoring drowns out the creaky board I accidentally tread on. He's sacked out on the armchair, hand on the hilt of his gun. I think he was serious about not letting Vaughn through that front door. He mumbles as we creep past him.

Elle is sleeping on the couch opposite him. She stirs when we pass, and I wonder if she's really asleep; she's so trained to be alert whenever Bowen makes a sound.

We bring our tea back up to the library. I don't think sleep will be an option, but Bowen's shriek of laughter startles me, and I open my eyes to realize there's daylight. My head is on Cecily's shoulder. She's hugging the arm of the couch, and I'm slumped against her, our bodies like collapsed dominoes. A blanket has been draped over us, and I wonder if Linden got up sometime in the night, having noticed her absence in that cramped twin bed, and found us together.

"Morning," Linden says softly. He's holding Bowen, who's gawking at nothing in particular. "Sorry to wake you, but Uncle Reed thinks we should get going."

As though in agreement, an engine splutters outside. The first several attempts to start the car fail. Cecily grumbles something unkind about the noise and buries her face in her arms, trying to hold on to sleep.

Linden carries Bowen to the window, and Bowen brings his face so close to the glass that it mists with his breath. There's sunlight and birds, so much to fascinate him. Linden watches with a sad sort of smile, like he knows that his son's happiness is a lie that must one day be dispelled. Linden loves his son, of course, but he can't show him the affection that Cecily does. After all the loss he's endured, all that await him are promises of death and good-byes. He's become very guarded.

He says just one word to his son, nodding into the daylight. "Look."

It's an astounding word. It's a gift.

Bowen looks, and for now everything he sees is beautiful.

PEOPLE USED to be connected to one another all the time. That's what my parents told me. Everyone had phones and computers. Everyone called and kept in touch. They used to be everything, these things that are barely remembered now. These things that mean nothing to me.

I imagine the world felt smaller when it was like that. When someone was away from home, they'd call. There were no brothers worrying that their sisters were dead.

Now we're left with old antennas, and radio signals. I know there's less land than there used to be, but without these connections the world seems impossibly big. I feel as though I'm always running, and my brother is always too many paces ahead. I call out, but he can't hear me. He's not even listening for the sound of my voice anymore.

And now it's morning, and I'm going to see some man

with opinions and a radio signal, yet another dead end, keeping hope alive like the frail pulse of a dying animal.

"Can I drive?" Cecily asks. She's sitting in the front seat of Reed's car, hovering her fingertips over the knobs and buttons.

"No," Linden answers from his place beside me in the backseat. "It's not safe."

"I wasn't asking you," she says, turning her nose up.

"He's right, kid," Reed says, pulling the car into gear. "It's not a good idea. But that knob controls the radio stations. Might be able to find something."

This doesn't pacify her for long, because as we start driving, none of the stations will come through. Sometimes there's a human voice in all the static, and my chest seizes up with dread and hope, but nothing comes of it. There's no more word about my brother. There's no sign of life out there at all.

Elle is small and quiet, holding Bowen in the seat beside me. She was cheerful and attentive when Bowen was first born, but now she's somber. The sunlight in her fine honey-brown hair does nothing to relinquish her from the grayness that overshadows her. I wonder if Vaughn has done something to her. I wonder if she knows what he has done to Deirdre, and I wonder still if any of that is real. And then my wondering turns to that dark, painful place, where I look at Elle and I see the young girl who should be making daisy crowns and daydreaming and living.

This isn't living, what all of us are doing.

We drive down long, dilapidated back roads. Reed ignores the stop signs, and the abandoned traffic lights stare at us like empty eye sockets. Fields have gone to weed. There's a little town of houses that have been haphazardly repaired by boards and scraps of metal. Linden is watching over my shoulder as they go by. He grew up in a very small, affluent town, and I doubt he could have imagined people living like this. I wonder what sort of world his father painted in his head for him. I bet it was all mansions and holograms, and then just clean white stretches of nothing in between. No matter. Nothing there.

He doesn't seem surprised, though. Just sad, in that dulled-over way he's adopted since Cecily miscarried. I think he's beginning to understand, and understanding is a horrible thing.

Linden clenches his hand into a fist. I want to make the world into something different so that he can be okay. I want to be the cure that doesn't exist. But I'm nothing. I can't even work up the courage to say something reassuring.

We come to another house that's similar to Reed's in that it's isolated. There are chickens squawking and meandering in an area fenced by wire, and they flap and flutter at the gurgling-popping sound Reed's engine makes when he shuts it off. There's a sign advertising fresh eggs for twenty dollars a dozen, a cup of churned butter for the same price. The pricing is outrageous but not uncommon. My brother and I would pay slightly less to the vendors in Manhattan, if we could haggle them down with the promise of repeat business.

Cecily is the first one out of the car.

Linden sees the guilt in my eyes as I watch her. "It's okay," he says softly. "She'll learn eventually."

When? In three years, when she's watching her husband die? When she's dying herself?

We wade through high grasses, and I watch Elle, two paces ahead of me, pertly landing on the stepping-stones that are half-buried in the weeds.

The house, despite its neglect, has small signs of care. There are red shutters, and window boxes that are full of wisteria blooms. Cecily presses her hand against her heart and says, "Oh, Linden, look. It's like the house you drew for me."

Linden is drawing houses for her now. I ignore this new wave of senseless jealousy and plod forward.

"Careful where you step," Reed says when we get to the porch. "The wood looks rotted."

Elle presses Bowen's head to her chest protectively, but he whimpers and resists. He wants to look over her shoulder at the morning light in the long grass.

Reed knocks on the door, which is fashioned from pieces of welded metal. Cecily is suddenly apprehensive. "You know this man, right?" she says. "I mean, not just know *of* him, but actually know him?"

"He's harmless," Reed says.

Linden is standing closer to her, but it's my hand she reaches for as we hear movement inside the house. Happy as she is to be Linden's wife, the ordeal of being Gathered still haunts her. She knows that unwanted girls can be made to huddle in dark vans and be shot. Like me, she's wary of shadowy places, and of strangers. Sometimes we don't know how afraid we are until we've reached a strange door and we don't know what will be on the other side.

The door opens just wide enough for us to see a pair of eyes blinking out at us.

"Reed?" a voice says. "Why the crowd?"

"I've brought my nephew," Reed says, clapping his hands on Linden's shoulders. "And the girls are with him. Girls follow him everywhere he goes. Poor boy's cursed with the family charm."

Linden's sullenness cracks to make room for embarrassment. He looks at the banister.

"There's too many of you," the voice says.

"Oh, hell, Edgar. Don't be crazy," Reed says. "Would it make you feel better if we all wore foil hats?"

The eyes look Linden up and down. "Your father is that doctor that's always on the news," the voice, Edgar, says.

Linden has nothing to say for himself. He knows less about his own father, it seems, than the rest of the world does.

Before I realize she's let go of my hand, Cecily steps forward and snatches Bowen from Elle's arms. "Yes," she says, exasperated. "Yes. His father is that doctor that's always on the news. And this is our son." She steps as close to the eyes as she dares, hoisting Bowen on her hip. "He's going to die. But you know that. We've heard you on the radio, and all you talk about is cures and theories. Well, this is what we're trying to cure."

There's a slight tremble in her posture. Linden stands behind her and touches Bowen's curls with one hand, her shoulder with the other.

The door slams shut.

There's the sound of a chain latch rustling, and then the door opens again, this time enough for us to see inside.

Though it's a bright, clear morning, no sunlight fills the room. The windows are blacked out, and instead there are lights strung along the edges of the ceiling like clumps of stars.

Edgar is tall, with wiry limbs but a round gut barely contained by the buttons of his flannel shirt. His eyes are dark and owlish.

"I have guns," he says to Cecily. "I don't care if you are a little girl. Don't try anything. None of you try anything."

We all look at Reed, as if to say we're wary. He waves us on. He's awfully calm, given the threat that was just made, and given how protective of me he's been against his brother. It occurs to me that Reed isn't fearful of many things, but his brother is one of those things.

Bowen is back in Elle's arms. She has plucked a blade of long grass to distract him so he'll be manageable. Lately all he wants to do is grab things.

Inside, the lights make everything warm and vaguely orange-brown. The walls are nothing but bookshelves. "Don't touch anything," Edgar says again. I wouldn't know where to begin, anyway. There are wires running across the floor, leading into another room, where they all assemble and cover a table like jungle vines. In that room there's a flickering television mounted to the wall and playing a grainy rendition of the news, as though we need another reminder of how bleak our world is.

I begin to wonder about the house Linden drew for Cecily. I wonder what was inside it—sometimes he offers you a peek through the windows. I wonder if he wanted to build it for her so they could live there. I wonder if she felt it come alive right there on the page when he put it into her hands. I wonder if anyone can see his houses the way that I do.

"You know how I feel about visitors," Edgar grumbles. He's hardly the assured voice I heard on the radio last night. He seemed to know what he was talking about when he went on about my parents. Now he seems scattered and unstable.

"Genius that you are, you sure have a way of missing what's right in front of your eyes," Reed says. "Have you even looked at what's in front of you?"

Edgar is looking us over, paying no real attention to any of us, more worried, it seems, about his things being stolen or damaged.

Reed grabs my chin, squishing my cheeks with his fingers and forcing my face into the light. "Her eyes," he says. "Look at her eyes."

Linden tenses, as though he wants to save me. I wish he would. I feel exposed. I feel the way I did standing in a line of Gathered girls on the side of the road.

Edgar gets a good look at my eyes. Reed lets go of me, and I stay frozen in that position. Best to get it over with. Best to prove that having one blue eye and one brown eye doesn't mean anything. It's the same view of the same world, no matter what color your irises are.

Edgar trips when he takes a step closer to me. Something falls and clatters against the ground. He doesn't seem to care. My eyes have hypnotized him.

"You're thinking I look like that boy," I say, feeling disparaged and brave. "That terrorist you've seen on the news who's blowing up research hospitals and labs, right? I look like him?"

In the corner of my vision, I see Cecily frowning. She realizes, finally, that she has subjected me to this with her hope, her desperation. She sees how it hurts me.

"Yes," Edgar says. He laughs. It's a humorless madman's laugh. A laugh of relief, maybe. "Yes. You're the dead one."

Reed thought I was Rose's ghost, and my brother

believes I'm dead, and now Edgar. Gabriel, wherever he is, probably thinks I'm dead too. Pretty soon I'll start believing it too.

But Reed says, "As you can see, she's alive. And she has some questions for you."

Edgar's mystified expression changes back into a guarded one. "Is this a trick?" he says.

"You know things about my parents," I say. "At least you sounded like you did on the radio. You said people were familiar with their research. The Ellerys."

"You're supposed to be dead," Edgar repeats. "That boy on the news said so."

"That was my brother," I say, surprised at how steady my voice is, how all the grief and the shock reaches a level so great that I'm unable to acknowledge it. "I disappeared more than a year ago. He just assumes because I haven't been able to reach him—"

"No," Edgar interrupts. "No, he said you were killed in an experiment that went awry."

My stomach drops. "What?"

"That's why he's doing this. He opposes the research labs."

"That couldn't have been Rhine's brother, then," Linden says. "You said on your broadcast that there are imposters, right? People who claim to be the children of experiments?"

"Only one way to find out," Edgar says. He ushers us into the room where all the wires lead. I feel as though my insides have been scooped out. My heart beats in a dark, empty space, and I think I'll be sick.

I see the television that's mounted to the wall, and I know what it means. Just when I'm sure I have no energy left, a moment before I'm about to collapse, Linden grabs one of my hands and Cecily takes the other.

Edgar fumbles through a box of video discs in a cardboard box.

When he finds the one that means something to him, he inserts it into the video player.

My body feels a rush of hot, then cold, hot, then cold.

The screen goes to static, and then there's an image of a crowd. It's amateur footage, which isn't uncommon for the nationwide news. Someone with a camera can make good money risking his life to film news footage.

I think it's the same clip we heard last night on the radio. Bodies blur out of focus as the camera tries to adjust. Eventually it does, and I see that the crowd isn't as big as I thought. It looks like new generations, from young children to those in their final year. There are two figures standing at a distance, not high up on a stage like I pictured, but on overturned wooden crates. I see the ocean behind them. This must be near the shoreline; bitterly I wonder how close my brother is to where Gabriel and I stood a few months earlier.

I recognize my brother immediately. There's a girl standing beside him that I don't recognize. She has chaotic black hair and eyes to match. Both of them are smeared with dirt.

No, not dirt. Ash.

The girl looks wild and dangerous. And then I realize Rowan does too. This is what happened to him when I left. Losing our parents had already taken away his hope, but losing me took away his reason.

The crowd knows him; they're saying his name, asking him to speak.

And then calmly, methodically, he begins to tell his story. Long ago he was a bright-eyed child with stupid delusions that the world could be saved. He had parents and a sister. His parents, trying to save the world, were killed in a bombing much like the ones he and his partners are responsible for now. So then, he asks the crowd, is it wrong of him to take away someone else's parents? Is it wrong to set fire to these buildings?

The crowd is silent, waiting for his response, because the venom has left the voice of this vigilante warrior. He seems so painfully, vulnerably human.

"No," he says. "A long time ago, maybe. But this is a world without right and wrong. This is a world that was someone's idea of perfection, and when that perfection didn't happen, this world was abandoned, and we were all left to run wild.

"And as for my sister," he says. "She was the opposite of me. While I was trying to keep us both alive, she was in a dead garden, trying to make dead things bloom. I didn't agree with it, but I thought, 'What's the harm? Why not let her pretend?'"

The girl standing beside him touches his arm. She's heard this story before. She noticed that falter in his voice.

He shrugs her off.

"Because I let her pretend, her imaginary faith in this cesspool of a world grew. Behind my back she signed up for an experimental procedure. She was lured into some primitive makeshift laboratory by promises of life." Any hint of an emotional edge has left him now. He speaks as though reading from a textbook. "Her heart began to palpitate first. And then her throat swelled shut; her eyes started to bleed. And when she died, several agonizing minutes later? Her body was dissected for even *more* research."

This has been Rowan's reality. While I was being laced into a wedding dress and was sucking on June Beans and napping comfortably on a fluffy blanket with my sister wives and daydreaming of home, that's the image of me he has carried.

My vision is tunneling around me, and I can't feel my legs, but somehow I'm still standing.

"Breathe," Linden whispers, reminding me.

"I'm here to take away your hope," Rowan says, "because hope will kill you. Every moment of this research is pointless. All this madness trying to find a cure is more dangerous to us than the virus itself. It kills people. It killed my sister."

I try to hear his next words, but the cheering crowd

cuts him off. They're in support of what he's doing, clearly. I almost can't blame them. A story like that is convincing; hope is so hard to come by and even harder to hold on to. Better to throw it away. Easier. After all, in his story there is the twin who tried to survive, and the twin who fell victim to silly hopes.

The film goes to static.

Edgar puts the disc back into its place.

"So you see," he says, "you're dead."

"Obviously she's alive," Cecily snaps. "Or are you even crazier than you look?"

Nobody chastises her for this.

"Seems like that brother of yours is the crazy one," Edgar tells me.

"I—" My voice is a rusty creak. "Where would he have heard such a thing?"

"Who else but the most respected doctor in modern science and medicine?" Edgar says, turning to face us. "Vaughn Ashby."

"That's impossible," I say.

"That's the rumor underground," Edgar says. "The rumor is that he wants to be rid of all the competition so he can find the cure himself."

"What underground?" Linden asks.

Edgar doesn't look entirely sane when he says, "I never reveal my sources."

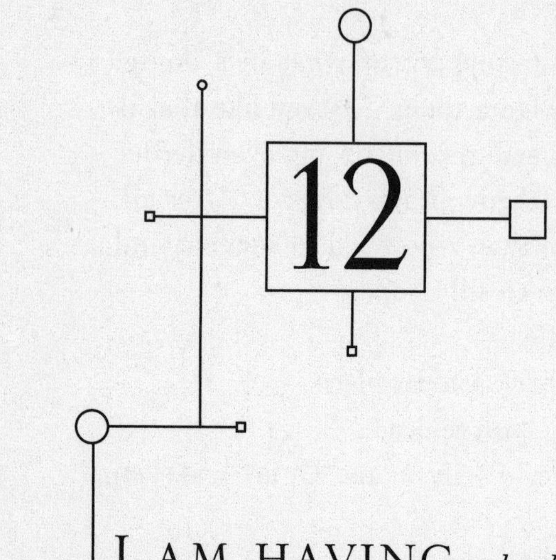

I AM HAVING *a hard time reading your twin because there is something about this person that you won't admit even to yourself.* That's what the fortune-teller said. Maybe she'd made a lucky guess, or maybe she really did have a gift, because she was right. I hadn't wanted to admit that my brother was capable of these awful things. I wanted to believe that I could find him again and it would be as before.

There are more things that Edgar can tell us. He has news clippings and a fascination with the work and progress of one of the nation's most prominent doctors and scientists, also known as my former father-in-law. But Linden takes one look at my bloodless face, and he says, "That's enough."

I open my mouth to argue, but before I can utter a word, he says, "If you want to know the truth about your parents, it sounds as though your brother has the answers."

My parents' notes, all missing from the trunk buried in the yard. Did Rowan make sense of them, or did he twist them to fuel his delusions?

Did he give them to Vaughn?

I feel as though I'm floating over my body. Even Cecily, who pressed for this, agrees with Linden that it's time to leave. If I want answers, I have to find my brother, and for now, at least, I have some idea where he might be.

But even with all of my unanswered questions, so much has been said and realized before noon. The ride home is quiet. We're all thinking, staring in opposite directions, in this car being driven by the brother of evil himself.

All I can think is, *I have to get to Rowan.*

Never mind all of the terrible things Edgar said after the broadcast was through. Never mind all the news clippings he showed us. What matters now is getting to Charleston, South Carolina, quickly, before Rowan is gone again.

"Why isn't anyone stopping him?" Linden blurts.

He looks at me. "Your brother has obviously gone crazy. Why aren't there any authorities stopping him?"

"He isn't crazy," I say with a calm I find disturbing. "He's right. We were abandoned when things didn't go as planned. Nobody really cares what we do."

"I can't believe that," Linden says.

"Believe it, kid," Reed says.

"You knew about this," I say to Reed. "Didn't you?"

His eyes meet mine in the rearview mirror for a moment. "All us crazy old men pay attention to the news, doll. I'd have told you myself, but I didn't have the heart."

Linden opens his mouth to say something, but the words fade away. I'd expect him to look hurt, or angry, but his eyes are blank. His whole face is blank.

I think he was going to defend his father.

He's watching Cecily's reflection in the glass as she stares out her window. He's watching the way her face disappears and reemerges in the scenery, and maybe he's remembering that his father is the reason she was almost gone entirely.

At least they still have each other, I think with the most bitter rush of jealousy I've ever experienced.

When we get back to Reed's, Linden quietly disappears into the house. Elle trails after him to feed Bowen; this is the sort of thing Cecily would normally want to be involved with, but instead we find ourselves sitting in the high grass and watching Reed toy with the car that's supposed to take me to Rowan. He thought it was ready to drive, but now something or other is overheating and he's not so sure.

"Linden is planning to go with you to find your brother," she says finally. "He thought you would object and try to run off on your own, so he didn't tell you." Her head feels heavy when she rests it on my shoulder. "But please let him do this. He thinks this whole thing is his fault. He thinks that he's the only one who can protect you if his father comes after you, and he's probably right."

Linden planned to come with me. I guess it's not much of a surprise. I think of all the times he tried to coddle and console me during our marriage. And I think of how many times, despite my resentment, he was the only one who helped.

"What about you?" I say.

"I've been thinking about it," she says, and sighs. "It would mean leaving Bowen here with Reed and Elle; I don't like the thought of leaving him behind. On the other hand there's this dream I keep having."

The sun breaks away from a wandering cloud, and she shields her eyes. "In it I'm chasing something. Some kind of shadow. And as it runs away from me, these pieces are falling away from it, crumbling into ashes before they reach the ground. The pieces come away, and the shadow gets smaller and smaller.

"I think the shadow is the cure. I think that the longer I wait, the smaller my chances are of ever reaching it. And don't tell me it's stupid to hope for a cure, because I know you're hoping too."

Thanks to Rowan, anyone who watches the national news knows that of the two of us, I am the one who was stupid enough to hope.

But am I still hoping? I don't know.

"Don't tell Linden I told you," she says.

"I won't."

By late afternoon the heat has escalated. The sun is burning my skin clean. The light has made hostages of Cecily and Reed, who stand a few feet away, their bodies reduced to shadow except for the strip of color that is Cecily's ponytail.

He's explaining his .22 caliber rifle to her. He's telling her about loading the chamber, and the gunpowder in the bullets, and the recoil. But she only has one question: "Can it kill?"

"It's a gun, isn't it?" Reed says.

He opens the chamber, and one at a time the gold shells fall into her waiting palm.

"But this isn't the one you carry around with you all the time," she says.

"That's because this one isn't as dangerous. It can catch dinner well enough, though."

I'm leaning on my elbows in the tall grass, and I close my eyes and roll my head back to catch the heat of the sun before it's swallowed by a wandering cloud.

I know a little bit about guns. My brother and I kept a shotgun for protection. Rowan greased the barrel because he said it made the shots louder. He wanted them to be a warning to intruders. He wanted everyone to think we were dangerous. It took months for me to stop being so afraid of that gun. The heaviness of it. The things it implied. I felt as though just being near it could kill me.

Cecily shows no such fear. She's never seen anything like Reed's arsenal, and after days of admiring it she's finally asking him questions. He's all too happy to teach her. He's patient; his answers are wise, detailed. Despite what he said about preferring dogs to children, I think he would have been a good father. A better one than Vaughn, for sure.

Reed puts the gun into Cecily's hands, and he shows her how to aim it at a dying dogwood tree several yards in the distance. "You always treat a gun like it's loaded, even if it's empty," he instructs. There's a pop as she pulls the trigger, draws back the hammer, pulls the trigger again.

"Keep practicing and maybe I'll let you shoot it for real," he says.

"Do you mean that?" she asks.

"Maybe I'll even show you the airplane I'm hiding."

"Now you're just messing with me," she says. "You do not have an airplane."

"I do so. And I'll have you know that with a few very minor tweaks, it'll be ready to fly. Put your eyes back on the target."

The screen door slams shut. Linden is running down the porch steps and toward us. "No, no, no," he's saying. "Absolutely no!"

"It's not loaded," Cecily and Reed say in unison.

Linden looks at me as though I am somehow responsible for this. I say nothing, and he bristles at Reed. "What are you thinking, letting her play with guns?"

"I'm not playing," Cecily says. "I'm learning."

I can see that Linden wants to tear the gun from her hands, but he's too afraid. Not just of the weapon but of this startling vision of the wife he's always coddled. His fingers stretch and clench. If we were married, I would try to reason with him.

"I don't know what's going on with you anymore," he says. "It's like you've completely lost your mind."

Cecily, remembering Reed's advice to always treat a gun as if it were loaded, takes her finger from the trigger as she lowers it. She regards him with resignation, maybe even annoyance.

"You could be killed. That thing could kill you," Linden says.

"It isn't loaded," Reed interjects. "We said that."

"And you! You should know better," Linden says. He looks like he wants to cry. When he's very frustrated, his eyes take on that sort of sheen. I want to comfort him. And I want to defend Cecily's actions, because I understand. I do. She's small, and she never had the opportunity of an education, and she just wants a little control. She wants to be taken seriously.

But this isn't my marriage. This isn't my battle.

"Let's get one thing straight, kiddo," Reed tells Linden. "I've never done a damn thing to hurt a soul in my life, and I wasn't going to let anything happen. You don't come out here barking orders at me."

"Linden just wants to protect her," is what I want to

say. She's all he has. I left him. I'm at arm's reach, but I've left him.

I flatten my back against the earth and hope the grass will hide me. I hope I'll disappear.

I hear them arguing. I close my eyes. Let the sun wash them away.

A loud crack jolts me back to earth. I sit up. Everyone has gone silent. Reed is holding his .45 caliber pistol skyward. Even without a bullet, the shot was loud. I think he meant to stop the argument, but the next moment Linden is calling him an insane old man, saying his father was right, which throws Cecily into hysterics and how-dare-yous and how-can-you-say-thats, because Vaughn is her sworn enemy now. I've never seen Linden and Cecily argue like this, and it makes me feel like the world is coming undone. I thought the world had already come undone, but now I realize that I still had faith in some things.

One thing at a time everything is falling apart.

My legs can't carry me to the house fast enough.

I find Elle sitting at the kitchen table, holding Bowen and staring at one of Reed's shelves of oddities. Her eyes are bleary. Bowen is lolling. He must have finally exhausted himself; he's been hyper all day, reaching for things, squealing, throwing anything he gets his hands on.

I think of what Jenna said about how he would grow to have Cecily's temper, and that it's a shame none of us would live to see it. I think she'd be surprised how happy he is, how excited to be alive.

Elle must be exhausted.

"I can take him," I offer.

"Huh?" She looks away from the shelf and blinks owlishly at me.

"I can watch Bowen, if you want to rest," I say.

"It's all right," she says. Her voice is wispy. "I like holding him."

I'm staring at her. I don't realize it until I notice her nervous intermittent glances back at me.

It's just that, with the light from the window in her hair, she somehow reminds me of Deirdre. She reminds me of the Once Upon a Time fairy-tale beauty of the mansion, and how that mansion sat atop its own parallel universe of horrors.

I pull out the chair opposite Elle's and take a seat. She flinches and stares into Bowen's coppery curls. She never used to be this nervous. At the mansion she was quiet and obedient, enduring Cecily's demands, but she wasn't frightened. I'm certain she rolled her eyes and told Cecily to sit still while she was trying to curl her hair or alter her skirts.

Elle is still wearing her uniform—a white button-down blouse and a black tiered skirt. She still calls us by our proper titles too—if she speaks at all. I think the routine gives her a sense of normalcy to cling to.

"Is it that you don't feel safe here?" The careless

question just comes out of me. It's been too exhausting a morning to skirt around things politely. "Reed is a little eccentric, but he isn't like Housemaster Vaughn. He wouldn't hurt you."

Elle purses her lips, stares at Bowen for a long time before saying, "Nowhere is safe, Lady Rhine. Especially not for you."

"And you aren't comfortable around me? Because you're afraid you'll get caught in the cross fire of the trouble I attract?"

She hesitates.

She nods.

"I never wanted any of it to turn out like this," I say. It's a flimsy excuse, but it's the truth. "I only wanted to go home again."

Bowen makes a sound, and Elle kisses his head.

"I didn't want anything to happen to Deirdre." I stop myself from saying anything more, because Deirdre exists as two people in my mind—my child domestic, and the ruined girl I met in the basement. I am still trying to tell myself that the latter was some nightmare, a trick. It's the only way I can move forward. I don't have many years left, and I have to choose which mysteries remain unsolved.

"Deirdre is gone," Elle says, standing and heading for the doorway. "She isn't coming back. I need to put Bowen down for his nap."

She can't get away from me quickly enough.

I can't very well blame her for that.

Down the hall the storm door opens, and footsteps pound down the hallway and toward the kitchen. Cecily is small, but she can rattle an entire house when she's mad.

Only, when she gets to the kitchen, she doesn't look angry at all. She looks frightened. "You have to hide," she says. "He's here. Housemaster Vaughn is here."

I'm huddled in the closet of the upstairs hall, buried haphazardly in Reed's coats, trying to breathe quietly despite the panic in my chest. I hate small dark spaces.

Vaughn's boots echo throughout the house, and when he stops walking, I feel certain that he's right beneath me, that any move I make will set off a creaky floorboard that will give me away.

"Before you ask, Rhine isn't here," Cecily snaps. Despite the authority in her tone, I know she's terrified of Vaughn, and she's facing him to protect me. "I didn't want her around my husband anymore," she says. "It wasn't right."

"She's gone," Linden says, with none of his wife's ire. "She left after Cecily was released from the hospital. She said something about going to Manhattan."

"Didn't it ever occur to you that your ex-wife isn't the one I care about?" Vaughn says. "I've been deeply concerned for your health, Cecily, and I miss my grandson. I've let this charade go on all this time because I wanted you to get the rest that you needed. I even allowed your domestic to come to your aid. But I see that you're back to your usual spirited self now."

"Nobody leaves this house by force," Reed interjects. "Except for maybe you, Little Brother."

"Who said anything about force?" Vaughn says. "Cecily. Linden. Be realistic. You can't stay here forever. This imaginary grudge you're holding against me has gone on for long enough. I'd like to put this whole mess behind us. I'd like to see my grandson again. I know he's here."

"He's napping," Linden says.

"I'd like to see him," Vaughn says, nothing forceful about his tone at all. "May I?" And I realize: Linden has the power here. Vaughn has always manipulated his son, but he's never used force. He's never showed his dangerous side to his son, and he won't, because he'd risk losing him forever.

"He's a light sleeper," Linden says.

There are more words, Vaughn trying to tear through Linden's newfound sternness, Linden refusing to comply, and finally Reed saying, "You've heard the kids. They aren't leaving with you tonight."

"Cecily, go check on Bowen," Linden says. He isn't asking. And in a few moments I hear the stairs creaking, her footsteps passing the closet as she heads into the bedroom, where she'll undoubtedly press her ear to the floor to hear why she's been dismissed.

"You wouldn't lie to me," Vaughn says. Then I could

swear there's a touch of doubt in his voice when he says, "Linden?"

"No, Father, I wouldn't. I've always felt that you and I could trust each other."

"Rhine is dangerous for you," Vaughn says. "You know that I was only trying to protect you, don't you? I saw how devastated you were by her absence. You understand why I didn't tell you when she returned."

"I understand," Linden says.

"Everything I have ever done has been to protect you."

"I know. Like I said, she's gone now." He lies so smoothly. I never would have thought him capable. "Let me talk to Cecily," Linden says. "Come back tonight, and I'll be sure she's ready to come home."

There's more talking, but I can no longer make out the words because they have moved out of earshot. Vaughn's voice sounds cooing, sympathetic. Despite every indication he gives that he is incapable of human decency, I've never doubted that he loves his son. His only living child is his greatest weakness; Linden is what he lives for, what drives him to madness and at the same time fills him with these rare bursts of humanity.

But he would destroy everything in Linden's life. He would dissect his wives. He would murder an imperfect child before he'd ever allow such a flaw to burden his son.

The front door closes. There's a long silence, and then footsteps come up the stairs and my closet door is opened. Linden and Reed are standing before me as

I climb out of the darkness, and Cecily comes from the bedroom, eyes full of tears, collar of her shirt in her fist. "I'm sorry I yelled at you before," she says to Linden. "Please don't bring me back there. Please."

Linden looks at her a long while, then at me. Reed puts a hand on his shoulder; he already knows what his nephew is thinking.

"We have to leave before my father comes back," Linden says. "Pack as quickly as you can."

13

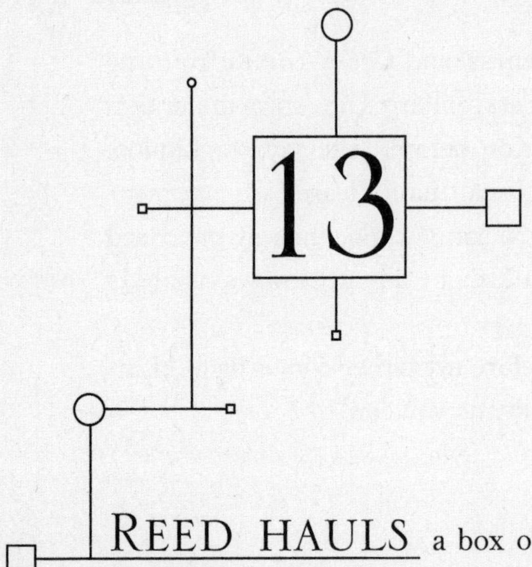

REED HAULS a box of dehydrated food into the backseat of the car.

Cecily frowns, hugging Bowen to her chest. "Is the top of the car made of plastic?"

"Vinyl. It's a Jeep. Been around for more than a hundred years and still totally weather resistant," Reed boasts, patting one of the windows. It shimmers as it ripples in the sunlight. "And the radio works. I've noticed that you're a little musical aficionado."

That gets a smirk out of her, albeit a reluctant one. "And you know how to care for an infant? You'll have enough formula and everything?"

"Formula?" Reed says, gently rapping his knuckle against Bowen's cheek. "A boy his age is ready for rum."

"Kidding," Linden says quickly, lugging my suitcase out of the house. "He's kidding, love." He kisses her cheek as he moves past. "My uncle took care of me when I was a baby. He knows what he's doing."

"And Elle will be here to help him," I remind her. Right now Elle is upstairs cleaning, as she's been doing all week; Linden emphasized that her only job is to care for Bowen, not Reed's house, but she insisted that the level of dust was unhealthy for an infant.

"I should make sure she has my checklist," Cecily says, and hurries inside. I can see that she's struggling to be strong about this. Bowen is as much a part of her as her own arm, and it was a difficult decision to leave him behind. But he wouldn't be safe. Who knows what we'll encounter.

Linden follows Cecily into the house, and I lean against the side of the Jeep. Reed leans beside me and says, "This isn't your fault, doll."

I know he's trying to comfort me, but I can't help my bitter laugh. "Right."

"Really," Reed says. "It was bound to come to something like this eventually. My brother was going to take things too far one day. I always feared that he would screw something up and Linden would be killed by Vaughn's efforts to make him healthy. But thanks to you, Linden is finally starting to gain some depth perception."

"Would it have been so bad letting him carry on in ignorance?" I say. "If I'd never come along, he'd have gotten some happiness, at least."

"Well, you're here now," Reed says. "You can sulk about it, or you can act."

He's right, of course. To die trying would be better than to die without purpose.

It was my brother who pulled me out of bed once before, who forced me to go through the motions until it became a comfortable routine. But he's not here to pull me together now; he's hundreds of miles away, murdering innocent people in the name of some anarchist cause. He can't hold me together this time. I have to do it myself.

Linden hauls a carton of water that's been bottled from Reed's well into the backseat amid all the other supplies. "Can I help with anything?" I ask.

He closes the door. "It's all done. We're ready to go."

Reed shows us how to use the phones, which are the pride of his homemade contraptions. There are three of them, one of which he'll keep. "They almost never work," he tells us. "They work on signal towers, and you'll only find those in cities. And here, of course, since I made one myself."

"So that's what that thing is that's always humming," Cecily says ponderingly. She's got her arms crossed and the hood of her sweater pulled up despite the heat. I think a strong wind could come and blow the hair across her face, and when it receded, she'd be gone.

"You can charge them with the cigarette lighter in the dashboard," Reed says. "Call me if you run into any emergencies. I'll come get you."

Everyone says good-bye. Bowen is complacent when

Cecily and Linden fuss over him, passing him between each other like a shared secret. He laughs, and Cecily frowns when she hands him to Elle, whom she bombards with a last-minute list of reminders. He likes being sung to. It's important to encourage him to crawl so he doesn't fall behind on his milestones.

"We'll be back soon," Cecily promises her son. "You'll hardly notice we're gone."

I feel a pang of guilt as I climb into the backseat. I don't want to be the reason anyone is separated from family.

I'm wedged between the plastic window and a pile of boxes and suitcases. Cecily takes the seat in front of me, and Linden gets behind the wheel.

Cecily asks, "So how fast can this thing go?"

"Fifty, maybe," Linden says.

She crawls over the armrest and peeks at the gauge. "The number goes up to one-forty," she says, pointing.

"It's an old car, love," he says. "Just because it says one-forty doesn't mean we should go that fast."

"Oh, Linden," she says, falling into her seat with a flourish. "Live a little."

When night falls, we don't stop. Linden puts the high beams on and keeps driving. The radio softly plays music that's cut by waves of static.

We took a brief stop at a diner to use the restrooms, and Cecily and I switched seats. Now she's asleep, snuggled against the luggage in the backseat. Linden casts worried glances at her in the rearview mirror. Despite her vigor, he worries. I think he's afraid she'll stop breathing again.

I think of my brother, out there somewhere. I think of time passing, and our lives slipping away. I think of my mother's handwriting, and Reed's gun in Cecily's fearless hands.

"Can't sleep?" Linden says.

It's only nine o'clock, according to the faded green numbers on the dashboard, but it feels much later. It feels as though we've been driving for an eternity, rather than four hours. It feels like there's no destination in sight, and maybe there isn't. I don't know. I've been thinking that Linden and Cecily would be safest if they could make it to Claire's. I've been wondering if Gabriel is still there, if he thinks I'm dead. And the wondering turns to worry turns to pain, and I have to shut down entirely and stare at the scenery blurring by. But now it's too dark to do that.

"No," I say. "Too anxious, I guess. I can drive if you'd like."

"I'm not tired yet," he says. "It's only a few more hours to Charleston. I'd like to make it there before we stop."

I notice his speed has increased. We're barreling down a tunnel of nothingness. Dead things all around. Broken buildings, civilizations that are hiding in their barricaded houses, if there's any civilization at all.

There's this sudden overwhelming need to hold on to something. This feeling that I'm falling forever and forever into nothingness, and I want to grab Linden's hand. I want to feel the pull of the steering wheel in his certain grasp. I want to feel like I have any control at all over where I'm going and what will happen next.

It takes all I've got to resist reaching for him.

He clears his throat. "I had a brother too," he says. "You knew that, right? My father told you?"

"He died before you were born," I say.

"Right. I never even knew his name," Linden says. "If I ask about him, my father shuts down, even gets angry. I don't know if he looked like me. I don't know if he was kind, or—or angry, or anything at all. But I think of him every day. He's not at the front of my thoughts, exactly, but he's like this weight I carry. This echo I hear sometimes when I speak."

I fold my legs, turning in my seat so that I face him. "I'm sorry that you never got to meet him," I say.

"It's a fact," Linden says, "that if my brother hadn't died, I would never have been born. My father wanted to have me so that he could have something to save."

I'm very quiet. I try to make my breathing inaudible. I know that what he's saying is important, and I don't dare disturb him; I think maybe he's never said these words out loud, and that he'll never say them again.

"Sometimes it makes me feel less than human," he says. "I don't tell my father that. He tells me that I'm the most privileged boy in the world because I'll be the one who lives. He tells me that everyone else is brought into this world because of the birth control ban, or because other wealthy families are naïve enough to believe they'll be the ones to produce the cure. He doesn't even understand that he's just like them. He doesn't understand that he has not only wasted his time, he's wasted mine. I'm just a wasted effort, and he won't accept that until I'm dead, until I've paid the price for his mistake."

"Don't say that," I tell him softly. "You aren't a waste."

"Your parents were scientists too, right?" His voice is so placid, I'm not sure if I've just imagined that slight tremble in it. "Didn't you ever want to resent them, even a little, for putting you here?"

"A little," I admit. "But we aren't asked into this world, Linden. We're here whether we like it or not. I can't let myself think it's for nothing."

"If you had been asked," he says, eyes always straight on the road, "would you have wanted to be born?"

I don't know what my answer will be until I've said it: "Yes." Soap bubbles between my fingers and words I wrote in window fog and my mother's fluttery good night kisses when she thought I was asleep, and my heart pounding when Gabriel and I first kissed, the warm buzzing going through my body when I had too much champagne and Linden unbuckled my shoe and told me I was beautiful. "Absolutely yes."

"I knew you were going to say that," he says.

"What about you?" I say.

"I don't know anymore," he says. "I hear Cecily singing the words of that poem sometimes—'And Spring herself when she woke at dawn, Would scarcely know that we were gone'—and I think it had the right idea. I think it's wrong of us to keep trying for something that will never come. I think it was cruel of me to try to have children. There's nothing out there, Rhine. There's no world. Only water that's full of dead things. Why keep trying to fill the empty space?"

Children. He's had three, and two of them are gone. I saw his eyes when Cecily had the stillbirth. He carried on as though the only thing that concerned him was her health, but I know losing that child devastated him. Our fake marriage taught me to read him very well.

"Try not to think about why so much," I say. "That poem was written more than three hundred years ago, you know. I bet that back when people lived to be a hundred and the earth was lush and the buildings were clean and new, people still questioned why they were here. I don't think that started after the virus."

I think that's a smile that comes to his lips, or maybe just a wry grin. "I can see why your brother said those things about hope," he says. "You have a way of looking at things. You make it seem as though everything's going to be okay. I can't imagine a more dangerous thing to have than hope like yours."

In the backseat Cecily coughs and stirs. Linden

glances into the rearview mirror. "Are you awake, love?" he asks.

She shuffles around for a while more before she sits up. "Your talking woke me," she complains. "Are we stopping here for the night?"

"No," Linden says. "We're going to try to make it to Charleston before stopping." I'm mystified by the tenderness of his words. For me he is openly bitter about the truths and troubles of the world, but he still adores Cecily.

"I want to sleep up front with you, then," she says. I can tell by her slur and stumbles that she's not entirely awake, but still she manages to climb over the seat and wedge her way between us, trailing a blanket after her.

She settles perfectly to Linden's side. "You don't mind getting in back, do you?" she says to me. "There's not enough room for the three of us."

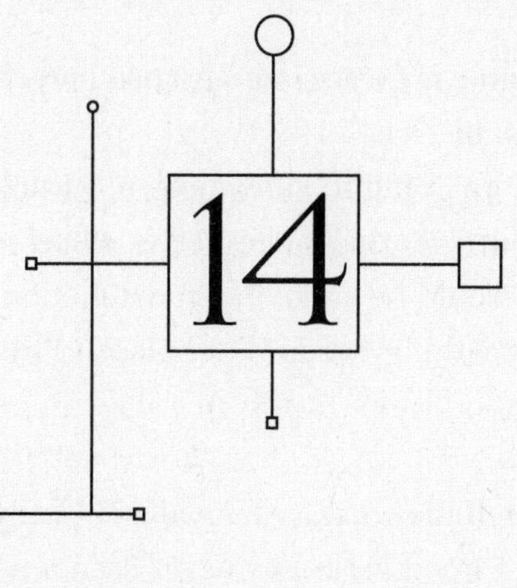

14

THE MUSIC makes my heart leap onto my tongue before I'm even awake. I'm pushing for consciousness through rainbow scarves and pale limbs and that music, that brass music that every nerve of me remembers.

Cecily is kneeling in the front seat, climbing over Linden to see out his window. "What is it?" she's asking.

It's dark. My eyes try to adjust. The car slows to a stop, and Linden says, "It's a carnival."

"Drive," I say. "Don't stop the car."

"What's a carnival?" Cecily asks.

"Drive!"

My tone startles Linden into accelerating. The tires squeal as we go forward, and I'm telling him to go faster, go a hundred-forty like the speedometer says we can, and he's saying "What, what's wrong?" as I turn in my seat and watch the shadows through the back window. Shadows that are full of Madame's guards, and broken girls, and Lilac, whose real name is Grace, who turned herself in so her daughter could be free.

It feels as though we're going in slow motion. I think we'll never get away. But eventually the Ferris wheel is far enough away that it could be a moving constellation.

I fall into my seat, breathing hard. "That place," I get out.

"What?" Linden says.

"Is anyone going to tell me what a carnival is?" Cecily says. "I didn't even get a good look. I've never seen anything like that before."

"You don't want to," I tell her.

Linden pulls the car off the road and stops. "We shouldn't stop here," I say.

"This is Charleston," Linden says.

My heart sinks. So Madame's carnival is in the same town as my brother. I don't know why I should be surprised. I try to quell the dizziness that comes from this wave of adrenaline.

"I'm not moving this car until you tell me what that was all about," Linden says.

Cecily turns on the overhead light, filling the car with a weak orange glow, and she spins in her seat to face me. Her eyes are wide. "What was that *thing*?" she asks excitedly. "It was beautiful."

Suddenly the air in here smells overwhelmingly like plastic.

I know that the air outside is like salt water and

garbage. I know because I've been here before.

"It's a Ferris wheel, okay?" I snap. "It spins around and people ride on it, and it used to make people happy, I guess, but it doesn't anymore. It's broken like everything else. It doesn't matter what happens there now. It's nothing good."

The engine is purring loudly under our feet. And Linden's voice is so soft that I barely hear him say, "You've been there, haven't you?"

"It doesn't matter," I say. "Please, let's just keep going."

"I just want to understand," he says.

I'm angry with him all of a sudden for being so oblivious. For all the awful things that happen in the world, all the effort that goes into day-to-day survival, and for having to explain it to him.

"There's a woman who lives there," I say. "She collects girls. It's a scarlet district."

"'Collects girls'?" Linden blinks. I doubt he's ever even heard of a scarlet district.

"For sex?" Cecily asks simply. She hasn't forgotten what the outside world was like before she became a bride.

"She turns them into prostitutes and makes it so they can't leave. And if the girls have babies, that's a good thing for her because she can use them like slaves."

I'm sorry for my brashness as soon as I've finished speaking. None of this is Linden's fault. And the Ferris wheel isn't the sole source of my misery; it's only a symbol of it. It's a pretty thing that used to be good, but none of that matters now. We're all living in a parallel universe of what the world used to be.

Without looking, I can tell that Linden has gone pale. "And you were there?" he says. "You—" He can't finish the thought.

"No," I say. "I escaped. The girl helping me wasn't so lucky, and I'm really in no hurry to go back there, or to talk about it, so please just drive?"

He puts the Jeep in drive and eases back onto the main road. "We can't waste fuel," he says. "But I'll go a bit farther and we'll stop for the night." He turns off the light.

Cecily reaches over the seat and squeezes my hand.

The radio is always on, low and warning like thunder before a storm. I keep expecting a broadcast to interrupt the song and tell us of another explosion. But nothing comes. I stare out the window at the shadows blurring by.

"I'm sorry," Linden says. The words come out firm and practiced, like he's been rehearsing them in his head this whole time. "It's just that Rose used to talk about a Ferris wheel. I know that can't be the same one, but it made me think of her, that's all."

"It's not the same one," I assure him. "Not unless the one she told you about was a nightmare." Madame's was the first and only Ferris wheel I ever saw, but they're big things, and probably too expensive and difficult to demolish. There could be several of them peppered across the country, just rotting for lack of purpose.

"No," he says. "The one she talked about was nice. Most things she told me about were."

Poor Linden. No one has ever thought he could handle hearing about the dark things; not even Rose, apparently.

"Her parents traveled a lot," he says. "I think she saw every state, which is a lot, if you think about it. Forty-eight states before she turned eleven." He's not counting Alaska and Hawaii, which were destroyed more than a century ago.

He thought it strange when I told him I was a twin, but I don't think his marriage to Rose was entirely different. There's this anomaly that happens sometimes with twins. It occurs in the womb when the fetuses are growing too closely to each other. The stronger twin develops normally, while the weaker twin crumples and is encased by the body of the stronger twin, where it becomes a parasite. The result is a single child, plagued by a twin-shaped fossil inside. Like a tumor.

In death Rose became Linden's parasitic twin. They were two separate organisms once, growing steadily beside each other. Two pulses. Two brains. But she has crumpled and died, and still he carries her inside himself. She goes where he goes, feeling nothing, seeing nothing, a shadow behind his ribs. I see the way his memory of her darkens his eyes when he glances at me and then abruptly looks away.

We agree to sleep in shifts. Because Cecily and I napped on the way to Charleston, we're wide awake. Linden stretches out across the front seat, and eventually I can tell by his breathing that he's asleep. If he's given any thought to his father finding us through Cecily's tracking device, it doesn't seem to be among his concerns. He has a better understanding of Vaughn's tactics than I do.

Cecily is beside me in the backseat, and she stares through her vinyl window at the darkness for a while before she says, "That's the first time he's talked about Rose in front of me. That story about the Ferris wheel and her parents traveling."

"It's painful for him," I say.

She shakes her head, still looking away. "That's not it. He knows that I get jealous sometimes."

"Jealous of what?" I say.

"It isn't easy competing with three other women for my husband's heart," Cecily says.

"There's no competition," I say. "You're the only wife he has now."

"I know Linden," she says. "He'll always love Rose. And Jenna was the beautiful one—I'll never be able to compare." She turns her head and looks at me, and there's so much pain in her eyes.

Softly she says, "And then there's you."

"Son, if you're listening to this, I'd like you to know that I won't stop until I find you."

Vaughn's voice emerges from the static, and at first I think I'm dreaming, but then I open my eyes. Linden and Cecily are in the front seat, listening intently to the radio as Vaughn tells the person interviewing him that his only son and his son's wife have disappeared, believed to be in immediate danger. He says there have been no demands for ransom, but he says he doesn't believe the pair left of their own free will. He says they were missing from their beds this morning. He says he'll offer a reward for their return.

"Why is he lying about everything?" Cecily asks. She's gnawing worriedly on the knuckle of her thumb.

"He knows I ran away," Linden says. "He just wants to put out a description of us so that we'll be found."

My stomach is twisting. Linden looks at me in the rearview mirror. "My father didn't mention you," he says. "But I bet he knows you're with us."

"What about Bowen?" Cecily says. "Linden, if your father has him—"

"Uncle Reed wouldn't let that happen," Linden says.

She doesn't look convinced. She's pale, and her arms are shaking.

There's a burst of static on the radio, and then some generic music starts to play.

It's early morning now, the sky a threatening shade of gray, the tides getting heavy along the littered shoreline. I know that beach. This isn't exactly where Gabriel and I arrived—we were closer to the carnival—but I recognize this dismal atmosphere. I've never seen it in the daylight.

Several yards away there's a brick factory building that looks abandoned except for the plumes billowing out of its smokestack. Something is being produced, which means there is civilization here other than Madame's carnival.

There's a cluster of buildings that could be an apartment complex, or they could be abandoned. It's hard to tell. There's no sign of any electricity. But I know from makeshift houses like the fortune-teller's that people live in this vicinity.

Linden shakes open the map and says, "We're about three miles from the research lab your brother—the lab that was destroyed. It's back in the direction of the carnival." He looks over his shoulder at me. "We should go to the site to ask if anyone knows where he went. Are you ready for that?"

I don't see how we have any other option. "Just as long as we stay away from the carnival," I say.

I don't allow myself to think that Rowan has seen Madame's Ferris wheel, that he may have ever spoken to that woman. That she's seen his eyes and made the connection that his dead twin sister isn't really dead but is the only girl who ever managed to leave her exquisite and demented prison. The first generations are good at making prisons. I suppose it's because they remember a time when things were as beautiful as the illusions they use to construct their cages.

I don't want illusions. I'm tired of feeling like I'm in a dream from which I can never awaken.

Cecily is trying frantically to get in touch with Reed through the cell phone, but there are no towers. Reed said there would still be some out there, though, particularly in places with strong radio signals, as that's the best sign of technology being nearby.

"I promise you, Bowen is all right," Linden tells her, putting his hand on her knee. "I wouldn't have left Uncle Reed in charge of him if I didn't have complete faith in him."

"It's your father I don't trust." Cecily's voice is tight. She's trying not to cry.

"I trust Reed," I say. "I bet he's not even in his house now. He has so many friends who are off the grid. I bet that as soon as we left, he took Elle and Bowen someplace where Vaughn can't even find him."

Cecily sniffles. "He better not be smoking around my son. I don't care that he says it won't make him sick, it's still vile," she says, but she has calmed down a little. She watches the world move by her window in ugly hues and crumbling pieces, and she glances occasionally at the cell phone's screen.

I can see the Ferris wheel again, purplish and faded against the sky. Madame's girls must all be sleeping now, as the children tend the laundry and patch tears and harvest crops. Jared is no doubt working on another invention.

I glance at Cecily. Times like these, when she's very worried, she looks about ten years older. She looks like a woman who has given birth, been married, witnessed death, and now carries the world on her shoulders.

Linden drives slowly, like we'll find clues on the side of the road. He asks me if I'm okay, if I need air. I shake my head and watch the world warped through the plastic.

Then I see the ashes. Far down a road that's barricaded by steel barrels and makeshift wooden fences, there's still the rubble from the explosion my brother caused. I see distant figures moving about it, a yellow crane hauling bits of wall into a dump truck.

This charred monstrosity will be a part of the scenery for months or years to come. And they probably won't build another lab. They didn't in Manhattan.

My brother won't be here. He's smart enough to stay moving; he'll stay just long enough to make his mark, maybe incite a riot, but not long enough to be caught by someone seeking revenge. He knows exactly how long it takes for shock to turn to anger.

I yank my door open, and Linden slams on the brakes a split second before I take off running. I wedge myself between the makeshift fence pieces, untangle my sleeve from a rusty nail, and run for the ashes of the laboratory my brother destroyed, only vaguely aware of the voices calling after me.

The road feels miles long. It feels like I could run it forever. But I'm hardly out of breath by the time I reach the heap of walls and broken windows that was once a laboratory. There are people working through it, all of them in plainclothes, probably just citizens trying to clean up the mess. Everyone knows the president won't offer any help, though maybe he'll make a speech or something if the explosions gain enough attention.

"If you're looking for anything salvageable, you're too late," a faraway voice tells me. "Place was picked clean apart yesterday."

I say nothing, kneel down, and press my hand to a crumbled column of bricks. It's warm—maybe from the sun, or maybe because it has somehow retained the heat of the flames. But I feel my brother there for just an instant, a rush of energy shooting through me, a sharp sideways pull as though he's trying to get me to follow him.

"Where are you?" I whisper.

A hand touches my arm, and I flinch. There's the hazy, sudden feeling of waking from a long dream.

Cecily crouches beside me. "Are you okay?" she says.

"My brother was here," I tell her. "Right here. Just a couple of days ago."

She frowns. "You shouldn't be running off by yourself," she says, and tugs me to my feet. "We're here to help you. You know that."

Linden catches up to us, gasping for breath. "What are you thinking, running off like that?" he says.

I say nothing. I watch the ashes swim around like

dandelion puffs, making swirls where bodies and walls once stood.

"Are you going to help or not?" a man snaps. "This isn't tourist hour."

Cecily draws a breath, and I can tell she's about to snap back something volatile, so I am quick to say, "Sorry. It's just . . ." My voice trails away. It's just what? I expected to find answers here? Clues? I've only found more of what my brother left at our house: some charred remains, more evidence that he's gone mad since deciding I'm dead.

"We're looking for someone," Linden says. "One of the people who caused this explosion."

"If they're smart, they're gone for good," the man says. "Are you helping or not?"

"Wait," a boy says. He's a new generation and hardly taller than Cecily. "Dad," he says to the man standing before us, "that's the one we saw on the news. He's that scientist's son."

I see a light of recognition in the man's eyes. Several others have heard this, and a circle has formed around us.

And there's silence, only silence. Linden and Cecily and I have orbited close together. It's all we can do, because we know it's too late to run.

Linden tries to leave Cecily and me behind. When the man shoves Linden into the backseat of the rundown car, Cecily cries out and rushes after Linden, and he tries to pull the door shut. But this is not an option,

and judging by the brute force used to throw us into the hot and stuffy car, I'd guess that the reward for Linden's return is exorbitant. The exact amount of money a town like this would need to build a hospital or rebuild the lab my brother destroyed.

"It'll be okay," Linden says. "I won't let my father harm either of you."

He hasn't been very good at this in the past, but I don't say that.

Cecily is pale and silent. I catch her glancing at her pocket, and through the fabric I can see the rectangular glow of the cell phone for an instant before she silently flips it shut. It's no use; there's no reception anyway.

The man and his son are in the front seats, and the son is pointing a gun at us, which would intimidate me more if I didn't suspect it was a pellet gun. I can see the CO_2 cartridge. Rather, what unnerve me are the several cars following us on all sides. There is a village of people making sure we have no way to escape. I can't imagine anything more unsettling.

Until I see the Ferris wheel getting larger as we approach, and the cavalcade of cars stops right at the chain-link fence that surrounds Madame's carnival.

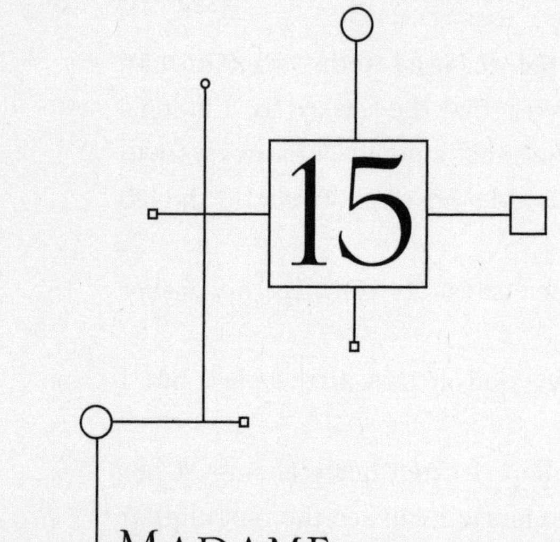

MADAME comes bursting through a wall of bodyguards like an actress through a stage curtain. Even from inside the car I can smell her perfume and the smoke ribboning off her cigarette. "Let me see them," I hear her gleefully cry.

She was expecting us, but how?

When the man and his son get out of the car, Cecily looks at me, all eagerness, and there's something she wants to say, but there's no time. The doors open on either side of us. Madame is saying, "I've never seen his son in the flesh before. I'm sure he's every bit as beautiful as his photo and then some."

The boy with the pellet gun is forcing us out of the car; Linden first, Cecily immediately behind him, and then me. And Madame's gasp of astonishment and admiration when she sees Linden in person is cut short when she sees me, her hands still outstretched to touch Linden's face. I recognize all her gaudy rings, her bun of gray hair that still has glimmers of blond.

"Where is your servant boy, Goldenrod?" she says. "Don't tell me you've returned to your husband here and left your servant boy jilted."

Cecily tries to wrap her arm around mine, but I move away. Madame hates affection. She sees love and wants to destroy it. I learned that the hard way.

I don't answer her question; instead I look beyond the chain-link fence, where curious eyes are blinking through the slit in the rainbow tent.

"It's all right," Madame singsongs. "Dear one, I won't hurt you. All the trouble you've cost me will be paid for in triplicate. Have you any idea the reward being offered for your safe return? Your photo and name aren't even mentioned on the news. That's how desperately Vaughn would like to keep you a secret. Wouldn't want someone else to snatch you up."

I look at Linden and see the way he's staring at her, like she means something to him. He doesn't seem at all afraid. I wonder if he's thinking what I thought when I first met Madame, that something is oddly familiar about her.

Madame exhales a cloud of smoke. Cecily stifles a cough, and Madame snaps to attention, grabs her face, and stoops to her eye level. They stare at each other for a long while, Cecily's eyes dulled of any emotion or fear. The night she lost the baby, she drowned in the sleepy gray waters of death and then swam scissor-kicking from its depths in defiance. Madame holds no power over her.

"You aren't much," Madame says. "Maybe once puberty sets in." She stands upright again, clapping, spurring her bodyguards into action. "Out of my way," she's telling them. "Someone make tea for our guests while I contact this beautiful boy's father."

"Your father and I go way back, Linden," Madame says. She has not used a single fake accent since we arrived. "Back in our school days, you could say we had something of a fling."

We're sitting on colored cushions in the peach tent where Gabriel and I were made to draw in a crowd. The gilded cage is still in place, and judging by the rumpled sheets inside it, I'd guess Madame has found new performers.

"And then a lover of mine became his colleague," Madame goes on, pouring tea into a quartet of teacups on a box crate table. "I see you've grown to have his charm, haven't you? Even if you are a man of few words."

She looks at Cecily, and her face dulls with disappointment. Perhaps she expected Vaughn's son to have a more glamorous wife. But she sees Cecily's ring, then Linden's, and her eyes brighten again. Though my sister wives and I had unique patterns on our wedding rings, they're of a similar design—vines and flowers etched in an endless loop—and Madame very much admired mine. Now she sees that I'm not wearing it.

"Where's your servant boy?" she asks me again. She begins polishing her silver pistol; it's studded with fake emeralds. I don't know if she means to threaten us. Probably not. In Madame's world it is perfectly normal to admire a lethal weapon over tea.

I speak my first word to her in months. "Gone."

"He was too weak for you anyway," Madame says. "You would have been better off staying with your husband." She smiles at Linden. Something has changed in his eyes, and she knows she's hurt him. That pain isn't enough, though. She must say something more. "When she first described you, I admit I pictured more of an impotent beast. She certainly didn't put you in a very flattering light. Drink your tea, all of you. I have a thing or two to tend to. Maybe you'll be chattier when I return."

She stands, skirts billowing around her, jewelry clattering as she makes her exit. And as usual I can see the silhouettes of her guards just outside the tent. Cecily and Linden see them too.

Cecily reaches into her pocket and stares at the face of the phone, distressed. "Nothing," she mutters, tucking it back. "You and your stupid broken junk, Reed."

Linden looks as though he'll be sick.

"There must be a way to use phones here," Cecily says, quietly so the guards won't hear. "How else could this crazy lady have gotten in touch with your father?"

"One of her guards is an inventor," I say. "I'm sure he worked something out."

Not that it matters. We're here now, and Vaughn is on his way, and he's bound to be less than merciful with us.

Cecily stares at the steam rising from her teacup.

"Don't drink that," I tell her.

She only stares at it, and her eyes start to fill with tears, because despite all the strength she has mustered and the brave face she's put on for Madame and even the way she stood up to Vaughn, she is still frightened.

Linden places his finger under her chin and coaxes her to look at him. "I won't let my father hurt you," he says.

Her voice is small when she says, "Do you still love me?"

"What a silly question," he says. "Of course I do."

I stare at the dirt floor, trying to erase these sudden memories of Gabriel. We were the Lovebirds, the illusion that Madame sold to her customers who crowded outside our golden cage. We were mesmerized by the smoky air, delirious from Madame's opiates, and as a result all my memories are feverish. But no matter how painful they are, I can't be rid of them. I can't forget his fingertips moving up my bare arms, all the hairs on the back of my neck rising with expectancy when he swept my hair away and kissed me.

I don't know if it was love or if it was illusion. I don't know if there's ever a way to be certain.

Madame returns, her jewelry like plastic bells

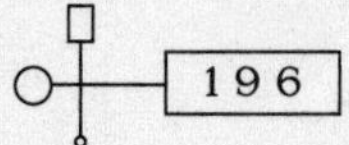

announcing her approach. She's holding something swaddled in a silk scarf.

Cecily swipes her wrist across her eyes, tears all gone.

"I met you once, when you were a little boy," Madame tells Linden. "You probably don't remember. My lover and I used to travel with our little girl. Back then we thought it would be good for her to see the world. You played with her one afternoon, when you were both just toddlers."

She unfolds the scarf in her hands, and I can see now that it has been protecting a picture frame. In my time here Madame confided in me that she had a daughter, but I never saw a picture. I assumed she didn't keep one, after all she said about how stupid it had been to love her. But now she stares longingly at the picture, and there's a smile on her neon-pink-painted lips before she hands it to Linden.

"This is my daughter," she says. "My Rose."

We all stop breathing. Cecily huddles close to Linden and stares at the picture he's holding. Linden's mouth is open, lower lip trembling just enough—just enough to register his shock. If not for that tremble, I would think he had no reaction at all. His eyes are green stones, his body a statue.

I feel as though I'm moving in slow motion when I inch closer to Linden so that I can get a better look at the picture as well.

There was a photo in Rose's bedroom. One afternoon

she took it off the wall and handed it to me. She was dying then, face painted up like a perfect china doll, lying in a bright sea of June Bean wrappers. The photo was of her and Linden as children in the orange grove. I remember how bright and healthy her smile was.

The little girl in Madame's picture is slightly younger, and rather than the toothy smile given in the orange grove, this one is slight, a coy little grin for the photographer. She's sitting on a merry-go-round horse.

I recognize that merry-go-round.

But more importantly, I recognize that little girl. She grew up and became Linden's bride.

Linden sweeps his thumb across the little girl's face, for a second covering it entirely.

Madame is perplexed by his somberness.

"Is this a trick?" he says. "I don't believe my father would be this cruel."

"A trick?" Madame says.

Linden opens his mouth, but his eyes are still on Rose's young face. Younger in this picture than when he was betrothed to her when she was eleven and he was twelve.

"Remind me," I say to Madame. "What happened to your daughter?"

Madame bristles. There's a moment of pain in her eyes, but she hides it quickly. She snatches the picture from Linden's hand, and he loses his wife all over again. He watches her go, watches her get wrapped hastily in

cloth and be crushed between Madame's jeweled fingers.

"She was murdered," Madame says. "Just as well. She was too good for this world."

You children are flies. That's what Madame said to me that day when she led me through her carnival.

You are roses. She told me that she had a daughter with hair that was every shade of yellow, like mine.

You multiply and die.

"She wasn't murdered," Linden says. "She was my wife."

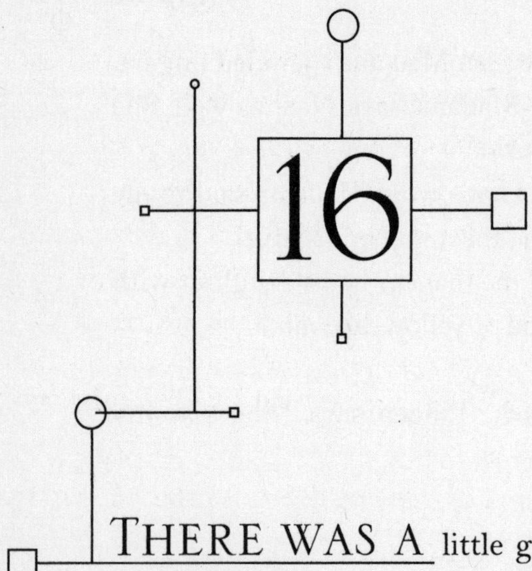

THERE WAS A little girl once who was very much adored.

Her existence was an act of carelessness, for Madame and her lover never intended to have a child, and in fact they had a long discussion about terminating the pregnancy. It seemed too emotional a venture to raise a child that would die on its twentieth or twenty-fifth birthday.

But neither Madame nor her lover could bring themselves to terminate the pregnancy. They decided that a short life would be better than none at all. And they would shower her with all the things a child could ask for. They would travel to every corner of the country, and they would fill her short years with a hundred years' worth of experience.

As a result their daughter grew to be fearless. She played among the tents and talked wildly about the ocean and the sky. She had dreams of leaving the country. If the rest of the world were destroyed, she wanted to visit the graves of the other countries. She wanted to start at one end of the world and sail all the way around until she came back again.

Madame blames herself for this. She raised her daughter to be discontent in this carnival of dying and broken girls. When Rose's father left on research endeavors, Rose pleaded to go along with him, and he most always relented. When Rose was eleven, he took her to the coast of Florida, where he would be meeting with several colleagues. Vaughn Ashby was among them.

"She was supposed to build sand castles on the beach and put her toes in the ocean," Madame says.

"What happened?" Cecily asks gently. She reaches for her teacup, but I put my hand on her wrist to stop her. Even if Madame is being civil, I don't trust anything she serves us.

Madame strokes the cloth-swaddled edges of the picture frame.

"There was a car bombing," Madame says. "I was told it was caused by pro-naturalists who opposed the research being conducted. I was told my lover and daughter were killed."

She looks at Linden now. He's so small and weary, and I worry that he'll collapse, but he doesn't. He says, "Rose thought that her parents were killed in that explosion. She thought that her mother met up with her father and that they died on their way to her. She had nightmares for—always. She always did."

"I can't help noticing"—Madame's voice is dry and lacking emotion, but ripe with expectancy—"that you are referring to her in the past tense."

Linden cannot speak. He only looks, bleary-eyed, into his teacup.

"Rose has been gone for a year now," I say.

"When she would have turned twenty, then," Madame says. "I let hope get the better of me for a moment."

"I—excuse me," Linden blurts, and before any of us can stop him, he's on his feet and stumbling through the slit in the tent, and Madame is yelling for her guards not to shoot, to keep the fences closed but to let him go wherever he pleases.

Cecily runs after him.

Madame looks at me, and I see a rare moment of humanity about her face. I see her brown eyes, and I understand now why she seemed so familiar to me when we first met several months before.

"Rose looked like you," I say.

During my time at this carnival, I was subjected to Madame's whims, treated like one of her girls. But not exactly. She put the pill down my throat but she never forced me to go quite as far as the other girls when I was with Gabriel. I never had to forfeit my virginity. Maybe that was her way of not sullying the image of her daughter. Maybe she still loved her after all.

Madame's mouth opens and shuts several times. She turns the picture frame over and over in her hands and says, "Vaughn asked me about arranging a marriage between our children. But I thought it would be a waste of time. Vaughn said that we could have grandchildren, but—burying Rose was going to be hard enough. I didn't want more children to bury."

This is the real Madame. I can see why she hides herself in accents and gems and exotic perfumes. I can see why she's grown to hate anything to do with love. She isn't evil or corrupt the way that Vaughn is. She's broken. Only broken.

"You remind me of her," Madame says. "Not just your hair and your face. You've both got that restlessness. Your eyes are somewhere else."

"I only knew Rose a little, toward the end," I say. "But she wasn't unhappy. She and Linden loved each other very much."

"All those years wasted," Madame says, and her voice is venomous. "I could have had her for nine more years. I could have said good-bye."

This is a woman who imprisoned me, who drugged me and betrayed me and nearly murdered a little girl right in front of me. And yet I believe that her grief is sincere. I believe that she loved her daughter. I don't hate her anymore.

"Vaughn lies," I tell her. "He took me away from my family too. He's the one I was running away from, not Linden. Linden would never hurt anybody."

"He was always off," Madame says. "That Vaughn.

Always trying to save the world, never mind what it cost. He has always believed he would cure the virus." She stares past me for a long time, and then, hesitantly, she asks me, "Did Rose have any children?"

"No," I say. That pain, at least, I can spare her.

I find Linden and Cecily at the old merry-go-round. Linden is staring at the horses that are impaled by rusted poles. "She told me about these," he says. "She told me stories about a Ferris wheel and a merry-go-round and women in extravagant dresses. My father told her it had been demolished. He told her that her parents were dead."

Rose told me many things, but she never told me about her childhood here. Too painful, I suppose. It must have taken years for her to speak of her past with her own husband.

Cecily's mouth twists as though the pain were her own. She can't bear to see him so sad.

"He took away everything she loved," Linden says through gritted teeth. "He wanted her to think there was nothing left for her so that she'd have no reason to run away."

I touch his shoulder, but he jerks away.

"Leave me alone," he says. "Both of you."

Cecily frowns. "Linden . . ."

"It's all right, Cecily," I say. "Come on. I'll show you the strawberry patch."

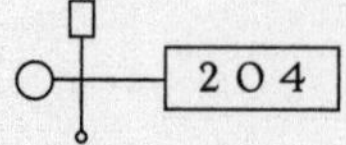

She follows me, looking over her shoulder at Linden, whose back is shaking with tears now that he's alone.

"He needs to grieve," I tell her. "He'll come find us when he's ready."

"Rose is never going to be dead," she says, too disheartened to sound bitter.

I didn't see Madame's carnival in the summer. Last time I was here, everything was dusted with snow. Now insects and Jared's machines are buzzing in the afternoon heat. The strawberries are fat and alive, not at all shriveled and mushy like they were in the winter. The flowers that frame the tents have multiplied in quantity and in color. The first generations have a fascination with keeping plants alive.

It's quiet this time of day, while all the working girls sleep.

Cecily and I sit in the tall grass. She shreds a leaf into ribbons. "I feel like I can relate to that woman," she says. "I feel like I lost a child too. It was never even born alive. I don't even know if it was a boy or a girl. I miss something I never even really had. Isn't that dumb of me?"

"It's not dumb," I say.

She tosses the bits of leaf over her shoulder. "I know it was wrong of me to try to bring another child into the world," she says. Her mouth twists into a smile that becomes a frown. "I wanted it, though. I would give anything to have it back."

I think she'll cry, but she doesn't. She only plucks a blade of grass and winds it around and around her wedding band.

She shakes her head. "Linden doesn't want me to talk about it anymore. He says it'll only make me sad. He says we need to move on now."

"We could have a funeral," I say.

"Have you ever seen a funeral?" she asks.

"No," I say. "Maybe I should've had one for my parents. It didn't seem necessary at the time; my brother and I knew they were gone. But it never felt final. I kept feeling like they'd come home."

Now I'm pulling at a blade of grass too, then peeling it apart.

"I don't think a funeral would have stopped that," Cecily says. "Those ashes I've been holding on to since Jenna was cremated? I know they probably don't belong to her. Even if they do, they won't bring me any closer to her. I know she isn't coming back, but I still think that she will. Nothing can make that go away. We figure out what death means when we're born, practically, and we live our whole lives in some kind of weird denial about it."

She's right. I hate that someone so young can be so right about death.

Eventually Madame finds us. Her eyes are reddened, thick layers of makeup melting tear-shaped rivers down her cheeks. "I've arranged for Jared to take you someplace safe," she says. Jared, the bodyguard who helped Gabriel and me escape the first time. She kneels before me and takes my cheeks in her hand. I'm caught off guard when she pushes forward and kisses my forehead, leaving lipstick residue so heavy that I can feel it. "I'm setting you free, little lovebird," she says. "Go enjoy the rest of your years."

Jared is not the same as when I saw him last. He somehow doesn't seem as tall, or as menacing. Though, the last time I was at Madame's carnival, I was under the influence of so many opiates that it's a wonder I have any memories of this place at all.

The sleeves of his shirt have been torn away, and I can see the scar from where the Gatherer's bullet hit. A rusted white car is idling beside us. Its windows are tinted black.

"You'll be taking them to the northern compound," Madame says. "See that they're fed and they have a chance to rest. Don't stop for anyone. The whole country's looking for them." She pats Cecily's shoulder blades with so much force that Cecily stumbles. "It's a good thing you were caught here, where people would think to bring you to me. They know better than to have kept you from me. I own these parts, Goldenrod. I told you that."

Back when she told me that, months ago, I couldn't tell if it was true or if it was more maddened nonsense from the woman who smoked too many hallucinogens and was perpetually rambling about spies.

"We need to get our car back," Cecily says.

"Consider it long gone," Madame says. "I'm sure the vultures have taken it for themselves by now, and if they haven't, they're even stupider than I suspect, which doesn't seem possible."

Linden looks at the dirt. He doesn't ask about his father. He doesn't say anything at all other than, "Thank you."

As we're climbing into the back of the car, Madame grips my arm.

She looks at me, and I can see all of the lines in her face. Now that I'm really paying attention, that neon pink doesn't hide her thin lips. I can see all the pain she's ever felt in her seventy-plus years. "When my Rose died," she says, "tell me, please—was she still pretty?" Beauty is Madame's obsession. It was Rose's also. I remember how she looked, languishing on the divan or in her bed, makeup always covering her illness, her hair always arranged in some way or other that was lovely.

I don't even have to lie. "She was beautiful," I say.

I can't tell if this eases the pain or intensifies it, but Madame takes my hand in both of hers and shakes it in gratitude. "Thank you," she says.

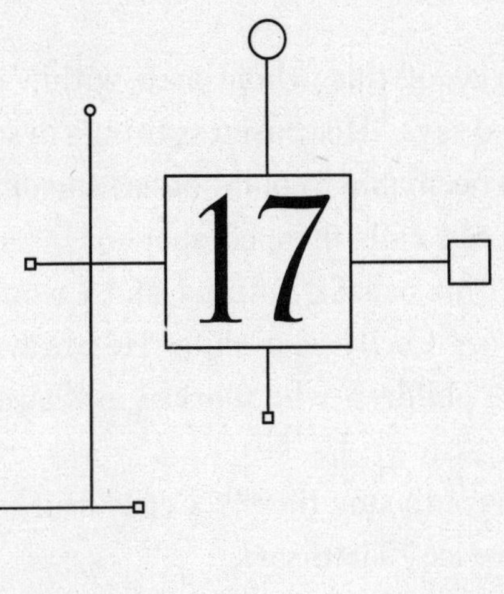

AS SOON AS we've pulled away from the carnival, Jared meets my eyes in the rearview mirror and says, "Maddie?"

"She's safe," I tell him.

He looks back at the road.

Cecily sits between Linden and me. She's twisting her shirt in her hands, and I know she wants to touch her husband, but she knows like I know that he's unreachable right now. Madame's berserk carnival has given him more painful revelations about his father.

I don't know what's going to happen when Vaughn shows up to collect us. I cannot imagine what revenge Madame will have for the man who took her only child away.

We're driving for several miles before Cecily, too restless to stay silent any longer, says, "She told you to take us to the northern compound. What's a compound?"

"Madame is in charge of this whole area within a thirty-mile radius," Jared says. "Her business brings in so much money that she's been able to build other, smaller scarlet districts nearby. She calls them compounds."

His tone has none of his usual gruffness, and I wonder if it's because he sees Cecily as a child. He always showed patience for the children who worked as slaves at the carnival.

"How long will we have to stay there?" Cecily asks.

"Until I'm told otherwise," Jared says.

"No offense," Cecily says, "but why do you get to be the boss of us?"

He laughs. "I'm not the boss of anybody," he says. "Madame's the boss. And I've learned that if she wants things done a certain way, there's always a reason for it."

Linden watches the ocean speeding by his window. He's thinking ugly things; I can see the reflection of his eyes, and I don't even recognize him.

The northern compound is not as grandiose as Madame's carnival. It's still comprised mainly of tents. Though, rather than a rainbow of colors, they are mostly earth tones. We stop at a high chain-link fence, and when Jared rolls down the window to speak to the armed guards, I can hear the buzz of electricity. Madame has a love affair with electric fences; Gabriel and I nearly got ourselves killed scaling one when we escaped the carnival.

The guards are new generation boys, baby-faced and

smeared with dirt. They push a button that opens the gate, and Jared drives us in.

There's still daylight, which would explain the lack of working girls. I see a few of them, though, scrubbing clothes in an old bathtub that has a hose leading into it. Somehow I can still smell the musk of Madame's perfumes. And there are no carnival attractions, though there are strings of lights decorating the tents, and brightly colored lanterns swinging on wires that form a fishnet pattern overhead. Still an upgrade from the standard scarlet district; Madame truly is a connoisseur of ambiance.

Jared stops the car. "Everyone out," he says. "It's about time for dinner anyway."

We're led to a green tent that has a matching green sheet for a floor, and more box crates for tables. The chipped paint on the boxes is advertising oranges, and I remember what Rose said about her father owning orange groves. I wonder how wealthy he was, and how influential; did he own the groves as a hobby when he needed a break from saving lives? And then a more sinister part of me wonders if Vaughn killed him not only to steal his daughter but also to be rid of the competition. Vaughn wants to find a cure, but would he accept it if someone else beat him to it?

Jared brings us bowls of oatmeal, which I eye warily. "They aren't drugged or anything," Jared says. "Look, see?" He takes the spoon from my bowl, helping himself to a hearty mouthful, even licking both sides before putting it back. I watch it sink into the oatmeal.

Cecily removes it, dangling it between her thumb and index finger before daintily laying it on the crate. "You can share my spoon," she tells me.

"There's an outhouse a few yards to the left if you need it," Jared says. "I'm going to go track down a radio."

As soon as he's gone, Cecily opens the cell phone again.

"Anything?" I ask.

"Nothing," she says, and sulks. "And the battery's going to die soon." She turns her attention to Linden, who is sullenly staring at his bowl. "Please try to eat something," she says.

It's as though he doesn't hear her.

"Cecily," I murmur, "let him be."

He does eat a little, though, because she's watching him. Because she's the only wife he has left, and he'd better appreciate her, because their time together will run out and there won't be a spectacular good-bye—only empty hands and a longing for more time.

When Jared brings the radio, there's music playing. "The regional news always updates at six o'clock," he says. "It'll be on in a few minutes."

Cecily has polished off the entire bowl of oatmeal; it's the kind of breakfast she'd complain about in the mansion, but after a day without eating, she wasn't picky. Linden, despite everything, has managed to eat a good deal as well.

Within minutes they're both asleep.

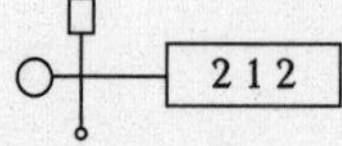

"You put something in their food, didn't you?" I say to Jared, who's fussing with the radio antenna.

"Madame told me about what that boy's been through today. I thought he could use the rest. And the little one just asks a lot of questions."

"You had no right—"

"Relax. It's a mild sleep aid. They'll wake up feeling in the best shape of their lives."

They *do* look peaceful. Linden had been withdrawing from human contact since he'd learned those things about Rose, but now in sleep he has his arm around Cecily. Her head rests in the curve of his neck. As long as he's close to her, she's happy. She's home.

It's true that they need the rest, but I suspect there's some deeper reason Jared wanted them out of his way.

Jared gets the radio antenna at the right angle, and the static gives way to music. "You told me Maddie is safe," he says. "Was that a lie?"

"She's at an orphanage in New York," I say. I don't tell him the whole truth about Maddie being with Claire, her grandmother, because I still can't figure out if this would be too painful for Lilac to learn, or if it's what she meant to happen all along. "She likes it there. She made a friend."

He looks like he doesn't know whether or not to believe me. I can't fault him for that; it's a rare thing for a malformed child to meet a kind fate.

"How's Lilac?" I ask.

"She's fine," Jared says. "Busy training some new recruits. Madame's been especially hard on her since that stunt you all pulled."

"You mean the stunt you helped us pull."

"Shh. Listen. This is what I didn't want them to hear."

The music has stopped, and a male voice is announcing the six o'clock regional news. As I expected, there's a recap of the Charleston bombings, guesses as to what type of homemade explosives were used, judging by the size of the blast and the state of the rubble left behind.

The nearest standing research laboratory, which doubles as a hospital, is the Lexington Research and Wellness Institute, approximately 120 miles northwest of the Charleston bombings. The researchers there have evacuated to an undisclosed location as a precaution.

If Lexington is the next target, then that's where I have to go to find Rowan.

"You're looking antsy, Goldenrod," Jared says.

"What do you know about it?" I say.

"I know that whenever trouble springs up, you're never far behind," he says. He looks right into my eyes, and his tone is practical. "This has something to do with you, doesn't it? And that scientist Madame is hiding you from?"

I look at my once-husband. In sleep his features have relaxed, but I can see that there's a weight on his chest that's laboring his breaths. He's got hold of Cecily's sleeve, because even in sleep he's terrified of letting go.

And he's in that state because of his father—I know this. It's his father who kidnapped Rose so his son would have her; it's his father who murdered his malformed grandchild. His father is the reason for all the ugliness in our lives.

But I'm the one who opened that door. I'm the one who forced these truths on Linden. He lied to his father and he ran away because of me. And Cecily followed, because where Linden goes, she goes.

I fear I've fueled her defiance against Vaughn. I fear he murdered her unborn child to either do away with her or tame her back into submission.

I fear it's all my fault.

I don't want to be the cause of any more of their pain. I want them to be reunited with Bowen, and I want for them to spend what's left of their years together. I've already ruined enough.

"Jared?" I say softly. "I'm in no position to ask for any favors, but if I answer your questions—all of them—I'd like for you to drive me somewhere."

"No can do, Goldenrod," he says. "I'm under strict orders from the boss lady to keep you safe."

"You're right to assume there's no coincidence that I'm always around when there's trouble," I say. "But if there's going to be a bombing in Lexington, I know I can stop it if I get there in time."

"Yeah?" he snorts. "How?"

"Because," I say. "One of the bombers is my brother."

I tell Jared everything that I know. I start with the day I was Gathered, and I tell him about the arranged marriage to Linden, the escape with Gabriel, which led to our capture by Madame. I tell him about the burned-down house that awaited me when I returned home, and the searches for my brother that reaped no results. I tell him about the orphanage where we brought Maddie, and my strange illness and how my father-in-law found and reclaimed me and subjected me to weeks of bizarre experiments all in the name of this elusive cure he's so sure he'll discover.

And I tell him about Cecily losing the baby, how we all suspect my father-in-law was somehow to blame, just like he was to blame for the death of my older sister wife. And as I tell this part of the story, I can't help the tremor of rage that moves through my arms. Cecily is fast asleep, safe now, but she's been victim to more horrors than a young girl should ever have to know. And it's my fault, all my fault, and my eyes are full of tears.

"It is not your fault," Jared says.

"And I don't know how, but Vaughn has gotten his hooks into my brother," I say. "He's made my brother believe that I'm dead. I don't know why, and I don't know how he knew I had a brother, but if I can just find my brother—if I can just explain, I know I can stop him from destroying another lab. But I don't know when he's planning to do it. I don't know how much time we have."

I don't realize how quickly the tears have begun to

overpower me, until Jared offers me a crumpled handkerchief from his pocket.

"Thanks," I sniffle.

"Well, it'll be dark soon," he says. "There's no sense leaving now. We can leave at sunrise. Your friends here should be awake by then."

Friends. That's the least complicated way to describe what they are to me.

"I've already dragged them through enough danger," I say. "Would they be safe here? At least until I come back?"

"Safe and sound," Jared says. "This place is heavily guarded."

I don't like the idea of leaving Cecily and Linden behind, but I know it's the only option I have. Rowan is my brother, my responsibility. Whatever damage he's done is because of this hatred he has toward hope, and I'm his symbol for hope. The sister who supposedly perished because of her stupid pro-science notions.

As the night progresses, Jared brings light blankets that smell of Madame's perfumes. I drape one of them over Cecily and Linden, who have barely moved at all.

I lie beside them and try to sleep, but all night I'm visited by images of flame and ash. There's no sense in calling out for my brother. In this wasteland of rubble and bodies, he's nowhere to be found.

We leave just before dawn. Jared tells the other guards that he's taking me on another of Madame's missions and that they aren't to let Linden and Cecily leave the compound.

"Sure you want to leave them behind?" he asks me as I'm climbing into the rusty car.

Right now I'd love nothing more than to have them with me. And I know they'll be angry when they wake up and realize I'm gone. But am I sure about leaving them behind? Sure that it will be safer for them? Sure that this is something I need to do alone?

"Yes," I say. And Jared turns the key in the ignition, and we're on our way to Lexington.

There's a little screen mounted over the dashboard that displays an electronic map of where we are, the red line of a road twisting and conforming to Jared's steering.

I can't help but stare at it. It's nothing like any of Reed's inventions, and I think it might be an antique from the twenty-first century. After the wars devastated the rest of the planet and before the virus took over, technology was at its most advanced. That much I know. Hospitals and businesses were sprawling. And then the virus was discovered, and it all deteriorated. What took generations to build took less than fifty short years to come undone.

Jared sees my interest. "Madame hates that thing. She says it's how the spies keep track of people." That last part is said as he rolls his eyes. Madame's fictitious spies are a recurring figment of her opium delirium.

"What is it?" I ask.

“It’s a positioning system. Like a digital map. It reads data from satellite signals.”

“I thought all the satellites stopped working years ago,” I say.

“Just one of many rumors,” Jared says. “The president still has use for them, I think. There are plenty of theories about what the president’s role really is. Then again, maybe he’s just this useless figurehead like everyone says, and the rumors are a way to keep hoping.”

It’s quiet for a while, and then I say, “I heard a theory.”

Jared glances at me before focusing on the road again.

“I heard that the other countries and continents still exist.” Reed’s theory seemed outrageous to me when I first heard it, but now nothing seems too crazy to be considered.

Jared laughs. “That one’s been going around for years,” he says. “Plenty have tried to prove it.”

“What happened to them?” I ask.

“Oh, they came back with tales of the wide blue yonder,” Jared says, and laughs. “They were killed, of course. What did you think?”

I set myself up for that. I ignore the sinking feeling in my stomach and watch the map twist and unfold.

The Lexington Research and Wellness Institute is the heart of a ramshackle city. It’s a multistory brick building, in pristine condition compared to the deteriorating housing complexes that surround it. Multifamily homes with boarded windows, a squat grocery store that doesn't appear to have any electricity, other buildings that could be more housing developments or orphanages. There are traffic lights still hanging from overhead wires, nonfunctioning.

As is the case with many research towns, the hospital and laboratory is probably the area's only source of income. Because the president is so adamant about the human race not dying out entirely, he funds these types of institutes, which create jobs locally and provide a shelter for the wounded or the dying.

Situations like Cecily's when she had her miscarriage, for instance.

If people still believe there's cause to heal, they'll believe there's a chance they'll be cured before the virus claims them or their children.

The president will fund these establishments, but not defend them from threats like my brother.

There's not a person to be found. "Did they evacuate the whole town?" I ask.

"They're probably all hiding indoors," Jared says. "Where would they evacuate to? We're just going to make them suspicious if we keep driving around in circles like this."

"I don't know where to start looking for my brother," I say.

"I'm guessing he's not just going to come out of his gopher hole," he says. "We'll have to wait for him to come to us."

"Where?" I say.

In answer he drives around to the back of the hospital, pulls into its dilapidated parking garage, and shuts off the engine.

The garage is silent. Even the birds have ceased singing. The positioning system goes black; the satellite can't find us here. I wonder about Jared. I want to ask him how he came to belong to Madame. I wonder what it is that makes him return to her even though she sets him free. He could easily keep driving and never look back. Why does he return? Is it because he wouldn't leave Lilac to face that woman alone? Because he has no place else to go? Because imprisonment is the safest existence in this world?

I think it's deeper than that. I think he loves Madame with the loyalty of a child who loves its parent.

Maybe hope isn't the most dangerous thing a person can have. Maybe love is worse.

I'm starting to think this is a senseless endeavor. Or some kind of trap.

Then I hear the voices accumulating outside. I hear the feedback of a microphone.

I twist around in my seat and look out the back window. From where we're parked, halfway underground, I can see the crowd of legs. They're setting up a makeshift stage with wooden crates. The scene is unfolding just like the one I saw on the news on Edgar's television.

My brother is preparing to make a speech.

I open the door, but Jared puts his hand on my arm to stop me from getting out of the car. "Think before you act," he says.

"But—"

"There's a crowd out there. A crowd who not only think you're dead, but also get off on the idea of this building going up in smoke. You're not dealing with a whole lot of sanity, Goldenrod."

"That's why I have to stop him," I say.

Jared smiles ruefully at me. "You can't stop what's already here. I've heard this kid on the radio and seen him on the television Madame keeps in her tent. He's beyond your control now."

"I refuse to believe that," I say.

"Come on," he says as he opens his door. "We can listen from here."

My legs barely work when I step onto the concrete floor of the parking garage. My vision bursts with moments of brightness as my pulse throbs in my temples.

Jared and I huddle at the opening to the parking garage, and I have to stand on tiptoes to peer out at the crowd.

It's a beautiful day, warm with a bright blue sky.

The crowd is mostly new generations, an even divide of boys and girls. "He's got quite the loyal band of followers," Jared muses.

"How did they know he would be here?"

He looks at me, smug. "Word travels."

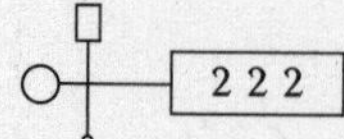

"You knew," I say. "Didn't you? Knew he'd be here at this exact time?"

"You didn't think I crushed sleeping pills into your friends' dinner simply because they looked like they needed a nap, did you?" he says. "There were rumors that this would be his next target. Information is always available if you know the right people."

The shrill microphone feedback forces me to cover my ears. And then it's replaced by a different sound. A voice I'd know anywhere, saying, "Hello. Welcome."

Rowan is standing on the makeshift stage.

His voice is booming through the speakers, thundering in the earth, forcing its way inside my skin. My bones shake with the sound. I feel dizzy and sick and unable to speak, unable to breathe, every neuron, every particle of me waiting.

He's standing just a few yards from me. But if I called his name now, he wouldn't hear me. The crowd is double, maybe triple, the size of the one I saw on the news. My brother notes this. He says he has benefactors now—benefactors that choose to remain nameless, but who are funding his cause because that's how important it is. He tells the crowd that each one of them is important, that they are not terrorists, as the news claims. They are a revolution. They are preventing more generations of suffering. He says that destroying these laboratories will end fruitless human experimentation.

Then I can't hear the words he says next, because the

crowd has gone wild with applause. It doesn't matter what he says. They're desperate for it, need to know that there's a leader among them. I try to cling to his words—I can feel them throbbing in my blood, but I can't make them out. Jared does, though. He's pushing me back toward the car, saying, "Go, go, go!" My door isn't even closed before he slams his foot on the accelerator.

We've just sped out of the parking garage in time to see the blast that dominates the rearview mirror.

The car is still in motion when I open my door. Jared is calling after me, but that's no matter. I'm on the ground now. I stumble forward onto my hands and knees, dizzy for a moment before I'm able to stand.

The earth is shaking under my feet.

The next explosion comes. And another, and another, and another.

I can feel the heat of the flames, the perfect morning appearing rippled and distorted by it. I'm coughing when I turn around to watch the burning building that just moments ago was the Lexington Research and Wellness Institute.

The crowd is absolutely wild.

They're glad.

That word they're chanting with such passion is "Rowan."

He did this. High up on the third story, a window shatters, barely audible in all the chaos. Something that was once a piece of wall lands before me.

Jared is pulling me back by the elbows, and I'm too numb to resist. Too stunned.

When we're far enough away, Jared lets go and I just stand there in the dirt, watching the destruction and the celebration intertwine, until I can't even tell which is which.

If Linden were here, he'd be telling me to breathe. I try to remember the motions of inhaling and exhaling. I try to slow my heart, because I'm sure it's going to burst through my ribs.

"Now do you see?" Jared says into my ear. "Whoever your brother once was, he's beyond your control now."

That brings me back to myself. I shake my head. "No, he's not," I say.

I run forward, and Jared doesn't come after me this time.

My brother has stepped down from his makeshift stage. The crowd is everywhere. They don't notice me, because on the outside I'm no different from any of them—a victim of the new generation, a kid in someone else's clothes with dirt on her hands. When people are in large groups, they lose what makes them human.

But I see him now. He's got his eyes shielded from the sunlight as he admires his handiwork. There's a girl wound around his arm, and I recognize her as the girl from the news, who stood beside him as he gave his speech about his dead sister. She seems fascinated by the sight of him now, though he's paying more attention to the flames.

When I call his name, it's a sound almost entirely out of my control. It soars over the crowd and hits him. Even from where I'm standing, I can tell that he recognized my voice. Hastily he unwinds himself from the girl, stands to attention like an animal sensing danger. And I try to call him again, but that word, that name, was all I had the energy for. I barely have the strength left to stand.

I wait helplessly for him to find the sound, and when he does, when his heterochromatic eyes meet mine, my mouth forms the word again, but just barely. The girl at his side disappears. The crowd blurs into senseless shapes and colors. I can't feel my heart or my body or the heat of the flames.

I can only see his face—his bewildered, beautifully familiar face.

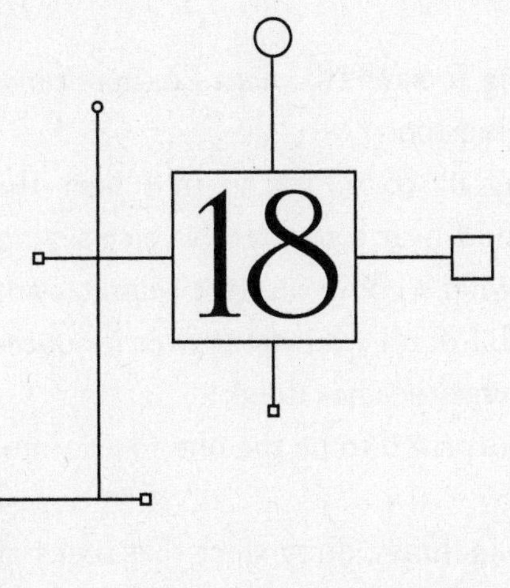

THE MONTHS FALL to shards at my feet. My legs move as though kicking to be free of them. I'm all arms and legs, all motion, and I can't move fast enough.

He catches me just before I'd crash into him. Grabs my arms, stares at my face, at my quivering mouth. His eyes are like mine and not like mine at all. They're sharper now than I remember. He's gotten taller, and I think so have I.

He opens his mouth, but before he can utter a word, I say, "Don't try to tell me I'm dead. I've heard that so many times, I can't stand to hear it again."

He tries to speak, but only a little cry comes out of him, like the inflection of grief I heard when he spoke about me on the news, and then he's pulling me to his chest and I'm throwing my arms around him.

He's shaking, and his breaths are hot sobs going down

my neck, and I'm trying to say, "It's okay. I'm here now; it's okay," but I'm sobbing too.

Reality is beckoning us to return to it. I hear the crackle of the flames and I hear a stranger's voice saying his name, asking him what's going on. But I don't want to return to that world. I don't want to answer its questions and face what my brother has done.

Which is why I'm surprised to be the one to ask him, "What did you do?"

I bunch his shirt—his flimsy, dirty shirt that reeks of ashes—in my fist. His collarbone is pressed against my cheek, so close that it hurts, but I don't pull away.

"I can explain," he says. "I can explain everything."

"Rowan," another voice persists. His name sounds so alien on her tongue.

He moves away from me, but wraps his arm around my back and squeezes me to his side. "Bee," he says to the wild-eyed girl. "This is my sister."

I can't tell from her expression as she looks me up and down whether she wants to spit at me or stare right through me like I don't exist. "The dead one?" she says. "Or is there another sister you haven't told us about?"

And that's when he draws away so he can look at me, and everything disappears around us again. "I thought you'd been killed," he says.

"I heard what you said on the news," I say. "None of that is true. None of it."

"But I—" He looks at the girl, Bee, and back to me

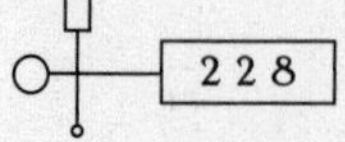

again. "I don't understand. I was *sure.* I talked to a doctor who saw you. Saw your eyes. And he knew the date that you disappeared, your name, that we're twins."

I can't bring myself to say his name out loud, that awful name that seems to follow me wherever I go.

"Reporters will be here soon," Bee says. "Wanna speak to them?"

"There's no time for that," Rowan says. "We have to get back." He looks over my shoulder, and I turn to see Jared standing at a distance, watching us. And now Rowan is looking at Jared the way the wild-eyed girl looked at me.

"I have to go," I tell Jared. "Thank you for the ride."

"You're sure?" he says.

I nod. "Tell Linden and Cecily—tell them that when they make it back to Reed's, I'll come and visit them." I'm struggling to keep my voice steady, because I don't know if what I'm saying is the truth. I don't know if I'll ever see them again. But I'm thinking of what Cecily said to me that night at Reed's. *We have our own lives to take care of, and there's only time to do so much with them.* I know she was right. I know that she belongs with Linden and that I belong with my brother, with my family. "And, Jared? Promise me they'll be safe."

"Sure," he says.

He turns into the crowd, and I cry after him, "Tell them both that I love them."

Jared waves over his head without looking back.

Rowan does not ask where I've been, just like I don't ask why he burned down our house or what course of events led him to be here, in the backseat of this hundred-year-old convertible that's being driven by a young man who seems nearly as wide with muscles as he is tall. That will all come later.

The driver eyes me as coldly as Bee, who is still glaring at me from across the backseat.

I feel as though I'm in a strange dream. My brother is my Eden, but something's amiss. There's something dark lurking behind the picture of this beautiful valley of waterfalls and lilies. But I don't want to acknowledge it. I want to be frozen here, where everything can be pretend-perfect, where I'm safe and Rowan's safe.

I pretend this year apart hasn't changed everything. I pretend that his eyes don't have some of the coldness I saw in that of his new friends.

The speakers and the assemblage of stage pieces were packed into the trunk, which is tied down with lengths of twine. My brother didn't have to lift a finger; he had fans in the crowd who were more than happy to help him. As he led me to the car, he didn't introduce me to any of them; he held my wrist and led me behind him, either protecting me or hiding me, or both.

He's become some kind of rebel celebrity. One girl asked if she could touch him, and then without asking she gripped his hand and shook it with desperation. She said he'd changed her life, and he thanked her and said he preferred that she admire his work rather than his person.

His work. Destroying the very thing our parents stood for.

And again I feel that darkness lurking. But if I look closely at him, I can see the pink around his eyes from the tears that ceased the moment we broke our embrace, and I know it's not like Jared says. The sunlight breaks in his hair that's every kind of blond, like mine. He isn't gone from me. Rowan can never be gone from me.

"We're home," Bee says as the car pulls up to a pile of rubble that was formerly a house. She hangs on Rowan's arm until he looks at her. She smiles at him, strokes his cheek with the back of her finger. "Should we rest before the doctor shows up?"

He regards her with only vague interest. "You two should go inside. I'll be along eventually."

"Sir?" the driver says. His voice is deep and menacing, even with that simple word.

"It's fine," Rowan says.

It's with hesitance that they get out of the car, looking over their shoulders, not making their suspicion of me a secret. I should look away, but I watch them because I'm dumbfounded as to where they are going to go. The house has crumbling walls that barely come to their waists, and there's nothing resembling a roof. All around us is a dead cornfield and the remains of what was once maybe a barn and a silo. The muscular one crouches down, undoes a padlock, and lifts a board that's hinged to the ground, and they descend the staircase it reveals.

Rowan squeezes my hands.

"It's like you're back from the—" He cuts himself off.

"I have been trying—" My voice fails me. I clear my throat. "I've been trying to find you. I saw what happened to the house."

He shakes his head, looks at our hands a moment longer, and then lets go and reaches past me to open my car door. "Let's go for a walk," he says.

There's a cool breeze that rustles the brittle cornstalks. Our steps sound like crumpled paper.

"So this is your home now," I say.

"I keep telling Bee not to use that word," he says. "This is just a temporary base. We've only been here a month or so. We go where we're needed and try to stay hidden."

I stoop to pluck a blade of grass and toy with it so that I have something to do with my hands.

"I want to ask you where you've been," he says, walking at an even pace with me and looking ahead. "I've believed the worst, but you seem as though you've been well."

Well. I've endured the blackness of a Gatherer's van, was married off to a stranger. I've been poisoned and swept up in hurricane winds. I've watched as a girl I cared for lay dying with her head on my knees, a girl whom my brother, who once knew everything about me, will never meet. I wore a wedding band, and I've had needles in my eyes.

But I don't know how to say any of this. I don't know what can make up for this lost time in which we both began living different lives.

"I'm sorry you had to see the house in that state," Rowan says. "I had no choice. I couldn't bear the thought of anyone else living there. It had to be done. I knew there would be no going back there."

"Why can't we go back?" I say.

"Things have changed," he says. "I've met this brilliant doctor, and, Rhine—" He pauses when he says my name. I wonder if he's been able to say it at all while I've been gone. "He knows things that I never would have thought could be true. Things about the world. Things about the virus."

Please don't be Vaughn. The thought is spinning frantically in my head. *Please don't let this brilliant man be the same man who separated us in the first place.*

"This is the doctor who told you I was dead?" I ask.

Rowan stops walking, catches my wrist to stop me in place. "He told me about a girl whose left eye was blue and whose right eye was brown, who signed up for an experimental procedure. She was a fraternal twin and she thought her eyes might be some sort of key, and she wanted to help find the cure."

I was Gathered because I responded to an ad that promised payment for bone marrow. It all turned out to be a ruse, though; there were no experiments—only Gatherers.

"Where did you meet this man?" I say.

"I thought you had been Gathered. I would take delivery jobs out of state so I could look for you in scarlet districts, but I always felt that you were alive. I always felt that you would find your way home, and so I always came back to the house. Several weeks after you disappeared, he showed up at the house. He had heard that I was looking for a girl who matched your description—a girl he thought had died in a research experiment. I didn't want to believe what he told me—of course I didn't. But while I had described you several times to strangers, I'd never said that we were twins. I'd never said your name. And he knew those things."

I feel dizzy. I take a steadying breath. Vaughn. It has to be Vaughn. Who else? But how would he have known about Rowan? How would he know that we were twins?

"He even knew about our parents being scientists. And he took an interest. It was several months before I started to believe what he was saying. I went through Mom and Dad's notes, and I found all of these things that we were too young to understand when they died. All these experiments. Notes about us, and about the children they had before us. I presented all of this to the doctor, and in exchange for my telling him about our parents, he employed me."

"Employed you?" I say. My voice is strange and faraway. It belongs to some other girl, in some other place. She can't possibly be me.

"He's a popular doctor," Rowan says. "He can't denounce research. He can't destroy laboratories. He needed someone else to do that."

"So he's using you," I say.

"No!" He rakes his fingers through his hair, frustrated. "When the time is right, he'll announce what this has all been about."

"What *is* this about?" I say. "How could you say that this research is pointless? How could you do those things for some brilliant doctor who's too much of a coward to do them himself?"

He smiles at me. It's been so long since I've seen him smile, but there's something unfamiliar about it. Something wrong. "Let me tell you about people," he says. "They don't know what's best for them. They need simple explanations. They need to be lulled into compliance, because they'll only rebel against it if they're forced. Of course I don't believe this research is pointless—not all of it, anyway."

"I'm not following."

"You're alive," he says. "But that doesn't change the fact that people die every day in experiments. It doesn't change that the world has fallen apart hoping for answers that won't come. All of these research labs—they've been recycling the same experiments for years. They aren't the ones that are going to find a cure."

"How do you know that?" I say.

"Because," he says. He takes my face in his hands and pulls me toward him and kisses my forehead roughly. There's wild delight in his eyes. "You have no idea the wonderful things I've seen."

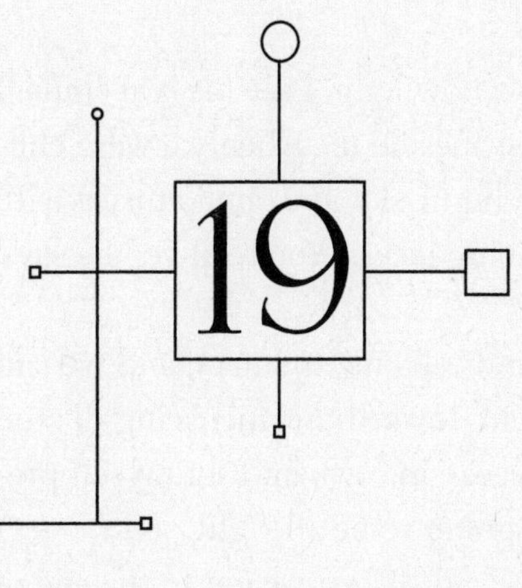

19

"ROWAN!" Bee is calling. When I turn in the direction of her voice, I realize how far Rowan and I have walked. I can barely see her standing at the edge of the dead cornfield. "The doctor is here!" she bellows.

In answer Rowan waves to her. "Come on," he says. "I can't wait for you to meet him. I can't wait to show him that you're alive."

"Wait," I say. "Doesn't it seem strange to you that this doctor knew all about me and he told you that I was dead?"

"If he lied about that, then he must have his reasons," Rowan says. "I know he can explain."

"It's not just a lie!" I say, and I have to pick up speed to keep pace with him, he's so eager to get to his perfect doctor. "He told you that your sister died a horrible death. You aren't angry about that?"

He stops walking and turns to face me. And for the

first time in I don't know how long, I see his real smile. I see the brother who slept beside me when we were children, who stared at the night sky and spun stories with me about the planets having faces. "You're alive," he says. "How could I be angry?"

He grabs my hand and tells me to hurry, and we run through the rustling field, toward this menacing doctor, but with the summer breeze in my hair, I let myself pretend that everything is going to be all right.

That feeling is short-lived. When we get to the end of the field, I see a black limousine parked beside the rickety car that brought us here. And my brother, squeezing my hand, has no idea that it's the same limousine that took me away from him. He has no idea that the doctor standing beside it has been the head demon of my personal hell.

Vaughn sees me, and I can't read his expression. He doesn't come to meet us but waits for Rowan and me to reach him.

"Dr. Ashby," Rowan says, "I'd like for you to meet—"

"Your sister," Vaughn says. "We've been properly introduced, haven't we, Rhine?"

Rowan looks confusedly between us. "Then, you knew that she was—"

"Alive?" Vaughn says. "Yes, of course. I had hoped to tell all of this to you when the time was right. But as usual your sister had her own ideas."

Rowan turns his back to Vaughn so that he can look at me, only me. "You know Dr. Ashby?" he says.

"I—" I look at my feet. How can I say this? How can I explain my hatred for this man my brother adores? How can I tell my brother that he's caused fires and murdered innocent people, that he's divulged our parents' lifework all for the man who has spent the past year of our lives manipulating him and imprisoning me?

"And she's been a delight to get to know," Vaughn says. "My son is quite taken with her. He was never a rebellious boy, but she brought out that side in him."

Rowan turns to Vaughn. "You have a son?"

"I'm afraid I'll have to explain all of this on the way to the airport," Vaughn says. "We're running behind schedule."

"Airport?" I say.

"You didn't think my brother was the only one with means to fly, surely," Vaughn says. "You'll like my plane. Much safer. And it'll actually leave the ground."

It horrifies me that Rowan doesn't question this, that when Vaughn opens the door for him, he gets into the back of the limo and waves me in after him. How many times has he sat here, in this place where my sister wives and I were drugged into captivity?

Any trace of my sister wives and me is gone. The leather smells of cleaning chemicals. The windows are spotless. I feel sick, but I climb in after my brother, because there's nowhere on earth I won't follow him, and because as much as I hate to admit it, I want to hear what my former father-in-law has to say for himself.

Bee and the muscular one try to follow, but Vaughn holds up a hand to stop them. "Not this time," he says. "This is a private party."

Bee frowns and looks into the limo. "Rowan?" she says.

"I'll fill you both in on the necessary details later," he says.

Vaughn climbs in after us, and I see Bee's face as the door is closed on her. She's got that unwavering adoration Cecily has for Linden, that lost look in her eyes because she doesn't know how to be without him.

Rowan seems unfazed.

As soon as we've begun moving, Vaughn says, "I've told you a few lies about your sister, as you can see. But I promise you that they were necessary."

Rowan is looking at me, taking in the way that I breathe, reminding himself that I'm alive.

"I'll start with something I never lied about," Vaughn says, "which is that she did sign up for an experimental procedure. A bone marrow donation, I believe, which promised compensation. Unfortunately, this was a trap set by Gatherers looking to make a quick dollar selling women to be brides. Imagine her good fortune when she was presented to my son as a bridal candidate. As soon as I saw those eyes of hers, I knew there was something special about her. Heterochromia might have occurred for a number of reasons in natural humans, but it's practically unheard of in new generations. If my son hadn't chosen her on his own, I would have been sure to convince him."

That's not entirely true. While he was experimenting on me in his basement, he told me that if Linden hadn't chosen me, he would have skipped that formality and kept me as an experiment.

"There were other girls in the van that brought Rhine to my son," Vaughn says. "After my son had chosen his brides, I paid good money to be sure the other girls were silenced. I couldn't take a chance of word getting out that a girl with eyes like Rhine's had been sold as a bride. The average citizen might think she was merely malformed, but imagine if someone well-versed in medicine—or worse, some deranged derelict searching for the cure—heard about it and tried to take her for himself? Imagine the danger she'd be in."

He made sure the other girls were silenced. I still hear the gunshots in my nightmares. I'm still haunted by the lost stare in Jenna's eyes when she thought of her sisters.

Rowan asks no questions; it's as though he's been trained to obey. How many other times has he taken Vaughn's words for truth? I've learned to smother my anger in Vaughn's presence, but this is especially challenging to take in silence.

"Rhine has lived quite comfortably as my son's bride. She's been to lavish parties and had a domestic to wait on her hand and foot. She's become quite close with her sister wives—one in particular, it seems."

"Rhine?" Rowan says. He peels back the curtain of my hair that's hiding my face. "You're married?"

There's no easy answer to that. Yes. No. Not anymore. I can't bring myself to look at him.

"I planned on telling you about your sister," Vaughn goes on. "But the opportunity hadn't yet presented itself. I didn't want to distract you. And I admit I was afraid that if you knew she was alive and well, you would lose sight of what's important. You would be so distracted with your own interests that you would forget that what you're doing now is saving something much bigger than yourself." He reaches right over me and pats Rowan's knee. He's showing me that my brother, the one thing I thought belonged to me, is in his control. "What you're doing is saving the world."

When I find my voice, I say, "How did you know to look for my brother at all? How did you know that I was a twin?"

He laughs, and all the kindness of his son's voice is in the sound. "From the stories you told our dear Cecily, of course."

I'm shaking when the limo finally stops. Vaughn steps outside and says that he'll allow us a few moments alone, but he reminds Rowan that we're on a tight schedule. There's a meeting we must attend.

When the door closes, leaving us alone, Rowan says, "I'm so sorry that I wasn't there to protect you."

I raise my eyes to meet his, and hope sparks in me. Hope that he sees Vaughn the way that I see him.

But he says, "Do you have any idea how lucky we are? If Dr. Ashby hadn't found you— I don't even want to think about what could have happened."

"Lucky?" I manage to blurt out. "I was stuffed into the back of a van and driven down the coastline and married against my will. You were left to assume I was dead. How is that lucky?"

"Because we get to be a part of something bigger now," he says. "We get to live."

"Rowan, none of this sounds unbelievable to you?"

"I've never been a believer in things I haven't seen for myself," he says. "You're smart to have doubts. I'm not asking you to trust Dr. Ashby. I'm asking you to trust me."

I feel like I don't know my own brother anymore. That's what I want to tell him. I open my mouth, but I lose my nerve. He looks right into my eyes, and, oh, how I want to believe everything he says. How I want to change reality to conform to what he's thinking. I can get us back to Manhattan. I can live with what he's done; I can find a way to rebuild our parents' home and spend the rest of my days planting lilies in the yard. I can never leave home again if that's what it'll take for us to be safe.

I cannot turn against him. I cannot leave him in Vaughn's clutches and say good-bye to him, because I've already lost my parents, and my husband, and a sister wife, and quite possibly Gabriel. But to lose faith in my brother would mean becoming a girl I wouldn't know how to be.

Vaughn opens the door and smiles that geriatric smile of his. "All set?" he asks.

"I think so," Rowan says, looking at me. "Rhine?"

"Okay," I say.

Vaughn leads us to the private jet that awaits us on the tarmac. It's got President Guiltree's emblem—the royal blue silhouette of an eagle flying across a white sun—printed on one of its wings. I add this to the long list of questions I don't know that I want answered.

Inside, the jet isn't very much bigger than the inside of the plane Reed has in his shed. It is fancier, though, with a beige leather wraparound seat and an oriental rug, and curtains that also bear the president's emblem.

Once we're seated, Vaughn orders the attendant to pour us glasses of champagne. When I only stare into my glass, Vaughn says, "I've found it settles the nerves for first-time flyers."

"I'm fine, thanks," I say.

"I've forgotten what a brave thing you are," Vaughn says, and takes a sip from his glass. "Remind me to tell you, Rowan, the story of your sister and the hurricane. For now I think I should tell her the story I told you. It's the only way to make her understand."

"Keep an open mind," Rowan says.

In response I stare at him. He's calm; he has already

accepted whatever Vaughn has laid out for him. But the Vaughn I know is different. The truth may be in his words somewhere, sure, but it's buried in his own version of reality, where things are never exactly as he would have one think. I should know. For a time I was married to a boy who lived in such a reality.

"Picture a world that's riddled with filth," Vaughn says. It isn't very hard.

"The world was divided into continents, countries, cities, towns. America was at its height more than two centuries ago. It was among the world leaders in medicine and technology. It also relied heavily on foreign imports.

"There was structure, a concept foreign to your generation now. You live among failed efforts and rotting crops, but once, there was order. The president at the time was more than a figurehead."

He takes a sip of his champagne and stares sideways out his window, as though the organized country he speaks of is directly below us.

"The order didn't last. History will tell us that it never does. War broke out, diseases, death. The president had a vision for what a precious commodity a country at peace could become. Maybe it would set an example and bring peace to the rest of the world. And while citizens were at their most vulnerable, he soothed them with promises of protection, promises that he could separate them from such devastation."

This isn't an act of Vaughn's imagination. History books have said such things, even though Reed tells me that the books aren't very reliable.

"The government began to confiscate things believed to cause disease—tanning booths, which you haven't heard of, darling, because they were worthless; specific chemicals that went into foods; water filters. Even sun exposure was limited. The towers that powered cellular phones were deactivated. There was once an infrastructure known as the Internet, through which anyone could have access to any information. This became a luxury afforded only to specific professions. There were hiccups of protest, of course, as was to be expected. But in the decades that followed, American citizens thrived. Its self-contained economy flourished."

I let myself picture this, though I shouldn't. It does no good to dwell on the things I'll never have. Time is too precious.

"It didn't last forever, as you can see," Vaughn says. "Every generation has its rebels, of course. It's the human condition to question the way of things. The president had no choice but to quell the tension that was arising among citizens. There were several ways he might have gone about this—finances, properties. But ultimately he chose the one thing he was certain no generation would want to lose—its children. He employed the finest geneticists to engineer the perfect generation of children that would be less susceptible to common bacteria. A flu epidemic that would once have been fatal would now be nothing but a slight case of the sniffles. As the technology progressed, the geneticists discovered a way to eradicate cancer and other genetic ailments entirely. The president announced that the illness-inducing devices that had been confiscated would be returned to society."

This part of the story I know. I was supposed to be perfect. I was supposed to live for decades and decades. There's no need for him to go on, but he does.

"As society changed, the president gradually arranged for new books to be distributed as old ones were filtered out. History was slowly being changed and rewritten; there's speculation that over the course of several decades he planned to wipe out any trace of the world that existed outside of America. Rather than having citizens believe that the rest of the world had been destroyed, they would believe it had never existed at all. No Internet and no international communications. The facts would be so muddled and disjointed that no one would know the truth."

I think of my father's atlas, and the boats Gabriel told me about in the history book in the library, and all the notes in Reed's library books. Full of lies. It wasn't enough that they stole our future; they had to steal our past.

"Don't look so crestfallen," Vaughn says. "You've heard stories about times when people lived well into their hundreds. The truth is that our country was suffering. Toxins in the air and in the water had already shortened the human life span to practically half of that. That's why you don't see anyone from before my time roaming around. The natural humans that remained when the virus was discovered were hardly fertile anyway. Really, the world was already a mess. This virus just made it slightly messier.

"And I suppose the rest you know. The first generations thrived and went on to have children of their own. It wasn't until more than two decades later that the fatal flaw was discovered. Females could not live past twenty, and males past twenty-five."

Twenty and twenty-five. Numbers we're all familiar with.

"There was a new president by then, our own Roderick Guiltree III, who inherited the title from his late father. With all our children dying off, the government lost its only leg to stand on. The police officers and doctors and lawyers it had bribed into compliance for so many years turned against the government. Pro-science and pro-naturalism stances formed. And then the very first laboratory explosion occurred, which, unfortunately, was the laboratory that started this whole affliction. And it was the only one that contained the research and technology that brought us the first generations. Because while natural children were gone for good, we might have at least been able to create more first generations, who are, as you know, living well into their seventies now. Some believe the research was destroyed by rebels, others by the government. A conspiracy to end the human race entirely, perhaps."

"That doesn't make sense," I blurt. "Who would want to end the human race?"

Vaughn, unfazed by my outburst, says, "Those who had grown tired of the endless cycle."

I don't want to believe him, and I hate that I do.

"But things aren't always as they appear. The rest of this story cannot be told. It can only be seen."

"Seen," I say, and my voice flutters down to the earth.

"I know it's a lot to process at once," Rowan says. "It's okay if you don't believe all of it at first. I didn't."

Without realizing it, I've downed my champagne. Vaughn refills my glass. "It's a long flight," he says.

"You haven't told me where we're going," I say. "Or is that also something that can only be seen?"

"I can tell you, though you might have to see it before you believe me," Vaughn says. "We're going to Hawaii."

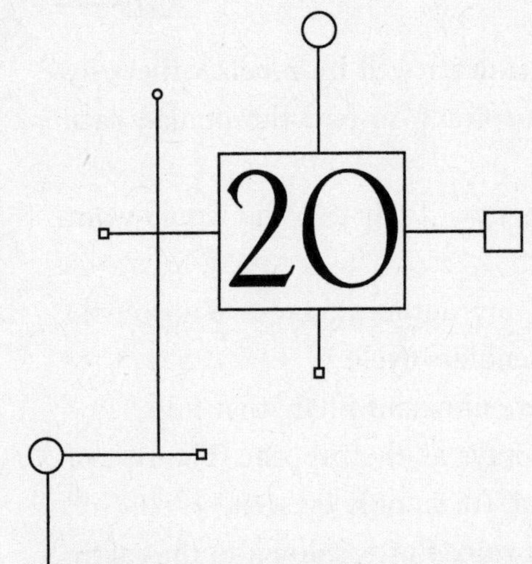

20

THE FLIGHT is eleven torturous hours long. Eleven hours spent face-to-face with my captor, and at first every moment brings a new question. *Were you ever really planning on reuniting me with my brother? Did you cause Cecily's miscarriage? How much of your story was true? What do Rowan and I have to do with any of it? What's happened to Deirdre? Where is Gabriel?*

"It's going to be all right," Rowan says. He's all softness now, coaxing me to take another sip of champagne, telling me to turn around and see what's outside my window, see the clouds.

Helplessly I look at him. He will never be just Rowan again. I will never be just Rhine. Everything has been tampered with. I can understand how the citizens in Vaughn's story must have felt, to have their lives invaded by the president's meddling. All of that happened long before I was born, and yet here is my life being invaded, broken into shards. I can catch glimpses and glimmers of what used to be, but the pieces will never be put back.

"It's not going to be all right," I murmur, but Rowan is listening to Vaughn prattle on about the altitude, and he doesn't hear me.

All this time during which Vaughn didn't tell Rowan and me about each other had nothing to do with me, I realize. I was just something to keep his son occupied, and another body to experiment with. Rowan had the brains Vaughn needed, and Rowan never would have cooperated if he'd thought I was alive; he would have been too busy worrying about me.

By the time we've landed, my head is throbbing. My ears feel strange, and my hearing is muffled. Even though we've been flying for eleven hours, it's still daylight where we are. Through the window I can only see water, green and blue and deeper blue. I've never seen water so clear as this.

"Our appointment is in an hour," Vaughn says. "I can see our Rhine needs a while to regroup. I'll arrange for your meals to be brought to you now, and I'll come and get you when it's time. How does that sound?"

"That would be best," Rowan says, speaking for both of us like I'm an invalid in his charge. I am grateful when Vaughn exits the jet, leaving us alone, though.

The attendant that brings our food is of Pacific Islander descent, which would only serve to verify that we've arrived in Hawaii, the supposedly annihilated branch of America, but I am so numbed to Vaughn's tricks that I haven't decided what to believe.

I barely notice the meal she brings at all, except for the aroma of lobster and melted butter. It's one of my favorite meals. Is it coincidence, or has Vaughn somehow stolen that knowledge from me as well?

"Before we get off this plane, I think Dr. Ashby meant for me to prepare you for the things you might see," Rowan says.

I cannot imagine how anything in this place will frighten me after what I've already seen. Rowan is still seeing the sixteen-year-old sister who was too naïve to understand that she was nearly stolen away when that Gatherer broke into our basement, who was dumb enough to answer an ad that was clearly a trap. He does not see what this year apart has shown me.

Or maybe he does. He tilts my chin so that I'm facing him, and he says, "But you're capable of seeing it for yourself. Right now I'm worried about other things."

"Other things?" I say.

He clears his throat, looks at his plate. "Sooner or later we'll both have to deal with the fact that things have changed. But right now you're alive, which is more than I thought when I woke up this morning. It's just that you're—you look older. This past year I've accepted that you were frozen in time, that I would grow older but you would always be sixteen. A child. We were both children when we saw each other last, weren't we? But you're somebody's wife now."

And now, strangely, I feel sorry for him. He hasn't forgotten what it felt like to mourn my death.

"I want answers and yet I don't. I don't know what I'm prepared to have you say about what you've been through."

"Sooner or later," I say softly. "You're right."

"For now I have one question, and it's—" His face has gone pale. He won't meet my eyes. "Your husband . . . has he been—kind? To you?"

I think of Linden. My sullen, elegant once-husband, who was so desperately in love with a woman who slipped through his fingers. Who came to my bed and held me when we both needed it. Who had been sheltered all his life, yet who ran away from the only parent and the only stability he's ever known, because of me.

I don't know that Rowan can ever understand the whole truth of my marriage to Linden. I don't even know if I can. So I say, "Yes."

And I can't help adding, "He's nothing like his father."

"You're angry with Dr. Ashby," Rowan says. "I can understand that. I want to be angry with him myself. He's kept us apart for a year, and yet—" He squints, trying to think of a way to reconcile this glitch in his great mentor. "And yet what he's giving us more than makes up for it."

"Why do you believe everything he says?" I ask. I

hesitate to say much more. I finally have him back and I can't risk losing him again.

"Didn't you notice anything unusual about the attendant who brought our dinner?" he says.

I wasn't paying attention. "You mean that she was Hawaiian?" I ask.

"I mean," Rowan says, "that she was older than new generations but younger than first generations. They don't even have those terms. The people here are born without the virus."

"That's impossible," I say. "It's a trick."

Rowan smiles at his plate. "You never used to be the cynical one. It bothered me that you were so trusting. Now I think I miss it."

I miss lots of things about him. But I don't say that.

"You should try to eat something," he says. "For energy, to combat the jet lag. It's ten p.m. back where we came from, but it's around dinnertime here."

We've just finished eating when Vaughn comes to collect us. He's brought a change of clean clothes for us: black T-shirts and olive-green shorts that fit perfectly. For a moment I'm foolish enough to hope Deirdre is somehow safe and that she made them for me, but then I feel the itch of the factory label against my hip.

"Your hair was always a bit unruly," Vaughn says, frowning as I exit the jet. I won't give him the satisfaction of patting my hair to determine what's wrong with it.

Vaughn walks several paces ahead of Rowan and me,

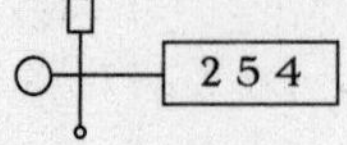

and I wonder if he means for us to talk. It's been more than a year since I've been this close to my brother, and now that I'm free to tell him about what I've endured, I know that it would be unwise of me. Whatever bond that has formed between my brother and Vaughn has been built on proof and on trust; Vaughn has justified his arguments and done so in a way that Rowan responded to. I'll have to be very careful about how I speak to my brother. As it is, he has decided that everything Vaughn has done will serve a greater good, that I am still incapable of understanding but that I'll come around.

Vaughn knows this, doesn't he? He knows that I'll have to bide my time with Rowan just as I had to bide my time with Linden. Vaughn is wise to my ways, and this time he isn't going to let me get away so easily.

"You don't look well." Rowan frowns.

"It must be jet lag, like you said."

He bumps his shoulder gently against mine. It's such a familiar gesture. It's something he always used to do. And it makes me so homesick that I could cry, but I won't, I refuse to. He has to see that I'm stronger now, that I'm not who I once was.

But who am I?

"Listen," Rowan says when we enter the building. He's leaning close to me, his voice a murmur. "You're going to see some things that may frighten you. But I want you to know that I agreed to it. I want you to know that, however it may seem, I'm okay."

"I thought you said I didn't need to be prepared," I say.

He bumps my shoulder again. "Just remember what I said."

We pass through several security checkpoints, and I pay attention to the armed guards, some of them male, some female. They all look as though they could be older than twenty or twenty-five, but I'm not convinced. I'm so tired and overwhelmed, and this entire day has been shrouded in unreal hues. It's almost too much to trust that this is really my brother beside me, that I'm standing on a ground I was told no longer existed.

And then we've stopped walking. Rowan is talking to a first-generation woman who is guiding him to a door that's as white and sterile-looking as everything else around us. This place is all white walls and sharp edges, so pristine that I think we must be ruining it with our shoes.

Rowan looks over his shoulder at me, and I see the thirteen-year-old boy who stood beside me when we felt the ground shake under our feet as our parents were killed. I see realization and fear. I see that we're all the other has. And then his eyes are unreadable. "I'll see you in a bit," he tells me.

"Wait," I say. "Where are you going?"

Vaughn puts his arm around me, steers me toward the opposite end of the hall. "Come with me," he says.

I look over my shoulder, but Rowan is already gone.

We pass another security checkpoint, and then we're in a dimly lit room that's no bigger than my bedroom closet at the mansion. One wall is almost entirely made of glass, and it shows us a room with neon lights and a bed with its mattress at an incline.

"I thought you and I might have a chance to chat," Vaughn says. "You and I have never gotten along very well, but now that the circumstances have changed, I'd like for us to start over. I underestimated you before, perhaps. I wasn't honest about the tests I conducted on you while you were married to my son. It's just that you were so stubborn, and I was sure you'd object. But I've enjoyed getting to know your brother. I see now that you're both bright children. Your parents would certainly be proud of how you've both turned out."

My arms are folded as I stare through the glass. "Don't talk about my parents," I say.

"Very well," he says. "Then, I'll only say that I have seen their notes and I admire their efforts. It may be more fitting for you to read what they wrote for yourself."

I hate the idea that he has read my parents' notes, that his eyes have invaded their thoughts and their handwriting the way his syringes and pills have invaded me. The way his promises have invaded my brother's mind.

"My life's work has been to find the cure," he goes on. "I won't bore you with the revelations and feelings I felt when I lost my first son, or the joy I felt when Linden was born. But every moment of that joy has been overshadowed by the fear of failing him. And it's that fear that has spurred me into action, and led me to become among the most revered in my profession, both as a doctor and as a geneticist."

That much is true. Vaughn is well established throughout the nation.

"And it's my hard work that captured the interest of the president. About thirty years ago, when it was discovered that our children were being claimed by this mysterious ailment, the president began compiling an elite team of only the best in their fields to go about understanding and fixing the problem. Just a few short years ago, I was selected.

"But it isn't enough to be selected. Each specialist to earn the president's interest must prepare a case study. Dr. Glassman did a fascinating presentation on the mutations in malformed children, for instance. And as a part of his study, Dr. Hessler prepared notes on the origin of how this affliction came to be known as a virus. It isn't exactly a virus, you understand. A virus is something that's contracted, not something that happens as a result of one's genetics. But when our children first started to die, we didn't suspect genetics. We suspected another outbreak like the tainted pesticides. Of course we know better now."

The lights in the room on the other side of the glass brighten. A door opens, and a nurse is wheeling a gurney in. My lungs constrict. My mouth goes dry. The boy lying on the gurney, as pale and still as death, is Rowan.

"I've been trying to come up with a case study that's worthy of the president's time," Vaughn says.

Four nurses are moving my brother from the gurney to the bed, propping him against the incline.

"First I tried to imagine a way new generations could adapt to their short life spans. I dabbled with the idea of females having full-term pregnancies before natural puberty. I was making some headway there, I thought, but none of the subjects could withstand the treatments."

This is what he did to Lydia, Rose's domestic, and to Deirdre. Lydia didn't survive the latest attempt, and I don't know that I'll ever be brave enough to face what happened to Deirdre.

And while these horrible things are being said, one of the nurses is taping Rowan's eyelids open. This setup looks familiar. So disgustingly familiar.

"Then your brother here introduced your parents' notes, about replicating the virus."

I can hear the muffled commands being given through a loudspeaker. A helmet is lowered from the ceiling, and the nurse positions it over Rowan's head, locking his chin in place. I can see the rise and fall of his chest, but otherwise he's paralyzed, his arms useless at his sides, an IV feeding fluid into his vein.

I don't want to see this, but I can't look away.

"Our Jenna was an interesting candidate to test your parents' theory," Vaughn says. "I won't go into the gory details; I know you were attached to her. Needless to say, she didn't survive."

That's when I stop listening. I stare at my brother, and I try to listen to the voice coming through the speaker over his bed. It's giving commands and words that mean nothing to me, but I will them to be the only thing I hear.

I know what's about to happen even before I see the needle reaching for his eye.

My hand is touching the glass. My mouth forms the word "Count." Count the seconds until it's over. I think that's what he's doing. I think I catch his bottom lip just barely moving. There's a second needle for the other eye, and just seeing it happen to him brings back every memory of my experience in that same position. Cecily was there to tell me her story about trying to make kites fly. There's no one to talk to Rowan. No one at all but the nurses who monitor his IV and hoist his limp body back onto the stretcher when it's through.

When the tape is removed from his eyelids, he blinks. I watch his fingers curl into an almost-fist, and I realize that in tandem I've made a fist over my heart.

Vaughn is still talking.

"Stop," I say, breathless. "You don't have to explain. I understand. We're your case study."

"Smart girl," he says. "Come, follow me. I'll let you see him now."

Rather than one armed guard marking the checkpoint to Rowan's room, there are two, and an authorization card

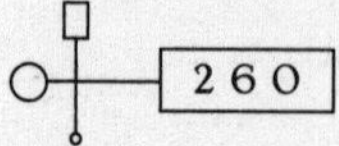

that Vaughn swipes through a panel to unlock the door.

Rowan is being kept in a room as soulless and sterile as the rest of this place. He's lying on a bed where a first generation nurse is monitoring the fluid that runs down a tube and into his arm. Everywhere are screens with wires that lead to his pulse points.

I'm not certain whether he's conscious. His eyes are closed, eyelids dark like bruises.

Is this how I looked when I was the subject of Vaughn's most invasive experiments? Rowan seems so fragile now, when less than an hour ago he was strong and his skin had color to it. I'm afraid to get any closer, afraid I'll damage him, but then Vaughn nudges me forward and I make my way to the bedside.

"How's our boy doing?" he asks the nurse. In answer she hands him a chart.

"Rowan?" I brush the tape residue from his brow with my thumb.

I can see his eyes moving beneath his eyelids, and then he manages to blink. He looks at me, and I'm not sure if he can register who I am; his eyes are all pupil.

Vaughn is asking him to clench his fists as best he can. Good. Move his toes. Good. Blink once, and again. Good.

I say his name, and he groans.

"He isn't in any pain," Vaughn says. "But he'll be down until the morning."

How could my brother have agreed to this? While Vaughn had me restrained and too sedated to put up a fight, my brother has been willingly enduring the same torturous regimes. How long did it take for Vaughn to manipulate him this much? How long will it take me to undo it?

Can it be undone?

When Vaughn leads me back into the hallway, I feel as though I'm the one who has been drugged. My eyes ache, and I can barely feel my legs carrying me forward.

Vaughn is talking about the heat, and his voice is so excited that it breaks into whispers at times. He loves his madness the way a bird loves the sky. And, oh, how glad he is that I'm here now. There are so many things he wants to show me; there's a world of things beyond my greatest dreams.

He has no idea what I am capable of dreaming.

We're in an elevator that's made of glass, going up. On one side are the sterile levels of the sterile building, and on the other side, the sky slowly going purple going pink.

For now we must remain in this place, he says. It's a secure building. Our business is within these walls, and then we must get back to our plane in the morning. From the door to the plane. But look, look at that view.

We've reached our destination, the thirteenth floor. One wall is made up entirely of windows, so much that I feel like I'm inside the building's skeleton. I stand before the glass, and Vaughn puts his hands on my shoulders and says, "Look. What do you see?"

I see an ocean that's spilled out of a wineglass, its body clear and sparkling and folding over itself. I see a ribbon of sand. I see clean buildings, tidy streets with streetlights that turn green, yellow, red. I see cars.

I don't have words to answer his question.

On a distant building, on a giant screen, a woman is washing her hands and then smiling as she holds the bottle up beside her face with its label clearly shown. The woman is much older than me, much younger than Vaughn.

"The people here have been cured?" I ask, not quite believing I've just said the words.

I see the reflection of Vaughn's smile in the glass, over the perfect ocean. "No, darling," he says. "Those people down there have never even heard of the virus."

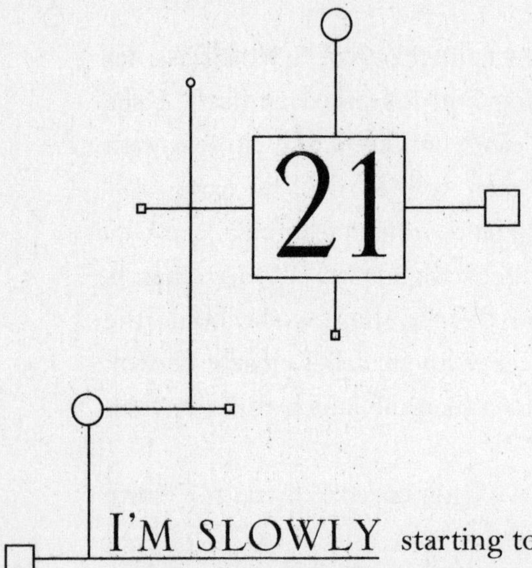

21

I'M SLOWLY starting to believe.

Rose was Vaughn's first true subject. She was his favorite—until Rowan and I came along, at least. He begins the story after we sit at a table in the cafeteria that's built into the fifteenth floor. All around us are doctors and nurses, all different ages but mostly first generation. Or is "first generation" even the term for them? What do you call someone who isn't a first generation or a new generation? What do you call it when death comes with a number attached to it that the person living cannot see?

Vaughn doesn't pressure me to eat what's on my tray. He saws a knife into his steak and goes on with his story.

He first saw Rose when she was a toddler, when her parents brought her along to a lecture on antibiotic resistance. She and Linden played together, crawling under tables and tagging each other and laughing. It occurred to him then that Linden should have a playmate, but more important, one day he would need to find a wife. This was before Vaughn knew about this place, before he had been contacted by the president, when he still believed his future grandchildren might hold answers that his own son did not. He proposed an engagement between their children, but Rose's parents declined.

"I could see even then that she was too good for her parents," he says. "They had no idea what they had in her."

Rose is alive for an instant in my mind. She has sharp brown eyes and a wicked smile. Her hair is alight.

And then I hear, once again, Linden's wailing as she stopped breathing.

She would have been free. She would have stuffed herself with fresh strawberries and teased Madame's guards and traveled the country with her father.

"They were always out there, her parents. They lived like gypsies rather than civilized professionals. And several years later, I saw Rose again when her father brought her to a conference on the Florida coast. She was growing to be every bit as beautiful as I would have expected. Looked a great deal like her mother.

"Her father pulled me aside and told me that the president had recruited him to do research for his team. He told me about this place. He wanted me to partner with him.

"And then, tragically, he was killed."

I don't ask about the car bombing that killed Rose's father. I can see in Vaughn's eyes that this tragic occurrence was less than accidental.

"You have to understand," Vaughn says. "I couldn't let that clever girl go back to her mother's brothel. You should have heard the mouth she had on her already. It pained me to think of her becoming a common street whore. No. I did what was best. She and my son were better for it."

Vaughn is polishing off his plate. "Before Rose came along, I'm ashamed to say I had a close call with Linden. One of my treatments made him ill. Fortunately, he recovered with little more than a few missing molars, but I knew that I couldn't risk anything like that again. If I wanted to cure my child, I couldn't also treat him like my guinea pig."

"That's why you used Rose," I say.

"'Used' is an ugly word. I don't know if I like that. No, I prefer to think that she was an invaluable learning experience for me. Thanks to my treatments, she lived several months after her twentieth birthday. Hers is the study that earned me the president's attention. I set a mortality record with her. But she wasn't the one. Not quite."

"And you think my brother and I are 'the one'?" I ask.

"Sadly, no," Vaughn says. "Once I came to this place, I discovered that someone else beat me to it. There have been several avenues of cures discovered."

The words don't even feel real. He says them so casually that I'm left wondering if I've misunderstood.

Vaughn sees that he's confused me, and he smiles in that disarmingly kind way. "You and your brother are my case study," he says. "Right now we're determining whether or not your bodies will be able to handle the existing cures. None of the cures have proven to be universal, I'm afraid. Some people are living into their thirties now. But in cases of others that have received the same cure, there have been some gruesome fatalities, depending on ethnicity, gender, and age at the time treatment is administered. Up until now there haven't been any tests done on subjects with heterochromia. And then, the heterochromia proved to be a dead end, sadly. But I remain convinced that there is something unique about your DNA; the heterochromia was just a surface side effect. There's no question that you and your brother were custom made. The only question is what your parents' intentions were."

All those times he left the mansion for days at a time—a convention in Seattle, a conference in Clearwater—was he really coming here, with my brother in tow?

I stare out the window that's behind him. *This is what an ocean looks like*, I think, *when there isn't a world buried inside it.*

The world isn't all gone. Only part of what we were taught is true. Wars and natural disasters have annihilated some landmasses, have reduced countries by halves and thirds and so on, have caused erratic weather in places that were temperate hundreds of years ago. Some things have changed. But not everything. Not the most important thing: There's still life left. There are still places to go.

"You and your brother were never meant to be ordinary," Vaughn says. "Your parents had plans for the both of you. Big plans. And I'm determined to fulfill them."

As we ride the elevator down, I think of Linden, Cecily, and Gabriel still trapped in that dying piece of the world, with them thinking it's all there is.

The question, Vaughn says, is not whether a cure will be found in time to save his son and grandson, but whether it will be perfected in time. Can I imagine the chaos, he asks, that would happen if people knew all of this was going on? No. Better to carry on his image of just another doctor working aimlessly, and to let the supposed rebels, like my brother, destroy labs and spread pro-naturalism. Better to let the people be ignorant and hopeless. And then, once the cure is introduced, they'll be so grateful and so desperate for a structured existence to save them from the cesspool that the country has become. They'll be back under the president's control.

"You've always had trouble with relinquishing control, haven't you?" Vaughn says as we exit the elevator. "But it's a rewarding thing. People need a leader. They need to feel that someone is in charge, that they're in the hands of someone greater than they are. It's far scarier for each of us to believe that we are the only ones in charge of our own destinies. We know our own downfalls."

"So you kept me in the dark," I say.

"I've told a few little lies I thought would be easier. The blue June Beans, for instance, were not giving you small doses of the virus. They contained minuscule doses of an experimental cure. The withdrawals after you ran away made you ill, like I expected. But it gave me an idea. I stopped administering the same treatment to your brother, to minimal effect. He hardly even developed a fever. It furthers the theory that the virus in males is entirely unrelated to the virus in females."

Suddenly I don't want to hear any more of this. My mind is spinning.

This white hallway is the same as all the others, but it seems different now. Everything seems different, even Vaughn. When he finally stops talking long enough for me to speak, I ask, "When can I see Rowan again?"

"In the morning," he tells me. "There's no need for concern. He'll be as good as new by then."

In addition to a cafeteria this building has a floor made up of bedrooms. I don't ask how Vaughn has arranged for me to have my own room, or how I was permitted to enter this secure building. I think he anticipated capturing me when Cecily was in the hospital; I don't think he anticipated that his son wouldn't abandon me. How do Cecily and Linden factor into this plan? He's left them in

Madame's care, but will they ever know about this place? What happens when we return?

"You're looking weary," Vaughn says. "Wash up, if you'd like. Rest. Enjoy the view. I'll come for you in the morning."

My bedroom, in contrast to the rest of the building, is warm and softly lit. The bed is lush and inviting, the bedding gold satin.

I step inside, and when the door is closed behind me, I hear the click of a lock.

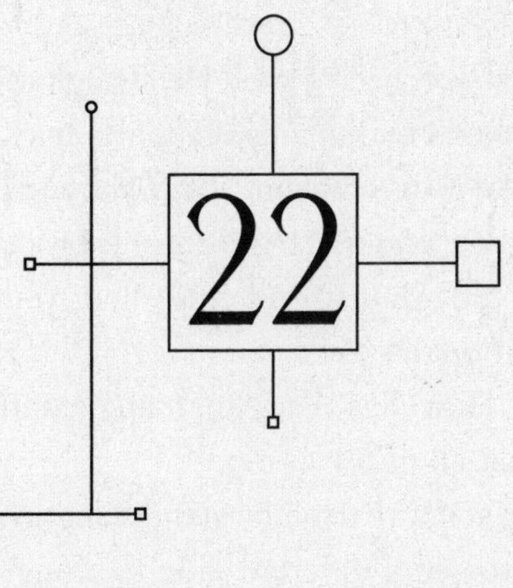

22

BEFORE I SLEEP, I think of the nurse that was monitoring Rowan's vitals. I thought she was a first generation, but maybe she isn't. Maybe she's just a person who was born and has reached a certain age. Maybe she just is.

What a thought.

I'm too tired to dream.

A knock on the door startles me awake. Daylight fills the room through the glass wall, and I have to shield my eyes.

"Rhine?" It's Rowan's voice. "Are you awake? Can I come in?"

"Yes," I say, pushing myself upright.

He closes the door behind him and sits on the edge of the bed. To see him now, bright-eyed and warm with color, I would never suspect the awful state I left him in yesterday evening.

"I'm sorry about what you had to see." He shrugs the backpack from his shoulders and unzips one of its pockets. The backpack has the lotus emblem. "Dr. Ashby told me this morning that you underwent the same procedure. He said that even though it wasn't entirely of your own will, you did exceptionally well."

Exceptionally well. How has Vaughn managed to convince my brother that all of this is okay?

Worse still is that I'm starting to understand Vaughn's methods. I'm starting to see a different side to things: a doctor who wants nothing more than to save the world, and the meddlesome daughter-in-law who foils his attempts and must be restrained, tracked, sedated if that's what it takes, because the world hangs in the balance.

I don't know what's worse—helping my former father-in-law or returning to the dying world that I've always known. As I begin to awaken more, I'm filled with a divine and yet horrifying feeling that something within me has changed.

"He admitted that he may have been wrong to keep you in the dark about what he was doing." Rowan is looking down as he speaks, and his tone is practical, but I know him and I know that he's contrite. For not protecting me. For letting himself believe I was dead.

"When Mom and Dad died, I gave up believing in everything they'd devoted their lives to. And then, once you were gone—it took me a while to dig up their things we'd buried. It wasn't that I wanted to understand their research. I just wanted to read their words. I wanted to remember how it felt to belong to them."

"Rowan . . ."

He inches onto the bed until he's beside me. Our mother's notebook is in his hands.

"I've always coddled you," he says. "But I shouldn't have. You're no more a child than I am." I'm older than him, in fact. "You have a right to see this."

He opens the notebook so that it falls into both of our laps. Before I see the words, I see his hands smoothing over the edges and then moving away like curtains parting.

I've never seen this before, and I have no idea, yet, what it means, but I would know my mother's handwriting anywhere.

In my nervousness the words all run together, and it takes a few seconds for me to read them.

And as usual the meaning of her words is over my head. My brother was the one who understood the science of things. But I try to hang on. I read and reread several pages about Subject A and Subject B, who were apparently children born in the lab where my parents worked. Subject A, female, was capable of loud wailing noises though she never learned to speak. Subject B, male, gave little to no indication that he was aware of any outside presences. By the fifth page, both subjects have died, the first generation of my parents' Chemical Garden project annihilated.

On the sixth page there's a photo of both subjects. They're lying beside each other in a crib, limp and pale. I can tell by their faraway stares that they're blind.

Before my brother and I were born, our mother gave birth to a set of malformed twins who only lived for five years. I never saw them before this moment, and I wish I could undo it, because this is an image that will always haunt me.

They look exactly like Rowan and me. The same feathery blond hair we had as children. The same heterochromatic eyes, only without any life to them. It's like staring at our corpses.

I realize my hands are shaking, but I go on reading, this time in a frenzy. I flip through the pages, skimming for words that will be of value to me. Words I'll understand.

There's a new set of Subject A and Subject B for round two of the Chemical Garden project. A photo of two chubby, healthy infants lying on a blue sheet. There is life to them. I should know; the baby on the left is me. For several more pages my brother and I are Subject A and Subject B. Then we learn to crawl, learn to walk, verbalize ahead of schedule. It becomes clear that we will live, and here is where my mother confesses that she and my father took the risky chance of naming us. *Rowan,* she writes, *is prone to violent tantrums.* He's three years old on this page; eventually they learned that his tantrums were the result of pain from persistent inner-ear infections.

Rhine has difficulty distinguishing reality from fantasy. Lately she tells stories of children in the bedroom walls. Turned out to be mice that had found a way in through the vents.

I go on reading about my brother's temper, and how dangerous it was for me to make friends with the little girl who lived in the house next door. I was too trusting, my mother wrote. I was cursed with her warm heart, she writes in parentheses, and that would have been a virtue a century ago.

And then I caught pneumonia, and my lungs filled with fluid. I remember that. I remember the steam bath in the bathroom with the tub with rusted knobs. It's rare for new generations to fall ill before their time, especially as severely as I did. Only, it wasn't pneumonia, my mother writes. It was a poor reaction to an experimental drug they gave me. My brother developed a rash behind his neck, but nothing more serious than that. Males have the better immune systems. Something is superior in their genes as a result of this virus. It takes five years more for their systems to shut down. My mother's handwriting has gone furious here. She's had a breakthrough. I can't read her tirade, because the words are running together, letters piling atop one another, many of them crossed out. Her daughter could have died from that reaction, but in these notes she has no daughter. Only subjects.

There are so many words. I feel like I could drown in what I don't understand of them, and it's getting hard to concentrate.

We were experiments. My brother and I were experiments. Round two. The twins that lived. And since our parents have died, we'll always be unfinished. Vaughn can pick up where they left off and run experiments of his own, but we'll never know what my parents might have gone on to do with us.

You and your brother were never meant to be ordinary.

I can't look at any more of this. Not now.

Rowan senses this, and he closes the notebook. "There's no point in trying to understand every word of it," he says. "Dr. Ashby has gone through it, and he's even tried to duplicate some of their work. He says it was advanced for the time it was written. He thinks they were on the path to becoming valuable in their profession."

My voice is small when I say, "They already were valuable."

"I didn't mean it that way," he says. "Rhine, you know I loved our parents."

I do know that, but I needed to hear him say it.

I slump back against the pillows and throw my arm over my eyes to block out the light. "God," I mumble. "Is all of this really happening?"

His weight jars the mattress as he lies beside me, and it's quiet for a while before he says, "I never stopped feeling like you were alive. I thought I must have been going crazy."

I prop myself on my elbow to look at him. "But I'm here now," I say. "You can stop destroying those labs. You can stop making people think there's no hope. You don't have to do everything Vaughn says anymore."

He tries to smile, but it fades as his eyes move up and down the length of my face. "Let's not talk about that now," he says. "Let's go back to the part where we're both alive."

I fall beside him again. "We are, aren't we?" I say. I don't know why it makes me laugh, but he laughs too, and outside the window there are traffic lights changing color and people throwing open their windows; there are buttons being buttoned and shoes being laced; there are clocks and calendars; there are fishing lines going out into the water.

It's a world worth fighting for. Set fire to the broken pieces; start anew.

"There is the matter of my son and grandson," Vaughn murmurs to me as I'm boarding the jet. "Keep that in mind."

This time as we ascend, I watch the world sinking below us. I watch the way the city fades into sand that gets washed by the ocean.

"It's like Dad's postcards," Rowan says.

It is exactly like that. It's like my father's postcards have become animated. And it's strange to see this alien world getting smaller and smaller as we head for the clouds. It's strange to think that this alien world is full of nothing but strangers.

An hour into the flight, Vaughn has immersed himself

in his notes. He has put in earplugs and turned away from us. He's asked not to be disturbed.

"He gets this way," Rowan says. "I can only imagine what it's like in his mind."

I've spent a great deal of this past year trying not to find out what's in Vaughn's mind.

"How are you feeling?" I ask.

He stretches his arms out over the back of the seat. "Great," he says. "And listen, there's a reason the others didn't come with us. The things that happened here are not for anyone else to know. The others don't know about the jet or about Hawaii or about any of what's been told to you since yesterday."

"Don't they get suspicious?" I say.

"People need to feel like someone else is in charge," Rowan says. "But those two need to feel like they're part of the bigger plan. They know that I'm working with Dr. Ashby. They think it's simply because I'm helping to rid him of the competition."

"That girl seems to like you a lot," I say.

"Bee? She clings."

He watches my left hand as I reach for my glass of water. "You're wondering where my wedding band is," I say.

"It had crossed my mind. But I meant what I said; you don't need to talk about it if you aren't ready."

"The marriage was annulled," I say. I take a sip of water, and it does nothing for how dry my mouth has become. How to tell the story of my marriage to Linden? Should I leave out Jenna and Rose? The horror of watching Cecily give birth? Or does he already know these things? Are my sister wives all Subjects A, B, and C in Vaughn's research? I don't know that I can stand the thought of summarizing them in that way. And I don't know that I can do justice to them either.

"I ran away," I say instead. "It wasn't that he made me unhappy; it was just that I wanted to go home."

"You made it all the way back home by yourself?"

I feel my cheeks burning as I gather my knees to my chest and look out at the clouds. "An attendant ran away with me. I—"

I don't know if he's alive or dead. That's what I was going to say, but my lip is quivering and the dryness in my mouth has been replaced by the taste of salt, and everything is starting to blur.

"Hey," Rowan says. He touches my shoulder, and just like that my limbs unfold and I fall against him in tears. It isn't just Gabriel. It's everything. It's Rose's blond hair spilling out from the sheet that covered her body, and Jenna's final breath, and Cecily, lifeless in Linden's arms, and all those mornings I awoke with a collar dampened by a night of my husband's tears. It's that all of these things happened because of one man, a man I decided was evil, but who has shown me the world I imagined as a little girl. It's that we're flying away from it, and I don't know what will await me when we land.

Rowan is saying, "Hey, shh. It'll be okay," with such compassion that it makes me fall apart all over again. And even though we've both grown, even though he's wearing different clothes and he's not exactly as I left him, he's the only certainty I've got, and I'm so afraid that something awful is coming for us.

He never used to let me get away with crying like this, but now he allows it. He wraps his arms around me and rests his chin on my head. I wonder if it's because he feels the same way.

Somewhere toward the end of the flight, Rowan fell asleep, and I think he was lying about how he's been feeling since yesterday's procedure. He always did see pain as a weakness.

His head is canted back against my shoulder. He's grinding his teeth, something I've never known him to do. I sit very still so I don't disturb him.

I turn the pages of my mother's notebook as carefully as I can. Rowan and I—Subject A and Subject B—were the results of in vitro fertilization. It was no accident that we were twins. Our parents needed a male and a female. So many of the notes are illegible, or just beyond my understanding. There are cross diagrams with notes in the margins about iridium. What it all comes down to is that we were born for a specific purpose. We were born for the same reason Linden was born—to be cured. Linden was ill as a result of his father's testing, but then, so was I.

If my parents hadn't been killed, would their desperation only have intensified as the years went on? Would they have earned the president's attention? Would they have taken the measures Vaughn has taken? Had they already begun to?

I have entirely new reasons for why Rowan and I were wise to bury our parents' things in the backyard. It's too late now to wish they hadn't been unearthed.

The jet touches down on an unfamiliar tarmac. But it's the same desolate horizon, everything shrouded in the smoggy blue of early dawn.

Rowan stirs and moves away from me. I close the notebook and slide it into his backpack.

"Where are we now?" I ask.

"We aren't very far from home," Vaughn says. "That's where we're headed."

"Home?" I say. It's a word that can mean anywhere and nowhere.

"Yes, of course," Vaughn says, rising to his feet and heading for the jet's door. "You'll always have a home. I told you that."

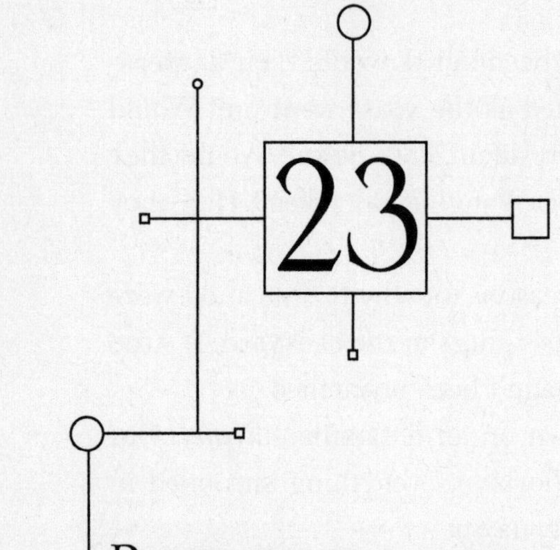

23

ROWAN IS blinking and sitting up very straight in an effort to keep from falling asleep in the limo. And despite persistent feelings of dread and anxiety, I feel myself fading as well.

"This will be the first time our Rowan has seen the property," Vaughn says. Our Rowan. I don't know what to do with the anger that causes in me. "Once you've both had a chance to rest, you must show him around. Everything is still as you left it, even that eyesore of a trampoline."

I stare out the tinted window as the mansion gates come into view. All around us are trees, some of them real and others a hologram meant to give the illusion that there's no way out from the inside. The gates open, and we drive straight through the illusory trees.

"You lived here?" Rowan asks as we drive past the mini-golf course. I wonder if any of my blood remains on the windmill from my escape attempt.

"Yes," I say.

Vaughn starts talking about how he's been thinking of ordering horses for the stables again, and he'd like to know what I think. He doesn't seem to notice that I don't answer him; he moves on to another speech about the rose garden thriving in the summer heat and this being ideal pool weather. Not that there's time for swimming, he says. Not now, at least. Later. There will be time for everything later.

The word "time" doesn't sound the same to me anymore.

We enter the mansion through the kitchen, which is dimly lit and empty. When my husband and sister wives and I were here, the head cook would be milling about preparing the day's menu at this hour. By her third trimester Cecily had developed so many food aversions that on an especially bad day she might send back four untouched breakfast trays.

Vaughn leads us onto the elevator. It was here that Gabriel stopped its descent so that I could tell him the story of how I came to be Linden's unwilling bride. Was Vaughn listening in and collecting information that would lead him to my brother? Looking back now, I realize how foolish it was for me to utter secrets within these walls.

The doors open, and I'm expecting to be met with the wives' floor; even after I became first wife and earned my key card, that and the ground floor were the only levels I had access to. But something different awaits me this time. Rather than the smell of incense, there's leather and a spice I can't exactly explain, but it's not unlike the smell inside the trunk that held my parents' things.

I've never seen this floor. Rather than lush carpeting, the floors are a dark, glossy hardwood. The walls are green and decorated with photos in gold frames. I immediately recognize the one of a young Rose and Linden in the orange grove. As we make our way down the hall, I watch them play together, run away from the camera with their hands knotted between them. I watch them get married, Rose in a billowing white dress that's both absurd and beautiful on her child frame, Linden an awkward boy concentrating deeply on the ring he slides onto her finger.

At the end of the hall, their story ends with their foreheads pressed together. He's got his hands on her swollen stomach, but the picture was taken a moment too soon; she will always be just about to smile.

Rowan isn't looking at the pictures. His eyes are dark and unfocused. "Rowan?" I say.

"Hm?" He raises his head but doesn't turn it toward me.

Vaughn opens the door that's in front of us, revealing a bedroom only slightly different from the ones on the wives' floor. There are dust-framed rectangles on the wall where pictures once hung. "I expected you might be tired," Vaughn says, wrapping his arm around Rowan's shoulders and leading him to the bed. "This room belonged to my son, but even when he's home, he doesn't much care for it anymore. Too many memories, I suppose."

There's no trace of Linden left in this room. I can see the empty spaces where things might have been once.

Rowan crawls under the sheets, and he's gone in seconds. Vaughn tucks the covers to his chin, as though my brother is a child in his care rather than a subject exhausted from horrifying treatments.

"He has your fire," Vaughn says. "I'm impressed that he was able to stand on his feet for as long as he did. Anyone else would be positively incoherent for at least two days following the sedation required for a retinal procedure. But time and again, the both of you exceed my expectations."

I watch Rowan turn onto his left side. It's how he's always slept, turned away from me when we shared a bed.

"You're looking tired," Vaughn tells me. "I could bring you to your room, but I was hoping we'd have a chance to talk first. There's something I'd like to show you."

After the thriving Hawaiian cityscape and my parents' notes and my brother, I cannot imagine what's left to see. But finding out is bound to be more tolerable than facing the wives' floor alone, so I agree to follow him.

I can't help but be curious about what's behind all of

the closed doors along this hallway, and wonder what was going on under my feet and over my head while I was trapped on the wives' floor every day. This level could almost belong to a different house.

We get into the elevator, and I'm not surprised a few moments later when the doors open to reveal the basement. But its chemical smell and flickering lights don't frighten me this time. I'll never trust Vaughn, but I can feel that things have changed. The world is not what I thought it was, and my brother is asleep upstairs, and somehow I know that I won't be harmed by this place this time.

There is a silence so great that I can hear the ice crystals cracking and falling from eyelashes of girls who will never blink again. Girls who used to braid my hair, wrap arms and legs around me in sleep, and ask me what the party lights were like in my rare evenings of freedom. They're here and not here.

And Spring herself when she woke at dawn,
Would scarcely know that we were gone.

Unlike two of my sister wives, I still have a pulse. I feel like a traitor.

As we walk, Vaughn says, "The hallucinations that caused you to harm yourself were very interesting. Your brother did experience some nightmares—I'd asked him to keep a journal—but he was, for lack of a better word, sane. I can't say the same thing for you."

He restrained me to a bed and filled me with drugs and took endless notes. The only company I had was my ailing domestic, who appeared to be even worse off than I was. But he wants to talk about sane.

"I'd like to try something different this time," he says. "I'd like to let you have more freedom. It occurs to me that I've treated you like a caged animal. I'd like for you to travel with your brother and me while you receive your treatments. I think you'd enjoy yourself."

I don't know how to answer. I'm scared to admit to myself that I might be willing to do as he asks. I do want to see what more is out there. I am starting to believe in the methods he's using to find this cure.

"You don't have to answer me now," Vaughn says. "Before we get to that, there is the matter of my son and grandson."

We've stopped before a closed door, and my heart starts pounding. My palms fill with sweat. Whatever is behind that door, I know it's going to be a bargaining chip.

I find my voice to say, "I can't force them to come back here; Linden has to decide for himself."

"So modest," Vaughn says, rapping his knuckle against the tip of my nose. "Still refusing to see the power you have over my son. And, perhaps more important, over your former sister wife."

"Cecily?" I say.

"Something tells me that she plays the biggest hand in keeping Linden and Bowen away from home. It's such a surprise because she used to be the obedient one."

I never would have described Cecily as obedient. But I suppose that's what she was to Vaughn. He earned her trust by being the parent she'd never had, and when she finally saw that she was being used, she ran as far and as fast as she could. Nothing will bring her back now.

"She'll listen to you," Vaughn says. "She'll follow you anywhere."

"She wouldn't follow me back here," I say.

"Let's just hope that she does," Vaughn says, and he opens the door.

At first I don't register what it is I'm seeing. I'm too afraid to let my eyes focus. But then I see a room like the one that kept me imprisoned the last time I was here, complete with a fake window that would show a fake horizon if it were turned on. Instead the screen is turned off. What's the point when there's no one to look at it?

There are several machines surrounding a bed, all of them with wires leading to a still body that breathes rhythmically. Colored fluids jolt back and forth through IV tubes. His skin is gray. His skin is gray, and my brain won't register what this is. Won't accept that this is happening, that the boy on that bed is the very same to give me my first kiss, and to show me the atlas with a river that has my name.

Gabriel. I rush to his side.

But there's nothing that my presence here will do. He doesn't feel it when I sweep my hand along the length of his face. He doesn't even know that I'm here.

"What have you done to him?" I say.

"He's seen my most valuable research. I couldn't very well let him run loose."

"How long has he been here?" My fingers make a fist around the bedsheet.

"Oh, goodness," Vaughn says, like it's a chore bothering to try to remember. "However long you were here. You wouldn't have known he was with you on the drive back home; you slept like the dead the whole way. He's fine, though, if that's what you're wondering. It's an induced coma, easy enough to undo."

"So undo it," I say through gritted teeth.

"I'm certain that once he awakens, we can all be one big happy family again," Vaughn says. "Once my son is home, of course."

"Rowan," I whisper. It used to be that a whisper would have him sitting bolt upright. The slightest noise would send him into high alert. But Vaughn's treatments have changed him. I crawl onto the mattress beside him and shake his shoulder. "Rowan."

He winces, and it takes a few seconds for the sleep to leave his eyes, and then concern takes over. He sees that I'm rattled. "What is it?"

"I have to go," I say.

He sits up. "Go? Go where?"

"I have to find my ex-husband." Ex-husband. The word sounds too strange and simple to tell the whole story.

"Are you worried about something happening to you?" he says. "I'll go with you."

Right now that would be the only thing to comfort me. But I shake my head. "You can't. House—" I hesitate. What do I call the man who's at the root of all this? Housemaster Vaughn? Dr. Ashby? But in the end it sounds strange to say it any other way than how I was taught. "Housemaster Vaughn says that you need to stay here and rest so he can monitor your progress."

"That's crazy. I feel fine," he says. "I'll talk to him—"

"No," I say. "Just do as he asks. Please."

I can't raise my eyes to meet his. I can't let him see that there are things I want to say to him, if only I trusted the privacy of these walls. I can't let him see that I'm being manipulated. I can't do anything to jeopardize Gabriel's safety.

But Rowan already knows something is up.

He puts his hand on my shoulder and stares me down until I raise my eyes. "Do you want me to come with you?" he asks.

Yes. A million times yes.

"I'll be all right. Housemaster Vaughn is sending his driver with me. He wants to supervise you and make sure you're all right." What I don't tell him is that Vaughn wants to allow me as much time as possible to convince his son and daughter-in-law to return to his clutches, and that I have to do as he says or Gabriel won't ever open his eyes again. "I'd feel better if you stayed here and rested. Besides, as you've pointed out, Housemaster Vaughn is doing so much for the both of us. We should trust him, right?"

Rowan falls back against the pillow. "I don't trust anyone," he says. "Except for you."

It hurts to breathe. "Trust me, then," I say.

"Always," he says.

He knows something is wrong.

I can tell, or maybe I'm just wishing.

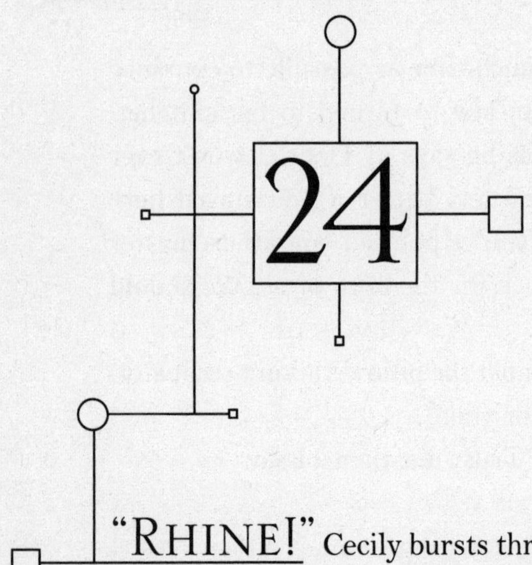

24

"RHINE!" Cecily bursts through two of Madame's guards and throws her arms around me, and we go spinning from the force. "Jared told us what happened. How could you run away and leave us? We were so worried!"

She's perfumed like one of Madame's girls, but without all the stench and decay. She's wearing a sequined dress that's too big for her, and blue eye shadow that drowns her eyes in their sockets. Costume beads are dripping from her neck.

All I can think as she's hugging me and telling me she missed me is that I don't want to force her back to the mansion. I don't want her to have to face the man who murdered our sister wife and quite possibly caused Cecily's brutal miscarriage. I'm working up the courage to assure her that I'll go with her back to the mansion, that I'll keep her safe. I'm trying to find the words, but all I'm finding is guilt. If anything happens to Gabriel, it will be my fault. If anything happens to her, it will be my fault.

When we break apart, she blinks and her eyes disappear and reemerge in all that blue. "You're wearing your green skirt," she says. "You went back there, didn't you?"

"Yes," I blurt, just to be done with it. "He wants to meet us at Reed's, so we can collect Bowen and Elle." We're standing at a distance from Madame, who is watching us between a curtain of guards but not approaching. She's far enough away that she won't hear us, and Vaughn's limo is idling out of sight while the driver waits for me. We're alone, away from the possibility of being overheard or recorded, and it may be the only chance that I get to tell Cecily the truth about Gabriel and what I saw in Hawaii, the frightening, amazing reality that there's more life out there than we were taught to believe.

I want to. I'm so desperate to tell someone, even if it's my little sister wife, who is as powerless as I am. But I know that I can't. She knew my secrets once before, and the consequences were devastating. This secret is too precious. I can't.

"Housemaster Vaughn caught up with me after I found my brother," I say. "My brother is back at the mansion now. It's a long story, and I'd like to tell you about it, but—"

"You've come to convince me and Linden to go back home, haven't you? It's okay. I thought about it, and Linden and I talked it through, and we can't go on like this—running away and leaving Bowen behind. The best thing for us to do is go home." She hugs me again.

She's abuzz with energy; I can't remember the last time she seemed this happy. "I'm so glad you came back," she says, and now she's pulling me toward Madame's carnival and calling out for Linden.

Madame grabs her by the back of the dress as we pass by. "Keep it down, child!" she growls in what I think is her Russian accent. "You want to wake up my girls?" I don't know that I've ever heard her call someone "child" before. Usually it's "stupid girl" or "worthless."

"And take off that dress," she says. "You're too scrawny. You're dragging it in the dirt."

Cecily fusses with the skirt, indignant but still in high spirits. I'd expected it to take more convincing to get her to return to the mansion, but it seems that Linden talked her into it before I returned. Stubborn as she is, she'll always be devoted to him.

We find Linden at the merry-go-round, and I begin to suspect that Cecily's willingness to return to the mansion has a lot to do with her wanting to take him as far from memories of Rose as she can. Or maybe she's willing to pretend his father isn't what she knows him to be, because then at least Linden can still have a father at all.

He sees my reflection in the metal at the heart of the structure. "Jared told us you found your brother," he says. "I'm glad."

"Thanks," I say, my voice as hollow as his. We always seem to be feeling the same way. "Your father sent the car for us. He's hoping you'll come home."

That gets him to turn around. His eyes are dead. He looks as though he hasn't slept at all while I've been away. "Is he? Cecily, you should return that dress and those things, then."

Cecily knows she's being dismissed, and for once she goes without incident.

Once she's gone, he struggles to speak, but the words don't come.

"I've learned some things about my parents too," I say. "Things I don't like very much."

"I used to read about the twenty-first century when I was younger," he says. "I wanted to know about things like cancer and muscular dystrophy and asthma. I wanted to know what could be so awful that we were so desperate to be rid of it. Did you know that the treatment for cancer was toxic? Parents would rather poison their children if it might save them than do nothing if it meant watching them die. I've been thinking about that, and I've been thinking about what you said about that poem and how hundreds of years ago people still must have questioned why they were here. I think humans have always been desperate. I think it has always been about doing something awful if it might help, when the only other option is death. Maybe that's what being a parent is supposed to feel like."

"Is that how you feel about Bowen?" I ask. "Would you hurt him if you thought it would help him?"

"I've never had to make a decision like that," he says. "Somehow I can't bring myself to imagine it."

"Maybe it *is* desperation," I say. "Maybe we can't let things fall apart without trying. We can't let go of the people we love."

He looks at me, and in the sunlight his eyes come alive with greens and golds. "Sometimes we can," he says.

Linden follows after Cecily, and I tell him I'll be there soon. I know we won't be coming back here, and there's someone I need to see before we leave.

I find her in the green tent, elbow-deep in a barrel of orange dye. Cloths are dripping from a clothesline onto her hair.

"You know," Lilac says, not looking up, "I've seen all kinds of foolish girls, but none so foolish they'd come back here if they got away."

Her dark skin is victim to the green tint. Her eyes are heavy with silver dust to match her frosty lips.

"I never stay gone, it seems," I say.

She laughs, holding up a square of tattered cloth and hanging it on the line. "So that boy is the tyrant you were trying to escape, huh?"

"It's not as simple as all that," I say. Her wry grin makes me uneasy. "He wouldn't have hurt me, but that's not enough of a reason to stay where I'm not meant to be."

"You didn't want to be a pretty thing on a shelf," Lilac says, plunging a little girl's dress into the barrel. Madame must be going through an orange phase. She likes the children to match as they do her bidding. "I get it. My husband wasn't a tyrant either. Not bad-looking, either, as first generations go."

Lilac was married. This doesn't surprise me as much as I'd have suspected. I knew that she was stolen off of the street, and like Claire and Silas I'd assumed she was sold into prostitution. But it would make sense that she was sold as a bride. She's a work of art; her teeth are straight; her eyes are sultry; she's intelligent. She's a commodity in a sea of broken girls.

"I stuck around for years," she says. "I didn't think I'd have a chance running away. I would have stayed until the end if it wasn't for Maddie. Something wasn't right even when she was in the womb. My husband wanted to have her destroyed as soon as we found out; he thought we could start over right away, have a baby that wasn't screwed up. So I left. Figured it was worth a shot."

"You knew I'd get her back to New York," I say. "Didn't you?"

"I hoped."

Hope, that risky, illustrious thing. It should have gone extinct by now, but we keep it alive. The girls who disappear but find themselves still breathing. The girls who will make it home. The girls who won't. We hope for things we may not get to see, and we hold on with both hands because it's one of the few things that can't be stolen from us.

"She made a friend there," I say. "I think she's happy."

Lilac wrings out the little dress, orange dye leaking like blood through her fingers. "I'm glad," she says.

I want to suggest that Lilac leave here while Madame is showing some humanity, but I think better of it. Lilac gives no indication that she plans to leave. She's rooted to that spot, dyeing cloths to set the atmosphere for Madame's latest whim.

She doesn't meet my eyes, and I suspect her skin is going sallow under all that makeup. I suspect her days are drawing to a close. So all I say is, "I spent some time with your family. They'd want you to know that you're still very loved, Grace."

At the mention of her real name, she pauses. Only for a moment, though, and then she kneads the fabric in the dye with vigor. "Thank you for seeing Maddie home," she says. "I hope you find what it is you're looking for. Take care of yourself, Rhine."

Her eyes are misting. I can tell she doesn't want me to see.

"Take care," is all I say.

Cecily and Madame are standing by the gate, holding both of each other's hands and talking in low voices. I find Linden standing at a distance, staring back at the Ferris wheel. "It is pretty spectacular, isn't it?" he says. "You look at it and you can almost hear all the laughter from another time."

"I think so too," I say.

When Cecily sees Linden and me, she breaks away

from Madame and waves. The blue has been scrubbed from her eyelids, rendering them gray.

"What are they talking to each other about?" I say.

"They've become friends," Linden says. Usually he's protective of Cecily, but he hardly sounds interested. He hardly even sounds like he's awake. His heart is broken, and only Rose would know how to mend it.

As we're walking toward the limo, Cecily shows me the fuchsia silk purse Madame gave her; it's fat with cosmetics. I don't know what to make of her high spirits; maybe it has something to do with the anticipation of being reunited with Bowen. He's all she can talk about on the drive home. She rests against Linden and dangles the purse over her head and checks off the things she misses the most about her son. His curls. His laughter. The colors in his hazel eyes that are different every day. She wonders if he has started to crawl while she was away.

Linden is watching my struggle to stay awake. I've disembarked from an airplane, discovered Gabriel in the place of nightmares, lied to my brother, and traveled from Florida to South Carolina. My mind is furious and awake, but my muscles will no longer oblige. The world is going in slow motion. Voices are muffled and far away. I hear Linden saying what sounds like "Come here," and I feel my cheek settling against his knee, and then everything in the world is gone.

A bump in the road startles me awake. The limo is taking us down all the back roads I've come to recognize. When we stop in front of Reed's house, the driver's voice comes through an overhead speaker to tell us that Housemaster Vaughn has requested that we wait for him here. He's tied up with an important project and cannot be disturbed until evening.

I wonder if the project is Rowan or Gabriel.

Cecily opens her door the moment it comes unlocked, and she's running for the front door calling out for Elle and Reed.

My muscles are stiff, and Linden patiently waits for me to stumble outside before following suit. He closes the car door behind us and waits for the limo to drive away, before turning to me. "Feeling all right?" he asks.

"Yes," I say.

"You're lying." He pushes the hair back behind my shoulder, his knuckles brush against my neck, and I don't know how I'm still standing. I want to fall into his arms. I want to tell him everything. My body aches and my heart is sick, and yet I'm excited about what I've seen. I'm excited to think that there could be a world better than what has been promised to us, and at the same time I'm frightened.

I want to take him with me. I want him to see that there's more to our lives than dying and being saved.

"Linden?"

"What is it?" he asks.

"There is something I'd like to show you, when I'm able. I don't think you'd believe me if I told you about it now." I look down at the grass drifting against our ankles, full of colorful weeds. "Until then you might think I'm crazy to say this, but I've been thinking about what you said earlier. I really am glad we were born. I can't imagine anything more important than being alive."

I venture to look at him, and he's not quite smiling. "You need sleep," he says.

He doesn't believe me, but that's okay.

You'll see, Linden. You'll see cities breathing and changing color at all the different times of day. You'll see what the world used to be and what it will be. You'll believe me then.

There's a loud crack like a gunshot. We turn in the direction of the sound. Another crack, and another. "Come on," Linden says, and we run after the sounds that lead us behind the house, where Reed is taking an axe to his giant shed.

"Uncle Reed?" Linden says.

Reed stops when he sees us, and waves. "Hey!" he says. "You're back! Come over and help me with this."

"What *is* this?" Linden asks.

"The plane is ready to fly," I say, daring to feel excitement.

"Damn straight, doll. There are axes in the other shed."

Cecily comes out of the house, Bowen straddled to her

hip. "What's all the noise? What's going on?" she says, handing the baby to Elle.

"We're going to fly, kid," Reed says, and hammers the axe into the shed again, causing it to shudder.

I can't tell if Linden disapproves of what we're doing, but he joins in anyway. It goes on for what feels like an hour, until we're sweating and gasping, and it's a wonder that it's taking so long to destroy this thing, when it was hardly stable enough to stand on its own in the first place.

Reed says, "One more push and I think we've got it, kids. Make it count."

With the last of our strength, we push our bodies against the same wall. Cecily's feet are slipping in the grass, and she kicks to keep herself from falling.

I've seen plenty of destroyed buildings in my life, but I've never seen them actually coming down in such a way. It's astounding the way the shed slants in one direction like a page that's closing. Linden pulls Cecily and me away, and we watch as the walls crack and splinter around the shape of the plane. Pieces fall amid clouds of dirt and dust.

Reed busies himself clearing all of the debris from the plane. Cecily is bursting with giggles because it's the greatest thing she's ever seen; she didn't quite believe Reed when he told her that he was hiding a plane in the shed.

By the time we've cleared away all of the shed debris

from the plane's wings and body, the sun is starting to set. "There's still enough light to fly it," Reed says. He's climbing into the open door that leads to the cockpit.

"Are you sure it will start?" Cecily asks.

"We're about to find out," Reed says. "Climb in."

Cecily moves forward, but Linden grabs her arm and says, "No, love. It isn't safe."

She wrests away from him. "Stay down here if you want to," she says. "But I'm tired of you always holding me back."

"Love . . ."

She sees that she's hurt him, and she softens. "It'll be fun," she says. "A little adventure."

He pulls her toward him and he stoops down, and she rises on tiptoes so their foreheads can touch. "I almost lost you once," he says.

"Nothing will happen." She kisses him. "When are we ever going to have another chance to do something like this?"

Reed is annoyed by their display. He starts the engine, and the little propeller at the nose of the plane starts to spin; the ground is vibrating, sending waves through my body. We're all choking on the dirt plumes. "Cowards!" he says. Just as he's closing the door by the pilot's seat, I hoist myself through it.

"I'll go," I say. Boarding this dilapidated plane without a tarmac and being flown by Reed won't be the craziest thing I've experienced this week.

"There isn't a runway," Linden protests, trying to appeal to my better senses. "And my uncle has never flown—"

Reed slams the door shut and pats the empty seat beside him. The cockpit is so cramped that I can't stand at full height. There are more gauges than I can count, levers pointing in different directions, but the pedals look at least vaguely similar to the ones in cars.

"You can be my copilot," he says, gesturing again to the seat beside him.

The engine is shaking the entire plane. My heart is pounding, but in the best way. I want to fly for that horizon like I want my next breath. I've spent my whole life on the ground looking up. I've spent so many afternoons on Jenna's trampoline reaching the greatest heights that I can. And now that I've had a taste of greater height, I don't think I'll ever have my fill.

Still, Linden does have a point. "Have you ever flown?" I ask.

Reed looks offended. "I've read," he says. "I know what all of these gauges and switches mean. And I've been on a plane before; they were still popular when I was a boy, you know. Don't look at me like that."

Cecily is pounding on the door, and when Reed opens it, she pushes her way inside, Linden on her heels. "I talked him into it," she says.

Linden looks less than enthusiastic.

"That's the spirit!" Reed says, and he pats the copilot's seat that was promised to me. "Best way to face your fears is to look straight at them with the best view in the house."

After Linden sits down in the copilot's seat, Cecily rakes both of her hands through his hair, and she kisses the top of his head and says something in a low voice. I see a nervous smile in his reflection in the glass.

There's hardly room for Cecily and me to be standing here, and Reed says, "You girls are going to have to sit in back, at least while we take off."

Cecily and I move through the curtain that takes us into the cramped passenger cabin, and we sit across from each other, knees touching. Cecily is gripping the edge of her seat. "I'm terrified," she says, like it's the greatest feeling to have.

The plane jerks and splutters, but then we're moving, and with a squeal Cecily grabs my skirt like it's a horse's reins. Through the oval windows on each wall, we watch the grass begin speeding past us; the house is getting farther away; Elle, standing in the grass, cradles Bowen's head in the curve of her neck to protect him from the wind we're causing as we go forward and then up.

We don't go nearly as high as Vaughn's private jet took me, but we can see the top of Reed's house, and then we're high enough that we can't see the cracks in the road or the weeds in the grass and we can't tell which trees are dying. Everything looks tidy and healthy.

When Cecily and I peek through the curtain into the cockpit, Reed is laughing and Linden is pale.

"See?" Cecily says. "It's not so bad."

Linden looks like he wants to throw up. He's focusing on his shoes. I wedge myself between the two pilot seats. "Pretend we aren't going to land down there," I tell him. "Pretend that we're going to fly straight across the ocean to a place where everyone lives to be a hundred."

In answer he raises his eyes to the windshield for the first time.

We fly over empty fields and little gray lakes and sparsely scattered houses. We go in a long loop that eventually leads us back to Reed's.

Linden is still too anxious to speak, but it's starting to register that he's flying, that there's more to the world than what we can see from standing in one place.

I lean over Linden, cup my hand around his ear, and say, "There's a whole world of this."

He turns his head to face me, and our noses almost touch. He sees my smile, sees that I'm hiding something, and I think he understands. "Really?" he says.

Cecily and Reed are talking to each other, excitedly pointing out the scenery, and they aren't paying attention to us.

"I've seen more than this," I tell him. "I know you don't believe me. I wouldn't either."

The skepticism in his eyes is intermingled with hope. A year ago he wouldn't have dared hope for anything beyond the mansion walls. I like to think I've had something to do with that.

"From the start I've never known what surprises you'd bring," he says.

"Not all of them are bad, are they?" I say.

"Mostly good," he says. "But I've developed a habit of believing you when I shouldn't."

"Give me a chance to prove it you," I say. "Give me time."

"For you, always."

He sits up straight to look out past the nose of the plane, and the happiness that was starting to form on his face is gone at once. Through the window I can see Vaughn's limo winding down the back roads that lead to the house. The only car on the road. From up here it's like a fish that's swimming upstream. "My father," Linden says. And so ends his rush from his greatest act of rebellion. He understands that no matter where he runs or how high he flies, he will always have to come home.

"I'll never hear the end of this one," Reed grumbles. "Back in your seats, kids. I have to figure out how to land this thing." He shoos Cecily and me through the curtain.

The plane was already shaking, but by the time we get to our seats, Reed's landing attempt has Cecily and me clinging to each other in horror. I feel it when we hit the ground, and then it's like we're speeding hopelessly through the field behind Reed's house, and I shut my eyes and will us not to go careening into the house.

I brace my legs against the adjacent seats, but when the plane makes its final jolt, despite my best efforts I go flying across the tiny cabin, and Cecily crashes into me. The storage cabinet flies open and rains little foil packets of food and lotus-embroidered handkerchiefs.

There's a moment of stillness. The engine has stopped, but things are still plinking and hissing under our feet.

"Everyone alive?" Reed calls to us.

We're stumbling as we all pour through the cockpit and out onto the grass. My shoulder is aching, but I'm otherwise intact. Cecily is inspecting her wrist that I'm guessing is sore from the way she braced herself in the last second.

Linden puts his hand to his temple, and it comes back bright with blood that's trickling down the side of his face.

"Oh!" Cecily says. "You're bleeding. Come here; let me see."

He takes a step toward her.

Everything happens in slow motion after that. He raises his foot for the next step, and then he's falling. I swear I can hear the sound of his bones hitting the dirt.

Blood is frothing in his mouth, and his eyes are closed and he's having convulsions.

Cecily drops to his side and she's screaming his name, but she's too afraid to touch him. I'm too afraid to move at all.

Reed takes a step forward but stops when he sees Vaughn running toward us. "Linden!" Vaughn is calling. "Son— Don't touch him! Don't touch him!" He says those words over and over, gasping them, whispering them as he drops into the high grass and forces Cecily out of his way. She crawls a few feet back and then watches, unsure what to do with herself.

Linden is still convulsing, making strained noises, and I'm not sure, but I think he's trying to breathe. And Vaughn, the only one of us who should know how to fix this, looks absolutely panicked. His hands hover over Linden's face, wanting to touch him, to soothe him, but he knows better. He can see that his son's injury is far more serious than the outer wound implies.

Blood is streaming out of Linden's ear, and it's so awful, so unimaginable, that my mind is trying to tell me it's only a trick of the light. Only, I know it isn't. Blood in his mouth, too. He's drowning in it.

There's a man who would drown for you, Annabelle the fortune-teller said, the light of all her metal and plastic treasures jumping around us.

And then Linden goes still, and Cecily is moaning, "Oh god, oh god, Linden," because she realizes before the rest of us that he isn't breathing. Vaughn tells her to shut up, and she does. He's checking for his son's pulse and then clearing the blood and the foam from his mouth. He's feeling for broken ribs, and then he's pressing his fists to the chest and forcing oxygen into the still lungs. For all the tools he has used, the equipment he has engineered, and the solutions he has concocted, all he has to save his son with now are his bare hands.

It isn't enough. Even I know that. The sun is coming down and everything is painted gold. The tiny airplane. Linden's curls.

Vaughn is persistent. It goes on like that forever and ever. But I know it's over when I hear his sob, baritone and booming. I've never seen him cry; I didn't think he could. It would have to take something greater than the end of the world to reduce Vaughn Ashby to tears.

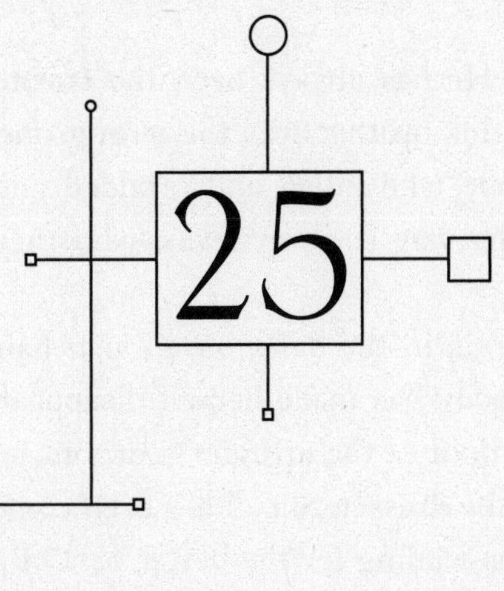

25

I WATCH VAUGHN scoop his son into his arms the way he probably did when Linden was small. I watch unresponsive limbs hanging slack, an open, motionless mouth that once told me "I love you." I watch Vaughn carrying him to the limo and yelling at the driver, who runs out to help what can't be helped. I watch the door close. I watch the limo getting smaller until it disappears.

And then, only then, I fall to my hands and knees.

When Vaughn returns after dark, the front door bursts open. His footsteps are thunderous and his voice is a hiss, and he's telling Reed that he's never, never going to let him see the children again. The children he's talking about are Cecily, Bowen, and me. Reed is broken. He says nothing. He's in his kitchen surrounded by mason jars, where watermelons and sprouts are growing beautifully according to his plan. He has always been the one to make things live while his brother was the wrong one. His brother was the one who killed and prodded and destroyed. That was the way it always was, who they always were.

I'm in the living room, in the dark, on an armchair that reeks of cigars. Cecily has made herself disappear. There's no lock on the door of the upstairs bedroom, so she barricaded it with the dresser. She didn't even come out for Bowen, who was wailing for the better part of a half hour before Elle found something to distract him in the library. She really is a skilled caregiver; she can open a textbook about air conditioner models and pretend to be reading from it, pointing to the pictures as she makes up a story about angels and falling stars. I was listening to her earlier, her young voice coming down the stairs as I focused on a crack in the ceiling. It took me away from the ugliness in my head for a while.

Vaughn breezes past me, and at first I don't think he realizes I'm here, but without looking back at me, he says, "Get everyone out to the car."

The screen door slams behind him. I hear a floorboard creak, and when I get to the base of the staircase, I see Cecily at the top step. It's too dark for me to see her face. All I see is the sheen in her eyes that are staring through me. She's got the fuchsia purse on her shoulder and Linden's suitcase in her hand. We brought clothes and supplies with us when we went to South Carolina, but things like Bowen's formula and Linden's sketch pads were left behind.

"It's time?" she says. They're the first words she's spoken to me all night. They might be the first words she's said at all since she has become a fourteen-year-old widow.

"Yes," I say.

"Elle," she says, not raising her voice, not looking back to see if her domestic is following as she descends.

We don't say good-bye to Reed, but I look over my shoulder and see him in the kitchen, staring through the table. This isn't his fault. I want to tell him that. I want to believe that the same way that I want to forget that I was the one who should have been sitting in the copilot's seat, and that the blood on the windshield should have been mine.

Cecily is quiet as we make our way to the idling limo. She's been quiet all evening, not a murmur, not a sob. But then she looks into the waiting car, and she sees the wraparound leather seat where the three of us sat just hours before, on our way back from South Carolina. The car smells like the mansion. It smells like the past year of our lives.

She turns around and looks at me, as if to ask what I make of this nightmare.

I can tell that she hasn't cried at all. I don't know if this is a healthy response, but I haven't cried either.

She opens her mouth to speak, but only a feeble

croaking sound comes out. Elle and Vaughn are waiting behind us.

"Go on," I tell her softly. "I'm right behind you."

She nods, crawls into the seat by the window. I follow her. Then Elle with the sleeping baby. Cecily watches him. "What will happen to us?" she says breathlessly. "I gave Linden everything I had."

"Don't be foolish, Cecily," Vaughn says. "You had nothing to give. You were nothing then, and you're nothing now." He closes the door on us.

Don't you dare believe that, is what I would say to her if I were brave enough to speak. She clenches her jaw, tightens her grip on the purse strap, and stares out her window.

I don't see Rowan when we make it back to the mansion, and I'm not foolish enough to ask about Gabriel, which would surely invite new wrath from Vaughn. I fear that he would kill Gabriel just to prove some sick point. In any case, Vaughn has vanished by the time an attendant opens the car door for us. We're guided through the kitchen, which is empty and tidy, though there is the faint smell of food. I think Vaughn had been anticipating a family dinner.

When we get to the elevator, the attendant hands me a plastic key card strung on a silver necklace. The same one Linden gave to me when he decided to make me first wife.

"Housemaster Vaughn has requested that you come

with me," the attendant says to Elle. Cecily takes the baby and the diaper bag from Elle before she's led away.

There's only one place in the world left for us to go. I swipe my key card, the elevator doors open, and I push the button that will take us to the wives' floor.

For what feels like hours, I sit in the library and listen to Cecily's brutal wails. She's finally found whatever it took for her to grieve, but whenever I knock on her door and call to her, she falls silent, waiting for me to leave her alone.

I pace the halls, missing the perfumed must of the incense and feeling unwelcome without it. Eventually I crawl onto my old bed and close my eyes against the light of my bedside lamp. Something deep within me cannot summon the wherewithal to grieve. I drift into a dream of Linden on the wet Hawaii sand, gray, eyes closed. The image gets closer like shutter clicks in a camera. A hundred pictures of a boy without life.

With a gasp I open my eyes.

I hear a rustle in the doorway, and I turn and find Cecily standing there. She's red-faced and wringing her hands. Wet hair sticks to her cheeks like bony copper fingers trying to pull her back. She opens her mouth to speak, but her lips are quivering, and only more tears come.

"Come here," I say. My voice is hoarse. She takes slow steps, and I pull back the blanket so we can both crawl beneath it.

After a very long time she says, "We're all that's left." And then she breaks down again, and I busy myself with holding her, saying, "I know" and "I'm here," because if I can just keep on this way, there's no time for me to face it myself. There is a dark place calling to me, but I will not go just yet. I know I can't return from it.

Eventually she exhausts herself and falls into a sleep so fragile that I wake her once with my breathing. Night deepens. There is no one to turn on the hall lights. No dinner is brought to us. There is no one keeping us trapped in this room, and it seems impossible that I ever could have wanted it that way.

I'm woken from my half sleep when Cecily moves toward me. My back is to her, but I can feel the mattress shift. Her breathing is matched by the heaviness of rain that has started outside. She weaves her fingers into my hair. She thinks I'm sleeping, and she doesn't want to wake me. She only needs to touch my hair, to make and undo little braids so that her hands can stop shaking. She only needs to not be alone.

And I stay very still, because I need it too.

Last year I was lying in this bed, half-asleep, when Linden climbed in beside me. He was warm, and he smelled like alcohol and the chocolate éclairs we'd brought home with us. This was where he burrowed against me and asked me not to leave him.

I thought I had it all worked out. I would run away. I went

through every scenario I could think of. But I never thought that he would be the one to leave me. I never thought being without him could hurt this much.

My muscles tighten. I break with a sob, and I'm surprised to hear his name come out of my mouth.

Cecily sobs too. We make horrible sounds echoing each other. I don't know how long this goes on before she crawls out of bed. The bathroom light comes on, but she closes the door, reducing the light to slivers.

She runs the water for a very long time. I listen as her sobs taper down to sniffles and intermittent coughs. She opens the bathroom door several minutes later, shaking, silhouetted. Her hair and hands are dripping.

"Tell me about the twins," she urges.

"What?"

"You and your brother," she says. "When your parents died, what did you do? How did you get to a place where you could just carry on? Tell me. Tell me, because I'm sure that feeling this way is going to kill me."

The last time I told her about the twins, she betrayed my trust. But she was a different girl all those months ago, still so easily coerced by Vaughn's promises that we'd all be a happy family. She's brutally wiser now.

"A feeling can't kill you," I say. "The twins thought the same thing as you, and they're both still alive."

"How?"

I go to her, and I mean to steer her back to bed, but she says that she needs air, and she leads me out into the hallway, and then onto the elevator. We go through the labyrinth of hallways, through the kitchen, out to the rose garden. I think she was hoping to find something here, but it's missing.

"I can't breathe," she says, gripping the railing of our wedding gazebo. Her words are fast and tight.

I stand beside her, all sympathy and guilt, remembering a day when I thought this demanding child of a bride was incapable of feelings.

"You are breathing," I tell her.

She shakes her head.

"I know what you're feeling," I say.

"Not like this you don't." She slides forward until her face is on the railing. Her back heaves with the weight of her breaths. All around us is the smell of damp spring, everything still wet from the recent rain. She's reduced to whispers. "Not like this."

I don't dare to touch her. Loss is a knowledge I'm sorry to have. Perhaps the only thing worse than experiencing it is watching it replay anew in someone else—all its awful stages picking up like a chorus that has to be sung.

It takes her such a long time to understand that her lungs and heart and blood are going to keep working. Nothing will stop. No feeling can be the end of a person, or else the virus would hardly be our biggest threat.

I sit on a wet step to wait for her, and to hold myself together. My own breaths are shaky; my head feels swimmy and light. I try to find shapes in the stars—only, they don't make sense tonight. I can't remember what they mean.

For a while everything feels still and unreal. But then I'm filled with thoughts of what the morning will have to bring. I'll make the bed, and then what?

When Cecily comes to sit beside me, we rest our heads together and I tell her a final story about the twins. The one whose grief drove him to set the country ablaze. And the one who found a way to love her captor.

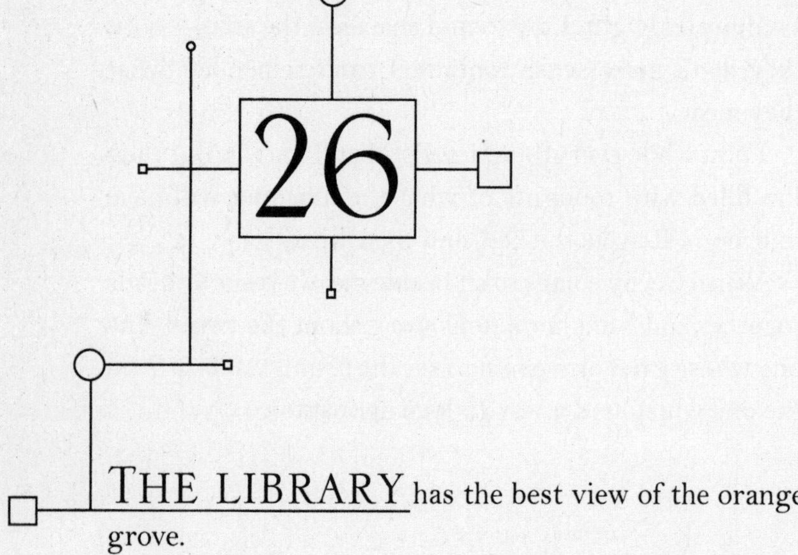

26

THE LIBRARY has the best view of the orange grove.

The morning is a gray photograph of a gray world where it is always raining; Cecily and I are standing at the window, watching Vaughn dig his son's grave.

"The orange grove is a good place," Cecily says, and her voice cracks. "Rose will be able to find him there."

Many deaths have happened in this house, but none of the bodies were ever buried. Linden once told me that his father said the virus might be detrimental to the soil, and I never quite believed that. I believed that the bodies became Vaughn's experiments. But after twenty-two years of working to save him, Vaughn is finally going to let Linden be at peace.

Linden is wrapped in a white sheet on a gurney, and for some reason I can't rid myself of the worry that he's going to be soaked by this drizzling rain.

It's going to be a shallow grave, but it will be enough. There will be room for roots to spread out and for things to grow over him.

When Vaughn lifts the body from the gurney, Cecily grabs my shirt in both her fists. My muscles tense. Vaughn kneels by the grave, and at first I think he's going to lower his son in and be done with it, but then he peels the sheet away from Linden's face. My mind goes numb. That is Linden and not Linden at all.

He hugs his son, rocks him, reinforces his grip. Cecily moves to hide her face in my sleeve, but then she changes her mind and we make ourselves watch. We have to. He belonged to us—we have to. The sheet is raised again and the body is lowered, and the dirt covers him.

As he's buried, my heart is a stone, burying itself in me.

So many things were said in the time I had with Linden. Lies were spun and things were whispered in the darkness of my bedroom. There was laughter, anger, party chatter, and occasionally the truth.

But now there are no words. Rain makes gentle noise against the house.

Cecily turns away from the window and sweeps her fingers over the table where the three of us as sister wives often took our tea. I hear a faint whimper as she moves out of the room.

For the rest of the morning I stay in the library, curled in the overstuffed chair that has always been my favorite, and I read one of the romance novels Jenna loved. Every so often I hear the first notes of a song Cecily is playing on the keyboard, but she can only go on for a few seconds before it becomes too much effort. She doesn't have the strength for an entire song.

She was right. There is no finality to a funeral. Linden is gone and I saw him go, but there's still the sense that he's somewhere. Everything in me is telling me to go outside and find him, bring him back.

It's thundering outside. Lightning flashes. I try not to think of Linden all alone out there. I try to read what's on the page, but I'm nearly halfway through the book, and I haven't retained a single name, a single word of what's happening.

An attendant comes for me. First generation, as most of them are. He stands in the doorway for a long time, hesitating. Maybe he thinks that I'm the House Governor's widow and I'll crumble and crack if he approaches me the wrong way. So he stares at me, and I stare at the page.

"What is it?" I say without looking up.

"The Housemaster has requested to see you downstairs. I was asked to escort you."

I close the book, set it on the chair, leave the desperate lovers therein to find their way back to each other, or to lose each other entirely. Jenna said those stories always either ended happily or everyone died. She said, *What else is there?*

Sometimes I can't help being angry that she left me behind.

The elevator chimes as its doors open, and Cecily comes out of her bedroom. She has changed into her nightgown, and her hair is a mess. I hope this means she's been sleeping. "Where are you taking her?" she asks the attendant.

He doesn't know how to answer her in a way that's safe. She is prone to temper tantrums, and Vaughn is surely on the warpath today already without having to deal with her.

"I'm only going downstairs," I say.

"You can't go," she says. "You won't come back."

"Of course I'll come back," I say.

She shakes her head furiously, barricades the waiting elevator with her body. "No," she says. "Rhine, please, no, no. I know that you won't come back."

"Cecily," I snap. I want to comfort her, but I am too exhausted. I want to find a lie that will soothe her, but I've run out. At this point I could use a nice lie for myself; nobody is ever kind enough to lie to me. "Go back to bed. It's fine."

She doesn't move. "You can't leave me by myself," she's whimpering as I push her out of my way. I don't want to leave her here. I don't. But Vaughn seems to have deemed her disposable. What use is she to him now? She can't give him another grandchild. I won't let her give him a final reason to do it. I won't bury her, too. She tries to get between the elevator doors as they're closing between us, but I give her a hard shove, and her recovery time isn't quick enough.

"Thank you." The attendant sighs, exasperated. "Something else, that one. She's too much to handle most days."

"This morning she watched from a window as her husband was buried," I say. "What did you do this morning?"

He clears his throat and looks straight ahead at the doors.

When the doors open on the ground floor, Rowan is waiting for me in the hallway, and I can see by his frown that he's all set to pity me. I steel myself.

"You're to go straight through the kitchen. The car will be waiting outside," the attendant tells us as I leave the elevator.

After the elevator doors have closed, Rowan says, "Dr. Ashby told me what happened to his son, your ex-husband. I'm sorry, Rhine."

"Linden," I say quietly as I start walking. "His name was Linden."

"You still had feelings for him, yes?" Rowan says.

I use the word that Jared said. "He was my friend."

I don't say anything further, and I don't look at him, though I feel his eyes watching me. My brother was never especially good with compassion. His idea of helping is to find the quickest way to overcome the loss, and

I'm not quite ready. I'm not sure it's possible.

I move down the hallway and through the kitchen and to the outdoors.

Vaughn is waiting by the limo's open door. The light rain makes little shadows on his gray suit. I can't bring myself to look at him, but he puts his hand on my shoulder to stop me from getting into the car, and he tells Rowan to go on ahead, and then Vaughn closes the door.

"It seems the terms of our agreement have changed," he says. "But I still have something you want, don't I?"

He lowers his face until our eyes meet, and he waits for me to answer with the obvious, as though I'm a child.

"Gabriel," I say.

"And you do still have something that I want. I still need your cooperation."

I don't know what more he wants from me. He already has my DNA, and the insides of my eyes, and my brother. He has enough fuel to take us all to a place where people go on living, indifferent or else oblivious to our misery. None of it is going to save his son.

"Can I still count on that cooperation?" he asks.

His eyes are almost kind. I have to look away from them, but I nod.

"Good girl," he says, and opens the door for me. As long as Vaughn is still alive, there will always be doors to open. There will always be something horrible waiting on the other side.

On the flight out to Hawaii, Vaughn tells us that he's sorry he didn't arrange for meals, but our next treatment is going to require a twelve-hour fasting. He has pills for us instead, and I am grateful when they make me feel drowsy. On some faraway level I'm aware of my body curling up on the seat, my eyes closing.

I'm barely conscious by the time we land. I try to call for my brother, but I can't move my tongue. Through a sheen of darkness I see the oriental rug rushing toward me as I fall, and then someone is holding me by the arms and I'm eased into a wheelchair.

I feel the mugginess and the heat. I hear the city noises and the ocean's waves, everything through a vacuum as I fall down, down, into the darkness I'm craving.

The darkness isn't perfect, though. Bits of reality peek through. A cold metal table under me. Surgical tools rattling on a rolling cart. Voices talking miles away from me, in a place where it still means something to be alive.

I wake up spluttering and gagging. A tube has just been pulled from my throat; when I manage to open my eyes, I see the nurse taking it away. It's bright in this room, and I can't see the nurse's face, can't tell if she's first generation or new or something else entirely.

She runs an ice cube across my lips and tells me that I'm brave. I want to ask her what's happening, but I can't speak.

"Rest now," I hear Vaughn say. "It's done, Rhine. It's all done."

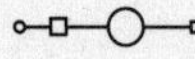

Linden is in the darkness with me, and he's trying to speak. But something isn't right. I can't hear his words. I can't understand them.

"You have to go now," I tell him, and he does. Even the dead know that we have to face certain things alone.

When I open my eyes again, I'm in a white room on an inclined mattress.

"Rhine?" Rowan says, and at once he has moved from the window to my bedside. He's all dressed in white like the walls and the curtains and the blanket that's drawn up to my chest. There's another bed on the other side of the end table, its blankets disturbed. I suppose Rowan recovered sooner than I did.

He takes my hand. Odd, he was never one for affection. I find that I have the strength to wriggle my fingers between his. The numbness of sleep is receding.

I try to speak. "What's happening to us?"

He smiles in a way I've rarely seen since we were children, when we were still foolish enough to think the world had anything to promise us. "Dr. Ashby has done it," Rowan says. "He's modified an existing formula for the cure. He made his official presentation to President Guiltree this morning. We were both supposed to attend, but you've been asleep, and I wanted to be here when you woke up. I wanted to be the one to tell you that we've been cured."

I must still be groggy, because I'm having trouble

understanding. "I thought none of the cures were universal."

He squeezes my hand. "We think this one is," he says. "He's spent this past week testing dosages on us and comparing his findings with other subjects. He's tested all of our hormone levels and our cell counts, and none of the abnormalities of the other treatments have appeared with this one."

All I understand from that is the word "week."

Linden has been dead for a week.

"Rhine?" Rowan says. I hear myself sniffle, and the room blurs through a rush of tears. "What's the matter?" he asks, and dabs at my cheeks with the cuff of his sleeve.

A week. Gabriel has remained frozen for all the things he knows and because I'm the only bargaining chip that could ever awaken him.

Cecily has been alone.

"How can anything be the matter?" my brother says. "You understand, don't you? We're cured."

"I don't care," I say, before the tears make it impossible to speak.

"Cure" is one of the most precious words in the English language. It's a short word. A clean and simple word. But it isn't so easy a thing as it sounds. There are questions like: How will this affect us in ten years? In twenty? What will it do to our children? Our children's children? Our immune systems are going to suffer, I'm being told. We may develop tumors. We'll be more vulnerable to toxins in the air. Minor ailments like colds run the risk of progressing into respiratory infections. Rowan and I have been fitted with tracking devices that will also keep track of our vital signs, which will be monitored around the clock.

In time the scientists are hoping the effects will take to female reproductive systems. There are already studies being planned to test the results of a new generation conceiving with a partner that wasn't born with the virus. This is not the conclusion, but only the beginning, the spark. We will undergo monthly physical examinations. And then there is the matter of certainty. The virus wouldn't have affected us until after my twentieth birthday and Rowan's twenty-fifth. There are fifty other participants in the study who vary in age, but we will all have to survive that fatal year before there's even going to be talk of starting to make these findings public. The hope is that more participants can be brought into the study annually as researchers build data on how the initial subjects are reacting to treatment.

All of this, of course, assumes that the formula for the cure that Vaughn modified will do what it's supposed to, and we won't all die a gruesome death like some subjects in other studies.

And because of the sensitivity and confidentiality of it all, we will not be allowed to return to the public. The president doesn't have the funds to keep all of us here, so we will return to the States, where we'll be monitored by the doctor assigned to our care—Vaughn, as far as Rowan and I are concerned.

I'm back to the familiar role of a prisoner, only this time without the formality of a husband. At least Rowan won't be free to destroy any more labs. He'll have to leave his friends behind, but he doesn't even think enough of them to mention it. Maybe that's why Bee stared at me with such contempt—she knew that for me, Rowan would abandon any life he had built elsewhere.

Rowan is the one who tells me all of these things. He talks softly, patiently, as I sit on the window ledge and watch boats with colorful triangles for sails scratch the ocean.

I don't touch the dinner that's gone cold on my nightstand. I don't ask any questions or give any indication that I've heard what he's telling me.

I watch the perfectly imperfect people several stories below, living their perfectly imperfect lives, and I think about how many decades will have to pass before the whole world can be like that again. I think about how many decades will pass before someone gets another idea to make the world perfect and destroys it completely.

"Rhine, please," Rowan says. He sits on the ledge beside me. "You have to care about this." After our parents died, one morning he interrupted my sulking by throwing the blankets away from me. The cold air made me wince. "I'm not going to spoon-feed you," he said. But I suppose that's what he's doing now—forcing me to take in this news, hoping it will cure this incurable grief I feel. It's not like him to say "please."

I'm quiet for a while, and then I say, "Do you remember when we were kids, and we used to look out at the sky and pretend we could see the planets? You said Venus was a woman whose hair was on fire. I said Mars was crawling with worms."

"I remember," he says.

I look at the sky, blue and cloudless. It doesn't seem as limitless as it used to. "I haven't seen Venus and Mars for a long time," I say. "I think they're dead."

I fall sideways and rest my head on his shoulder.

"You're really in pain over Linden's death," he says, putting his arm around me and gently tugging at some of my hair. "But your own life hasn't ended. You have to go on."

"You can go ahead and say that I'm too sensitive now. I know you're thinking it."

"What I was thinking," he says, "is that you've grown up while we were apart, but maybe you haven't changed that much."

"I'm still weak, you mean."

"You were never weak," he says. "Just empathetic. I've always worried about you. It's dangerous to become attached to anyone in our world. To trust anyone."

"I don't know how you think it's something that can be helped," I say.

"I just hate to see you like this," he says. "Isn't there anything I can do?"

You could murder Vaughn. You could free Gabriel. You could help repair the damage that's been done to our home. By you.

This room is surely being recorded, though, and all I say is, "No."

He tilts my chin, and then he cups his hands around my ear and whispers, "I don't believe that."

I look at him, and I see the same look in his eyes as on the morning when I told him I was going to bring Linden home. Vaughn may be Rowan's benefactor, but I'm his twin sister. Even after this time spent apart, he can read me. He knows as well as I do that walls have ears. He knows there's something I can't say. And if I know my brother at all, he's going to find a way to hear it.

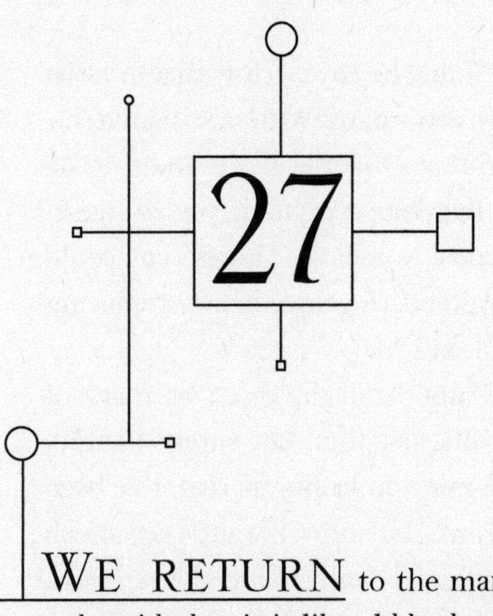

WE RETURN to the mansion on an afternoon so humid, the air is like old bathwater.

Vaughn has updated my key card so that, in addition to the ground floor and the wives' floor, I'll have access to the guest level where Rowan will be staying. I didn't even know we had a guest level, but according to Vaughn, it's one down from the wives' floor. But there will be time for Rowan to explore his new accommodations later. For now Vaughn has asked me to show Rowan the gardens, turn on the pool holograms if I'd like. Just be inside and cleaned up by five p.m., in time for dinner.

I think my former father-in-law just wants to be rid of us for a while, and although I'm in no hurry to reenter those walls anyway, there's something I have to deal with. "Wait here," I tell Rowan, and I run into the kitchen after Vaughn.

Vaughn stops walking when he reaches the hallway.

With his back turned to me, he says, "How nice it must be, darling, that the boy you ran off with is still alive."

My heart is in my throat. "Gabriel has nothing to do with all this," I say. "And I've done everything you've asked."

"Yes," he says. "I suppose you have. Though you could allow a little time to pretend to grieve before replacing my son with the hired help."

The word "pretend" hits me in the chest. So much of my time with Linden was just that, but surely Vaughn can recognize that this pain I'm feeling is real. I've been angry with Vaughn before, but now I want very much to take a swing at him, and I really think that I could. But the moment of satisfaction wouldn't be worth the repercussions.

"Gabriel is not a *replacement*," I say, in a measured tone. "He's a person, and he's done nothing to deserve what you're doing to him."

Vaughn's shoulders tense. I think he's going to turn around and face me, but he doesn't. "It isn't wise to make me angry with you right now," he says. "I intend to hold up my end of the bargain, but there's a certain etiquette to this matter."

The elevator doors open, and he's gone.

"Etiquette," I say under my breath.

I return to my brother, furious and sad and drained.

"Are you feeling sick?" he asks. "Your eyes are a little glassy."

"Let me give you the grand tour," I say.

Things are buzzing in the gardens. I wonder if Rose and Linden have found each other in the orange grove, if they're the ones rustling the leaves, if the orange that falls from its branch and rolls along the dirt is part of a game they're playing. It taps my shoe.

"Hi," I tell it.

"Who are you talking to?" Rowan says.

"I don't know. Come on; I'll show you the golf course."

I lead my brother through the loveliest avenues of my prison, which will now be shared with him. It seems silly that I ever thought I could be free. If this cure really does what it's supposed to, maybe I'll outlive Vaughn. Maybe I'll be free then.

And what will happen to Gabriel? How long is he going to remain in that state, gradually growing closer to his twenty-fifth birthday?

When we get to the pool, I turn on the hologram machine. The still water comes alive with guppies weaving anxiously through corals.

We sit at the water's edge and watch them go.

"They look so real," my brother says. I try to imagine how the two of us would look from Reed's plane. Two little forms with blond hair. The color of our eyes wouldn't matter. Whatever Vaughn has put into our blood wouldn't matter. We'd be nothing but a moment flashing by.

I'd like very much to fly again. I close my eyes, try to remember that dizzying moment of weightlessness when I first felt myself lifting off the ground.

It's quiet for a while, and then Rowan says, "We could talk now. We're alone out here. No walls."

"There are always walls," I say.

Shortly before dinner Rowan uses his own key card to access the elevator. Once he's made it to the guest floor, I ride the rest of the way to my own floor.

"Cecily?" I call as I step out of the elevator.

There's no answer. I find her bedroom empty, one of Bowen's bottles lying in her unmade bed. A sick feeling begins to form in my stomach. I hurry down the hall, and I check all the aisles in the library and the sitting room. The keyboard is on, its keys lighting up one by one as it waits for hands to play it. I check Jenna's room, which remains pristine and untouched.

When I open the door to my own room, I'm greeted with the familiar smell of baby powder, and I find Cecily sleeping on my bed. Bowen is napping under her small, protective arm.

She's wearing one of Linden's button-up shirts; the open collar falls over her shoulder; the hem just about reaches her knees.

"Cecily," I whisper, and sit on the edge of the bed.

She flinches and opens her eyes.

"Rhine?" Her voice is scratchy. "Rhine!" She sits upright. "Where have you been? Nobody would tell me anything. They wouldn't even talk to me."

"We can talk about it downstairs at dinner." I frown and clear some of the tangled hair from her face. She doesn't look well; if I hadn't found her napping in my bed just now, I would think she hadn't slept at all since I left.

"Dinner?" she says. "Downstairs?" She looks as though she's just tasted something sour. "Then that means Housemaster Vaughn is back?"

"Come on," I say, guiding her off the bed. "Let's get you cleaned up. We don't want Housemaster Vaughn to see you in Linden's clothes." I don't know how it's possible, but she smells like Linden and Jenna and Bowen, and nothing at all like herself.

She stumbles as I guide her to my bathroom. She sits on the edge of the tub, staring through me while I take a warm, damp towel to her face. She doesn't seem to mind when I brush the knots from her hair, and there are a lot of them.

"Do you want your hair up or down?" I say.

"Is he very mad at me?" Cecily asks.

"Who?"

"Housemaster Vaughn. Does he blame me for what happened?"

I unwind the hair elastic from the handle of my brush. "I think he blames Reed, and himself."

"He should blame me," she says.

"Shh." I tie her hair back and wind it into a bun. "Dinner is in a few minutes. We need to figure out what to wear."

She nods, but there are tears in her eyes as I hustle her out the door. "You can wear one of my dresses if you'd like," I tell her.

"I'm not filled out enough," she says. "I want my yellow dress. The one with the lacy sleeves."

"Concentrate on getting Bowen dressed, then, and I'll find your dress."

We each help with the other's zippers, and I tuck a silk flower into her hair for a bit of color. She looks half-asleep, but when I smooth the arches of her eyebrows with my thumbs, she makes an effort to smile.

"Ready to head downstairs?" I say.

She holds her breath for a few seconds, nods, and smoothes out her dress. She wore it the night of the party in the orange grove, the night she and Linden stole away to be alone for the first time. It's shorter on her than it used to be, and it's getting tight at the chest and the waist. She's outgrowing her memories. We both are.

I catch our reflection in the elevator doors on our way downstairs; husbandless brides in sundresses, hair upswept, eyes determined. We are stronger than we've credited ourselves to be. We have been the victims and the witnesses. We have said a lifetime of good-byes.

She holds Bowen to her hip, doesn't stop him from reaching for the fake flower in her hair.

"You'll get to meet my brother," I say.

"What's he like?" she asks.

"Condescending, mostly."

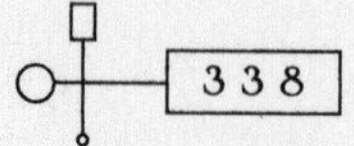

That gets a little laugh out of her, but it turns into a sharp breath, and she rests her head against my shoulder.

"I love you, Rhine," she says.

"I know," I say. "I love you, too."

She has composed herself by the time we make it to the dining room, where Rowan and Vaughn have already been seated. Vaughn's eyes brighten as soon as he sees us, and he breaks his own decorum to leave the table, arms outstretched, to take Bowen from Cecily. I see a moment of resistance before she relinquishes him.

Vaughn keeps Bowen in his lap through the first two courses, marveling at the way he can keep himself seated upright with minimal assistance, spooning him bits of applesauce and strained carrots, applauding every swallow.

Cecily says nothing, but her ears are turning red.

"Cecily," Vaughn says as our plates are being cleared away, food hardly touched. "Must you bring that eyesore of a purse to the dinner table?" He doesn't even want to allow her the small comfort it provides.

She raises her head for the first time all through the meal and smiles sweetly at him. "Bowen will be crawling soon," she says.

"Will you?" Vaughn asks Bowen. "No doubt you'll be walking before we know it."

"I'll teach him to walk," Cecily mutters under her breath. "Far, far away from you."

"Say something, darling?" Vaughn asks.

"I was wondering what the occasion was," she says. "It's been a long time since we've had a family dinner."

The word "family" is a staggeringly flawed way to describe us.

"Yes, it has, hasn't it?" Vaughn says. "I was hoping to have a talk with all of you last week, but certain events caused the evening to go differently than I had planned."

Linden's death, he means.

"I wanted to announce that I, along with a team of respected colleagues, have developed a cure," he says.

"A cure?" Cecily says.

"For the virus," he says. "Rhine and Rowan here are among the first participants. It's still experimental, but I'm confident that it'll take."

She looks at me, not understanding. "You're cured?" she says. "Right now?"

"Supposedly," I say. Maybe my brother is right to think I'm too empathetic or too sad to appreciate this, because I don't feel a drop of excitement. I still haven't decided if I believe it. Vaughn is something of a master at ulterior motives and catches.

"Dr. Ashby has been working on it for the past year," Rowan says. He's trying to help; I don't know what Vaughn has told him about my sister wife, if he's mentioned her at all, but I think Rowan feels sorry for her. Cecily looks at him like he's a strange creature that somehow found its way into her home. And I suppose that's all he is to her. A stranger who looks something like me.

"It's best not to overcomplicate it for our Cecily," Vaughn tells Rowan. "She never has been very good with the how and the why of things."

Cecily stares with disenchantment at the slab of chocolate cake that's been set before her. She hasn't eaten a thing all evening. I can see that she has questions, but she's too afraid to ask them. And she is still in the thick smog of grief, where everything, even the promise of a cure, means nothing to her. The husband who spoke sweetly to her is gone, and she's left at the mercy of a father-in-law who no longer makes his disgust with her a secret.

"You're going to stay here, then?" she asks me. "For how long?"

Vaughn laughs, holding Bowen up close to his face. "For now the project is top secret. Nobody who knows about it will be leaving here. The twins will remain in these walls for years, most likely. Perhaps for the rest of their lives."

Vaughn calling us "the twins" is an entirely new violation somehow. Maybe even the worst one yet. Even Rowan casts a displeased stare when Vaughn isn't looking.

"What about Bowen?" Cecily asks.

"What about him?" Vaughn says. He's playing with Bowen's curls now. They've got Linden's shape, but they're blond and beginning to take on Cecily's shade of red. I think he looks the way she must have looked as a baby. Vaughn, with all his genetic expertise, must think this as well. Surely it fuels his hatred for her.

"Is he going to be cured also?" Cecily says the words like she doesn't believe any of this.

"He's too young yet," Vaughn says. "This study isn't open to infants, but I am certain that he'll be as right as rain when he's a bit older. Won't you, Bowen?"

Cecily doesn't ask what will become of her. She already knows.

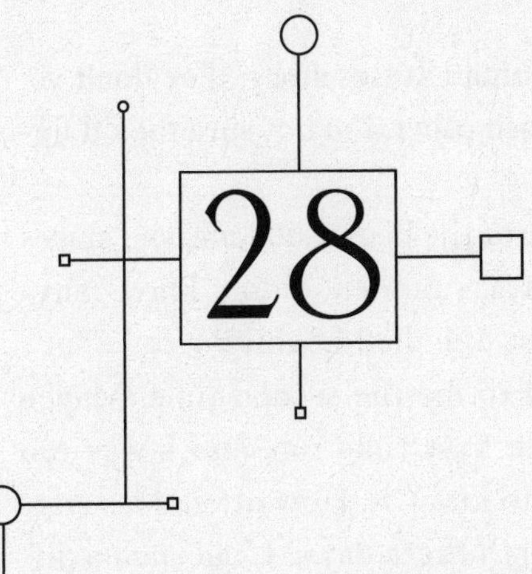

28

"HOUSEMASTER VAUGHN is going to murder me," Cecily says.

She's been soaking in my tub for the better part of an hour. I can smell all of the salts and soaps from where I'm lying on my bed, Jenna's romance novel open in my lap. I'm trying to ignore that the bath smells like the hours I'd spend getting ready for Linden's parties. I'll never be on his arm for another one. I'm trying to forget that he isn't coming home.

"Nobody is going to murder you," I say.

"Did you see the way he was looking at Bowen, like he wants him all for himself?"

"That bathwater must be ice-cold by now," I say.

"I was never anything but an incubator for his grandson," she says. "He has no use for me now." I hear the water rushing down the drain after she pulls the plug.

While she dries her hair, I try to focus on the

ill-fortuned man and woman in this story; they don't yet realize that they love each other. I'm not sure they'll figure it out in time.

When Cecily falls into the bed beside me, she stares at the ceiling and says, "Linden didn't know anything about his mother. She died in childbirth. That's what almost happened to me the second time. Maybe it almost happened the first time too, and I was too exhausted at the time to know it. How often does anyone even die in childbirth these days? I had such a difficult time giving birth to Bowen, and I was so ill after. You remember—"

"Cecily, stop," I say.

"Do you remember when Vaughn taught me to play chess during that hurricane?" she says. "A pawn is the littlest piece. He told me that. It was right in front of me, and I didn't see that I was his pawn. And now I'm not even that. I have no use, except to interfere with how Bowen is raised."

I roll over so that I'm on top of her, and I put my hand over her mouth and bring my face close to hers. "Listen," I say, very quietly. "There are certain things you shouldn't say out loud in this house. I'm here now, and I am not going to let anything happen to you, so no more of this talk. Understand?"

She stares at me, breaths heavy and warm, and there is such desperation in her eyes, such loss. But whether she believes me or not, she nods.

"Good," I say. "Come on. Get under the covers. We both need to sleep."

After we've both settled under the blanket, I turn off the lamp. "I thought you could read your book out loud until I fall asleep," she says.

I don't think she could bear a tragic love story right now. "It isn't very good," I say.

"I don't care about that," she says. "I just can't stand the quiet."

So I tell her a story of my own. I tell her about a little girl, named Maddie, who doesn't speak because, although she's just a child, she has learned that this world has nothing to offer her. She's found a way to hide herself in a world of her own, a world where there's always music, a world that's on the other side of the ocean, where the water is the most unreal shade of blue. In that world there are entire walls made of windows, and when the people awaken and pull apart the curtains, there is everything they've ever wanted laid out in front of them. It isn't a perfect place. There are no perfect places. But nobody cares about perfection when there are sand castles to build and kites to chase, children that are being born, old hearts that are giving in.

It's not long before she's asleep. All she needed was for someone to stay in the bed with her, someone to make her feel protected and tell her nice things.

I'm the one who's awake now, head full of ugliness. For most of the last week, any sleep I've gotten has been the result of heavy medication. And now, cured or not, I am haunted by my once-husband's final moments. I'm wondering what his thoughts were before we spilled back to earth in Reed's plane. I'm wondering if he was in pain in his last seconds, or if he had already left his body, the world getting smaller and dimmer below him until we had vanished into the greenery as we watched him die. I'm wondering if there's any truth to this word I hear sometimes: god. People say it when they're frustrated or when they're sad. It implies that there is something, someone greater than us. Greater than the presidents we used to elect or the kings and queens we used to throne.

I like the idea of something greater than us. We destroy things with our curiosity. We shatter with our best intentions. We are no closer to perfection than we were one hundred years ago, or five hundred.

I want to think that Linden has gone to the place that god implies—even if that means he's just in the orange grove with his first love. I hope that Linden will be able to hear Bowen laughing in the gardens as he plays.

As the night wears on, I find that it's impossible for me to sleep. I feel I'll go crazy if I'm made to lie still much longer.

Cecily barely stirs when I move away from her and climb out of the bed. I'm quiet as I make my way to the elevator and press the button that will take me to the ground floor.

Outside it's a beautiful night, warm and starry. The buzz and chirp of insects gives the feel that the grass is alive under my bare feet as I make my way to the orange grove.

I don't know why I've come here. I think I was hoping that the night would make it someplace different from what it is in the day. I was hoping to overhear a murmur or the whispered secrets of the dead.

I was hoping for guidance.

But when I hear footsteps worrying the earth behind me, it's no ghost that says, "A bit late for a walk, isn't it?"

Vaughn moves out from the shadow of the branches and into the light of the three-quarter moon.

Normally there is something menacing about his presence, but tonight I suspect he is just a father visiting his son's unmarked grave.

"I couldn't sleep," I say.

"You need your rest," he says. "I'll have an attendant send a sleep aid up to your room."

"Thanks," I say, "but I've had my fill of medications."

He laughs, and for once there is nothing dark about it. It's sad and defeated.

"I was pleasantly surprised this evening by how big my grandson has gotten," he says. "Even if I don't see much of his father in his features, there's something hopeful about babies. It's a joyous thing to watch them grow. I've missed him."

He paces under an orange tree and reaches out to touch a branch, but then withdraws. "I would have liked for my granddaughter to be here as well. She would be talking by now. I'd take her for walks and I'd teach her the things ordinary children out there aren't privy to. Maybe I'd tell her how many countries still remain. I'd promise to take her to whichever ones she liked when she got older."

He's talking about Rose and Linden's only child together. The scary part is that I believe him.

"Why couldn't you have just let her live?" I say. I feel that we're past the formality of lies; we both know that baby wasn't a stillbirth.

The branches are rustling; Linden and Rose are waiting for his answer.

For a moment I feel certain there is someone hiding there.

"A curious thing, malformed children," Vaughn says. "One can never be certain they'll live for a full day, a full year. There's no certainty that they'll speak, or that they'll be able to draw a single breath without agony. My granddaughter wouldn't have been the child her parents had been daydreaming about. She was bound to be nothing more than a heartbreak for the both of them."

"That wasn't your decision to make," I say. "That wasn't your child."

"Linden was my child," Vaughn snaps. "Everything that had to do with him concerned me. If he'd had time to fall in love with that baby, only to lose it, he would have come apart."

Maybe that's true. Maybe. But, one way or another,

he was still damaged. He was so shaken by that loss, so shaken by all of his losses, that every bit of love Linden felt for his own son was also filled with guilt for bringing him into this world, where nothing lasts as long as it should.

"There are different types of malformations," Vaughn says. "My granddaughter's was severe. But your older sister wife's was hardly noticeable."

"Jenna?" I say.

"Yes, darling."

And just like that the small bit of belief I mustered in my former father-in-law comes undone. He must have a very low opinion of my intelligence if he expects me to believe there was a thing wrong with Jenna. "Jenna wasn't malformed," I say. "She was perfect."

"She was a convincing one," Vaughn says. "When my son chose her from the lot of you, my first thought was that her features would complement his nicely when they had a child. But that thought was short-lived. Before any of you were married to my son, you underwent a physical examination, and that's when I realized that she wasn't as perfect on the inside as she was on the outside."

I'm beginning to feel sick. I'm not sure I want to hear this, but I listen anyway, because she was my sister wife, and because there's nobody left to hear her secrets now but me.

"Her uterus was as viable as a lump of scar tissue. She would never have been able to bear children," Vaughn says. "I was going to have to find another use for her.

And for a while I did, didn't I? I learned that one avenue of treatment proved fatal. I might have been able to save her life, if only she hadn't been so meddlesome. My efforts were better saved for something more important."

So there it is. Jenna's big secret. Though I'm sure it's only one of many.

"Was Gabriel involved in this?" I say.

"Not very," Vaughn says. He begins walking away from the orange grove, and I follow him. "I tell each of my workers the details necessary to their specific tasks. I never reveal the full picture."

"What will happen to him, then?" I say, keeping pace beside him. "You've gotten everything you wanted from me. I've cooperated."

"Yes, I've been meaning to ask you about that," he says. "What is it that you saw in him? What has he got that my son couldn't have given you? Is it just that running off with an attendant felt like the romantic thing to do?"

"I wanted him to know freedom," I say. "It wasn't about what he could give to me. It was about what he should have had for himself."

"Freedom," Vaughn says. "My son had one small taste of freedom, didn't he? Before he died? An entire lifetime of keeping him safe, and it only took one—one moment to end his life." I notice a beat of hesitation from him. He is a beast of a man, but even with his last son in the ground, he's still a father. "Freedom is dangerous," he finishes.

Of course it is. Rose's life in her mother's carnival would have been dangerous. And Cecily's life as an orphan, and Jenna's life with her sisters in a scarlet district, and my life in Manhattan. And Linden would still be safe and alive if he'd stayed on the ground, but our safety came at the price of being caged. There's a limit to how much living can be done in a life without freedom.

There was more freedom in the moment that plane came down than Linden had experienced in his whole life. I want to believe that's worth something. I have to believe that's worth something.

If Vaughn has more to say, it's lost by his sharp breath. He stops walking and turns to look at the orange grove, its leaves and branches silver and black in the moonlight, its oranges the only vague bits of brightness.

Then I realize that wasn't just a breath. It was a sob.

Maybe it's my own grief that's clouding my judgment, but I believe that Vaughn is human.

He's through talking, I can tell, and the grief is creeping up on him again. He should be alone with it.

Just after I've taken a step away from him, a loud crack splits the air, making me jump. Something rustles in the orange grove, but it isn't a ghost.

Vaughn puts his hand to his chest, and that's when I see the dark stain of blood on his shirt. Another shot comes, and then he drops to the ground, astonished eyes open and unblinking.

I'm too startled to scream.

Footsteps come toward me, and as she gets closer, I see my sister wife's red hair in the moonlight. I see the opened purse at her hip, and the gun in her hand, and her unflinching stare as she looks at what she's done.

She presses the gun's safety switch with her thumb just as she was taught, and as she lowers it, I see the fake emeralds studded around the handle. Madame's gun.

I also see that her bottom lip has started to tremble. She presses her lips together and stares at Vaughn's motionless form, either to make sure he's dead or because she can't bring herself to look away.

"Cecily." I put my hands on her shoulders, and she looks at me.

She opens her mouth to speak, but nothing comes. How can she explain? How can words ever be enough? There's a space in her womb where her unborn child died inside her. There's a place in the orange grove where her husband is buried. There's a world out there that nobody has bothered to promise to her.

I understand. It wouldn't have ever been enough for Vaughn that I bled into tubes. It wouldn't have been enough that Cecily gave him a grandchild and nearly died to give him another. It wouldn't have been enough that Jenna was destroyed, or that Rose was in so much pain that she didn't want to endure his measures to save her.

We were his disposable things. Brought to him like

cattle. Stripped of what made us sisters or daughters or children. There was nothing that he could take from us—our genes, our bones, our wombs—that would ever satisfy him. There was no other way that we would be free.

29

SHE HAD BEEN dreaming of this for a long time. But Madame was the one to put the gun into her hands. Madame looked at Cecily, and she saw the latest of Vaughn's victims. She saw a girl with vengeance in her eyes. And so they whispered and convened in colorful tents. They hugged good-bye at the gate and wished each other well, all the while a gun hiding in that innocuous pink purse.

It takes her a long time to tell me about Madame, and for her to admit that Vaughn's murder might have only been a daydream of hers if Linden were still alive; she knows it isn't what he would have wanted. She tells me that as angry as her husband was with his father, he was disgusted by the violence and the deceit. He wouldn't have wanted another death. But without Linden, she's certain that Vaughn was going to kill her if she didn't act soon, and the idea of Bowen being orphaned was too much for her to stand. She might not have been brave enough to do it at all if she hadn't used the key card she blackmailed off an attendant and followed me outside. She was only going to join me on my walk; she was too scared to sleep upstairs alone. But then she saw Vaughn and she hid. She heard what he said about Jenna.

We're sitting on the trampoline, in the darkness, and she finishes with the words "I had to." She's shivering now. In the moonlight her eyes are dark and worried.

I think she's brave. I think that nobody has ever believed what she could be capable of. All her life, nobody was listening.

I put my hand over hers.

In the morning the lotus gate is wide open. There's an emerald-studded gun in the grass, wiped clean of any fingerprints. There's a prominent doctor lying dead a few feet from the weapon that killed him.

It makes sense. He had become a member of the president's elite. There would be competition. There would be jealousy. There would be people that he had, in his fervor of research, shorted or stolen from or wronged.

Cecily and I are playing chess in the library; we aren't supposed to know any of these things yet. We're supposed to be waiting for breakfast.

Her fingers are shaking as she selects a pawn; she's far more competent at this game than I am, but neither of us is paying attention to the board. "I've seen your brother on the news," she says, "but seeing him in person—I wasn't prepared for how much he looks like you. It's jarring."

I watch her set down the pawn on the same square.

"I bet it makes you feel like you belong somewhere," she says. "I've never had brothers or sisters. It must be nice."

"You've had sisters," I say.

She raises her head to me, and she isn't quite able to smile, she doesn't have the strength, but I know my words have reached her.

A nervous attendant bursts into the room, uncertain what to do as he explains the catastrophe with the Housemaster. Without a Housemaster and without a House Governor, there is no order to follow.

We tell him that Vaughn has a living relative. A brother. We tell the attendant where he lives, how he can be reached.

Several floors below us the chemicals are slowly filtering out of Gabriel's system. His mind is slowly awakening, his eyes blinking. Elle is familiar with the practices of nursing, and she has access to the basement.

When Reed arrives, Cecily and I run from the kitchen door to greet him. And for the first time in well over a decade, he's invited into the building his father had reconstructed into a home. We don't have to explain. He can see in Cecily's eyes that she's the reason his brother is dead. Maybe he already knew she had it in her when he taught her how to pull a trigger.

When she puts her arms around him, she finally breaks into tears.

"It's okay, kid," he says. For an instant her feet are off the ground, she's holding on so tight. "It'll be okay."

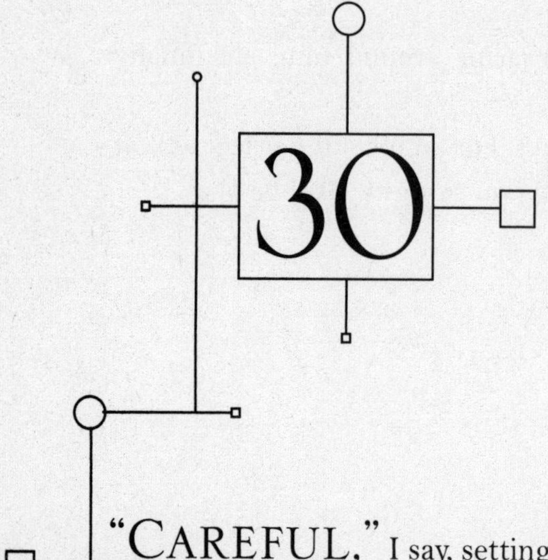

30

"CAREFUL," I say, setting the tray on the nightstand when Gabriel tries to stand. I tuck my comforter back over his legs. "You shouldn't be on your feet."

"I could say the same for you," he says, but he accepts the kiss I place on his lips.

"I'm fine," I say. "I made tea. And you"—I poke his chest, pushing him back against the headboard—"need to drink some of it."

His eyes are wandering the length of me, and he mouths "Okay" and closes my hand in his. He wants to ask if I'm all right, but he won't. That will only make it worse. It is taking all I have to keep my eyes dry. Staying busy helps.

"It's chamomile," I say. "It's supposed to make you sleepy. I think it's only a placebo effect, though."

His eyes are bright, so bright and blue like the water sparkling around Hawaii as I looked down from the plane. His cheeks are pink again, and I follow a prominent vein in his wrist that disappears halfway up his forearm. When we're alive, life consumes us. But when we die, all of the color and the motion is gone so quickly, it's as though it can no longer stand to be wasted on us.

"Rhine—" Gabriel says, at the same time that I blurt out, "I wanted to ask you—"

My fist clenches inside his hands.

"You go," he says.

"I wanted to ask you what happened the night Vaughn found me at Claire's," I say, finally meeting his eyes. "It's fine if you don't want to discuss it, and I suppose it doesn't matter, but I've been all over the place these past few months wondering what happened to you after I left. I thought it would be nice to have at least one chapter I could close."

"I woke up and you weren't in bed anymore," he says. "So I came looking for you."

With his free hand he takes a sip of tea. Steam swirls about the rim as he exhales.

"And then Vaughn knocked you unconscious," I say. I think of the syringe that was emptied into my arm, the sick feeling and then the blackness.

"No," Gabriel says. "Housemaster Vaughn was waiting on the sidewalk. He knew I'd be coming to find you. And there you were in the backseat. You were sick while we were at Claire's, but that was the worst I'd seen you.

He told me that you would die if he didn't tend to you."

"And you believed him," I say.

"Of course I believed him. It turned out to be true, didn't it?"

"But did he threaten you?" I say. "You knew a lot of his secrets; that's what he told me. Did he tell you that you had to come back?"

"Maybe he would have if I'd refused," Gabriel says. "But I didn't."

"You went," I say, and only when I hear the anger in my voice do I realize how upset this makes me. "Willingly. After all that effort to be rid of him."

"I wanted to be rid of him," he says. He raises my chin with his thumb. "But not if it meant being rid of you. I climbed in beside you, and you put your head in my lap. You can't think I would have left you like that."

"Look what it got you," I say.

"Tea in bed and you here in front of me," he says. "It was a terrible decision, and I confess I'd make it again."

It's impossible for me to resist his smile. One day after awakening from the coma, he is doing astoundingly well. Vaughn's strongest chemicals are no match for the will to live, it seems.

"I'm not through being angry," I say, my words muffled when he kisses me.

"Stop ruining it," he says, and kisses me again, and again, until I let go and I move into his waiting arms.

His parted fingers move up my neck and through

my hair, and the rush of nerves is overwhelming, and I freeze, stop breathing.

After all the months without him, my bed somehow kept Linden's scent, and I've just found it in the pillow.

"Rhine?" Gabriel says.

I'm sitting up now. My eyes are aching. "I should make dinner," I say. "Cecily and Rowan probably haven't eaten, and you should try something solid. I'm sure your stomach will handle it now."

He means to say something, but I'm on my feet before he can get the words out. I kiss his forehead and hurry away, to the scent of incense in the hall. Cecily has been lighting the sticks.

The kitchen is empty when I enter it, but the moment I make the slightest noise, the head cook is there, swatting at me with a wooden spoon and telling me to stay away from her ingredients. She'll make whatever I'd like if I get out of her hair, she says.

No one eats, though. Rowan is out exploring the grounds somewhere, and when I bring dinner to Cecily's room, she pretends to be asleep. I set the plate on her nightstand, kiss her forehead, and close her door on the way out.

Gabriel doesn't press me. I tell him about Hawaii and he listens. We don't discuss the fact that Vaughn was the one to bring me there, or the things that happened to my brother, or the things that happened to me. We talk only about the colors, and the blinking lights, and how from up high the ocean looks like a giant spill.

We stay away from words like "cure" and "hope." Hope has been especially cruel.

When I close my eyes, I see the traffic lights changing and the triangular sails moving across the water. Gabriel sweeps the hair from my forehead as I lie with my head on his chest. Here I am telling him about these beautiful things, and I don't deserve a single one of them.

"It's my fault that Linden's dead," I say. "He was in my seat. I don't even know why I let him have it; the view terrified him."

"If he was sitting there, it wasn't your seat," Gabriel says. "Rhine. Look at me."

I open my eyes and tilt my face toward his. My vision is blurred and I realize I'm crying, my throat heavy with the taste of it.

Gabriel tightens his arm around me, gathers me close. And I wrap my arms around him, because I am human and selfish and breathing. I'm still alive and I don't know for how long, or what for. I shudder and sob, and the guilt and the hurt are so heavy, but not so much that it stops my heart from beating.

A feeling can't kill you. That's what I told Cecily. That's what I've told myself so many times before.

"He wouldn't want you to feel this way," Gabriel says. "I didn't know him very well, but I'm sure of that."

"It's because he was better than me," I say. "He never wanted to hurt anyone. I didn't want to hurt him, either.

I only wanted to go home, and instead I made a mess of everything. I killed him."

"You didn't," Gabriel says. But he says nothing more, because I'm sobbing and he knows that I'm in no state to listen to his reason. He rubs my back and he says impossible things. He tells me that I'm strong and that I deserve to be here. He tells me that I'll never have to be alone.

As the day turns darker, I weave in and out of sleep, dreaming of the world through an airplane window. I try to find Linden, but he's not on the crowded beach or in any of the gleaming windows. I listen for his voice, but I only hear Gabriel's whispers filling the clouds and turning them pink as the sun goes down.

"I've loved you since the day I stole the atlas for you," Gabriel says, because he thinks I'm asleep.

The door creaks open, startling me awake.

Timidly, Cecily moves into the doorway. "I knocked but you didn't answer," she says. "There's a man downstairs to speak with you and your brother."

Even before I'm fully awake, my heart is pounding. "What does he want?"

"I don't know, but he's rude," she says. "He won't tell me a thing. He just demanded to talk to you."

She glances at Gabriel sleeping beside me, but her blank expression doesn't change.

"I'll be right down," I say.

Once she's gone, Gabriel, with his eyes still closed, says, "I heard her moving around all last night."

"She's having a terrible time with everything," I say.

"What about you?" Gabriel says.

"Me? I slept well last night."

"That isn't what I meant."

"I know," I say, climbing out of the bed, seeking out my reflection in the mirror and gathering my hair into a ponytail. "I'm not ready to get into all of that. You're here, I'm here, my brother and Cecily and Bowen are here." I tug the wrinkles out of my shirt and jeans. "I'd like to focus on being grateful for all of that, if you don't mind."

He gives me a wan smile.

"Maybe over breakfast I'll tell you what Madame has been up to. I guarantee that most of it isn't what you'd expect." I smile at him as I leave.

The man waiting to speak to me is an official sent by the president—a doctor-slash-scientist who has been assigned to monitor Rowan's and my progress and escort us to our monthly physical examinations in Hawaii. He won't be staying with us, only monitoring our vitals via our tracking devices. It turns out that there was never any rule about us staying on the property; that was something Vaughn devised to keep us contained. While we're bound to confidentiality on penalty of execution, we are, as the official puts it, free to go where we please, provided we are here in time for our monthly flight.

I would just as soon cut the tracking device out of my body and be done with it, but Cecily comes out from her hiding place in the hallway and begins an eager round of questions about what she can do to participate in the study. She insists that she was Vaughn's protégé, that he planned to include her as soon as a new round of subjects was recruited. Though this isn't true, Rowan and I readily agree. There's no reason to suspect that a man as in love with research as Vaughn was wouldn't have planned to save his other daughter-in-law.

After the official leaves and Cecily has gone upstairs, Rowan and I sit at the kitchen table.

"Why did Dr. Ashby hate Cecily so much?" he asks.

"He told you he hated her?"

"He didn't have to. I could tell by the way he treated her that night when we all had dinner. That, and he never expressed any interest in trying to cure her."

I stare at my tea that's gone cold. "I think he was jealous of her," I say. She endured much of Vaughn's venom, and perhaps the worst part of it was that he once pretended to love her. "Linden was finally beginning to grow up. He was making decisions that had nothing to do with his father's wishes, and she was the reason for much of that. He chose her over his father."

Rowan nods into his tea. I don't know if my explanation makes sense to him. He only knows Vaughn as a brilliant doctor. He wasn't here for all the gory affairs of the family dynamic. And part of me doesn't want to sully the image of his hero, because the fact is that we may all live beyond our expectancy because of that man.

"Someday I'll tell you all of it," I say.

"I'd like that," he says.

"No," I say. "I promise you won't."

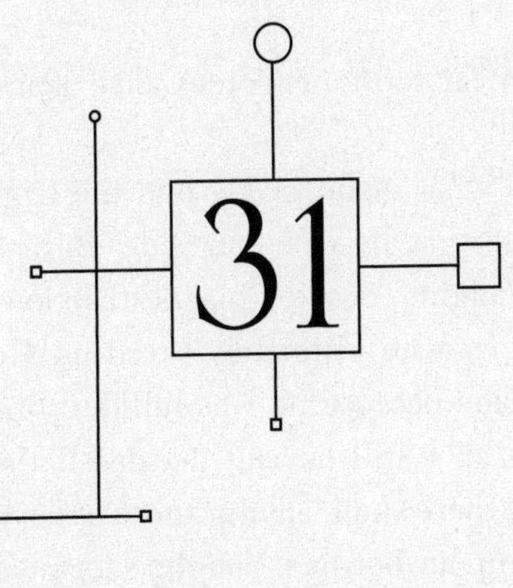

31

IT'S NEARLY a year before there are openings in the study and Cecily is able to sign up. Gabriel joins her. By then the years of careful planning that went into Vaughn's basement experiments are undone. We've searched every room, and while we found every manner of machinery, we never found any bodies. I decide that's for the best; there are some questions I never want answered.

Reed does away with the key card system, and he opens entire rooms and levels of the house that I never saw before. He fills them with his strange and wonderful things. He turns an entire wing of the basement into a sort of greenhouse.

Cecily and I keep our old bedrooms, and we still call ourselves sister wives, or sometimes just sisters. Eventually Cecily decides that Jenna's room would make the perfect nursery for Bowen. And our sister wife's room, which was stagnant for far too long, comes alive again, in an entirely new way.

Rowan understands what made Cecily pull the trigger. He's made it clear that he's on our side. But he still maintains that Vaughn, despite his destructions and downfalls, is the one who ultimately saved us. He resorted to drastic means because he was fulfilling his calling to save the world. I still haven't decided if the world can be saved, but there's talk among those of us in the study now of opening our borders. Vaughn's formula for the cure is bound to reach the rest of the country if the cure works.

Gabriel has stopped trying to understand Vaughn. He says that we have to move forward, and I agree. We don't talk of revenge or bitterness anymore. We don't forget our losses, but we've stopped counting them. There are so many other things to live for. We still aren't allowed to explore the countries outside of our own—not just yet. But President Guiltree grants the study's participants access to his private Hawaiian beach sometimes. From there we can hear the traffic. We can feel the pull of a thriving world that we will one day be able to join. The hope is most palpable there, and sometimes Gabriel and I disentangle ourselves from the others. We go as far out into the water as we dare, and only when we're alone in this way do we talk to each other of love, like it's a faraway city.

Remembering the address for Grace's Orphanage,

I send word to Silas about the study. He shows up one year as the study's newest participant, and he takes an immediate liking to my sister wife; every day she's growing more into a woman, becoming something lovely and enchanting. She meets Silas's advances with annoyance, although sometimes he manages to get a laugh or a smile out of her. "Be careful with her," I tell him one afternoon as we're wading in the ocean's shallows. "I know how you can get around girls." He kicks ocean water at me.

Cecily is just as hesitant about these things as I am. She still wears her wedding ring and maintains that Linden will always be her only love. But maybe one day that will change; everything is already starting to change all around us.

I'm still uncertain. I'm still untrusting that I'll live long enough to know what it means to love the way that my parents loved.

On the morning of my twenty-first birthday, though, I awaken with a feeling that the whole world is possible.

That's the morning that Cecily bursts into my room with Linden's sketch pad and tells me her greatest plan yet to keep Linden alive. She wants us to build one of his houses.

Every day, we've looked for ways to keep Linden alive. It's especially important to do this for Bowen, who doesn't remember. Cecily has an exceptional memory for detail; she can make stories of even small moments. She writes things down so that she won't ever forget, and sometimes, late at night, she comes to my doorway unable to sleep, fearing that he's slipping away from her, and we put our memories together—the way he held his sketch pad at an angle, and his small, frustrated sighs as he erased the lines, and how at a glance his hair was black, but then the sun made it bright with auburns. I remember the things she can't, and in that way he's still our husband, the thing that once did and always will bond us together.

Reed has his memories too. He tells us of the quiet, inquisitive boy who wanted to know how things were made, who built houses out of old books and towers out of cards. He tells stories that make us laugh, and more still that have us in tears.

I didn't think the house would happen so quickly, but one day Reed started building it, and he hasn't stopped. Once he hired the contractors, the skeleton of the house seemed to appear overnight. I help wherever I can, and Cecily makes sure that the details are exact. The number of steps. The gingerbread trim.

"Maybe it will give you some closure too," Gabriel says, and I let him pull me into his arms.

We let Bowen help with the painting, and though he's only four, he moves with patience, taking care with his strokes. Cecily's convinced he'll grow up to do something great, something that will impact the world. She won't let him waste a second of his potential, because just being able to grow up at all is a gift.

Each new year, each new day, is the chance to do more. I try to remind her that she's still young herself. We all are. Once the house is built and Bowen is older, we'll all travel. We'll see the things we thought only existed in books. We'll scale mountains and parachute from planes, and visit the river that has my name. Rowan believes our parents always meant for us to see it, that they knew it was out there waiting for us to find; it won't be the way they intended, but we'll get there. We'll squeeze every second that we can from our lives, because we're young, and we have plenty of years to grow. We'll grow until we're braver. We'll grow until our bones ache and our skin wrinkles and our hair goes white, and until our hearts decide, at last, that it's time to stop.

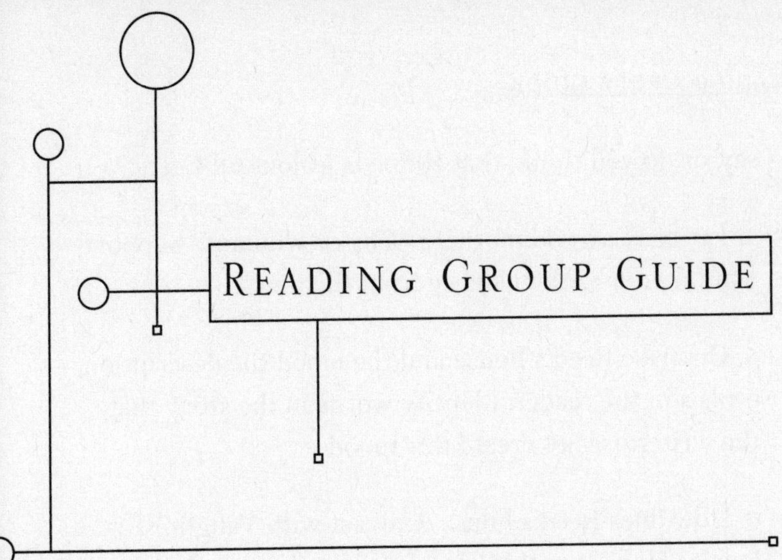

PREREADING QUESTIONS

1. To what extent would you go to save a loved one?

2. What does the title of the final book in DeStefano's Chemical Garden Trilogy suggest about the plot?

DISCUSSION QUESTIONS

1. When the story opens, Rhine is in the hospital and is being visited by her husband, Linden, and her sister wife Cecily. Why is she in the hospital?

2. Who is Reed and why does Linden suggest Rhine stay with him for a while?

3. Compare and contrast Cecily's relationship with Linden and Rhine's relationship with him. Would you

say, or do you think, that Rhine is jealous of Cecily?

4. Is Cecily a good mother? Why or why not? Support your answer with evidence from the text.

5. Describe Reed's house and the mood the description evokes in the reader. Identify words in the story that the writer uses to create this mood.

6. How does Reed's house contrast with Vaughn's house? How does this contrast contribute to the mood?

7. What role does Reed's airplane play in the story?

8. Why does Vaughn come for Cecily? What power does Vaughn hold over her?

9. Why do Linden and Rhine rush Cecily to the hospital? How does the author create tension in this scene? Identify passages and/or dialogue that help build this tension.

10. Why does Reed wonder if Vaughn knows that the Ellerys are Rhine's parents? How does he assist Rhine?

11. What does Rhine learn about her brother? Why is she unsettled by his work? Why does she decide that she has to find him?

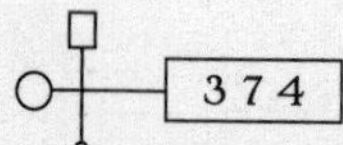

12. How does Linden's attitude toward his father change and why?

13. Linden, Cecily, and Rhine pass through Madame's carnival on their way to find Rowan. When they are taken to Madame, what do they learn about her connection with Linden and Rose? How does the writer create a more sympathetic character in Madame in the final volume of the trilogy?

14. How does Rhine find her brother? Describe the scene in which they first come together. How does the author use dialogue to evoke emotion when they reunite?

15. What surprise is in store for Rhine when she is reunited with her brother? How does she manage the shock?

16. Where does Vaughn fly Rhine and Rowan? Why? What does Rhine discover about this place?

17. Why does Rhine return to the mansion with Vaughn? What does she learn about Gabriel?

18. Why does Cecily believe that Vaughn plans to murder her?

19. After Rhine learns the truth about Vaughn and his relationship with Rowan, Rowan says to her, "I've always worried about you. It's dangerous to become attached to anyone in our world. To trust anyone." Does this statement accurately describe Rhine? Why or why not? Is Rowan as stoic as he presents himself? Support your answer with evidence from the text.

20. How are Rhine and Gabriel reunited?

Questions for Further Discussion

1. In the first two books in the Chemical Garden Trilogy, Vaughn is determined to keep Rhine prisoner and/or hunt her down. How does he change in the third installment? What contributes to this change? For what reason does the author make this change?

2. When Rhine learns that her brother is still alive, she insists on finding him. How has he changed since they were separated? How has Rhine changed? Are they able to reconcile their torn relationship?

3. How does Linden feel about Rhine? Is the feeling mutual? Explain. How is Linden similar to and different from his father?

4. What happens to Linden? How does Rhine deal with this loss?

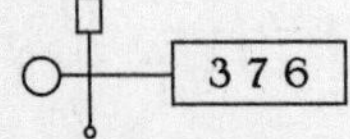

5. DeStefano uses imagery to create a dystopian world. Identify two examples of strong imagery and explain what they contribute to the story.

6. By the end of the trilogy, the reader gains a clearer understanding of Vaughn's scientific mission. Is Vaughn good or evil? Explain and support your answer with evidence from the text.

7. How does Cecily grow throughout the story? What contributes to her maturity? How do her feelings change toward Vaughn and why?

8. Does Vaughn love his son and grandson? Support your answer with textual evidence. Does the story have a satisfying ending? Why or why not?

9. What does Rhine learn about her parents and how does this information change her?

Guide written by Pam B. Cole,
Professor of English Education & Literacy,
Kennesaw State University, Kennesaw, Georgia

Turn the page
and find out how far you can fall for
Lauren DeStefano's new series,
The Internment Chronicles.

You have all heard the warnings about the edge. We have been told its winds are a song that will hypnotize us, and by the time we awaken from that trance, it will be too late.

—"Intangible Gods," Daphne Leander, Year Ten

WE LIVE ENCAPSULATED BY THE TRAINS. They go around in a perfect oval at all hours, stopping for thirty-five seconds in each section so the commuters are able to board and depart. Beyond the tracks, after the fence, there's sky. Engineers crafted a scope so that we can see the ground below us. We can see tall buildings and other sorts of trains—some of which disappear underground or rise onto bridges. We can see patches of cities and towns that appear stitched like one of Lex's blankets.

We've never been able to craft a scope advanced enough to see the people—it isn't allowed. We've been banished to the sky. I'm told they can see Internment, though. I wonder, what must we look like to them? A giant oval of the earth with rocks and roots clinging to the bottom, I suppose. I've seen sketches of what Internment looks like as a whole, and it's as though a giant hand came down and took a piece right out of the ground, and here we are floating in the sky.

When I was a child, I used to think about the day Internment was ripped from the ground and placed in the sky. I used to wonder if the people were frightened, or if they felt fortunate to be saved. I used to imagine that I was a part of Interment's first generation. I'd close my eyes and feel the ground under my feet going up and up and up.

"Ms. Stockhour," Instructor Newlan says, "you're dreaming with your eyes open again. Page forty-six."

I look at the textbook open before me and realize I haven't been keeping up with the lesson since page thirty-two.

"I don't suppose you would care to add to our discussion." He always paces between the rows of desks as he lectures, and now he's stopped before me.

"The festival of stars?" I say, but I'm only guessing. I have an incurably wandering mind, a fact that has given Instructor Newlan much cheerful cause to torture me. The chorus of chuckles from my classmates confirms I'm wrong.

"We've moved on to geography," Pen says from beside me. She glances from me to the instructor, curls bouncing around her cheeks and creating a perfect ambiance for the look of contrition on her face; if Instructor Newlan thinks she's sorry for speaking out of turn, he won't give her a demerit. He likes her; she's the only one left fully conscious after his geography lectures—she'd like to work on the maps when she's older. He gives her a wry glance over his glasses, flips my book to the correct page, and goes on.

"I do realize that it's December first," Instructor Newlan says. "I know we're all excited for the festival of stars to begin, but let us remember that there is plenty of class work to be done in the meantime."

The festival of stars is a monthlong celebration, and in the excitement and preparations, it's common for students and adults alike to daydream. But while the rest of Internment daydreams of normal things—gifts and requests to the god of the sky—I dream of things that are dangerous and could have me arrested or killed. I stare at the edge of my desk and imagine it's the end of my little world.

After the class is over, I wait for Basil before I move for the door. He always insists on catching the same shuttle to the train so he can escort me home. He worries. "Where does your mind go?" he asks me.

"She was thinking about the ground again," Pen teases, linking her elbow around mine and squeezing against me. "I swear, with all your daydreams about the ground, you could be a novelist."

I will never be disciplined enough to write a novel, not like my brother, Lex, who says I'm too much of an optimist to have any artistic prowess.

We walk quickly. Pen is trying to avoid Thomas, her betrothed, and the way she keeps glancing behind us, she isn't even being inconspicuous.

We make it into a shuttle with hardly a second to spare.

The shuttles are electric vehicles that are much smaller than train cars and therefore are usually crowded. We stand huddled by the door. Pen deflates with a quiet sigh of relief. Thomas is just leaving the academy as we depart.

Basil grips the overhead handle, and I grab his arm as a jolt knocks me into him. The reason for our betrothals is never explained to us, but I like to think the decision makers knew Basil was going to be taller than me. It can only be an act of good planning, the way my head fits into the hollow between his neck and shoulder.

I keep hold of Pen's wrist so she doesn't stumble, but she has no problem keeping her balance. She's staring out at the clouds full of evening sunlight. They meander alongside Internment, but just when I think they'll hit us, they evade, slipping under or over our little world like we're a stone in their waters. Internment is encased by a sphere of wind that prevents the clouds from entering our city, though they seem close enough to touch.

The shuttle stops, pushing strangers into us. We're lucky to be so close to the door, because everyone rushes to get out at once, hoping to catch the train so they won't have to wait for the next one.

The train is not very crowded when we board, aside from the seats at the head of the car that are occupied by a group of pregnant women, chattering with one another about the details of their birthing class. Judging by their stomachs, I'd guess they're carrying a round of January births.

The higher grades let out an hour after most work shifts

end, and the younger children have another hour yet of classes. We find an empty row of seats wide enough to fit the three of us, and I deliberately usher Basil in first so that Pen won't be the one to sit by the window. She has spent enough time staring at the clouds.

"They've already started decorating for the festival of stars," I say, nodding to the silver-colored branches that frame the ceiling of our train car. From the branches hang little metal toys and trinkets that are meant to symbolize human desire—toy trains and books and miniature couples holding hands, the brass silhouette of true love.

The festival of stars overtakes the city in the month of December. It's a time for giving gifts to our loved ones to show our gratitude for having them in our lives. And on the very last day, we're allowed to make one big request of the god in the sky. Each request is written on a special piece of parchment that we aren't meant to share with anyone else. The entire city gathers together, and our pieces of parchment are set on fire and cast into the sky, like hundreds of burning stars. We cling to one another and watch as our greatest desires are carried off and eventually extinguished, to be answered or denied.

"They've asked me to help with the murals this year," Pen says, raising her chin in a modest show of pride. "Apparently one of the instructors recommended me to the festival committee."

"It's about time," I say. "You couldn't keep your talent a secret forever."

She smiles. "I'm a bit nervous, if I'm going to be honest

about it. All those people telling me what to draw. I've never been good at taking orders."

She takes my shoulders and faces me away from her so that she can weave my straight dark hair into a braid. She says I waste my beauty, letting my hair fall over my shoulders like a mop.

Basil doesn't comment on my appearance at all, although sometimes he says he hopes our children have my blue eyes; he says they make him think of what the water on the ground must look like. We've never seen it from up close, but we have the lakes here, which are sort of green.

"If they boss you around, just call it artistic license," Basil says. "You can convince them to see it your way. You're a good debater."

"That is true," Pen says cheerily. "Thanks, Basil."

The train stops, and everyone getting off at the nearest section rises to their feet, but their haste is replaced by confusion. This isn't the platform. Basil cranes his neck and tries to see ahead, but Pen is the one to notice the lights first. She abandons my braid, and my hair falls, undone. She jabs my ribs and says, "Look."

Red-and-white medic lights are flashing off in the distance.

People around us are murmuring. There are medical emergencies sometimes, and despite the organization of the shuttles, accidents happen when people get too close to the moving vehicles. Once, there was an hour's delay after one of the cattle animals broke through a fence and was struck by a train.

Pen and I start to get to our feet for a better look, but a jolt forces us back into our seats. We start moving again. But something is wrong. The scenery moves in the wrong direction.

We're going backward.

Pen is alight with excitement. "I didn't even know the train could *go* backward," she says. "I wonder if it puts any strain on the gears." At times her curiosity makes her brave.

I bite my lip, look out the window because no matter which direction we go, the sky looks the same. And the sky is familiar. The sky is safe.

There's a half mile of land on the other side of the fence that lines the train track; I've never set foot on the other side of the tracks—we aren't supposed to—but Lex has.

On Internment, you can be anything you dream—a novelist or a singer, a florist or a factory worker. You can spend entire afternoons watching clouds so close that it's as though you're riding them. Your life is yours to embrace or to squander. There's only one rule: You don't approach the edge. If you do, it's already over. My brother is proof of that. He has successfully quieted any delusions I held about seeing the ground for myself.

My stomach is doing flip-flops, and I can't decide if it's excitement or fear.

I force myself to look away from the window, and my eyes find Basil's.

Some of the other passengers seem excited, others confused.

A man several seats down, in a black suit, has begun talking to Pen about how trains have emergency systems, and shuttles too. He says that the train has moved backward before, several years before she was born, when repair work needed to be done on the track.

"So it could be that something just needs to be fixed," he says.

One of the pregnant women is staring past Basil and me, out our window at the sky. Her lips are moving. It takes me a few seconds to realize that she's talking to the god in the sky, something the people of Internment do only when they're desperate.

"All this backward motion is starting to make me dizzy," I say.

"It's only because you're worried," Basil says. "You have great equilibrium. What was that spinning game you used to play when we were in first year?"

I let out a small laugh. "It wasn't a game, really. I just liked to count how many times in a row I could spin without falling down."

"Yes, but you would do it everywhere you went," he says. "Up and down stairs, and in the aisles of the train, and all along the cobbles. You never seemed to get dizzy."

"What an odd thing to remember," I say, but it makes me smile. I would spin around the apartment from the time I awoke in the morning, jumping around my older brother and spinning after each step as we shared the mirror in the cramped water room. It drove him mad.

One morning as he was fixing his tie, he warned me that

LAUREN DESTEFANO

earned a BA in English with a concentration in creative writing from Albertus Magnus College in Connecticut.

VISIT HER AT

LAURENDESTEFANO.COM.

THECHEMICALGARDENBOOKS.COM

if I kept spinning, I'd be stolen by the wind and carried off into the sky. "We'll never get you back then," he said. The words were meant to frighten me, but instead they filled me with romantic notions that became a part of my game. I began to imagine being carried on the wind and landing on the ground, seeing for myself what was happening below our city. I could imagine such great and impossible things there. Things I didn't have words for.

The madness of youth made me unafraid.